SHEILA

CW0092 2750

HUNTING
SHADOWS

'Marks the entrance of a major new talent.
Sheila Bugler delivers a chilling psychological twister of a novel,
laced with homespun horrors, a compelling central character in
DI Ellen Kelly and a strong contemporary resonance. Fans of
Nicci French and Sophie Hannah, prick up your ears.'
Cathi Unsworth

'Truly a *tour de force.*
Imagine a collaboration between Ann Tyler and AM Homes.
Yes, the novel is that good. Sheila Bugler might well have
altered the way we view families and
the very essence of mandatory Happiness.
This is great writing.'
Ken Bruen

Sheila Bugler grew up in the west of Ireland. After studying Psychology at University College Galway, she left Ireland and worked in Italy, Spain, Germany, Holland and Argentina before finally settling in London, where she lives with her husband, Sean, and their children, Luke and Ruby.

In 2008 she was one of four writers to be offered a place on the UK Arts Council-funded Apprenticeships in Fiction programme – a mentoring scheme designed to nurture emerging writers in the UK and Ireland. When not writing, Sheila works as an online editor and writer and is also a regular contributor to the writing magazine *Words With Jam*.

Hunting Shadows is her first novel. She is currently finishing a sequel.

Hunting Shadows, by Sheila Bugler, is the first book in a series featuring Detective Ellen Kelly, and continues a strong tradition of acclaimed crime fiction published by BRANDON.

CORNWALL COUNTY LIBRARY	
38009047545519	
Bertrams	11/09/2013
AF	£8.99
BOD	

BUGLER SHEILA
Never to forget: Sheila Bugler
737843/00014 - 1 of 3

HUNTING SHADOWS

AN OBSESSION FOR HIM. LIFE AND DEATH FOR HER.

SHEILA BUGLER

BRANDON

AN IMPRINT OF THE O'BRIEN PRESS

First published 2013 by Brandon, an imprint of The O'Brien Press Ltd,
12 Terenure Road East, Rathgar, Dublin 6, Ireland.
Tel: +353 1 4923333; Fax: +353 1 4922777
E-mail: books@obrien.ie
Website: www.obrien.ie

ISBN: 978-1-84717-366-9

Copyright for text © Sheila Bugler 2013
Edited by Rachel Pierce at Verba Editing House
Copyright for typesetting, layout, design ©
The O'Brien Press Ltd.

All rights reserved. No part of this publication may be
reproduced or utilised in any form or by any means, electronic or
mechanical, including photocopying, recording or in any information
storage and retrieval system, without permission in writing from the publisher.

1 2 3 4 5 6 7 8 9 10
13 14 15 16 17

Layout and design: The O'Brien Press Ltd.
Cover photograph: iStockphoto
Printed and bound by CPI Group (UK) Ltd, Croydon, CR0 4YY
The paper in this book is produced using pulp from managed forests

The O'Brien Press receives assistance from

To my parents, Harry and Adrienne, for everything

Acknowledgements

Svetlana Pironko, Michael O'Brien, Rachel Pierce and everyone at O'Brien Press.

Fellow writers: JJ Marsh, Gillian Hamer, Catriona Troth, Pete Moran, Justine Windsor, Amanda Hodgkinson, Chris Curran, Marlene Brown, Lorraine Mace, Marion Urch, Martyn Waites, Cathi Unsworth, Ken Bruen and everyone I've met at the Writing Asylum.

My 'perfect reader', Michelle Romaine. I'm hoping a baby isn't going to get in the way of the serious business of reading early drafts of my books ...

Chioma Dijeh of the Metropolitan Police, who advised on police procedural issues; any mistakes are mine.

Luke and Ruby: Chessington is booked – you deserve it for putting up with a mother who writes.

Finally, Sean: love you.

From: Briony.Murray@LewishamPsych.nhs.net
To: Ebaxter@met.police.uk
Subject: DI Ellen Kelly

Ed,

As promised, please find attached my report on Ellen
Kelly. In it, you'll find my professional assessment of
Ellen's mental health, along with my recommendation
that she continues her counselling sessions for a further
six months. I've also stated that I believe Ellen is ready to
return to work, but in a reduced capacity.

Off the record, though, there's something you need to
be aware of.

As you know, Ellen only agreed to counselling because
it was one of the recommendations of the IPCC investigation following the fatal shooting incident last year.
Despite the compulsory nature of the sessions, I think
Ellen has enjoyed them more than she expected and I
hope she has found them useful.

She is a compassionate, intelligent woman who clearly
loves her two children and is still mourning the tragic
death of her husband three years ago. Dealing with any
death is difficult, but coping in the aftermath of a murder
can be an unmanageable burden. In general, I would say
Ellen is dealing with her loss as well as can be expected.

As you've already said, she is remarkably modest.

I read the official report on the Hope investigation. It's clear that Ellen was solely responsible for saving the lives of Katie Hope and her son, Jake. Ellen's bravery in confronting the man who abducted them is the single reason they are still here today. And yet she refuses to acknowledge that.

At first, I put this down to guilt. The only way she was able to save Katie and Jake was by killing William Dunston, the man who abducted them. However, at the end of ten counselling sessions with Ellen, I am doubtful now that this is the case.

And here's the thing you need to be aware of, Ed. I can see no sign that Ellen feels any guilt at all about what she did. As you know, I've worked with several men and women who have killed in the line of duty. In every case, the officer in question struggles to come to terms with what they've done. Taking another person's life leaves its mark. And there seems to be little correlation between the 'sort' of victim and the level of guilt. Drug-dealers, child abusers, murderers – many of your colleagues would say they got what they deserved. And yet ... One officer, for example, shot dead a serial killer in self-defence. His guilt was such that he couldn't face returning to work and, eventually, packed it in altogether. Every time he thought about it, he saw the face of the man he'd killed and he just couldn't do it.

So what makes Ellen different? Normally, I'd say this lack of remorse might indicate a psychopathic personality, but with Ellen that's categorically not the case. (And yes, I did run some standard tests – it's all in the report.)

There is another explanation but it's not one you'll want to hear. You see, far from showing signs of guilt, Ellen seems glad about what happened. And knowing what we do about who she blames for her husband's death, I am left with a question: did Ellen kill William Dunston in self-defence or did she kill him deliberately?

I know the IPCC cleared Ellen of any wrong-doing and there is no reason to dispute that ruling. And what I'm telling you now is just a hunch and – very occasionally (!) – my hunches are wrong. I like Ellen. I can see why you rate her so highly. But there's something not quite right about her reaction to Dunston's death. You and I go way back, Ed, otherwise I wouldn't even mention this. But I owe it to you to be as honest as I can. Plus I trust you to treat what I've told you in confidence.

I've done my best, but I'd really like to get to the bottom of this. Until I do, I would strongly recommend Ellen continues her counselling sessions and you keep her off frontline work until further notice.

All the very best

Briony

MONDAY, 14 FEBRUARY

09:45

They were coming. Brian couldn't see them. Not yet. No problem hearing them, though. Their voices drifted towards him, breaking the silence of the empty street. Daddy shouting and Marion's little voice answering back.

Brian tensed. He wanted to warn her, tell her not to talk back. Daddy didn't like it. It wound him up something terrible. And you didn't want that.

They turned into Lenham Road and now he could see them. He stepped back into the garden behind him, breath held, waiting. Daddy would leave Marion, like he did every morning, and let her run on her own to the school at the other end of the street.

They were late. The other kids had already gone in. If you looked up and down Lenham Road, there wasn't a soul about. Apart from Daddy and Marion. And Brian himself, of course. Except hidden in the garden like this, you'd have a problem noticing him there at all. Which was the idea.

He'd chosen this place on purpose. Behind him, the big house was derelict – windows smashed or boarded-up, no sign of anyone having lived here for a long time. No fear of anyone lurking inside, watching what he was up to.

Daddy looked different, but Brian had expected that. He'd probably changed his appearance on purpose. Trying to disguise himself. Doing all he could to confuse Brian. Daddy was clever that way. Not like Brian, who took after his Mam and was a brainless twat. Or so Daddy said.

In fact, Brian was cleverer than Daddy gave him credit for. Fair enough, he'd made some mistakes, messed things up from time to time. Especially with Molly. It would be different this time, though. He could feel it. This time, he knew exactly what he was doing.

Daddy leant down, like he was trying to give Marion a kiss. It was all Brian could do to stop himself jumping out from his hiding place and screaming at Daddy to take his hands off her. But he didn't have to worry. Marion had already turned away and was running down the street towards the school.

Daddy called after her but she didn't stop, didn't even slow her stride or look back. Couldn't wait to get away from the mean old bastard.

'Just go!' Brian whispered, willing Daddy to walk away.

Marion was getting closer.

'Go!'

His hands clenched into fists, fingernails digging into his palms. Marion slowed down. Not running anymore. Daddy turned and started walking, disappeared around the corner. Gone. Only Marion left. Nearly here now.

His heart was thumping so loudly it was a wonder she couldn't hear it. But she showed no sign of hearing anything except the song she was singing. It was that stupid song she sang every morning. Something about a man and a mirror. And when she got to the middle bit she'd squeal – dead loud – like someone was hurting her. He hated that song. Especially the squealing. It drilled into his head until he thought he'd do anything to get it to stop. She wouldn't sing that when they were together. He'd get her to sing other songs for him instead. Songs like *Over the Rainbow* or *Endless Love*. Proper songs without all that bloody squealing.

His heart was really going for it now, banging away like a drum. The palms of his hands were damp. He kept wiping them on his jeans, but it made no difference. Moments later they'd be all wet again. Nerves, that's what it was.

What if she didn't recognise him?

He shook his head, smiling at himself for being so daft. Hadn't he gone over this again and again?

She'd be a bit shocked to start with, of course. He'd prepared himself for that. It had been a while, after all. That's why he'd decided to do it this way. Once they got home, he could explain things properly to her. Plenty of time for chatting then.

Now, he had to concentrate on Marion.

He glanced behind him — at the house with the boarded up windows; at the white van parked on the gravelled driveway, its doors open, ready and waiting.

Marion's voice. The words growing clearer as she drew close.

'I'm starting with the ma-an in the mirror ...'

One.

'... I'm asking him to cha-ange his ways ...'

Two.

'... *No message could have been any clearer ...*'

Three!

He jumped from his hiding place, reached out and grabbed her, all in one smooth action. He swung her in the air and lowered her gently into the back of the van, hand covering her mouth the whole time so she couldn't scream out. Holding her down while he wrapped the thick tape around her was a bit tricky, but nothing he couldn't handle. She kept wriggling and trying to hit him, but he got there in the end. As he closed the doors, he couldn't stop smiling.

Humming quietly to himself, Brian climbed into the van and reversed out of the driveway. Lenham Road was still deserted. Even if someone did happen to pass by, he doubted they would be able to hear the feeble thumps coming from the back of the van.

Let's see who's the brainless twat now, Daddy.

13:30

He called her Blue. Because of her eyes, he said. Told her they were the bluest things he'd ever seen. Later, when he knew her real name, he still called her Blue. She liked it. Blue. Vinny's name for her.

He was gone now. Only his voice came back to her. During the long nights of jumbled sleep and tumbled dreams, she'd hear his voice whispering in her ear: 'What you up to, Blue?'

She'd lie there, eyes closed, still asleep, head twisting from side to side on the pillow, trying to follow the sound, trying to see him. But she never did. There was only the voice. So close she'd imagine she could feel his warm breath on her cheek as he whispered to her.

'What you up to, Blue?'

And even though she couldn't see him, she'd try to answer. Try to tell him what she'd been up to. Struggling out of sleep as she used every bit of strength to get her mouth working, get the words out.

Except every time, every single sodding time, she was too late. By the time she managed to say something her eyes were open and she was awake and he was gone. Always gone.

Vinny. Ellen thought of him the moment she got out of her car and looked up the length of Lenham Road, to the school at the other end. Maybe it was the black and yellow lines of police tape blocking access, or maybe the alien army of white-suited, silent SOCOs inching their way along Lenham Road, examining the scene meticulously for traces of forensic evidence. Most likely, though, it was the unmistakable sense that something terrible had happened here, and that the lives of those directly affected had changed forever in ways they could never have foreseen.

An icy February wind cut across South-East London, rustling the protective plastic boots Ellen had put on and causing the ends of her blue Reiss winter coat to flap against her legs. When she shivered, though, it wasn't because of the wind. It was the sight of a child's black shoulder bag lying on the pavement, like it had been thrown there.

It was similar to the bags her own children had, with a round school logo on the front. This bag had opened and some of its contents had fallen out, including a slim paperback book. It was too far away for Ellen to read the title, but she recognised the image. The shadowy outline of a man and a young boy, with aeroplanes flying overhead. *Goodnight Mister Tom*. Waterstones in Bromley had it on special offer before Christmas. She'd bought a copy for Pat, her eldest child.

It seemed wrong, somehow, for the bag and its contents to be left on the ground like that. The mother in Ellen wanted to run down the road and pick up the bag, carefully put everything back inside and hand it back to the little girl who'd dropped it.

Except there was no little girl.

'Boss!' A familiar voice rose above the low moan of the wind. Ellen turned around, saw a short man with cropped ginger hair and a large stomach charging towards her like a bull. She held up her hands, protecting herself, as he slid to a halt in front of her, his white face shiny with pleasure. Malcolm McDonald.

'Baxter said he'd called you,' Malcolm said. 'He wasn't sure how soon you'd be able to get sorted, though. It's true then, is it? You're coming back? About bloody time. Hasn't been the same without you, Ellen.'

Ellen cocked an eyebrow.

'Sorry,' Malcolm said. 'It hasn't been the same without you, *Ma'am*. Pretty bad business to come back to, though. You sure you're up to this? I mean, can't be easy. Another missing kid on your first day back. I mean, it's bound to bring back some memories, right?'

'You been on training to become more tactful?' Ellen asked.

'Huh?'

Ellen smiled. 'Didn't think so. Right, let's get to it. What's happened here? I got the basics from Baxter, but go through it again for me. From the beginning.'

'Jodie Hudson,' Malcolm began. 'Ten years old. Father took her to school this morning, like he does every morning. Left her at the top of the road – here – for her to walk the last bit by herself. School's down there. Look, you can see for yourself. Three hundred metres max. You can't see the road from the classrooms, but anyone standing at the school gates would have been able to see Jodie walking the whole way along the road. Except she never got there.'

'When she didn't turn up for school, they phoned the mother, who called the father, only she couldn't get through to him. She wasn't too worried at first. Assumed the girl was sick and Dad had forgotten to call the school to let them know. Sadly, that wasn't the case. Father wasn't tracked down till two minutes past eleven.'

Ellen interrupted him. 'Okay. Questions. One, why didn't anyone notice her? When I drop my kids to school the road is packed with parents and children rushing to get there before the bell rings. Two, if the girl was sick, why wouldn't the mother know that already? Are the parents separated? Three, where the hell was the father between dropping the daughter off and eleven o'clock?'

'The street was empty,' Malcolm said. 'They were running late. A regular occurrence, according to the school. Girl's parents aren't separated, but the mother works in the City and leaves early every morning. She's the breadwinner. Dad stays at home and looks after the kids. Two kids. Jodie and her older brother, Finlay – fourteen years old, goes to Thomas Moore in Eltham. Catholic family, as you've probably gathered.'

Ellen nodded. St Anne's, the school Jodie was trying to get to, was a Catholic school, like the one her own children attended in Greenwich. Plenty of Catholic schools in this part of London to meet the large population of first- and second-generation Irish and Poles.

'And the father?' she asked.

Malcolm shrugged. 'Not sure yet. Claims he was shopping in Lewisham and had his phone switched off. We've no idea yet if that's true or not. He's at the station now being questioned. Mother's there too. Baxter's with them.'

Malcolm said something else, but Ellen had stopped listening. She turned away from him, looking down Lenham Road as she tried to picture the scene. The little girl skipping down the road, father standing where Ellen stood now. She imagined him watching his daughter for a moment and then – reluctantly, maybe – turning and walking away. And after he was gone, the girl keeps going, her bag over her shoulders, slapping gently against her back in time with her footsteps. And then ... What?

Or maybe it didn't happen like that at all. Maybe the daughter had said something to upset or anger her father. As she walks away from him, he can't stop thinking about what she's said. He's angry. Really angry.

Jodie's bag lay beside the entrance to one of the houses on Lenham Road. The house was boarded-up. Looked as if it hadn't been lived in for years. What if the father ran after her? Grabbed hold of her and dragged her into the garden? She fights back and in the scuffle, her bag falls to the ground. Neither of them notices. She's too scared, he's too angry. And then the red mist descends and something terrible happens and afterwards, he doesn't have a daughter anymore.

Ellen looked at Malcolm. 'What do you think happened?'

'Thought we was meant to keep an open mind,' he said. 'Isn't that what you're always telling us?'

'True,' Ellen said. 'But a good detective also follows their gut instinct. What's your gut telling you, Malcolm?'

Malcolm ran a hand over his tight haircut and sighed. 'There's a part of me, right, that keeps thinking it must be the father. I mean, that's the most likely explanation, right? Except there's something else I keep thinking about as well.'

'Go on,' Ellen said.

'Something about it reminds me of Molly York,' Malcolm said. 'Remember that case? I know this is different because Molly was over three years ago and there's been nothing like it since.

But in here,' Malcolm thumped his chest. Hard. 'In here, I can't help thinking the two things might be related. And that makes me feel sick, El– I mean, Ma'am. Sick as a dog. Because if the same person who took Molly has taken Jodie, then, well, you know what that means.'

Ellen knew exactly what it meant. She remembered the photos of Molly's dead, mutilated body. The thought of the same thing happening again. She hadn't seen a photo of Jodie yet, hadn't spoken to her family or friends or formed any clear picture in her head of what the child was like. But that paperback lying on the ground was all Ellen needed. In her mind, Jodie was already there. Her head buried in Michelle Magorian's classic story of war and friendship.

Other images were there, too. Images Ellen tried to push aside. Jodie without her book, her face unrecognisable from fear and terror and pain. The sound of her voice, screaming inside Ellen's head, begging Ellen to find her, to save her from the unimaginable hell.

Ellen blinked twice. The images faded until the only thing she could see was Malcolm, a frown creasing his shiny forehead as he stared at her.

'We'll find her,' she said. 'Even if it is the same sick bastard. We'll find Jodie and we'll make sure, whoever he is, he'll never harm another child for the rest of his miserable life. Okay?'

The frown disappeared.

'It's good to have you back,' Malcolm said.

14:30

Ellen got out of the car, locked it and hurried towards the white building at the end of the car park. At the entrance, she held her security pass against the door, waited for the red light to flash green, pushed the door open and stepped inside.

Keeping her head down, she strode quickly to the lift. When she pressed the button, the doors slid open and she crossed over into the narrow space, only allowing herself to breathe once she'd pushed the button for the third floor and the lift started to ascend.

Her hands had a slight shake, as if she'd been drinking the night before. Being back here, in this building, it affected her more than she'd expected. She thought she'd prepared herself. Had run through any variety of situations and anticipated emotions. The one thing she hadn't expected was that she'd feel so damn scared. Nerves she'd expected. Excitement, too. Apprehension, of course. And even a bit of uncertainty. But this? Fear was something new. She didn't like it one bit.

Pushing it aside, she tried to focus on the positives. Over the past two months, she'd built up this moment, going over it again and again. Her return to the job. A sure sign that she was starting to put the past behind her and move on with her life. It was good to be back. It had to be. Because the alternative – that she wouldn't be up to the job, anymore – was unthinkable.

Malcolm had wanted to come back with her, but she'd made

him stay at the scene to co-ordinate things at that end. A team of uniforms had already arrived and were conducting the door-to-doors. Ellen had told Malcolm to set up the school interviews, questioning staff and pupils, looking for any clue as to where Jodie might be or who had taken her.

The lift stopped, doors opened and Ellen stepped out. The corridor stretched out in front of her, limitless in length. Or so it seemed at that moment. Behind her, the lift doors closed with a *whish*. Part of Ellen wished she could turn and go back, pretend she'd never been here. The other part of her said she needed to get a grip. Quickly.

She took a deep breath and started walking.

Her footsteps were loud against the tiled floor. The sound echoed around the corridor, competing for Ellen's attention with the flood of memories. People, cases, sounds, emotions – a rush of everything, making her light-headed, almost giddy.

Suddenly, she had reached Room 3.03. The door was closed, but she could hear the buzz of voices inside the room. Alastair Dillon's low, Scottish growl; Raj Patel's rich, resonant rhetoric; and Abby Roberts' high-pitched, girly voice, as grating as finger-nails on glass.

Ellen pressed down on the handle and pushed open the door.

A burst of noise hit her, short and sharp, like a slap. Then silence followed, just as startling, as all the faces in the room turned and stared at her. She stared back, unable to speak. She wanted to move forward, make the moment pass, but she was

23

incapable of doing anything.

There were just the three of them. DC Raj Patel, DC Alastair Dillon who, by some odd coincidence, came from the place as Malcolm McDonald – a small town on the Scottish island of Orkney. And, at the front of the room, separate from the others, Abby Roberts, the family liaison officer.

Ellen's eyes locked briefly with Abby's before the other woman turned back to her computer. Her fingers tapping on the keyboard sounded overly loud in the surrounding silence.

There was a scraping sound as Raj pushed his chair back and got to his feet, face breaking into a smile, transforming it. Before Ellen could react, he started clapping. Suddenly, Alastair was on his feet, clapping as well, the sound drowning out the tap-tapping of the keyboard as Abby continued typing, ignoring what was going on behind her.

The noise and the subsequent embarrassment was enough of a trigger to get Ellen moving again. She stepped forward, face burning, and told them to behave. As the clapping stopped, Raj moved towards her, hand outstretched.

'Good to have you back,' he said. 'Pleased as anything when I come in this morning and the boss says you'll be part of this. Between you and me, he looks like he's feeling the pressure.'

Ellen managed something approaching a smile, although she felt closer to crying. The reaction from her team was so unexpected. During the dark days she'd been away, she'd thought about them a lot. Missed them and wondered how they were.

It had never occurred to her they might be thinking of her too.

She glanced through the glass panel that split the room in two. On the other side of the glass, a row of uniformed officers were on the phones. Following up statements taken on the door-to-door enquiries, taking calls from the usual selection of well-meaning members of the public and a significant number of nutters who seemed to have nothing better to do with their time. Ellen knew if she went through the list of callers, she'd see a smattering of names she recognised from earlier investigations.

On this side of the glass a massive whiteboard took up one side of the room. At the centre, a blown-up photo of a young girl with dark hair, blue eyes and a cute, crooked smile. The name Jodie Hudson written underneath in blue pen, alongside the date and time of her disappearance.

Ellen turned back to Raj, avoiding eye contact. He had this way of looking at people, like he understood what they were thinking. It never failed to unsettle her.

'Right,' she said. 'I'm anxious to get stuck in, but I need to talk to Baxter first, then we can go over what we have. Where is he?'

'In his office,' Raj said, nodding towards the door.

She thanked Raj and scowled at Abby's back, still tensed over the keyboard, still typing furiously. Then she got the hell out of there as quickly as she could.

Ed's office was two doors down from the incident room. Unusually, his door was closed so Ellen knocked and waited for him to answer. She was about to knock a second time when she heard his voice, telling her to come in.

He was sitting at his desk, head in his hands. At first, he seemed barely aware she'd entered the room but when she said his name, he looked up.

'Ah, Ellen,' he said. 'Good. Take a seat.'

She sat down, grateful for the support for her shaking legs. Despite the chill of the day, she was hot. Her hands were clammy and she wiped them several times on her trousers in a futile attempt to dry them off.

'Black no sugar, right?' Ed said. He stood and moved across to the coffee machine on the shelf beside his desk.

Ellen nodded, thinking a hot drink and a rush of caffeine to her system was probably the last thing she needed right now.

'Here you go.'

He placed a mug on the table in front of her and, despite her reservations, she breathed in the rich smell of fresh coffee with relish. She didn't reach out for the drink, though. She had to wait until her hands stopped shaking.

'You okay?' Ed settled back in his seat the other side of his desk.

'I think so,' she said. 'I was fine until I got up here. It feels,' she searched for the right word before shaking her head. 'I don't know how it feels, to be honest. It's good to be back, though. I know that.'

'It's good to have you back,' he said. 'Even if it is part-time for now. Thirty hours, right?'

Ellen nodded.

They both knew the reality would be more than that. She didn't care. It was thirty hours better than nothing.

'I'm ready,' she said.

He nodded. 'Good. Of course, if we find her within the next day or so, we can review the arrangements. Oh, and you need to continue with the counsellor as well. Another six months.'

'Why?'

Ed wouldn't look at her when he answered. 'That's between you and her, Ellen. If she says you need some more sessions, then who am I to argue with her?'

'What did she say about me?' Ellen asked.

'She said you're good to return to work,' Ed said. 'Or else you wouldn't be here. Okay?'

Ellen shrugged. 'Guess it'll have to be.'

In truth, the counselling sessions weren't as bad as she'd expected. It was possible they were even helping. A little. Would probably help more if she applied herself to doing the small tasks Briony, the counsellor, set after each session. Except somehow, Ellen always found excuses not to find the twenty minutes it took to sit down each week and write about her feelings. She just wasn't that type of person and being asked to do something she found so difficult, well, it was easier simply to resent being asked in the first place and ignore the request. Over and over.

'Kids okay?' Ed asked.

'Great,' she said. 'Hard work as well. But lovely. Perfect, in fact.'

Ed nodded. 'You know Ellen, you should only be here if you're sure it's what you want. I used to think work was what gave meaning to my life. It's only recently I've realised it's a distraction. Nothing more than that. Family's what matters. If you want to be with your kids, then don't let me or anyone else stop you. Okay?'

'Hey.' She held up a hand. 'Shouldn't you be giving me a pep-talk instead of encouraging me to go home again? Seriously, it's great to be back. I've found it really tough these last few months. I don't know how other women do it.'

'Everyone's different,' Ed said. 'My Andrea never worked a day in her life once Melissa came along. And I don't think she regrets a moment of it.'

His voice trailed off and he gazed off to the side. Ellen waited, hoping he'd change the subject. The last thing she wanted was a cosy chat about his home life. Things might be better between them, but she wasn't ready for that. Not yet.

She waited for him to say something else. But he stayed quiet, lost in his own thoughts.

'Are you okay?' she asked.

'Sorry,' he said. 'Got distracted there for a minute. Right. Where were we?'

He looked exhausted. Ellen thought she knew why. The case felt like Molly York all over again – girl disappeared, no clues or leads, dead-ends everywhere they looked. Only this time, they had a chance to get it right. To find the missing girl before it was too late.

'Jodie Hudson,' Ellen said. 'I've been to down to Lenham Road. So far, no witnesses, no leads. Nothing.'

The tremor in her hands was gone and she felt safe enough trying the coffee. It was good. Just the right side of bitter, with a kick to it.

'It's as high-risk case,' Ed said. 'Obviously. That's why we're leading on it.'

Missing children cases were routinely handled by CAT, the child abuse investigation team. If SCD1 Homicide command were leading, it meant this was being treated as a stranger abduction. Or possible murder. Given the girl's age, the chain of command made sense.

Ellen pictured the smiling ten-year-old she'd seen in the incident room. She thought of her own children, the visceral love she felt for them, and shivered. The thought of anything happening to them was beyond anything she could comprehend.

'What about the parents?' she asked.

'They've gone home,' Ed said. 'For now. Roberts will go and stay with them. She'll be the FLO on this.'

Ellen drained the rest of her coffee. Felt her face flush.

'Is that a problem?' Ed asked. 'If it is, I need to know now.'

He'd promised her, hadn't he?

'It's fine,' she said.

Ed nodded. 'Good. You'll need to speak to her as soon as we're done. In fact, you'll probably be working closely with

Roberts the whole way through this. Who knows? Might turn out to be a good thing. Give you girls a chance to get over your differences.'

Ellen stared at him, not trusting herself to speak. Her face was still hot. This time, she knew the cause. Anger. He had a bare-faced cheek trying to turn this into some spat between 'the girls'.

She recalled the scene earlier in the room down the corridor. Two of her colleagues standing up to welcome her back. The other one sitting stubbornly at her desk, the angry clatter of her keyboard telling Ellen everything she needed to know about what Abby Roberts thought of her.

The image faded, replaced by another one. Abby Roberts and Ed Baxter. Abby on her knees, face flushed red as she turned to look at Ellen. Baxter, eyes wide with shock, realising he had – quite literally – been caught with his trousers down. The incident happened two days before Abby's application for transferral to CID had been approved. By none other than DCI Ed Baxter.

He had the grace to drop eye contact. Clearing his throat, he shuffled the papers on her desk, refusing to look at her.

'That sounded wrong,' he said. 'And patronising. Sorry. I'm trying here, Ellen, but it's not easy. I made a mistake. I told you that already. Can't we at least try to move on?'

What about your wife? Ellen wanted to ask him. Did you ever tell her what you did? Except she knew it was none of her business. Not really. So she kept her mouth shut and waited for him to continue.

He sighed. 'Right then. I'm the SIO and I'll be as hands-on as I can, but I've a lot on my plate at the moment. I need you. I know you're only part-time for now. Even part-time, you could run rings around anyone else in the place.'

The praise worked. Her anger faded. Damn him. He always knew which buttons to push.

'Thanks,' she said.

'Don't thank me,' Ed replied. 'I mean it. It's bloody good to have you back. Here, do you fancy a top-up?'

He lifted the cafetiere and Ellen shook her head. The surge of caffeine, combined with the familiar rush of adrenalin as she focussed on the challenge ahead, was more than enough.

'How did the parents seem?' she asked.

'Kevin and Helen Hudson,' Ed said. 'Good question. There's something off there. Something I can't quite put my finger on.'

'Can you be a bit more specific?'

Ed's forehead wrinkled, the way it always did when he concentrated.

'I don't like the father,' he said after a moment. 'But it's more than that. I don't like lots of people, but it doesn't make them criminals. He's got form, though. Previous. Maybe that's what my problem is.'

'Doesn't mean he'd harm his own kid,' Ellen said.

'Maybe,' Ed said. 'Maybe not. He did time for GBH. So we know he's got a history of violence. Couple that with the fact he's not the kid's real father and I'd say we've got a pretty good case

31

for keeping a close eye on him. They're hiding something. Him and his missus. That's the impression I got when we interviewed them.'

'Not the real father?' Ellen asked.

'Kevin's the second husband,' Ed said. 'First husband ran off to Dubai when the marriage broke down a few years back. When Kevin and Helen got married, he adopted the kids and, seemingly, has raised them as his own. Husband number one is still in Dubai. We've already checked that. No record of him being back in Blighty over the last few years. No contact with his kids at all, apparently. Helen Hudson's taste in men obviously leaves a lot to be desired.

'Kevin doesn't work. Helen's the breadwinner. Happy to earn the money while her husband lays about the place doing nothing.'

'Hardly laying about if he looks after the kids,' Ellen said. 'Why doesn't he work? Do we know?'

'He's an ex-con,' Ed said, as if that was all the explanation that was necessary. 'Right. I've got a lot to get through. I need you to get over to the Hudsons' as soon as possible. Question both of them and see what you come up with. Speak to Roberts first. Get her view on things.'

Ellen knew she was being dismissed. Before she left, she had one last question.

'Ed, you haven't mentioned Molly York yet. Why is that?'

'I'm not convinced,' Ed said. 'It was flagged up on HOLMES. But that's hardly a surprise. Two girls go missing from the same borough. Both the same age; both pretty middle-class girls. That's what HOLMES does, Ellen. It connects those dotted lines. But it's not that simple.

'It's three years since Molly was taken. Nothing between then and now. To focus all our resources on finding a nonexistent link between the two disappearances would be foolish. I won't ignore it, of course. But I'm going to make sure we explore every other angle, too. No path unfollowed, no stone unturned. You know the score.

'And that starts with the family. Let's focus on them, Ellen. Kevin Hudson's hiding something. I want to know what that is. And soon. Time's already slipping past us. I want Kevin investigated and either discounted or arrested. If he's done something to Jodie, let's find that out as quickly as we can. If he's innocent – which I very much doubt – then let's clear him from the investigation so we can focus our efforts elsewhere. Got that?'

15:15

Back in the incident room, Raj and Alastair were still at their desks. Malcolm was here as well, shouting something about Rangers' performance the night before. He stopped talking abruptly when he saw Ellen.

Ignoring him, she walked to the top of the room.

'Where's Roberts?' she asked.

'Gone across to the Hudsons' place,' Raj said.

A surge of anger rose inside Ellen. She'd come back here, bracing herself for a confrontation. And now the stupid cow wasn't here. Even though she knew – she *knew* – that Ellen would expect to speak to her first.

'Why the hell did she do that?' Ellen asked.

Raj shrugged and looked embarrassed. She scanned the rest of the faces in the room. No one would look at her. Ellen didn't push it. Abby's attitude wasn't their problem; it was hers. A frank conversation was on the cards the moment she got her hands on Abby bloody Roberts.

'Never mind,' she said. 'We've got more important things to focus on. Malcolm, how did you get on at the school?'

'Nothing very helpful,' Malcolm said. 'Jodie's a bright, popular kid. Lots of friends, no issues as far as anyone's aware. Two close friends ...' he consulted his notebook, '... Grace Reed and Holly Osbourne. Both claim to have no idea where Jodie could be. I don't think they were hiding anything. A few of the teachers mentioned that Jodie's father, Kevin, is a bit odd. Parents at the school gate shared the same view, by and large. Couldn't get anything definite, though. Just the sense that not many people liked him. Oh, and several of the parents said they'd seen him shouting at Jodie more than once.

'The head mistress, Celia Roth, wasn't around. She's on compassionate leave. Mother died last week. She'll be back at work on Monday.'

'What about door-to-doors?' Ellen asked.

Malcolm shook his head. 'One old bird thought she saw a white van around the time Jodie was meant to have disappeared. Couldn't be specific on model or anything else. Apart from that, nothing, I'm afraid.'

Nothing.

Ellen bit back her frustration, forced herself to concentrate. Focus on the family. That was Ed's instruction. And yet how could she do that and ignore what was staring them in the face?

'Right,' she said. 'Here's what happens next. Malcolm, get the contact details for all the families in Jodie's class. Speak to the school admin and get them to give you whatever you need. Then I want you to visit every single family and see what you can find out about Jodie and her family. Parents will have a totally different perspective from the kids and teachers.'

'Alastair and Raj, I need you to start going through CCTV. See what we've got. There's a garage on Lee High Road, several small businesses. We're looking for anything out of the ordinary. Especially any sightings of a white van. You'll need to co-ordinate the door-to-doors. Have we got anyone doing Dallinger Road yet?'

Raj nodded. 'Team went out half-an-hour ago.'

'Good.' Ellen turned to the other detective in the room. 'Alastair, do you remember Molly York? Good. When you're done with the CCTV, I want you to dig up everything you can find on that case. Make a list of all the similarities between this case and that one. Note down anything and everything. Got that?'

Alastair's eyes widened. 'You think there's a connection?'

'I don't know,' Ellen said. 'All I know is it's something we should consider. Just in case. Remember Katie Hope? We only found Katie and her boy because we dug deep into her past and followed leads that, at the time, seemed pointless. We found Katie and we'll find Jodie, too. We just need to work at it.'

'What about you?' Alastair asked. 'Where will you be if we need to speak to you?'

'I'm going across to see the Hudsons,' she said. 'I need to speak to them as soon as I can. And I'm keen to have a word with Roberts, too. I'm on the mobile. See you later.'

She said goodbye to the team and left them to it. Fear clung to her, wound its way inside her, sat in the pit of her stomach; a dead weight. Fear that she couldn't do it. That she would mess up and a little girl's life would be lost. It was good to be scared. Ellen knew that. The fear would push her forward and keep her focussed. Help her find Jodie. Before it was too late.

16:00

Lee, South-East London. A sprawling suburb on the edges of Lewisham and Blackheath. Ellen's old stomping ground from way back. Not the most exciting place in the world, but it had plenty of green space, good schools and a strong sense of local community. There were worse places to bring up children. Unless you happened to be Kevin and Helen Hudson.

The Hudsons lived on Dallinger Road, a quiet street of

detached and semi-detached 1930s houses in the heart of peaceful, prosperous SE12. Their house was at the top of the road. As Ellen stepped from the car, she was hit with a blast of icy wind, full of the promise of snow.

So far, there was no sign of any press. Ellen knew that would soon change. Right now, Ed was sitting down with Jamala Nnamani, Lewisham's Media and Communications Officer, to finalise the media strategy. This time tomorrow, the road would be crawling with reporters.

Ellen ran through the biting cold to the house and rang the doorbell. As she waited, she looked along the road for Abby's car, before remembering she had no idea what it looked like.

The anger she'd felt back at the station resurfaced. Abby was good at what she did. Even though it killed Ellen to admit that. It was why she'd wanted the FLO's insights into the Hudsons before meeting them. Not after. Still, nothing Ellen could do about that now.

Inside the house, she heard footsteps. The door swung open and Ellen was face to face with Abby.

'Oh,' Abby said. 'You. No one told me you'd be here. I could have warned Helen and Kevin.'

The expression on her perfect face was utterly guileless and Ellen wondered if the FLO almost believed the lie herself. Then she got a grip. Abby manipulated everyone to her own means. Everyone except Ellen, who knew only too well how far Abby would go to get what she wanted.

'Warn them?' Ellen asked pointedly.

Abby blushed. Some people didn't suit blushing. Abby Roberts wasn't one of those people.

'You know what I mean,' Abby said.

Ellen pushed past her into the house without bothering to reply. There was an unnatural stillness in the house, something Ellen recognised. During times of great trauma, people's behaviour became muted, speaking to each other in low voices, moving slowly, as if they'd been drugged.

The hallway was bright and airy, decorated in a pared-back, Scandi style: stripped floorboards, white walls and minimal clutter.

'This way.' Abby led Ellen through the hallway, into the kitchen. Like the hall, the kitchen was modern and minimalist. The wall between the kitchen and sitting room had been knocked down, creating a large, open-plan living area.

A man, woman and young boy all sat on red chairs at the white dining table. The woman was short and slim with thick dark hair and huge brown eyes. When she saw Ellen, she jumped up.

'Helen.' Abby went over and put her hand on the woman's arm. 'This is DI Kelly, Lewisham CID.'

Briefly, Helen's face lit up. Just as quickly, it crumbled again. She grabbed the back of the chair, as if she might fall otherwise.

'Is it ...?' her voice trailed off and she seemed to be struggling to breathe.

'No,' Ellen said. 'I'm sorry. It's not that. I just need to ask you a few more questions. You and the rest of the family.'

She looked at the man and boy. Kevin Hudson was tall with thinning, mousy-brown hair. His son – step-son – sat beside him, holding his father's hand. The boy looked like neither parent and Ellen assumed he took after his father. A good-looking kid, with long dark hair that flopped forward over his pale face. He had striking green eyes with long, thick black lashes. Like his father and mother, the boy's face had that shell-shocked look to it that Ellen had seen so many times before. Had seen it in her own face, staring back at her from the bathroom mirror, the night Vinny had been killed.

'Do you mind if we sit down?' Ellen asked. 'I'm sure Abby would be happy to make us all a pot of tea.' She gave Abby her sweetest smile. 'Wouldn't you?'

Ellen waited until Helen sat, then pulled out one of the red chairs and sat down herself. As well as being ugly, the chair was uncomfortable. Made her wonder what the Hudsons had been thinking when they chose them.

'Are you any closer to finding her?' Helen asked. 'That's what we need. Not more questions. We've already told you lot every-thing we know. And what about her?' She nodded at Abby. 'Why do we need two of you here? You should be out looking for Jodie, not sitting here drinking cups of fucking tea.'

'DS Roberts is the family liaison officer,' Ellen said. 'Her role is to be the link between you and us. That's what she does. My job is to find Jodie. That's what I do and that's why I'm here.'

'I recognise the name,' Kevin said. 'Ellen Kelly. You found that woman who went missing a few months ago. Her and her kid. That was you.'

'That's right,' Ellen said.

'And now you'll find Jodie,' Kevin said, as if he had no doubt about this.

Abby came across with the tea, handed out mugs. When Kevin picked up his, Ellen noticed the way his hand shook.

'You killed him,' Kevin continued. 'The guy who was after her. I remember. What was his name – Billy something?'

Dunston. Billy Dunston. Vinny's killer.

The explosion. Warm blood splattered across her cheeks. Dunston's face disappearing. His body falling on top of her. Holding the gun to his shattered head and pulling the trigger. Again. And again.

'It was self-defence,' Ellen said, recycling the same old lie she'd used ever since that day.

Kevin put down his mug and stared at her. 'Isn't that what we all say?'

Ellen wanted to drop eye contact, but she waited. Eventually, he turned away.

'I can't imagine what this must be like for you both,' Ellen said. She looked at the boy, who'd so far remained silent. 'Or you, Finlay. You must be so worried.'

He tried to say something, but his mother cut in first.

'No one can,' Helen said. 'And you're not helping. All this time spent asking questions, you could have found her by now.'

'We're doing everything possible,' Ellen said. 'I promise you.'

'No,' Helen said. 'That's not true. You're spending all your time focussing on Kevin. Don't pretend you're not. It's why you're here now, isn't it? To see if you can dig up some more dirt on him. And while you're doing that, some ... some maniac has got my child and instead of looking for her, instead of tracking that animal down and castrating him, you're here asking your stupid questions when you should be out there finding my little girl!'

'Helen.' Abby put her hands on the woman's shoulders. 'Don't let yourself get stressed. You're under enough pressure as it is. That's it. Deep breaths, remember?'

If it had been Ellen, she would have thrown Abby across the room for laying a hand on her. Helen Hudson, on the other hand, seemed grateful for the FLO's intervention.

'Let's get this over and done with, then.' Kevin said. His eyes flicked to Helen. 'My wife really can't take much more.'

'Tell me about this morning,' Ellen said.

The white table had traces of past meals on it: a faint brown circle from a bottle of red wine; children's fingerprints. Ellen pictured a happy family, sitting around it sharing a meal.

Helen moaned and the image faded.

Kevin reached out and squeezed his wife's hand.

'It was my fault,' he said. 'Helen starts work early, so I get the kids ready and take Jodie to school. Finlay can make his own way. He gets the bus at the bottom of the road. There's a gang of them who go together. I get him out the door and then walk Jodie down to St Anne's. We leave at just after half-eight to get there for nine. She's always asking to walk by herself, but I've never felt comfortable about that. She's in Year Five now. Some of her friends already walk on their own, but we've told her not till Year Six.'

'But you let her go part of the way on her own, right?' Ellen asked.

Kevin nodded. 'We compromise. St Anne's is at the top of Lenham Road. I leave her one end and let her walk up to the school on her own. She likes that. Loves the independence, you see. It's not much, I know. But that's London for you, isn't it?'

Helen snorted. 'Independence? It had nothing to do with independence. It was all to do with you wanting to get her off your hands as quickly as possible so you could ...'

'Could what?' Ellen asked as Helen stumbled to a halt.

'Get to the park,' she mumbled. 'He likes to have a coffee in Manor Park after dropping Jodie at school. Can't wait to get rid of her most mornings.'

Kevin buried his face in his hands, but his wife, on a roll now, wouldn't let up. 'If you'd stayed with her, this would never have happened.'

'What I need are the facts,' Ellen said. 'There's no point thinking about the *what ifs*. They'll just tear you apart. Kevin, how far down Lenham Road did Jodie go before you left?'

He lifted his face. 'I don't know. I've gone over and over it in my head. I think she was nearly at the school.'

'But you can't be sure?' Ellen asked.

He shook his head.

'Nobody saw a thing,' Helen said. 'How is that possible? How can a little girl just disappear into thin air like that?'

She reached across and grabbed Ellen's wrist. 'Someone must have seen something. The police say they've already spoken to everyone living on Lenham Road, but I don't believe them. You've got to help us. Someone, somewhere has my baby girl and I want her back. I need her back. And I keep thinking about poor Molly York. Every mother around here remembers her. What if the same person has taken Jodie? Oh God, I can't bear it. Please, DI Kelly. You've got to find her. You're our only hope.'

16:30

It was a typical girl's bedroom. Bright yellow walls covered in posters and drawings. Most of the posters were of a teen boy band that Ellen recognised from videos her own kids watched on YouTube. The drawings, obviously drawn by a child, were good, nevertheless. She made a note to find out if there was an art club at school. If the art teacher had noticed Jodie's talent and taken an interest, maybe he or she might have some insight into the child that they'd missed so far.

There was a cabin bed, like the one Pat had. Underneath the

bed was a desk and chair. Ellen sat down on the too-small chair and looked at the work laid out precisely on the desk. A white sheet of A3 paper, three pens lined up neatly beside it. On the A3 paper, a new drawing. This one of an old man with a beard and a young boy. The man had a paper bag in his hand and from this he was pulling out a book with the word BIBLE written across it.

It was a key scene from the early part of *Goodnight Mister Tom,* when Mister Tom and Willie meet for the first time. Ellen's own children often drew scenes from books they were reading. The only difference was that their drawings were nowhere near as accomplished as this one. Somehow, Jodie had managed to show the distress on Mister Tom's face as he tries to understand the contents of the bag.

Ellen pushed back the chair and stood up. Frustration ate away at her as she paced the small room, looking inside the wardrobe, pulling open drawers, searching – in vain – for anything that would give an idea of where Jodie might be: a letter from a pen pal, a copy of an email from someone she'd met online, a photograph, a train timetable, something that would help. She found nothing.

Being in this room, feeling Jodie all around her, heightened her sense of urgency. Jodie was in her head now. Not the made-up image she'd had earlier. Now, she was a real person. A white Ikea shelving unit ran along one wall. Both Ellen's children had the same shelves with similar collections of childhood junk on them. She moved across to this one, examining the photos, books, games and clutter.

More drawing and painting materials here: glue, scissors, pens, paintbrushes and an expensive-looking set of oil-based paints. Framed photos lined the top shelf. Different versions of Jodie at different stages in her life grinned out at Ellen. Jodie in a sheep's costume aged about five or six, on a stage with a group of children the same age; Jodie with two other girls on a beach, all three wearing swimsuits and big, happy smiles; Jodie with her brother on a windy hill somewhere, dark hair blowing over her face, blocking out those blue eyes; Jodie on a donkey at the top of Blackheath, the same place Ellen used to take her own children when they were younger. Jodie, Jodie, Jodie, everywhere she looked.

Ellen stared at the photos until she was certain each and every image was burned onto her brain. Then she left.

In the landing, she nearly collided with Finlay, who was standing right outside the door. It was obvious the boy had been waiting for her.

'Hey,' Ellen said. 'I was looking at some of your sister's artwork. She's very talented.'

He nodded. 'She loves drawing. There was this competition last year in Lewisham Library. You had to draw a picture that represented what it was like living in Lewisham and the winner had their drawing in the newspaper. Jodie won it.'

'What did she draw?' Ellen asked.

His eyes filled with tears and he shook his head. 'I heard what

Mum said,' he whispered. 'In the kitchen. You think my dad has something to do with this. Just because he was in prison before. But he's not like that. He's not some perv or, like, someone bad. He only went to prison 'cause he was trying to protect this girl. You're not going to arrest him, are you?'

Ellen wished he was younger so she could give him a hug. But his body language, so tense and confrontational, told her this would be utterly the wrong thing to do.

'Finlay,' she said. 'I promise you I'm not going to arrest anyone for something they didn't do. I want to find Jodie and I want to find the person who's taken her. If she's been taken. You know, it's possible she's just run away or there's some perfectly normal explanation for where she is. It's far too early to start worrying about things that may never happen.'

For the first time since she'd been here, the boy's face showed some sign of life.

'Do you really think that?' he asked. 'That she might have run away? She could have, you know. She had this big fight with Dad this morning. I heard them at it before I left.'

Easy, Ellen thought. Don't rush it, don't let him know this is important or he'll clam up.

'I row with my kids all the time,' she said. 'Especially my son. It's part of family life, I guess. So what was this row about then?'

'She has these new trainers,' Finlay said. 'She wanted to wear them to school, but Dad wouldn't let her. And sometimes when she goes on and on about something he gives in and lets her do what she wants. It drives Mum mad when he does that.'

Ellen smiled. 'I do the same. Sometimes it's easier than listening to the constant moaning. I take it your Dad wasn't so easy-going this morning?'

Finlay shook his head, but before he could say anything else, his father appeared at the bottom of the stairs.

'Everything okay up there?' he shouted up.

'Fine,' Ellen replied. 'We were just chatting, that's all.'

But the moment was gone. The boy had already turned and was running down the stairs, two at a time, to where his father waited. Almost, Ellen thought, like he was scared of what his father would do if he realised Finlay had been talking to her.

17:15

Downstairs, Ellen found both parents in the kitchen with Abby. There was no sign of Finlay.

'What happens now?' Kevin asked.

'Jodie's photo has been sent out to police stations across the country,' Abby said. 'Police officers will be working through the night, doing everything they can to find her.'

'There'll be press coverage, too,' Ellen said. 'DCI Baxter's been working with our press team this afternoon, devising a media strategy.'

'So there'll be journalists poking their noses into our business?' Kevin asked.

'It's unavoidable, I'm afraid,' Ellen said, thinking if it was her child, the last thing she'd care about would be intrusive journalists. Not if it helped find her daughter. She nodded at Abby. 'DI Roberts will be with you the whole time. She'll handle any press enquiries.'

'Absolutely.' Abby cut in, not seeming to care that Ellen hadn't finished. 'Listen, Helen and Kevin. It's very possible we'll find Jodie sooner rather than later. In that case, you've got nothing to worry about.'

'What if we don't?' Helen's voice was barely more than a whisper.

'We'll find her,' Ellen said, meaning it. She had Jodie's smiling face in her head now. They would remain there until the girl was safely back home again.

Ellen left soon after, instructing Abby to call her later with an update.

'Walk me to my car first,' she said. 'I need a word in private.'

Abby looked like she was about to protest but, wisely, she kept her mouth shut and followed Ellen outside. At the car, Ellen unlocked the door before turning to the FLO.

'Listen,' she said. 'We're going to have to work together, Abby. Whatever differences we've had in the past, I suggest we put those to one side for now and concentrate on the case. What do you say?'

Abby flushed. 'You went around telling everyone I'd slept with the boss. A bit difficult to put that to one side and just pretend it never happened. Do you know what a hard time I had when I started in CID because of that?'

'Two things,' Ellen said. 'One, you never should have slept with Baxter. It was unprofessional and stupid. Two, I damn well didn't go around telling everyone what you got up to. However your grubby little secret got out, it wasn't from me.'

The expression on Abby's face made it clear she didn't believe that. Ellen didn't care.

'I'll ask Baxter to assign a different FLO,' she said. 'If that's what's required. I need someone I can trust. Not someone who'll ignore explicit instructions from the boss because she's got some misplaced grudge against me.'

'What instructions?' Abby demanded. 'I don't know what you're talking about.'

Like hell you don't, Ellen thought.

'Baxter told you to brief me before coming over here this afternoon,' Ellen said.

Abby shook her head. 'No he didn't. If he had, I would have done that. What sort of idiot do you think I am that I'd ignore a specific order?'

She sounded genuinely aggrieved, but unless Ed was seriously losing the plot, Ellen didn't believe Abby. But getting into all that now would be petty and pointless. She needed to focus on Jodie. They both did.

'Bottom line, Abby. We have to get on. Somehow. So let's put our differences aside for now and concentrate on what really matters. Okay?'

Abby nodded. 'Fine with me. But you're wrong about T– Oh Lord, it doesn't matter.'

'What doesn't?'

'Nothing. Things are complicated, that's all.'

Abby looked like she was about to burst into tears. Dear God, Ellen thought, she's not in love with him? Sex for promotion was one thing. A soppy love affair something else entirely and the last thing Ellen needed right now.

'Tell me about Kevin,' she said.

'What about him?'

It was like prising open a pit bull's jaws.

'Do you think he's capable of killing his step-daughter and hiding the body?'

Abby frowned as she considered her answer. 'He is a bit odd,' she said. 'But he doesn't strike me as nasty. More nervous, really. Like he's scared of something.'

'Scared of what?' Ellen asked.

Abby gave a withering look. 'What do you think? His little girl's missing. Of course he's scared. Wouldn't you be?'

'He says he was in Lewisham this morning,' Ellen said, ignoring the question. 'Do you believe him?'

'Not sure,' Abby said. 'But I'll find out. I've already got Helen on side. And Finlay. Kevin's taking a bit more work, but I'll get there. I always do.'

I bet, Ellen thought.

She looked down Dallinger Road, spotted the pair of uniforms carrying out the door-to-doors. She needed a quick word with them, then back to Greenwich to get the kids.

'Call me tonight,' she told Abby. 'We'll talk then. In the meantime, get back in there and work your magic on Kevin Hudson. Find out what he's hiding. Got that?'

'Got it.'

The FLO turned and went back into the house. As she watched her go, the image of Abby and Ed rushed to the front of Ellen's mind again. She hoped this wasn't going to happen every time she had to deal with Abby Roberts. If it did, Ellen might have to seriously reconsider her decision to come back to work.

18:00

It's cold. I want my mum. I don't know where I am. There's this man. He ... I was on my way to school. My dad was angry because we were late. I hate when he gets like that and maybe it was my fault. Because I was angry with Dad and I was thinking about that instead of where I was.

What's that noise? NO. Go away! But he won't go. The light comes into the room and I go under the quilt. I'm praying to God, really begging him, but He doesn't listen. The man's right close to me now. I can hear him. Breathing.

'Marion?'

Please. Go.

He starts to pull the quilt back and I'm screaming at him but he's not listening and he's so big. He's so big, he's a giant and I'm remembering that film we saw with the big giants. What was it called?

He's on the bed, beside me. I'm trying to hit him, to keep him away, but it's like hitting a statue or something.

'Look what I've got.'

He's big and ugly and his teeth are all yellow and there's this stinky smell, like an onion.

'Fairy cakes. The ones you like, with pink icing.'

I'm going to be sick. I can taste it. I can't be sick. He's got this weird look on his face and I'm thinking about what Mum said about never talking to strangers, but if I don't tell him, then I'll be sick all over him and he'll get angry.

He's holding up a fairy cake and the smell of it. The sick comes and it's on me and my tummy hurts and I'm crying and I can't stop and he's saying something but there's this noise in my head. Like a hurricane. And I can't hear anything else properly.

He puts his hand on my shoulder and I scream. I think I scream. I can't hear anything except that screaming wind inside my head.

18:30

'Ah, there you are.' Mrs Flanagan came to meet Ellen as she let herself into her parents' house.

'You look exhausted, pet. I thought you were meant to be getting back into it slowly? And only doing part-time hours. What's happened, Ellen?'

'Did you catch the news this evening?' Ellen asked.

'The girl?' Her mother nodded. 'I thought that's what it was. Listen, Ellen, isn't it too soon to be taking on a big case like this? Another missing person, too. There's no shame in saying you're not ready. I'm sure Ed would understand.'

Ellen gave her mother a hug. 'I'm fine, Mum. To be honest, it feels good to be back. Although, of course I wish it was working on something less horrible. She's only ten. Not much older than Pat.'

'Well I know you'll do your best,' her mother said. 'Just like always.'

A shriek from the sitting room made them both jump.

'Your dad,' Ellen's mother said, smiling. 'He's playing that ridiculous game. Buckaroo. In there on his hands and knees, running around with the two of them on his back, trying to buck them off. He looks a right eejit, I can tell you. And at his age. He'll do his back in and that's all we need. Then I'll have him to look after along with your two.'

Ellen followed her mother down the narrow hallway of her childhood home and into the sitting room. She remembered Buckaroo from when she was young. Even then, it hadn't been a game her mother had approved of. Although in those days, Ellen was sure her mother's protests had to do with damage to furniture and not concern for her husband's back.

Her mother opened the door and, sure enough, there was her

father, on his hands and knees, with Eilish on his back. As Ellen watched, her father gave an almighty roar – 'Buckaroo!' – and reared up onto his knees. Eilish flew off his back and landed on the carpet in a giggling heap.

Ellen lifted her daughter into the air, swinging her around before pulling her in for a hug.

'Mummy!' Pat jumped off the sofa and joined them, wrapping his arms around Ellen's lower body. She dropped to her knees and managed to grab Pat into her embrace as well. Together, all three of them tumbled to the ground, legs, arms, bodies coiling around each other. Ellen, on her back, gazing at the plaster cracks in the ceiling, pulled her children close and listened to them telling her about their day, shouting over each other to get her attention.

Outside, it was dark. In the furthest parts of her mind, she had a memory of being left in the dark, as a very young child – herself and Sean, before they were adopted. Locked in a room with no electricity, not knowing when, or if, anyone would come and get them. Trying to block out the sound of their baby sister, crying. She was always crying.

Ellen's mind drifted to Jodie Hudson. Was she alone somewhere? At least Ellen always had Sean, someone to stick with during the worst, early years of their childhood. She hoped Jodie wasn't alone. Hoped that no matter where she was, she was with someone who would protect her and make her feel safe. It was foolish and naïve to think like that, she knew, but she held onto the thought anyway, not wanting to consider the alternatives.

* * *

Ellen gave Pat a final goodnight kiss and switched on his night light. After checking on Eilish, fast asleep in her own room, she came back downstairs. This was the worst moment of each day. She suspected it might never get easier.

A lot of things had become bearable. She could walk down a street now, without imagining every man with red hair was Vinny. The smell of garlic no longer induced overwhelming memories of Saturday evenings, relaxing with a glass of wine while he cooked dinner. Hours at a time could pass now without his death being foremost in her mind.

But this, coming downstairs to an empty house after the kids had gone to bed, this felt as hard as it had the first night. Both children had slept in her bed that night, and for many nights after as well. She'd stayed with them, Eilish already asleep, not really old enough to realise what had happened, Pat sobbing as Ellen stroked his head.

Later, long after Pat had gone asleep, she had come down to the kitchen. She'd stood here, drinking wine and staring out at the garden, thinking that she'd never felt so alone. Not knowing then that this was how she was always going to feel from now on.

She wasn't alone, of course. Not really. She had her parents practically down the road in Fingal Street. Sean and Terry were only across the river in Limehouse. And she had the kids, who, more than anything else, kept her going.

She wasn't alone and she was lucky. Her parents helped so much. They'd always been there for her. Never more so than in those dark months following Vinny's death. And now, here they were again, propping her up so that she could satisfy this need to return to work.

Thinking of her parents, Ellen's thoughts shifted – briefly – to the first mother she'd had. Noreen. Mostly, she managed not to think about her but there were occasions, like now, when her birth mother pushed her way through to the front of Ellen's mind.

It was inevitable, Ellen supposed, given the day she'd had. A missing child was bound to trigger memories. But she was damned if she was going to indulge those memories. Her sister was dead; her mother long gone. There was nothing she could do about either of those things and, in the case of her mother, nothing she would want to do anyway.

Pushing Noreen to the back of her mind, where she belonged, Ellen switched on the kitchen light, walked to the wine rack and withdrew a bottle at random. Côtes du Rhône. She poured a healthy measure into a John Rocha wine glass and breathed in the smell – liquorice, vanilla and forest berries. Lovely. She took a sip, letting it linger in her mouth, savouring the flavour.

Glass in hand, she wandered through the dividing door that separated the kitchen from the sitting room. Since Vinny's death, the kitchen seemed obscenely large for one person. In the evenings, she never stayed there any longer than she had to.

She switched on a side lamp and sat in front of her laptop. Her head was full of Jodie and she needed to write everything up, get her thoughts in order. She worked solidly for two hours, going through her emails, writing notes, making a list of outstanding tasks.

When she'd finally done as much as she could, it was ten o'clock. She was tired but wired, not ready for bed yet. She'd been expecting a call from Ed but, so far, he hadn't been in touch.

Her glass was empty. In the kitchen, she refilled it, then went back in the sitting room and called Ed. When he answered, he didn't sound pleased to hear from her.

'What is it?' he barked.

'I've sent you my update,' Ellen said. 'But I thought you might want to talk things through as well. You usually do.'

Any other time, Ed would ball her out for not keeping him updated during an important case like this. Damned if she did, damned if she didn't.

'It's a quarter-past ten at night,' Ed said. 'Unless you've got something worth telling me, I'm sure it could wait.'

'You're right about Kevin Hudson,' Ellen said. 'He is hiding something. The only problem is, I'm not sure if it's got anything to do with Jodie.'

Ed snorted. 'Course it has. What else could it be?'

'All sorts of things,' Ellen said. 'What if he's having an affair, for example? Wouldn't that be a reason to be so evasive? Or maybe he's got some sort of dodgy job or he's running drugs or, oh I don't know. But there could be all sorts of reasons he's being evasive.'

As she was talking, she opened her internet browser and typed Molly York's name into the search engine. A moment later, the first page of 1,090,000 results flashed up on her screen.

'I've asked Malcolm to look for any connection with Molly York,' Ellen said. 'Just in case.'

'I thought I told you to concentrate on Hudson,' Ed said.

'And that's what I've done,' Ellen replied. 'But we should check other angles as well. No stone unturned, isn't that what you're always telling us?'

'I also expect you to do what you're told,' Ed said. 'And right now that's to find out whatever the hell it is that Kevin Hudson is hiding. Got that?'

Then he said something that really riled. 'I've just spoken with Abby. She's doing a great job with the Hudsons. There's a café in Manor House Gardens. Apparently Hudson goes there every morning after dropping Jodie to school.'

'I know,' Ellen said.

'The only morning he hasn't gone there recently was today,' Baxter continued, ignoring her. That cannot be a coincidence, Ellen. I want you to get your arse down there first thing in the morning. Speak to the staff in the café. Find out what he does there each day. Find out why a grown man spends half his morning drinking cups of coffee and staring at kiddies running around the playground beside the café.'

'You're not suggesting ...'

'I'm suggesting nothing,' Ed said. 'It's facts I want, Ellen. And I guarantee you, the facts in this case all point to Kevin Hudson. And when you're finished, come back to the station. Full team briefing at ten a.m. McDonald can give us his update on Molly York then. If there's a connection, we'll follow it. If not, we focus on Hudson. All right?'

No it was not bloody all right. Far from it.

'Why did Abby call you?' Ellen asked. 'I told her to speak to me.'

'She tried you,' Ed replied. 'Said the call went straight to voicemail.'

Lying cow.

'Anyway, that's beside the point,' Ed said. 'All that matters is she's making progress. Which is more than can be said for you.

'You know the stats, Ellen. Nine out of ten kids who die are killed by a family member. Hudson's got form. History of violence. A loner with crap social skills. Unhappy marriage. He's already done six months for GBH. What more do you need?'

'You don't like him,' Ellen said. 'That's what this is about, isn't it?'

'It's not a question of liking,' Ed said. 'The man's the most obvious suspect. All we have to do is prove it.'

'And what if we can't do that?' Ellen asked.

'There's always proof,' Ed said. 'You know that, Ellen. It's just a question of finding it, that's all.'

She threw her phone down on the desk, stared at it for a moment, then went back to the internet. A few minutes later, she had two images on the screen. Jodie Hudson on the left, Molly York on the right. Two young girls with dark hair, blue eyes, a gap between their two front teeth and a dimple. They weren't identical, but it would be foolish to say there weren't similarities between the two girls.

Ellen's gaze lingered on Molly's pretty face, thinking how bloody awful life could be. There was a connection there some-where. She could feel it. Now all she had to do was find it.

22:00

Brian didn't know what to do.

She wasn't exactly making things easy for him. There was all that business with her name, for starters. And all that crying! It was wearing him down, so it was. Truth was, she was starting to remind him of Molly. And that was bad because he didn't want to think about her. Not ever.

He could hear Marion now. Crying and banging on the door of the shed, screaming at him to let her out.

It wasn't fair. He'd come out here, thinking he would pop down to the shed and keep her company for a bit. He was all prepared, with his *Rainbow Parade* videos, two bottles of Coke and a packet of cheese and onion crisps. But then he'd opened the back door and heard her.

A right old commotion she was making. The sound stopped him dead. He stood there in the dark, trying to make sense of it.

And the language out of her! She sounded like a mad thing. Nothing like the sweet girl he'd kept at the front of his mind all this time. If he was honest with himself, this wasn't quite how he'd planned it. Sure enough, he knew there'd be the odd hiccup, but this carry-on? Well, it was a bit more than he'd anticipated.

And it wasn't like any of this was easy for him. When he thought of the things he'd done, the risks he'd taken to bring her home, not to mention the mistakes he'd made.

And Molly.

He closed his eyes, groaned. No. Quick. Think of something else. Anything. He pressed the heels of his palms against his eyes, as if doing that might squeeze her from his head.

In the shed, Marion had calmed down. She was still crying, but it was quieter now. He had to listen hard to hear her.

He opened his eyes, squinting through the trees as if he'd be able to see her if he tried. Which was stupid. It was dark out here. No moon tonight, and the sky hanging low over the flat fields all around him.

It was easy to get lonely out here. If you weren't careful, you could think you were the only person left in the whole world. Which was exactly what he'd thought after they'd first left him here ...

Wasn't that why he'd been so keen to get her back? With Marion here, he thought he'd never be lonely again. Except now look at him – stuck out here in the dark on his own, waiting for her to stop acting like a bleedin' baby.

She'd definitely calmed down. Not a buzz from the shed now. Maybe he'd go down, after all. The videos and snacks were in a pile at his feet. He bent down to pick them up, then hesitated. She'd only start up again the moment he went in there. Like she always did. He wasn't ready for any more of that.

Instead, he collected up his stuff and went inside. At the door, he thought he heard her, calling out again. He shook his head. Best leave her for now. They'd both feel better after a good night's sleep.

As he turned off the lights and made his way to bed, Brian realised he was smiling. Everything was going to work out fine. He just knew it.

TUESDAY,
15 FEBRUARY

09:30

Manor House Gardens was a pretty park situated amidst the tree-lined streets of Victorian terraces in the heart of the Lee conservation area. There was something peaceful about the park that made Ellen feel as if she was somewhere else, instead of a grimy suburb in South-East London.

Not that you would describe this corner of Lewisham as grimy. Leafy, suburban, quiet, safe. Apart from that business with the priest last year, Ellen couldn't recall ever having much work in this area.

The café where Kevin allegedly had his morning coffees was at the far end of the park, near the old manor house. The rain had eased off but the day remained cold. Ellen didn't loiter, hurrying along the path that wound up through the park, towards the café.

There were two people working inside – a stunning blonde in her late teens and a surly guy a few years older, with long dark hair and face fluff. When questioned, their view on Kevin Hudson seemed to back up everything Ed had told her. The blonde was particularly loquacious on the topic of Kevin's perversions.

'He's a creep. All shifty, if you know what I mean? Sort of looking at you all the time, even when he's pretending not to. Giving you these sideways glances, like he's eyeing you up.' She shivered dramatically.

'Always sits outside with his coffee,' she continued. 'Staring at the kids in the playground. Pretending not to, like I said. But you know that's what he's doing.'

She smiled. Face like an angel, mind like a sewer.

'I'm confused,' Ellen said. 'If he's always looking at you, how can he be staring at the kids at the same time? I mean, no matter how – *shifty* – he is, he can't look in two different directions at the same time.'

The smile dropped from the angel face, replaced by a sullen scowl.

'I'm just saying he's a creep. That's all. Don't know why you're having a go at me. You're the one asking the questions. I'm just trying to help, isn't it?'

Ellen turned her attention to Face Fluff. 'Anything to add?' she asked.

He moved his shoulders into something that might have been a shrug if he'd put a bit more effort into it.

'It's like Steph said. Guy's a weirdo. Seriously, he should be out working, shouldn't he? Any other blokes his age, they come here with their kids. Not on their own like that. It's not right, is it, just to sit out there every morning when you don't have kids?'

Stephanie's face lit up. Less angelic this time, more smug 'told you so'. It made Ellen want to reach across the counter and slap her. She looked at the seated area outside the café.

'He sits out there, you say?'

Stephanie nodded.

The chairs and tables overlooked the playground.

'Does he smoke?' Ellen asked.

'Yeah,' Stephanie said. 'What's that got to do with anything?'

'Well if he's a smoker,' Ellen said, 'that could be why he chooses to sit outside. I mean, it's not like he's allowed to smoke in here, is it?'

'Suppose.'

Ellen pretended to think for a moment, then turned to Face Fluff. 'What time did Kevin arrive yesterday morning?'

The boy frowned. 'He weren't here yesterday. We already told the other bloke. The fat one.'

'And that was unusual?' she asked, already knowing the answer.

Stephanie nodded, a little too eagerly. 'It's like we said, he's here every morning. A bit of a coincidence the one morning he doesn't show his little girl goes missing. You lot need to listen. He's a perv. Should be locked up.'

Ellen left soon after that, unable to listen to any more. The easy way the two youngsters vilified Kevin irritated her. Her mood darkened as she walked across the park to her car. What gave them the right to adopt such a self-righteous attitude? Barely out of nappies the pair of them. It was the parents' fault, of course. Ellen would bet any money they grew up hearing shit like that at home.

She was so preoccupied, she barely noticed where she was going. She didn't even see the white van coming directly towards her along the path until the driver braked abruptly in front of her.

Briefly, she clocked two men in the van. The driver, a short bloke with the red cheeks and angry face, pushed his head out the window.

'Look where you're going, would you?' he shouted.

'What do you think you're doing?' Ellen shouted back. 'It's a park not a racing track. Or didn't you notice?'

'And we're the bloody people who keep the park looking the way it does,' the man said. 'At least we try to. Not easy with birds like you walking around with your head so far up your arse you can't see where you're going.'

Rolling her eyes, Ellen flicked her middle finger at the man and moved on.

'Oi!' he called. 'Come back here. I'm not finished with you.'

Well I'm finished with you, tosser, she thought. Behind her, she could hear the engine starting up again. She tensed, half-expecting him to come after her, half-hoping he would. She'd slap a pair of cuffs on him before he knew what was happening. It didn't come to that. Instead, just as she was psyching herself up for a confrontation, the van drove off in the opposite direction.

At the end of the park, she turned and looked back. The van was still there, driver's head stuck out the window, shouting at someone else. From where she stood, Ellen could just make out the name on the side of the van – Medway Maintenance. She would remember that name.

Driving back to the station, Ellen switched on the car radio and caught the news. Jodie was the main story.

'Police leading the investigation into the disappearance of missing schoolgirl Jodie Hudson made a further appeal today for witnesses to come forward,' the female news reporter announced.

Ed's familiar voice filled the car. 'Jodie's been missing for twenty-four hours. Every minute that passes is another minute her family go without knowing where she is. People don't just disappear into thin air. Someone out there knows what's happened to her. If that's you, if you're the person who knows where Jodie is, or even if you suspect you might know something, then come forward. Help us find Jodie before it's too late. Please.'

His voice faded and the news reader moved on to another story – something about escalating tensions between rival drug-dealers in Bromley. Ellen zoned out. Bromley was nothing to do with her.

Twenty-four hours. Fear gnawed her insides. What had she missed? Concentrate on Hudson, Ed had said. What if he was wrong? Worse, what if he was right and she'd refused to listen? Questions spun around her head. The worst sort of questions. Ones she had no answers for.

As she pulled into the car park at the back of Lewisham station, she decided Ed was right. Kevin Hudson was hiding something. They needed to bring him back in for questioning.

As she headed into the station, her thoughts returned fleetingly to Medway Maintenance and the angry van driver. She realised she couldn't be bothered making a complaint. She couldn't spend her time obsessing over every idiot who got in her face.

Better just to put it behind her and move on. Let it go. Life was too short.

10:05

Brian kept his mouth shut while Simon raged beside him.

'Should have gone after her,' Simon said, parking in the spot behind the café. 'Stupid cow. First she walks in front of us and nearly gets herself killed, then she pulls that stunt. You'd think she'd be grateful we didn't run her over. Not her, though. Oh no. Just starts shouting like she owns the park. Cunt!'

Brian winced. He hated that word. It was the worst swear word there was. Daddy used to shout it at Mam sometimes, usually right before laying into her with his fists.

'What the hell's wrong with you?' Simon asked, punching him in the arm.

'Ow.' Brian rubbed the spot where Simon's fist had struck. 'That hurt.'

Simon snorted. 'Bloody sissy. Jesus, Brian. Look at the size of you. How could a little tap like that do you any harm? You need to toughen up, mate. I'm telling you. No wonder the other lads take the piss. You have to be able to stand up for yourself. I can't always be there for you. I do my best but I've got my own life too, Brian, know what I mean?'

Brian didn't really know what Simon meant but he said nothing. He'd learned a long time ago not to answer Simon back when he was in this kind of mood. He might be bigger than Simon now, but it hadn't always been like that and even now, when he should be old enough to know better, Simon still scared him.

'You need to be a bit more like your old man,' Simon continued. 'Never met a tougher bloke. Wouldn't have found him moaning like a little kiddie over a tap to the arm. Nah. Your old man, right? He would have whacked me right back.'

Hot tears filled Brian's eyes, making it difficult to see. He wanted to wipe them away but didn't want Simon to see him crying. Simon was right. He was a sissy. What was wrong with him? Crying. And he a grown man!

He couldn't even stand up to Marion. Choosing to avoid her instead of going down there and dealing with her. Daddy was back inside his head as well, telling him to sort her out. Brian couldn't even do that.

Daddy wouldn't let it go, though. Whispering away at him, getting on at Brian the way he always used to. Telling him to pull himself together, stop being such a baby.

It wasn't right. Brian knew Daddy couldn't really be there. Knew Daddy hadn't stepped foot inside the house since he'd run off, taking Marion, all those years ago. Except ever since they'd gone, it was like Daddy had left part of himself behind. Lodged himself in Brian's head and stayed there, having a go and nagging and bullying and never shutting up.

Suddenly, he got this image of a little miniature Daddy sitting up in his brain somewhere, on a rocking chair, with a fag in one hand and a can of lager in the other, ranting and raving and spilling ash and spitting beer all over Brian's brain. It was such a stupid thing, but now he'd started thinking of it, he couldn't stop.

He thought of telling Marion about this and smiled, imagining her reaction. She'd giggle like anything, most likely. And just thinking of her laughing like that set Brian off, too. He tried to stop, thinking he must look like a right pillock sitting there laughing away to himself. But then he pictured the little man in his little rocking chair, surrounded by brain and bits of blood and God knows what else, and he was off again, laughing so hard the whole van shook and his face was all wet with the tears running down it.

'Brian? Get a grip, would you?'

Brian jumped. He'd forgotten all about Simon sitting beside him.

'Jesus, mate.' Simon was angry now. 'You don't do yourself any favours, do you? What were you laughing at? It better not be me because I'm in no mood for your bullshit today. Got that?'

'Sorry,' Brian mumbled.

He glanced over. Saw Simon's hands clenched tight on the steering wheel, even though he'd turned the engine off ages ago. Brian shivered. He knew what those hands were capable of.

Simon breathed loudly through his nose.

'You sure you're okay?' he asked. 'You haven't been yourself recently. It's not only me that's noticed. The other lads have and all. It's like you're on a different planet half the time. Even more than normal, like.'

'I'm fine,' Brian said. 'Just tired, Simon, that's all. Finding it a bit hard to sleep. House gets very cold at this time of year.'

Simon shifted in his seat, turning to face Brian directly.

'You should move back to the village,' he said. 'That house is there for you, whenever you want. I don't know why you insist on living where you do in the middle of nowhere.'

Brian said nothing. The truth of the matter was, this business with Marion wasn't working out the way he'd planned. He'd only just found her and already it was turning out like the last time.

Molly's face fluttered through his mind. He closed his eyes tight, trying not to think about her. Except it was hard not to. She used to wet the bed. Brian had tried not to get cross with her about it, but it wasn't easy when she kept on doing it, night after night. He hoped Marion wasn't about to start with all that nonsense. Wasn't sure he could stick it.

'What about this missing girl?' Simon asked, like he could read Brian's mind and saw all the horrible things that were there.

'What about her?' Brian said. His voice was shaking. Had Simon noticed? He could feel his insides going all soft, the way they did sometimes when he got scared. He let off a loud fart before he could stop himself.

'Jesus Christ, Brian!'

Simon wound down the window as the stink filled the car. He turned away, making a big show of taking in breaths of cold air.

Brian was relieved. He could feel patches of red blotches on his face, the ones that appeared whenever he got nervous. Or scared.

He had to stay calm. Whatever happened, Simon couldn't find out about Marion.

'See, I just think it's funny, that's all,' Simon said then. 'Whenever I think of this girl – Jodie, right?'

Not Jodie, Brian wanted to scream, Marion. Her name's Marion!

'Well, I can't help asking myself if you've got anything to do with it.' Simon swung around and stared at him. 'I've really stuck my neck out for you this time. I told the police you were with me yesterday morning. Now that's some favour I'm doing. If I find out you've been lying to me, Brian, I can't let that go. Right?'

'Swear to God, Simon. It's nothing to do with me. Swear to God.'

Simon reached across and grabbed Brian by the collar of his jumper, dragging him across the seat until their two faces were so close, Simon's spittle hit Brian's face when he spoke.

'You'd better not be lying to me, Brian. If I find out you have this girl and you've been lying to me, I will make you regret the day you were fucking born. Have you got that?'

Brian wanted to tell Simon he got it, but the other man's hold on his neck was so tight he couldn't get any words out. So he nodded like a wild thing, thinking he'd do whatever he could to prove to Simon that he was telling the truth. Because he knew Simon, and he knew exactly what Simon would do if he ever found out about Marion.

Brian had already lost her once. It had taken him all this time to find her. Okay, things were a bit difficult right now, but they'd get easier. He'd made mistakes in the past, but they were behind him. And Marion would come around eventually. Her mind was half shot with the pain of losing Mam. She was too young to understand what was happening. It was okay for him. He was a big boy. More than that. He was a man now. It was his job to look after her, just like he'd promised Mam he always would.

He'd brought Marion back home and there was no way Simon Wilson or anyone else was going to take her from him a second time.

10:30

'Okay, people!'

Baxter clapped his hands to get their attention. 'Quick update from everyone, then let's sort out our priorities for today. We'll start with the school. McDonald?'

'We're working our way through a list of all families in Jodie's year to start with,' Malcolm said. 'And I've left two uniforms on site for another day.'

'Which ones?' Ed asked.

'Beaumont and Robinson.'

Ed nodded his approval and Malcolm continued.

'General consensus amongst parents is there's something

dodgy about the parents, especially the father. How much of this is down to gossip? Hard to tell. Parents definitely not part of the 'in' crowd. There seems to be a group of parents – mothers, mainly – who spend a lot of time together and do a lot of fund-raising and stuff for the school. The Hudsons are definitely not part of that clique.'

The description was familiar to Ellen, made her think of the cliquey group of parents at her own children's school and how she always felt like an inadequate outsider in their company.

'Interestingly,' Malcolm continued, 'this isn't a view shared by Jodie's friends, who all seemed to quite like her parents. Said the dad was a bit of a laugh, in fact, and that visiting Jodie's house was more fun than most.'

'What about staff at the school?' Ellen asked. In her experi-ence, it was usually the teachers who best knew what went really went on in the homes of the children they taught.

'Teachers all very positive about the family,' Malcolm said. 'The Hudsons are supportive and approachable and pleasant to deal with, apparently.'

Ed snorted. 'Looks like Hudson's managed to pull the wool over their eyes, then. Anything else, McDonald?'

Malcolm consulted his notebook.

'Three more families to interview this morning, but I'm not holding out we'll get anything else from them. I spoke to the Head on the phone last night. She's on compassionate leave. Her mother died last week.'

'When will she be back?' Ed asked.

'Not till next Monday,' Malcolm said.

'Can't we get someone out to wherever she is in the meantime?' Ellen asked.

Malcolm shook his head. 'Afraid not, Ma'am. Her mother lived in Australia. So unless the CID budget can stretch to a trip to Sydney, we'll have to wait.'

'Bollocks,' Ed muttered. 'Right. Who's next? Patel, anything from CCTV yet?'

He was deliberately leaving Alastair until last, Ellen realised. She had to endure ten minutes of Raj droning on about the lack of leads from CCTV, and another ten minutes of Jamala Nnamani instructing them on what they could and couldn't say to the press before Ed finally turned his attention to Alastair.

'Dillon, did you dig up any connection with Molly York?' Ed made a show of looking at his watch. 'And keep it brief, for God's sake. We're running out of time.'

Alastair scraped his chair back from the table and stood up. Ellen hid a smile. Alastair was the only detective on the team who insisted on standing when he was briefing the boss. Ed seemed to like the respect. Ellen always found it slightly ridiculous.

'Molly York,' Alastair began. 'Disappeared August 2009 from Mountsfield Park. Out for a walk with her father. There one minute, gone the next, according to him.'

'Right,' Ed interrupted. 'We all know the background. Let's just deal with this Fletcher bloke. Can we discount him or do we need to take another look? Quickly. We haven't got all day.'

The boss was tense. Not unexpected given the circumstances, but out of character for it to be so evident. Ed Baxter was usually adept at hiding his feelings.

'After her body was found,' Alastair continued, 'the investigation focussed on one suspect, name of Brian Fletcher. It was a joint investigation by then. Our lot teamed up with Rochester because the body was found on their patch. A DCI called Cox headed up their side. But you know that because ...'

Ed groaned. Loudly. Alastair blushed. Furiously.

'Sorry. Where was I? Fletcher, aye. He worked for the firm contracted to look after Lewisham and Greenwich parks. Looked likely on paper, but turned out he had nothing to do with what happened to Molly.'

Briefly, yesterday's angry encounter with the Medway Maintenance worker flashed through Ellen's mind.

'What made them so sure?' she asked.

'Fletcher had an alibi,' Alastair said. 'He was working down in Belvedere the day Molly disappeared. Nowhere near Mountsfield Park when it happened.'

'We should still follow it up,' Ellen said. 'Find out where he was yesterday morning.'

'Already done it,' Alastair said. 'According to his boss, Fletcher was working all morning.'

Ellen frowned. 'Is this the same boss who gave him an alibi when Molly was taken?'

'Yeah,' Alastair said. 'But not just him. Another guy who works there also confirmed Brian was working.'

'Where?' Ellen asked. 'Working where?'

'Greenwich Park.'

She rolled her eyes, frustrated. Another dead-end.

Alastair finished speaking but continued standing, waiting for a sign from Baxter that he could sit down. After a moment, and still nothing from Ed, he sat down anyway.

'Boss?' Ellen said.

Ed frowned. Ellen realised he'd been miles away. What the hell could be more important than this, she wondered.

'Good work, Dillon' he said. 'Right. Let's put Fletcher to one side then and focus on Hudson. Ellen, any insights for us?'

'I think you're right,' Ellen said. 'He's hiding something. But I'm not sure it's got anything to do with Jodie.'

'Let's get him in again this morning,' Baxter said. 'Put the shits up him. Do a formal interview, tell him he'll need a solicitor.'

'What about Fletcher?' Ellen asked. 'Sure you don't want me to look into his background a bit more? See if there's anything that was missed first time around?'

'No,' Baxter said. 'Get across to the Hudsons' and drag his arse in for questioning. Okay?'

Ellen wanted to say no, it wasn't okay, but she decided to wait. When the briefing finished, she stayed at her desk until Baxter went back into his office, then she called across the room to Raj.

'I'm going to have a word with Ed,' she said. 'When you get a

moment, can you find the number for this Ger Cox, the Rochester DCI that Malcolm mentioned?'

'Sure thing,' Raj said.

Satisfied, Ellen left the room and walked down the corridor to
Baxter's office.

'Got a minute, boss?'

Baxter looked up and nodded. 'Grab a seat,' he said. 'You don't
mind if I eat when we talk, do you? Don't want my bacon sarnie
going cold.'

'From the canteen?' Ellen looked at the soggy sandwich Baxter
was biting into. Appetising wasn't the first word that sprang to
mind.

'I've had worse,' Baxter said. 'Was over at a mate's house last
week. Made the mistake of sampling one of his veggie offerings.
Word of advice, Ellen, never let a vegetarian tempt you into
trying that fake bacon. Terrible stuff.'

Ellen smiled. 'I'll take your word for it.'

She wondered if Baxter resorting to the staff canteen was a sign
of discord in his personal life. Andrea, his wife, was known for
lavishing the greatest care on her husband. In all the time Ellen
had worked with him, he'd never once come to work without
a lunchbox packed with homemade food. She'd long given up
the demoralising process of comparing the ham sandwiches and
supermarket biscuits in her own kids' lunchboxes with the exotic
salads, gourmet wraps and home-baked delights that Baxter con-
sumed on a daily basis.

Maybe he'd finally confessed about Abby and he was being punished. Ellen hoped so. It would serve him right.

'What is it?' Ed asked. 'I'm keen to get Hudson in. Whatever you want, make it snappy.'

'Two things,' Ellen said. 'First off, we need another body on the team. We're all stretched too thin and I'm worried we're going to miss something because of it.'

'That's for me to decide,' Ed said. 'Not you. What else?'

'I think you're wrong about Molly York,' Ellen said.

Ed put his sandwich down and wiped his mouth carefully with a napkin.

'Sounds like you're trying to tell me how to do my job, Ellen.'

'No,' she said. 'Just telling you what I think, that's all.'

Like you've always told me I should, she added to herself.

'Listen,' Baxter said. 'I didn't bring you back so you could start investigating three-year-old cases. Jodie's been missing for almost twenty-six hours and so far we haven't come up with a single concrete thing that will help us find her. Time's running out.'

Ellen started to speak but he held his hand up, silencing her.

'Enough. I've told you what to do. I want Kevin Hudson here within an hour. Do I make myself clear?'

She left Ed's office, slamming the door behind her. Hard. He wouldn't like it but she didn't care. For reasons she couldn't work out, Ed was being totally unreasonable. It was like the Baxter she knew had metamorphosed, during the months she'd been away, into a different person entirely.

He'd been distracted this morning. Not the first time since she'd been back, either. Ellen recalled her conversation with Abby Roberts the day before. The FLO was adamant Baxter hadn't briefed her. Was it possible Abby had been telling the truth? And this bullshit about him deciding whether they needed extra support. It was a missing child investigation, for Christ's sake. It was clear to anyone with eyes that they needed as much help as they could get.

She walked down the corridor. By the lift, she leaned against the wall, closed her eyes and took several slow, deep breaths.

'Having a bad day?'

She recognised the voice instantly. Opening her eyes, a flood of warmth rushed through her when she saw the big man standing in front of her. Dai Davies, her colleague from back in the early days at Ladywell.

'Dai! What are you doing here?'

'Just passing, wasn't I? Thought I'd drop by, see how you were.'

Stepping into his embrace, she hugged him tight, breathing in the smell of cigar smoke clinging to his clothes.

He was taller than any man she'd ever met. She remembered him embracing her at Vinny's funeral, the top of her tidy bob brushing off the bottom of his chin as he lowered his head to whisper condolences. Funny the things you remember. She couldn't recall what he'd been wearing or what he'd said to her, but the memory of his chin against her head was as strong as if it was yesterday.

She stood back to get a better look at him – dark eyes, thick white hair and a face more lived in than any she'd ever seen. Apart from the hair, he looked pretty much the same as he had the first time she'd laid eyes on him, her first day on the force. Dai Davies, Paul Conlon's partner at Ladywell. That was nineteen years ago and Dai Davies was already an experienced detective. He must be nearing retirement by now, she guessed. Sad to think he wouldn't be around for much longer.

'No one just passes the third floor,' she said. 'Come on, what's your real reason for prowling around up here?'

He nodded in the direction she'd just come from. 'Hard at it, are you?'

She sighed. 'Missing girl. Jodie Hudson? You've probably heard about it already.'

'Ah yeah. Tough case that. I don't envy you. Don't suppose you can spare a few minutes to have a coffee with me?'

She thought about Baxter's directive to get herself down to the Hudsons' and back here as soon as she could. She shook her head. 'I'm sorry, Dai. It's not a good time right now. I've loads to get through this morning.'

He nodded. 'Fair enough. I suppose I just wanted to see how you were. This is your first case since that business last year, isn't it? You holding up okay?'

She swallowed the lump in her throat, and smiled. 'I'm fine. And I'm glad you've dropped by. Really glad. I can't remember the last time I saw you. I'd love a proper catch-up. Find out what's happening over in Greenwich. How about a drink sometime?'

'I'm free tonight, if you fancy it.'

'Can I call you later?' she asked. 'Tonight might be tricky, but a drink sometime soon sounds good.'

'Sure,' Dai said. 'Why don't I give you a call this evening and we can arrange it?'

'Yes, do that.'

He leaned down and gave her a peck on the cheek. 'All right. See you later, then. Look after yourself, you hear me?'

The smell of his aftershave triggered a rush of memories. Dai Davies and Paul Conlon. Already sergeants by the time Ellen joined as a fresh-faced rookie. Seen it all, done it all. At first, they'd intimidated the hell out of her. Both so cynical, they seemed to know everything about everything. But they were kind to her, especially Dai, who took her under his wing and showed her the ropes, made sure she didn't mess up.

Paul died six years ago. Cancer. Diagnosed one warm summer afternoon in June. A week after Eilish's first birthday. Three months' later, he was gone. There was only her and Dai left now. Survivors, the pair of them, as he'd put it one bleak afternoon after Vinny's funeral.

It was exhausting being a survivor. Sometimes, Ellen wished there could be an easier way to go about life. Surely it was meant to be about living, not just surviving? If so, she wasn't sure she'd found out how to do that. Not yet.

11:45

Kevin stood in the garden, smoking, sucking nicotine into his lungs, trying to ignore the noises from the kitchen behind him. Helen moving around, banging plates on the table, slamming drawers as she prepared lunch. Abby was in there too, acting like she was Helen's new best friend. Kevin didn't like – or trust – the FLO, who was too slickly charming for her own good.

He took another drag, held the smoke in until the blood rushed to his face and he felt like if he didn't breathe out, he would explode. Smoke burst from his mouth and hung in the air in front of him, before drifting away across the garden. As he watched, the smoke seemed to wobble, fade and finally it disappeared entirely, until there was nothing left at all. Gone. Just like Jodie.

He heard a car drive down the street and stop near the house. As the car door slammed shut, a cacophony of voices rose through the air. Bloody reporters. When he'd woken this morning the street was full of them. All gathered outside the front of the house, like vultures at a fresh carcass.

Helen shouted something from the kitchen. He pretended not to hear. A sudden blast of music made him jump. Finlay in his bedroom. Probably using the music to block out the sounds on the street. Poor kid.

Kevin had tried – unsuccessfully – to persuade Finlay to go to school this morning. Said it was better than hanging around the house all day. Of course, Finlay refused and Kevin didn't blame him for it. It was pointless, anyway. Going to school, getting an education, all the stuff they told the kids was so important. When it came down to it, you had to ask yourself, what did any of it matter? In the end, the number of A-levels you got made shit-all difference. People fooled themselves, thinking if they obeyed the rules – eat well, cut down on the booze and fags, be careful with your money, get a good education – then somehow they could protect themselves from the bad stuff. It didn't work like that. Kevin just wished someone had told him that a long time ago, so he hadn't wasted half his life believing he was in control.

He'd smoked every last bit of the cigarette. Flicking the still-smouldering stub onto the damp grass, he turned and went back inside. Abby flashed him a dazzling smile. He didn't return it.

'Can you give us a moment?' he said instead. 'I want a word with Helen. In private.'

The smile disappeared and Abby with it a moment later. Thank Christ. He turned to Helen.

'Why didn't you tell me you'd called Davies?'

She sighed. 'Does it matter? I thought maybe he could help.'

Dai bloody Davies. Jesus.

'You slept,' Helen said. 'I lay beside you all night wondering how you could do that. How could you sleep, Kevin, when this is happening to us?'

She broke off with a sob. Kevin wanted to put his arms around her, comfort her and tell her he was sorry, so very sorry, but before he could do any of that, Finlay appeared in the doorway.

'Has something happened?' the boy asked, edging his way into the room.

Helen wiped her face and stood up. 'Nothing, darling. Are you okay?'

'Dad?'

Finlay looked at Kevin so innocently, like he still believed his father was capable of doing something good and worthy of his admiration, even after everything that had happened. Kevin felt a sudden rush of love for this boy-man. His son. Not his son by blood, just as Jodie wasn't his biological daughter, but surely the love he felt for them was as much as any parent could ever feel for their children?

Helen lifted the remote control and aimed it at the TV mounted on the wall above Finlay's head. Jodie's face filled the screen, smiling down at her family sitting around the kitchen table. When she appeared, it felt like Kevin's insides were being vacuumed from his body.

'Police are still no closer to finding the whereabouts of ten-year-old Jodie Hudson, who disappeared on her way to school in Lee, South-East London yesterday morning.'

After reiterating the police plea for anyone with information to come forward, the report ended.

Helen flicked the remote and Jodie's face disappeared. Kevin wanted to ask her to leave it on but when he tried to speak, he couldn't.

That photo of Jodie was his favourite. Until recently, it had been in a frame on the mantelpiece. It showed Jodie on Christmas morning, right after they'd opened their presents. She was sitting, surrounded by wrapping paper, posing for the camera. In the photo itself, you could see all of her. She was still in her nightdress, her *Hannah Montana* one. In the photo on TV, the image had been resized so all you could see was Jodie's face, smiling at you like she was the happiest little girl in the whole wide world.

Finlay started crying, his head bent, shoulders shaking as sobs racked his body.

'Oh Fin,' Kevin murmured. He went over to the boy and wrapped his arms around him. 'We'll get her back, son. I promise.'

He would have said more, but just then bloody Abby appeared. And she wasn't alone, either. Beside her stood the woman detective they'd met yesterday. Ellen Something.

Kevin's heart lurched, but as she started to speak, he realised it wasn't the news they were waiting for. Anger replaced hope. They wanted to question him. Again. With a lawyer.

Damned police. He hated them. So predictable. So utterly lacking in imagination. Just because he'd fucked up once, they assumed he was capable of something like this. And all the time they wasted on him, was time they could be spending finding Jodie.

When the Ellen woman took his arm, Finlay jumped forward, crying and grabbing hold of Kevin, begging him not to go. Gently, as gently as he could, Kevin prised his son's hands off him. And when he'd done that, he did something he swore he'd never do. He lied to his boy.

'It's okay,' he said. 'It's okay, Fin. I'll be back soon. There really is nothing to worry about. I promise.'

12:05

'It's only me, Marion. Okay if I come in?'

I want to tell him to go away, but my voice won't work. My throat is sore from all the vomiting, but it's not that. There's all this stuff in my head, but when I try to speak, I can't get my mouth to work. Later, after he'd cleaned up all the sick and went away, I tried saying my name. It's weird. In my head I know what my name is, but when I try to speak, it's like I forget right at that moment.

The room smells of sick. He was angry about it but tried to hide it. The way Mum does sometimes. Like, you can see she's really annoyed but she puts this stupid smile on her face and when Dad asks if she's okay she says: 'Of course. Why wouldn't I be?' And you can hear the way she says it that she's not okay at all.

I can hear the key turn and then bolts being pulled back. Click. Bang, bang.

Please God, no. Make him go away.

I'm praying in my head, begging God, wondering what I have to do to get him to listen. He should hear me even if it's only inside my head, because He is always with you. If you believe in Him. I didn't but now I do, and I'm begging Him so hard to make him go away.

But He doesn't listen and the door's open and his big shadow is everywhere and he's smiling that stupid smile.

I hadn't even seen him. You're not meant to talk to strangers because not everyone is kind and if they try to give you a sweet, then that's a bad thing and not a good thing and you're never, ever meant to take a sweet from them.

His hand was on my mouth and I couldn't breathe. I wanted to scream, but his hand was against my mouth and nose. He put me in a van and we drove for the longest time and there was this stuff over my mouth and I couldn't scream and I thought, I thought he was going to kill me.

He's right up close now. Too close. Sitting beside me on the bed, making it rise up. I don't like his smell. I try to pull myself further into the corner, away from him.

He's saying something, but it's not easy to understand the words because he's got this funny way of speaking. He's talking about this room I'm in.

'It'll be easier in a bit,' he's saying. 'When you can have your old room back. We can't go there yet, though. There was this other girl, see ...'

He shakes his head.

'No, best not. You don't want to be hearing about that.'

There's this funny noise. Like the cat that sits in our garden sometimes at night, wanting to come inside. The noise is me. It's coming from inside me, but I don't know how to stop it. He acts like he can't hear it, but if I can hear it, then he can hear it too, unless there's something wrong with his ears.

There are posters all over the wall. Fairies and puppies and kittens. They're all looking at me and him on the bed. Tinkerbell is smiling at me, like she thinks this is really funny.

He grabs my arm. His fingers dig into me, hurting me. I'm crying again and I want to scream at him to stop but nothing works anymore.

'Marion!' He's shouting and the fright makes me stop trying to pull away. I'm frozen.

'It's okay,' he says. 'It's me. Brian. Don't you recognise me?'

I think really hard, but the only person I know called Brian is Ruby Rice's dad and it's not him.

'Marion?'

I'm not Marion! I'm screaming that inside my head but he can't hear me. He thinks I'm this Marion, but he's got it all wrong. I concentrate really hard on getting my mouth to work. My lips move, I can feel them. But I can't get it to do anything else.

I growl, like a dog now, not a cat. Growling when I want to scream. He's still holding my arm, but I get my other hand to my mouth and push my fingers inside, pulling at my tongue, trying to get the stupid thing to work.

It hurts. Especially when my nails scrape the top of my tongue. I don't care.

'Marion, stop it. What the hell are you doing?'

I'm crying now. My whole body shaking and my face and neck and the top of my school blouse are all wet with tears. I want a towel, but I can't ask for one.

He has both arms then and he's holding me tight and it hurts, but I can't tell him to stop. When he speaks, his voice rumbles through my body, like an earthquake.

I hate it.

'It's okay,' he says. 'It's okay, Marion. I'm here now and everything's going to be okay. Daddy's gone and he's not coming back. It's just you and me now.'

13:40

'Ready?'

Ellen looked through the glass window in the door, at the two men sitting in the interview room. Kevin Hudson and his solicitor, Tom Abbot. Tom was a Lewisham-based criminal lawyer. Ellen had sat across the table from him in countless interviews. He was a good bloke and she'd often thought if she ever ended up the wrong side of that table, she'd like to have Tom Abbot sat alongside her.

'Ed?'

At the sound of her voice, he jumped, as if it was the last thing he expected.

'Sorry,' he said. 'What were you saying?'

'I asked if you're ready,' she said. 'Listen, are you okay? You seem distracted. I'm happy to do this without you, if you'd prefer that.'

Truth was, she'd prefer to do the interview alone. She was certain she'd have more luck on her own with Kevin.

'No,' Ed said. 'I need to be here. Come on. Let's get this over with.'

He pushed open the door and walked into the room ahead of her, not bothering to hold the door open for her. Ellen had to rush forward to stop it slamming in her face.

Greetings out of the way, Ellen set up the tape recorder and spoke into it, stating the date and time, along with the names of the four people in the room. Then she paused, waiting for Baxter to take the lead.

Baxter placed his hands on the table, palms down, and looked at Kevin.

'Let's start with Monday morning,' he said. 'Talk us through what happened. From the beginning.'

Kevin looked at his lawyer. 'Do I have to go through this again?'

'Just answer the questions,' Tom said. 'And remember, you've nothing to worry about. Okay?'

Kevin didn't seem convinced, but after a moment he shrugged and went through the same story Ellen had heard several times already.

'It was the same as every other morning,' he said. 'Helen went to work and I got the kids ready for school. Finlay left at the usual time and Jodie and I left about half-an-hour later. We were late, I remember that. And I remember being angry with her.'

'Angry?' Baxter interrupted.

Kevin sighed. 'Jodie's a dreamer. It's always difficult to get her out the door in time. That morning, I had to keep nagging her to get dressed. She just kept saying yes, then going and doing something else.'

Pat was like that. Nine times out of ten, Ellen ended up shouting at him on school mornings. Then hating herself for it for the rest of the day.

'Do you get angry with her a lot?' Baxter asked.

'I don't think that's relevant,' Tom said.

'Can't be easy, I suppose,' Baxter said, ignoring the lawyer. 'Doing all the childcare yourself like that. Especially when they're not even your own kids. It's no wonder you lose it with them every now and then. Can't say I blame you. Was that what happened on Monday, Kevin? Did Jodie just push you too far? Tip you over the edge? Kids can do that. I remember it with my own. They have this knack of pushing and pushing. And then the red mist comes down and before you can stop yourself – *bam!* Happens to all of us.

'See, the thing is, Kevin, if you're just straight with us, tell us what really happened that morning, you'll feel a lot better. No one could blame you if you lost it. It's part and parcel of being a parent.'

Baxter leaned forward, eyes boring into Kevin, face the very definition of empathy.

'Talk to us, Kevin. She was playing up, wasn't she? Ten-year-old girl, I bet she played up all the time. Bet she ran rings around you the moment her mother was out of the house every morning. Must have been a nightmare. All sweetness and light one minute, then the devil incarnate the next. And you couldn't talk to Helen about it, of course. Because Jodie's her little princess. Her little angel. And you had to go along with that. Didn't have any choice because if you didn't, Helen would show you the door and then where would you be?'

Kevin's face was twisted as if he was in physical pain and even though she knew this was what they had to do, Ellen felt sorry for him.

'Stop it!' Kevin shouted. 'Stop it! You don't know what you're talking about. It wasn't like that. I love Jodie. And Fin. Don't try to pretend you know what it's like for me. Because you don't. None of you do. Watching my wife go out the door to work every morning, knowing it should be me instead. Knowing how she'd much prefer to be at home with the kids but she can't. Because I'm a no-good loser who can't even get a job stacking shelves in Tesco because they won't have me. Because there's twenty other people applying for every bloody job I go for and none of them has a record so they all get favoured above someone like me.'

Tom put a hand on Kevin's arm, stopping him in mid-flow. A bit late for that, Ellen thought.

Baxter leaned back and nodded. 'So,' he said, 'now we're getting somewhere. Why don't you tell us a little more about your attempts to get a job and how frustrated you got when you were turned down, again and again, for positions you knew you were over-qualified for?'

Kevin rubbed a hand across his face and sighed. 'Look,' he said. 'I know why you're doing this. You think because I've a record, I must have taken her. But I haven't. I swear to you. And all these questions, you're just wasting your time. I don't know where she is. I wish to God I did, but I don't. You've got to believe me. Someone else did this.'

He was telling the truth. Ellen glanced at Ed, but his face gave nothing away. She leaned forward in her chair and cleared her throat.

'Kevin,' she said, 'what happened after you dropped Jodie off?'

He frowned. 'Are you serious? You want me to go through it all again? Why? What possible good can it do?'

'Please,' Ellen said. 'Just take me through it step by step.'

Kevin groaned, but after a moment he started talking.

'We got to Lenham Road. I said goodbye to Jodie and left. She likes to walk the last part on her own and I don't have a problem with that.'

Ellen thought of her own kids, of Pat in particular. Wouldn't any normal parent wait and check their child made it as far as the school gates?

'At what point did you leave?' she asked. 'How far down Lenham Road had Jodie got before you walked away?'

Kevin shook his head. 'Not far. I mean, I know I should have waited until she'd reached the school, but I was in a hurry …'

He stopped, realising his mistake. Too late.

'Why?' Baxter asked. 'Where were you rushing off to in such a hurry? We know you didn't go to the park, so where did you go?'

'I've already told you,' Kevin said. 'I went shopping in Lewisham. I was rushing because I wanted to get it over with. I hate shopping.'

'What did you buy?' Ellen asked.

'Nothing,' Kevin said. The answer was too quick, but he'd had a day to think about it now. To get his story straight. Ellen gave it one final try.

'Kevin,' she said. 'We've gone through all the CCTV footage from the shopping centre for yesterday morning. You're not there. And we've shown your photo to people working there and no one can remember seeing you. You weren't there. You accuse us of wasting time but while you refuse to tell us where you really were, what choice do we have?'

She maintained eye contact with him the whole time she spoke. When she finished, something in his face told her she'd made a connection. She felt a brief flicker of hope that was quickly dashed when he spoke again.

'I've already told you,' he said. 'I went to the shopping centre and after that I went home. I can't help it if no one saw me there, but it's the truth. I'm telling you the truth. Why won't you believe me?'

14:35

Kevin shook hands with his lawyer outside Lewisham station.

'I'll be in touch,' Tom said.

Kevin nodded, not trusting himself to speak.

'It'll be okay,' Tom continued. 'If you've got nothing to hide, then you've got nothing to worry about.'

Except he had something to hide. And he suspected his lawyer knew this too. Just like that prick, Baxter.

'Are you sure there's nothing else you want to tell me, Kevin?'

Kevin shook his head, desperate to get away from Tom Abbot's probing stare. Any more interrogation and he'd crack.

Tom shrugged. 'Have it your way then. Call me if you change your mind, okay?'

After the lawyer left, Kevin looked up, breathing a shaky sigh of relief. The clouds had cleared, replaced by a clear blue sky that offered the promise of warmth but didn't deliver. As he hurried away from the police station down Lewisham High Street, Kevin wrapped his arms around his shivering body in a futile attempt to stop the icy wind cutting through him.

At this time on a Tuesday afternoon, Lewisham was busy. Kevin pushed his way through the throngs of school kids and shoppers, barely noticing them.

He'd lied to the police. And to his solicitor. It was a stupid thing to do, but he didn't see that he had any other choice. It was the same lie he'd told the first time he was questioned yesterday.

He hadn't been thinking straight. Thoughts all muddled with what had happened and then the shocking realisation that his daughter was missing. Somehow, in his mind, he couldn't separate it all. So when the police had asked him where he'd been, his first instinct was to lie. And once he'd told the lie, he couldn't untell it. Every time he repeated it since, it grew harder and harder to force the words out in a way that sounded convincing.

'I went shopping in Lewisham.'

Five words. Five simple words that could get him into a whole lot of trouble. Sooner or later, he'd be found out. Tom told him the police would continue to check the CCTV footage. Going through all the cameras in Lewisham shopping centre, looking for images of Kevin from yesterday morning. There wouldn't be any, of course. And at some point, they'd bring him back in. Ask him more questions about what had really happened the morning Jodie disappeared.

Kevin tried to work out what he'd tell them, but his mind wouldn't let him think that far ahead. All he could do was what he was doing right now. Move forward, putting one foot in front of the other, focussing on the here and now. And hope that, somehow, if he kept it up, he would make it home.

16:00

The decision to start smoking again was unconscious. Ellen hadn't deliberately woken up this morning and thought she'd buy a pack of cigarettes. Yet, somehow, she'd found herself standing in the tobacconists across the road from the station, buying twenty Marlboro Lights. So far, it wasn't a decision she'd regretted for a single moment.

At the back of the station there was a small, covered area for officers who smoked. Normally, this was packed with people getting their regular ration of nicotine. Today, for once, it was mercifully empty. Ellen sat on a wooden bench, damp soaking through her woollen trousers, freezing her backside. She didn't care. Anything was better than the frenetic, chaotic atmosphere of the incident room. She'd come outside to think.

The interview with Kevin Hudson had been a waste of time. His word against theirs. Most frustrating of all, Kevin's obvious evasiveness about his whereabouts yesterday morning made Baxter more certain than ever that Kevin was behind Jodie's disappearance. Which made it even harder for Ellen to persuade her boss they needed to explore other angles as well. It was so frustrating to watch as Kevin messed up the investigation, pulling all the focus onto himself. She wasn't sure how aware he was of what he was doing, but he was doing it anyway.

Twice today she'd noticed a tremor in Baxter's hands. Almost like he'd been on a heavy session the night before. Except in all the time she'd known him, Ed Baxter rarely drank alcohol and never to excess. And yet …

The shakes, coupled with the irritability. Maybe the stress was getting to him and he was hitting the bottle in the evenings as a way of coping. Ellen was hardly in a position to point fingers if he was.

She took a drag on her cigarette and sighed. She'd been so looking forward to coming back to work, but so far nothing was working out the way she'd hoped. Maybe it was this case. A missing child case was never easy. The only thing worse was a dead child investigation. And the way things were going, they'd be dealing with that soon enough if they weren't careful.

'Penny for them?'

Raj was standing in front of her, pack of red Marlboros in his hand.

'Alright?' Ellen said.

Raj lit up, took a drag and blew a thin trail of smoke into the air before answering.

'Been better,' he said. 'Can't stop thinking about Jodie, wondering what we're missing. It would help, of course, if we had an extra pair of hands. We're drowning under the workload at the moment, Ellen.'

Her insistence that the rest of the team refer to her as Ma'am never seemed to work with Raj and she didn't push it. Older than the others, there was a mature air about him that would have made it difficult if she'd tried to force the issue. Not that she wanted to. She'd always viewed Raj Patel more as a friend than an employee she was meant to manage.

'I have raised it,' she said. 'But Baxter's not playing ball. Not yet, anyway.'

'What's going on with him?' Raj asked. 'You worked it out?'

'You've noticed then,' Ellen said.

Raj nodded. 'Everyone has. There's been a bit of gossip, if you must know. General consensus is that Abby's dumped him and he's not taking it very well.'

Ellen groaned. 'Come on, Raj. Can't you put a stop to it? That sort of talk doesn't help anyone. Least of all Jodie Hudson. The team should be focussing on her, not on some tawdry office fling that was over nearly as soon as it started.'

Raj took another drag and looked out across the grey, empty car park. He was wearing a pale blue shirt, without a jacket. Even though it was February, he showed no sign of feeling cold. When he moved, the muscles across his shoulders rippled, reminding Ellen why so many of the women at work had a crush on him. As far as she knew, he'd never shown the slightest bit of interest in return. Privately, she suspected he was gay.

'I like Abby,' he said eventually. 'She's a good cop and decent with it. Yeah, she uses her charm to get what she wants, but who doesn't? Can't blame her for that, especially in a place like this.' He turned to Ellen, intense brown eyes boring into her. 'I've tried to put a stop to the gossip, Ellen. Not just because I like Abby but because, like you, I don't think it's very helpful. But someone needs to have a word with Baxter. Find out what the hell is going on and make it stop. He's totally lost his focus. Have you noticed?

'This obsession he has with Kevin Hudson, it's not right.

There are loads of other leads we need to be following up. I'm scared, Ellen. Scared we'll mess up and this will turn into Molly York all over again.'

'It's partly because of Molly that he's so focussed on Kevin,' Ellen said. 'I think he's desperate. Like the rest of us, he can't bear to think we won't find Jodie in time.'

'And I get that,' Raj said. 'But speaking frankly, that's not much help to anyone. You need to speak to him. And soon. Before it's too late.'

Ellen threw her cigarette onto the ground and stubbed it out with the toe of her shoe.

'You're right,' she said. 'I'll go in there now, see if I can find him and work out what's going on. How about that?'

Raj smiled. 'Thanks, Ellen. I knew I could count on you. Hey, before you speak to Baxter, I've got something for you.'

He pulled a slip of paper from his pocket and handed it to her.

'Ger Cox,' he said. 'The detective who led the Rochester end of the Molly York investigation. You asked me to get the number.'

'What would I do without you?' Ellen asked, grabbing the slip of paper from Raj's outstretched hand.

'Hey,' he said. 'It goes both ways. It's really good to have you back, you know. This old place just wasn't the same without you.'

She felt better for talking to him. He had that affect on people. Something about the calm way he dealt with problems, preferring to address them head-on instead of burying his head in the sand. There was a time he'd been her sounding board, her first port of call when she had a problem or issue that was bothering her. Since Vinny's death, she'd let that friendship slide, like so many things. It was only now, when it was probably too late to get it back, that she realised how much she missed him.

Still, no point worrying about what might have been.

Ellen pulled her phone from her pocket and, reading the number on the slip of paper, called DCI Ger Cox.

A woman's voice, gravel-throated and with a strong Kent accent, answered after three rings.

'DCI Cox, how can I help you?'

A woman. Stupidly, Ellen hadn't expected that.

'DI Ellen Kelly,' she said. 'Lewisham CID. I'd really like to speak to you about a case you handled a few years ago. Molly York?'

'Lewisham,' Cox said. 'It's that missing girl, isn't it? Jodie Hudson. Please tell me you've found something.'

'It's just a hunch at the moment,' Ellen said. 'But there are similarities between the two cases. Things I'd like to follow up with you.'

'Whatever you need,' Cox said. 'Just tell me what you want and I'll make sure it happens. I'll do anything if it helps nail the bastard who killed poor Molly.'

'Could I come and see you?' Ellen asked. She was rapidly warming to DCI Cox.

'Tomorrow morning,' Cox said. 'We can meet on the Hoo, where Molly's body was found. I think it's important you see it.'

After making arrangements to meet the next day, Ellen hung up. She considered whether to tell Baxter what she planned, but decided against it. She would investigate the Molly York angle by herself and only tell her boss about it if she uncovered some link with Jodie. In the meantime, she had more pressing issues to discuss with Baxter. Following Raj Patel's example, she decided to go back inside the station and confront those issues head-on.

17:00

Ellen left work early enough to have tea at her parents' house. She had hardly seen the children since Sunday and she missed them. She made a mental note to fit in some more time with them over the next few days. The case was important, but so was her family. She'd made the mistake once before of putting work first. It wasn't something she was about to let happen ever again.

'We're running a bit late,' her mother called as Ellen let herself in. 'Come into the kitchen and tell me how your day's been.'

As she passed the sitting room, Ellen heard voices. Her children's and a man she assumed was her father. She thought about popping her head around the door to say hello, but decided to speak to her mother first.

In the kitchen she found both her parents: her mother standing at the hob stirring something in a big pot; her father sat at the table, face hidden behind *The Guardian*.

Ellen frowned. 'Who's in the sitting room with the kids?'

'Jim O'Dwyer,' her mother said. 'We've been having problems with the hot water. Your father called Jim earlier and he came straight over. He's a good lad, is Jim. You look tired, Ellen. Are you sure you're not working too hard?'

Her first day at school. She hadn't thought about it in years. Rage and confusion. Everything made better by a smiling boy with a kind face and a dimple that appeared under his left eye when he smiled. She hadn't seen him in years.

'Positive,' Ellen said. 'What about your water? Has he managed to fix it? And what's he doing in the sitting room if he's meant to be sorting out your plumbing?'

'Relax, Ellen.' Her father's voice rose from behind the newspaper.

'The water's all sorted,' her mother said. 'I told him you'd be here soon and he stayed to say hello. I didn't realise you'd be so exhausted or I'd never have suggested it.'

'I'm not exhausted,' Ellen said. 'I've already told you. I'm fine.'

Her mother tut-tutted and Ellen gritted her teeth, knowing there was more to come. She was frustrated, not tired. Her attempts to catch up with Ed had all been in vain. No one knew where he was and her phone calls had all gone to voicemail.

'I don't understand why you do it,' her mother said. 'It's not like you need to work. Vincent left you with more than enough. I mean, I'd understand it if you needed the money, but you don't.'

It was true. Vinny had been sensible with money. Two life assurance policies and a comfortable income from the stocks and shares he'd invested in had left Ellen with no money worries. Which was why her mother revisited this same old argument again and again. It was partly Ellen's fault, of course. She'd never properly explained why she needed to carry on working. Didn't know how to admit that she was scared. That even with all of Vinny's money, the constant fear of not having enough drove her to keep going. She remembered what poverty felt like, real poverty, and it terrified her. Over time, the memories had faded but they were still there, like a stubborn scar after an accident.

She never spoke about her early life, before the adoption, not even with Sean, but she remembered it. Days passing without any proper food, the electricity gone because there was no money to pay the bills, the cold and the darkness and the fear. And the tormenting, ever-present sound of their baby sister crying.

'You were always the same,' her mother continued in a softer voice. 'Independent as bedamned. I remember the day you and Sean started school. You were a bit later than the other kids because of everything that had gone on. Neither of you wanted to go, although you'd never have guessed it by the way you behaved. Sean screamed the place down like we were about to kill him. You, though, you walked in as cool as anything. Like you were meant to be there. Do you remember that?'

Ellen smiled. 'Only because you never stop reminding us. Or the fact that I insisted on walking to school on my own after the first couple of weeks. How you had to walk behind with Sean, not close enough for me to see you but close enough so I wouldn't get lost.'

Her mother nodded. 'Sure maybe I was a bit like that when I was a girl myself. I just want you to know you're not on your own. If this job is too much for you, give it up. Your father and me, we'll help out anyway we can. Sure, we don't care if you get a job stacking shelves in Sainsbury's. We just want you to be happy. That's all.'

'I am happy,' Ellen replied. 'I promise. And you and Dad have been great. You are great. Now then, where are these kids of mine?'

'Playing cards as far as I know,' her mother said. 'Go on in. I'll call you when the tea's ready.'

At the door to the sitting room, Ellen paused. Inside, she could hear Eilish's girly squeals of laughter. Ellen and Jim had been at primary school together. St Joseph's in Greenwich, the same school her own children now attended.

Apart from that first day, her memories of him had grown foggy over the years. She could recall one incident where he'd pulled another boy's pants down in the playground and got into trouble for it. Apart from that, nothing. His friend, Anthony Mendoza, she remembered more vividly. She'd had an unrequited crush on him through most of her primary school years.

She pushed open the sitting room door and three faces turned to her. Her spirits lifted the moment she saw the children. Pat jumped up and raced across to give her a hug. She held him tight, smiling a hello to Jim and Eilish. Her daughter, playing it cool for Jim, nodded briefly before turning her attention back to the cards she was holding.

'We're playing Gin Rummy,' Pat explained. 'Jim's teaching us. It's really fun. Will you play with us?'

'Ellen?'

He'd put his cards, face down, on the table and was walking across the sitting room towards her. The corner light was behind him and his face was cast in shadow, features only coming into focus as he stopped in front of her. She felt a sudden, unexpected flutter in her stomach.

'Jim O'Dwyer,' she said. 'It's been a while.'

'Ellen Flanagan.' He leaned forward and kissed her on the cheek. The gesture surprised her. Without noticing, her hand stroked her face where his lips had been.

He stood back and smiled, his hands still on her shoulders. Big hands that felt good, like they might ease all that tension from her upper body if she let him.

She wondered if she should move back, away from him, or if that would seem rude. He made the decision easy by looking down at her shoulders and laughing.

'Seems I can't let you go,' he said, lifting his hands away, leaving her shoulders suddenly bare. 'Sorry about that. It's a shock seeing you after all these years, that's all. You haven't changed a bit.'

She rolled her eyes and thought how much she liked his smile.

'Bullshit,' she said. 'You have. Changed lots, in fact. Last time

I saw you, you were a chubby little kid with glasses and a whole load of attitude.'

The smile turned into a grin. 'Still got the attitude. A bit too much, some people might say. Of course, others think it's part of what makes me so loveable.'

'By others you mean your mother, right?'

He frowned, mock-serious. 'Not just my mother. There's a whole army of chicks out there who find me pretty irresistible, I'll have you know.'

'Yeah, right. You were always delusional. I remember that now. It's got worse over the years then? And it's Kelly, by the way. Not Flanagan.'

This time the frown looked real. 'Right. Sorry. And I was sorry to hear about your husband as well. I heard what happened. It must have been tough. Still is tough, I guess?'

She was saved from answering by the cacophony of noise from her children piling around them.

'Mummy!' Eilish jumped into her arms, wrapping herself around Ellen's body, little arms squeezing tight across the back of her neck, little legs clamping around her middle, all her pretence of coolness forgotten in her efforts to win back Ellen's attention. 'Come and play with us.'

'I don't know how to play Gin Rummy,' Ellen said, laughing as she hugged her back.

'Mummy's not very good at cards,' Eilish informed Jim. 'But that's okay. She can be on my team.'

'We don't have teams,' Pat said. 'It's not football, Eilish. Every-one plays by themselves.'

'Yeah, but Mummy's not good enough for that so I have to help her,' Eilish replied.

Jim bent down and stage-whispered in Pat's ear. 'Do you think Mummy would like to get trashed?'

'In your dreams,' she said. 'Come on, Eilish. Let's show these two how it's done. You too chicken to face us, Jim?'

They squared up, facing each other. He smiled. The dimple appeared and something inside her went soft. Then she got a grip. She unwound Eilish and put her gently down on the floor.

'Come on,' she said. 'Let's trash these boys, Eilish.'

22:00

Brian was dreaming. Even as it was happening, part of him knew it was only a dream. He would have woken up if he could but, like all the other times, the dream had to follow its course first.

... He was playing by the railway line. He liked it down there. It was only the other end of the field behind the house but it felt like another world. Once he'd climbed over the fence and clambered far enough down the slope so the house was out of sight, he always felt safe. As if no one or nothing could touch him down here. It was his secret place. Even Marion didn't know about it. It wasn't safe for her, not with the trains and everything. If she slipped and fell onto the

track when a train was approaching, well, he didn't even want to think about that.

Throughout the afternoon, he counted five trains. Two heading towards the sun, which was gradually sinking lower in the sky, and three going in the opposite direction. Only freight trains used this line, so he never saw people, apart from the occasional glimpse of a train driver.

Even still, every time a train approached, he would clamber further up the hill, away from the track, scared that the driver would see him and wonder what a boy was doing out here on his own, in the middle of nowhere.

No one was allowed to know where they were. That was one of The Rules. Because if They found us, Daddy said, They would come and take Marion. They would leave Brian here with Daddy, because who would want a pillock like him, but They would want Marion. They would tell Daddy that little girls needed mothers and, as their mother wasn't with them any longer, they would need to put her in a new home with a new mother.

The idea of being without Marion terrified Brian.

He stayed down by the railway line for as long as he could that afternoon. Until the sun disappeared completely, and the sky had faded from pink to a pale grey. He would have stayed longer except he was starving and knew he should go back to the house and start getting dinner ready.

He ran home as quickly as he could. The sky was getting darker. He was late. Daddy would kill him if dinner wasn't on the table in *time. As he ran, he tried to remember what food was in. They had potatoes and he was sure he'd seen some ham in the fridge that morning. Yes! There was definitely ham. He'd been tempted to take a piece for himself but had managed to resist, knowing Daddy wouldn't be happy to find a big chunk taken out of it.*

So, potatoes and ham. Daddy would have the ham but that was fine. There were more than enough potatoes for him and Marion. By the time Brian reached the house, he had the whole meal planned out in his head, was already working out how many potatoes he'd need to boil.

He pulled open the back door and went into the house, feeling pretty pleased with himself for working it all out. Not realising the house was empty. That Daddy and Marion were gone. That he would never see either of them again.

He started looking for them, calling out their names. But no one answered. As he moved from room to room, things started blurring, then fading. Until there was nothing left. And then, just as the house itself disappeared, he woke with a jolt.

Awake, it made no difference. He was still alone.

22:30

By the time the children were settled, Ellen was good for nothing except a glass of wine and some crap TV. She nodded off on the sofa, midway through the second drink, and might have stayed there all night if it wasn't for the phone call.

She'd been dreaming about Vinny and when she woke, she thought for a moment he was in the room with her. She hated that. The little slice of time when life was as it once was, followed by the gut-stabbing realisation that everything was different now.

She looked around for the ringing phone, images of Jodie over-riding everything else. She grabbed her phone and answered it without checking the caller ID.

'Hello!' she barked. 'What is it?'

'Hello to you too.' The familiar voice was a balm, instantly soothing her.

'Dai.' She leaned back on the sofa, smiling. 'Thank God. I thought it might be Ed.'

'No news then?' Dai said. 'About Jodie, I mean.'

'Nothing,' Ellen said. 'You okay?'

'No change since we spoke this morning,' Dai said. 'Just hoping I could pin you down sometime soon for that drink you promised me.'

In her mind, two girls' faces appeared, side by side. Both smiling. Ellen blinked and they disappeared.

'Tomorrow?' Ellen said. 'I'll just need to check it's okay with my mother. She's already helping out more than she should.'

'I could come to yours if that would help,' Dai suggested. 'See, the thing is Ellen, there's something I need to talk to you about.'

'We can talk now,' she said.

'It's a bit awkward,' Dai replied. 'I'd be more comfortable

doing it in person, if it's all the same to you.'

What the hell, she thought. She could do with a night out and a drink with an old colleague wouldn't be too much of a chore, surely?

'No,' she said. 'Let's go out. I'm sure it'll be fine. Besides, Mum likes you. She'll be delighted to hear I'm meeting you. Although I must warn you, she's mad keen for me to find someone new. She might get ideas about us.'

Dai laughed, a rich, warm sound that Ellen hadn't realised she'd missed until she heard it.

'You could do a lot worse,' he said. 'I'm still considered quite a catch, you know.'

'Yeah, right. At the Welsh Pensioners' tea parties, you mean?'

'Enough of that,' Dai said. 'Or you'll find yourself drinking alone tomorrow night.'

'And I wouldn't want that, obviously. So, where shall we meet?'

There was silence as Dai appeared to consider the question seriously before answering. 'The Dacre?'

Ellen laughed. 'Why did I bother asking?'

'Listen, when you find a decent local you stick with it. Too many poncey pubs springing up all over the place these days. The Dacre and me have a long history. Why would I mess that up by drinking somewhere else? Especially at this stage in my life. I'm assuming you'll want to put the kids to bed first?'

'Yes.'

'Okay. So why don't we say nine o'clock?'

'Nine o'clock it is. See you then.'

When Ellen hung up, she was smiling. It had been a long time since she'd got together with Dai Davies. Too long. And it would be her first proper night out in a while. She was, she realised, really looking forward to it. It was only later, after she had gone to bed and was struggling to fall asleep, that she wondered what was so awkward Dai couldn't tell her over the phone.

WEDNESDAY,
16 FEBRUARY

09:15

The press conference was scheduled for nine-thirty, Wednesday morning. Forty-eight hours since Jodie's disappearance. Ellen turned up early, hoping to catch Ed. Unfortunately, someone else had the same idea and got there first.

Press briefings took place in the conference room on the first floor. When Ellen arrived, the room was already filling with reporters and camera people, all keen to get the inside story on the missing girl. She recognised a few of them, including one particular female journalist she despised. Keeping her eyes averted from the visitors, Ellen walked up the centre aisle towards the raised platform at the front of the room. This was already set up with five chairs, a table and microphones.

Behind the platform, a door led into a smaller room, off this one. In a few moments, Baxter and the Hudsons would emerge from this room and take their places at the table. At the door, Ellen knocked first, then went inside.

The three Hudsons were in here, sitting close together on low, black chairs. Kevin jumped up when he saw Ellen.

'Are they ready for us?' he asked.

Ellen shook her head. 'Not yet.'

She wondered how they were holding up. And what the hell Abby was playing at leaving them alone in this dismal place.

'Abby's gone to see about getting us some water,' Helen said, pre-empting Ellen's question. 'She's been brilliant, actually,

117

hasn't she, Kevin?'

'When will it begin?' Kevin asked, ignoring his wife's question. 'It's not very nice sitting here with no one telling us anything.'

'Let me find Abby,' Ellen said. 'And see about that water. Is there anything else I can get you? Coffee or tea or anything?'

All three shook their heads and, excusing herself, Ellen slipped out through the far door. This one led to the corridor. Out here, she found Ed and Abby huddled together. Abby was speaking forcefully, using hand gestures to emphasise her point. There was no sign of the drinks she was supposed to be getting.

'Abby!'

Abby stopped speaking and turned to Ellen.

'The Hudsons are sitting in there on their own,' Ellen said, striding towards the pair of them. 'They're anxious as hell. You need to be in there reassuring them, not hanging around out here. I thought you were meant to be getting them some water.'

'I was,' Abby said. 'I am.' She turned back to Ed. 'Just think about what I said? Please?'

'It's none of your business,' Ed said. 'Now get back in with the Hudsons and do your job instead of sticking your nose into things that don't concern you.'

Abby flushed and looked as if she was about to respond. In the end, she obviously thought better of it and turned without another word and walked off. Fast. Footsteps banging loudly on the tiled floor.

'What was that about?' Ellen asked.

'Nothing,' Ed said. 'What do you want, Ellen? Briefing kicks off in a moment, so it's not exactly a good time.'

'Did you get my messages?' Ellen asked. 'I need to talk to you.'

'Is it about the case?' Ed asked. 'Have you got something for me?'

'Not exactly,' she said.

'Well in that case I'm not interested,' Ed said. 'Now if you'll excuse me.'

'It's important,' Ellen said.

'The only important thing is Jodie,' Ed replied. 'Now I'm going in there and doing something I hate because we have to do it. You need to put whatever personal issues you're having to one side and focus on the case. Get focussed or get out, Ellen. The choice is yours.'

The comment was so unjustified, Ellen couldn't think of a suitable response. Instead, she stood there with her jaw hanging open as Ed brushed past her and disappeared into the room she'd just left.

* * *

Half-an-hour later, still fuming, Ellen was driving east along the A2 to the small village of Cliffe, on the Hoo Peninsula in Kent. Ed's words repeated over and over in her head. Each time, her anger intensified.

Personal issues? He was the one with issues, not her. It was *him* who was losing his focus. *Him* who'd got embroiled in some pathetic affair at work and was now dealing with the fall-out. Because that's what this was about. Ellen was sure of that. Baxter and Abby had had some sort of bust-up and it was affecting the way they worked together. Christ only knew what effect it was having on Abby's performance as FLO. One thing was for sure, Ellen was going to get Abby Roberts on her own and give her an earful. This was all her doing and now that things had gone pear-shaped, Abby could damn well sort it out.

The Hoo Peninsula was a stretch of land situated between the Thames and Medway rivers, on the very edge of the North Kent coast, where the two rivers met the North Sea. Turning off the A2 towards Cliffe, Ellen found herself driving through a flat, bleak landscape that bore little resemblance to the 'Garden of England' Kent she was more familiar with.

Cliffe was a nondescript village with a smattering of Kent clapboard houses scattered amongst a few half-hearted streets of modern, red-brick council housing. Less than thirty miles from London, it was another world entirely.

Ellen had arranged to meet DCI Cox outside the church on the edge of town. She'd thought she might have problems finding it, but the four-sided spire was clearly visible as she approached the village.

She pulled up outside the church, beside the only other car parked there – a red Mazda convertible. A tall blonde was lean-ing against the car, smoking a cigarette. As Ellen switched off her engine and climbed out, the other woman stubbed out her cigarette and came forward, hand outstretched.

'Geraldine Cox,' she said.

Her handshake was firm, bordering on scary. Ellen tried not to wince as she introduced herself.

'Thanks for agreeing to meet me, DCI Cox,' she said, pulling her hand free. 'I appreciate it. Great church, by the way.'

'Eight hundred years old,' Cox said. 'See the brickwork? Layers of Kent flagstone alternated with black flint. And as for meeting you, it's a pleasure. Any friend of Ed Baxter's is a friend of mine. It's Geraldine, by the way. DCI Cox makes me sound like some fat copper off an old-fashioned TV show.'

Ellen turned away from the church and gave Cox a closer examination. Tall, probably as tall as Ellen herself, but with a fuller figure, cropped blonde hair, strong, Slavic cheekbones and ice-blue eyes. DCI Geraldine Cox was a stunner. On top of which, even though she looked no older than Ellen herself, she'd already made DCI. Comforting herself with the thought that the woman probably didn't have any kids – let's face it, if she did, how on earth did she find time for the gruelling hours expected of a DCI? – Ellen got straight to the point.

'You said you'd take me to where Molly's body was found?'

Geraldine nodded. 'I did. Leave your car here. I'll drive. We could walk there, of course. It's not far. But I've got my shoes to think of.'

She held up one foot, revealing a killer patent black stiletto underneath her tailored trousers.

'Vivienne Westwood,' she said. 'Divine, aren't they?'

'How do you know Baxter?' Ellen asked, once she'd settled herself in the passenger seat of the DCI's quite-frankly-ridiculous tiny car.

'We go way back,' Geraldine said, revving the engine and pulling away from the church with alarming speed.

'I met him on a training course about ten years ago. Something about performance metrics and KPIs. I remember next to nothing about the course, but it was worth it for meeting Ed. I was only a humble DI then. It was Ed who persuaded me to go for DCI when Bruce Audley, my old boss, retired. And ever since then, Ed's been a bit of a mentor to me, really. You know what he's like, right? Can't do enough to help. Then we worked together on Molly's case. I guess you could say we have a bit of a special relationship.'

The green-eyed monster in Ellen expanded and threatened to take over if she wasn't careful.

'Although he's been a bit reclusive lately,' Geraldine said. 'There's nothing wrong, is there?'

'Not that I'm aware of,' Ellen said. Thinking, but not saying, *apart from the fact he's screwing a female officer young enough to be his daughter.*

'I've been following the case,' Geraldine said. 'And I can understand why you've made the link with Molly. Christ, if you manage to catch that sicko, you'll be doing the world an almighty favour.'

The monster receded, pushed back by the image of two dark-haired girls with blue eyes and dimples.

'Here we are,' Geraldine said. 'Told you it wasn't far.'

Ellen got out of the car and looked around. Behind and either side of them, flat marshland stretched out as far as the eye could see. In front of them, right on the riverbank, were the ruins of what might once have been a prison or an army barracks.

'Cliffe Fort,' Geraldine said, walking towards the ruins. 'Built in the 1860s to stop the French invading. Later, it was used as an anti-aircraft battery during the Second World War. A crying shame they let it get into this state. No money to repair it. No one cares enough. Right dangerous it is down here. The whole place is falling down. Entry strictly forbidden – see the sign over there? This whole area,' she flung her arm in the direction of the marshes, 'was used as the paddy fields in *Full Metal Jacket*. Vietnam-on-Thames, hey? This way. Follow me.'

Geraldine walked across to the stone wall surrounding the fort. Ellen watched as she crouched down and pushed her way through a gap in the wall. Once through, she started walking towards the river, any concern for her Vivienne Westwoods suddenly forgotten. Ellen ran forward and did the same.

'Local youths come here all the time. Can you imagine if you're a teenager in a place like Cliffe? Nothing to do except get wasted. A group of drunk teenagers was having a party here one Saturday night. Saw Molly's body right over there.'

Geraldine stopped and turned to Ellen.

'My first case as DCI,' she said. 'On my good days, I still believe we'll catch the fella who did this. You got any kids, Ellen?'

'Two. Boy and girl.'

Geraldine nodded. 'I've got three. All boys. A five year-old and three year-old twins.'

Another time, Ellen might have asked how, with three young boys, Geraldine managed to find the time to look so damn good, dress so well and make DCI. Right then, however, standing beneath a grey February sky and looking at the spot where little Molly's body had been found, she didn't much care about things like that.

'She was raped,' Geraldine said in a voice every bit as bleak as the place where they stood. 'Repeatedly. Early signs of malnutrition. The bastard didn't even feed her. He smothered her. Put something over her face and held it until she stopped breathing. And then, when she was dead, he washed her – inside and out – with bleach, getting rid of every trace of his DNA. Then he brought her out here and dumped her.'

Until now, Ger had been looking not at Ellen but down at the spot where Molly's body had been found. Now, she turned and looked directly at Ellen.

'When you find him,' she said, 'I want ten minutes alone with him. In return, I'll give you everything I have on Molly's case. I'll go through the old files, pull out everything we've got. Every little lead we followed. It's yours. In return, when you find him, you let me have that.'

Ellen shivered. Not from fear or repulsion or anger. She shivered because the rage and determination in Ger Cox's face and voice was something she recognised. It was exactly how she used to feel about Billy Dunston. And when that rage was directed at someone, there was only one way to quench it.

'Sounds like we've got ourselves a deal,' Ellen said.

Ger nodded. 'Good. We've got a lot to talk about, then. Do you mind if we go somewhere else? I don't know about you, but I'm freezing.'

It was a cold day but Ger Cox's wool coat looked expensive enough to ward off anything. Ellen knew the real reason Ger suggested going was that it was just unbearable standing in this desolate place, thinking about a little girl's body being dumped here, without a second thought. As if she wasn't, like all children should be, absolutely the most important person in the entire world who deserved to be loved and cherished and protected from all harm. Always and forever.

They went to a country pub on the edge of the marsh where they sat beside an open fire and drank cups of milky hot chocolate.

'Our prime suspect was a guy called Brian Fletcher,' Geraldine said, leaving a chocolate moustache on her mouth as she sipped the hot chocolate. 'Weird sort of bloke. Backward. Suffers from a range of learning difficulties, I'd say. Lived in this shack of a place outside Higham. That's a village not far from here. Parents seemed to have dropped out of mainstream society. Travellers, I suspect, although that was never confirmed.

'Brian never went to school, never had any chance to integrate properly with society.' She shrugged. 'These things happen. Especially back then, and especially if you had a kid that wasn't, you know, normal.

'Anyway, like I said, our investigation focussed on him initially. He did some occasional work for this firm that's got the contract managing the park Molly disappeared from. All employees were questioned initially, but a few things pointed to Fletcher. Not least the fact that several witnesses reported that he seemed to have been watching Molly in the weeks leading up to her abduction.'

'Watching?' Ellen asked. 'How exactly?'

'Apparently when he was meant to be working, he'd loiter near wherever she was – watching her. It got so bad his boss had to have a word with him about it. The thing is, the day she was grabbed, Brian was nowhere near Mountsfield Park. He'd been on a job in Foster Park, down in Belvedere. We had several witnesses confirming he was there all day. We searched his house as well. Nothing. Then forensics confirmed what we knew already – Fletcher didn't do it.

'I mentioned the killer had done his best to get rid of all traces of DNA? Despite this, Forensics were able to get a semen sample. We checked this against Fletcher's DNA. It wasn't a match. So, no DNA, no evidence and witnesses who swore he was somewhere else the day Molly was taken. Fletcher didn't do it.'

'What made you focus on him in the first place?' Ellen asked.

'Profiling,' Geraldine said. 'We got this damn profiling expert in to help us. Guy was certain Fletcher had done it. Said he fit the profile. The thing is, Ellen, even at the time I didn't feel comfortable bringing him in. My kid brother, right, he's Autistic. Drives me nuts every time there's some sort of sex crime and the profilers go for the loners and the people with poor social skills.'

'Yeah, but there's a reason they do that, surely?' Ellen said.

Geraldine sighed. 'I know. It's just, not everyone who's a loner is some sort of sexual predator. A lot of loners are just people who can't get a handle on how society works. They don't fit in, so they find it easier to live on the outside, keep themselves to themselves. Just like Fletcher.'

Ellen thought of her own investigation and Ed's single-minded focus on Kevin Hudson. What she was hearing now confirmed what she already believed: focussing on one suspect at the expense of all other leads just wasn't the way to do it.

'Before you knew he couldn't have done it,' Ellen said, 'what was your gut telling you when you questioned him?'

'Good question,' Geraldine said. 'To tell you the truth, there was just something not quite right about him. At the time, I was certain he was hiding something from us. In hindsight, it's no wonder he went so funny on us. I mean, a guy like that – he's completely under the radar most of the time. No NI number, doesn't pay tax, probably can't even read or write. Suddenly being dragged in by the police and questioned for a serious crime, he must have been terrified.

'But I can tell you this, even when I thought he might be hiding something, I never once, not for an instant, got the impression he was capable of hurting someone the way that little girl was hurt. No way.'

'So if Fletcher was your main suspect and he didn't do it,' Ellen said, 'then it stands to reason that whoever killed Molly is still out there?'

Geraldine nodded. 'Which means, in my book, there's every chance it's the same person who's taken Jodie. Whoever he was, he was a monster ... the way that little girl suffered. Jesus. I hope you find him, Ellen.'

'Ed thinks it's Jodie's father,' Ellen said.

'I've known Ed a long time,' Geraldine said. 'He's not like me. You asked me a moment ago about my gut reaction to Fletcher? The reason I liked the question is that I'm an instinct sort of girl. Always trust my gut. And I'm guessing you do too, if you asked the question in the first place. Not Ed. He's a fact man. Keeps his mind open until every shred of evidence is gathered in. If he says Kevin Hudson's your man, then he'll have spent so long working up to that decision, nothing is going to change his mind.'

'The problem is, I think he's wrong,' Ellen said.

Geraldine lifted her mug and drained the rest of her drink.

'In that case,' she said, wiping the smear of chocolate from her upper lip, 'I'd say you've got a problem, Ellen.'

14:30

Rob York lived in a row of red-brick Council houses along a tidy cul-de-sac just off Mountsfield Park in Lewisham. Ellen drove straight there after her meeting with Ger. She wanted to hear, first-hand, his account of the day Molly disappeared. Her conversation with Ger had strengthened Ellen's belief that the two disappearances were connected. Hearing Ger's account of how Molly had suffered made her even more determined to find Jodie before the same thing happened to her.

Mountsfield Park was at the Hither Green end of Lewisham, an up-and-coming area notable for its good housing stock and strong community spirit. Ellen knew the park vaguely. When she'd first joined the force the place was a no-go area, full of druggies and winos and God knows what else. The park had improved a lot in recent years. Lewisham Council had invested serious money into cleaning it up – building a new playground, adding a coffee shop and employing a full-time park-keeper to monitor it. Glancing across as she got out of her car, Ellen was pleased to see young kids running around, a group of school children playing football, and not a druggie or wino in sight. Even Lewisham was becoming gentrified.

She ran through what Ger had told her about Rob York. A widower, his wife had died of cancer two years after giving birth to Molly, the couple's only child. Since then, Rob had raised his daughter single-handedly. He had, Ger said, been a devoted father who'd adored his only child. Before his daughter's death Rob York had run his own painting and decorating business and the family had lived in a large, Victorian house overlooking the park. After Molly's death, Rob fell apart.

'Makes you wonder about people who believe in God,' Ger had said. 'What sort of God would inflict that on a man, do you think? First he loses his wife, then this happens. If God's got something to do with it, then he's not any sort of god I want anything to do with.'

Despite her Catholic upbringing, it was a sentiment Ellen shared.

She approached York's house with apprehension. It was a horrible thing she was about to do – asking Molly's father to revisit the circumstances surrounding his daughter's murder. But if it helped them track down Jodie Hudson, she couldn't see that she had a choice.

In her jacket pocket, she felt her mobile buzzing. When she pulled it out, she saw Abby's number on the display. She switched the phone off and put it back in her pocket. She hadn't told Abby – or anyone else – about this morning's visit to Hoo. It would be on Ellen's head, and hers alone, if Baxter found out what she was up to.

At the front door, she paused. There was still time to turn around and go back to the station. Or to the Hudsons' house and spend the day doing what she was meant to be doing. Trying to get underneath the skin of Kevin Hudson.

She rang the bell and moments later the front door swung open. A man stood there. Tall and thin, much too thin, with yellow teeth and faded hair. He smelled of rotten fruit. It was like coming face-to-face with a dead person.

'What do you want?' he asked.

Ellen swallowed. 'Mr York? DI Ellen Kelly.' She flashed her warrant card. 'I called earlier. Left a message on your phone. When you didn't call back I drove over on the off chance you might be here.'

He stepped forward and she nearly gagged as his foul breath hit her nostrils.

'I asked you what you wanted,' he said. 'Not a load of bollocks about who you are and how many times you've called. I don't care what your name is. I just want to know why you're here.'

'I need to talk to you about Molly' she said.

His body sagged. 'Have you got him?' he rasped. 'Is that why you're here? You've found the bastard who killed her, is that it?'

'I'm sorry,' Ellen said, hating herself more and more as every second passed. 'That's not why I'm here. Not exactly. Could I come in, do you think? I'd rather not talk about it out here.'

He stood back to let her pass, motioning for her to go forward into the sitting room.

Inside the house, the smell was worse and Ellen tried to breathe through her mouth.

The sitting room was a small, dark room at the front of the house with tightly drawn curtains. It was all Ellen could do not to turn around and run back outside.

York switched on the single bare bulb in the ceiling as he followed Ellen into the room. She wished he hadn't. The room was
definitely better in the dark.

'Drink?' He waved a can of supermarket-brand lager at her.

She shook her head. 'No, thanks. Okay if I sit down?'

He shrugged. 'Help yourself.'

She sat on the very edge of a sticky armchair and watched him
open the can and take a long slug from it. He belched loudly,
then sat opposite her on the only other chair in the room.

The mantelpiece over the gas fire was covered in photos. The
same girl in each one – a smiling child with thick dark hair, a shy
smile and a gap between her front teeth.

'Molly?' Ellen asked. A rhetorical question, but one she felt
obliged to ask.

York took another swig of beer and nodded.

'Sam didn't tell me you lot would be calling,' he said. 'He usually calls when it's something like this. Mind you, I haven't heard
from him since the ear-bashing I gave him last time. No news, he
said. Just phoning to see how I was doing.'

He shook his head. '"How you doing, Rob?" he says. Like we
were mates and he was just phoning for a chat. How the fuck did
he think I was doing?'

'Sam's your liaison officer,' Ellen guessed.

'That's right. DS Sam Spade. His real name, I swear to God.'
York paused and peered at Ellen. 'But you'd know that, wouldn't

you? You said you had news. Come on then, spit it out. I haven't got all day, you know.'

Ellen remembered Sam Spade – it was hardly a name she'd forget. A Lewisham old-timer who'd retired a couple of years back. She had no idea where he was now, but was sure she could track him down if she needed to.

'A young girl has gone missing,' she said.

York sprang forward in his chair. 'I knew it!' he cried. 'I told your lot over and over. Pull your fingers out and find the bastard who did this. Otherwise, he'll do it again and some other poor family will be destroyed.'

'We don't know if this has anything to do with Molly,' Ellen said.

Despite her best efforts, she couldn't drag her eyes away from the photos. There must have been twenty or more, all crowded onto the small mantelpiece, the images jostling for attention, each one determined not to let Ellen forget about the little girl who'd been strangled and dumped in the Thames.

York followed her eyes to the photos and his body sagged again. 'She was my world. My little princess. Me and Molly, we were a team. When Sheryl died, I thought that was it. Didn't know how I'd manage to keep going. Except you've got to, don't you? No choice when you've got kids.'

'It's them that keeps you going,' Ellen said.

York nodded. 'That's what Molly did. Mornings I thought I'd never find the energy to drag myself out of bed and there she'd be, with that smile of hers and I'd manage it. Couldn't do it for myself, but I did it for her. Did it over and over again.'

'It was the same for me,' Ellen said. 'After my husband died, I only kept going for the kids' sake. You don't have a choice, do you?'

'What did he die of?' York asked. 'Your husband, I mean.'

'Hit and run,' Ellen said.

'They ever catch who did it?'

Ellen's fingers twitched with the memory of pulling the trigger.

'Yes,' she said. 'They got him eventually.'

York drank more beer and wiped his mouth with the back of his sleeve.

'So this missing girl,' he said. 'You think it's the same bastard who took my Molly?'

'No,' Ellen said.

She shifted uncomfortably on the chair. She should never have come. She knew that now, but it was too late. The man was destroyed by grief. What had she expected? She had no right, none at all, turning up like this and expecting him to go through it all again.

'Course you do,' York said. 'It's why you're here, isn't it? You think he's after doing the same thing to someone else's child. Jesus!' He slugged back the rest of his beer, crunched the can with his fist and pushed himself from his chair. Suddenly, standing over her like that, he seemed very tall.

'You lot fucked up,' he snarled. 'You should have found him, but you didn't. Spent all your time focussing on that poor backward bloke when it was never him who took her. You don't give a toss about me or my little girl. You don't have the first idea what it's like for me, waking up day after day after day. Waking up and realising all over again that she's gone and there's another twenty-four hours I have to find a way of surviving through. And then you turn up, telling me *it's happened again*, like I should ... what? Thank you or something? Come on, out!'

York grabbed her arm, dragging her from the chair and pushing her towards the front door. He was strong, but she was stronger. She thrust her elbow back into his stomach and he staggered back, clutching his middle.

'Assaulting an officer,' Ellen said, panting, 'never a good idea, Mr York. I'm sorry for what you've been through. Really I am. But please, don't ever try that again.'

He looked up at her, face full of pain and rage.

'She's going to die,' he whispered. 'That poor little girl. He's got her and he'll do the same things to her he did to my Molly. He's probably doing them right now. And instead of trying to find him, you're here in my house talking shite I don't want to hear.'

'We'll find him,' Ellen said. 'Whoever he is, wherever he is. We will find this man, Mr York. And when we do, we'll make sure he can't ever hurt another child. I promise you.'

York threw his head back and growled. 'You're all the same. Lies, lies and more fucking lies. Acting like you care when all this is to you is a job. People like you, with your cosy little lives and your lovely houses and your perfect bloody children. You haven't got a clue. Not a fucking clue. You tell me your husband dies and you want me to believe that's the same thing as losing a child the way I lost my Molly. Listen to me, lady. I lost my wife. I lost my kid. And let me tell you, the difference between those two things is like the difference between a grain of sand a fucking *planet*. Can you imagine it? What it's like to think about someone doing those things to your kid? To the one person you wanted to love and protect more than anything?

'He raped her. Everywhere he could. She had anal injuries, lesions inside her mouth. Two fingers broken on her left hand. Three ribs broken. And you know what I can't stop thinking about?'

Ellen wanted him to stop. But she couldn't speak. The noise he'd made, more animal than man, and these things he was telling her, things she knew but did her best never to think about, made words impossible.

'I think about her little face,' York said. 'What she used to look like when she cried. And I can see her. And hear her. And that's all there is. Her little face full of pain. Her screams. Begging him to stop. Begging me to come and rescue her. That's all there is inside my head. And it makes me sick. Literally. But I can't stop it and part of me doesn't even want to because if I stop it, then she's gone altogether.'

'I'm sorry,' Ellen said. But he didn't hear her. He was crying now, his body shaking, tears running unchecked down his face. When she opened the front door to leave, he showed no sign of noticing.

15:00

'Here. Have a cake.'

He's sitting beside me on the bed. Too close, like he always does. The smell of him is disgusting, but I'm so hungry. My tummy's rumbling and grumbling. And beside Brian's smell, I can smell the cakes.

He shifts away from me a bit, making the bed shake, and puts the bag of cakes down between us.

I'm remembering the last time, when he grabbed my arm, and I don't want to go for a cake in case he does it again. Except my tummy hurts I'm so hungry and the sweet smell of them is inside my nose, making my mouth water.

I grab one. Quick. Keep my head down so I don't have to look at him. He doesn't do anything. Oh God. It's so good. I stuff it into my mouth and it's gone too quick. I lick the crumbs off the paper case and scrape the little bits of pink icing off with my teeth.

He's got a thing about pink. This room I'm in, it's some sort of shed but it's all decorated like a girl's bedroom. And everything is pink, I swear to God. Absolutely everything, except those stupid posters. Pink stupid walls, a pink stupid rug and stupid, horrible pink sheets on the bed.

'Marion.'

I don't want to look at him, even though I know by the way his voice is that that's what he wants. I keep my head down, but then he says it again.

'Marion.'

I look up. He's staring at me with a funny look on his face. Like he's smiling except his eyes are wet and you'd think he was about to burst into tears.

He stands up and the bed moves. I can't breathe, waiting to see what he's going to do.

'Do you still like The Rainbow Parade?'

Am I meant to say yes or no? I don't even know what the stupid Rainbow Parade is.

I nod my head, praying that's the right thing to do.

He smiles and my body goes loose and I can feel the cake sitting in my tummy and I feel a bit sick, but not so bad like the last time. I don't think I'll vomit.

'I've got some old videos,' he's saying. 'I could bring them out for you to watch. Would you like that?'

I nod again, knowing now this is what he wants. It helps. Knowing what he wants and what I have to do. If it was like this all the time, then it wouldn't be so bad, maybe.

'I just want my mum.' My voice! It's working again. I can't believe it. Oh thank you, God. Thank you.

Brian sighs and my whole body goes cold and now I really think I might be sick. Except when he speaks he sounds sad, not angry.

'I know you miss her, Marion. I miss her myself, love. But you

know what Daddy did to her. I told you, remember? You can't see her. I'm sorry.'

And now I'm angry because he's not listening and if he doesn't understand I'm not this stupid Marion person, he'll never let me out of here. So I'm shouting at him and my voice sounds horrible and angry, but I can't help it. And I'm telling him that I'm not stupid Marion and my dad would never hurt Mum so why is he saying that and is he so stupid that he can't see I'm Jodie not Marion and what's his problem, anyway?

And I'm doing all that before I can stop to think that it's the wrong thing to do because what I need to do is what he wants so that I don't make him angry because if that happens, he'll hurt me.

But then just when I think something bad's going to happen he walks away from me and I know he's going to close the door and lock me in again and I really, really can't bear it if he does that.

I jump up from the bed and run after him but I'm not fast enough. By the time I get to the door he's outside, and I can hear the lock turning and the bolts being pulled across and I'm banging at the door, screaming, begging him to come back, even though I can't bear him, anything is better than being locked in here on my own.

Except he doesn't come back.

I can hear his footsteps and they're moving away from here and I beg, please, please, please, please, please, but the footsteps keep moving, until I can't hear them at all.

15:10

Ellen was shaking as she walked away from the house. She got as far as the car before she realised she was in no state to drive. Not yet. She remembered the café in Mountsfield Park. Just the business. A cup of tea while she pulled herself together. A quiet moment to indulge in a spot of self-loathing before heading back to the station.

The café was a prefab building at the top of the park with great views across London. In the distance, if she tilted her head, she could even make out the silvery curve of the London Eye. It was, she thought, as she took her tea to one of the tables outside the café, quite beautiful here. Not as dramatic as Greenwich Park, perhaps, but lovely in a different, more unexpected way.

She had messed up. The interview with York couldn't have gone any worse. And she'd learned nothing new. Worst of all, there was something about his grief that reminded her of how she'd been after Vinny died. No wonder Rob York was the way he was. Driven mad with grief.

She finished her tea and decided she was still too jittery to get back in the car. So she walked along the top of the park, past the two playgrounds and down the hill that wound its way to Catford at the bottom.

As she walked, her mind turned to that day in Bristol. She remembered Dunston's warm blood splattered across her face, and the weight of his body as it fell on top of her. And then, as he lay half-dead on top of her, his raggedy breath rasping in her ear, the feeling of jubilation surging through her as she pressed the gun to his face and pulled the trigger a second time. Turning her, in an instant, from a copper to a killer.

Enough.

Shivering against the wind, Ellen turned and walked back up the hill, pushing Billy Dunston from her head for now. Her thoughts returned to Rob York. The encounter left her feeling dirty. She wanted to rush home and jump in the shower, letting the hot water wash away every trace of York's pleading eyes, booze-ruined breath and unfathomable rage.

At the playgrounds she stopped for a moment, watching the small children running around. Molly York would have come here when she was little. Ellen imagined a different, happier Rob lifting his daughter onto the swings like the little girl in there now, shouting at her father to push her higher and laughing as her feet swung into the air before dropping down again.

Beside the playground, a group of men in green overalls were throwing bits of broken branches and other park debris into a trailer at the back of their van. One of them caught Ellen's eye, nodded at the playground and smiled.

'Hard to believe we were all that young once,' he said.

'Isn't it just?' she said, smiling back.

There was a logo in green on the side of the van. Medway Maintenance. Ellen frowned, recalling her encounter in Manor Park the previous day.

The man turned and waved goodbye to Ellen.

'Maybe see you around again sometime,' he said, giving her a grin.

She laughed and waved back. Cheeky bugger was young enough to be her son. Still, at her age a girl had to take whatever she could get, and a handsome young man flirting with her was something to enjoy, no matter how briefly.

The cold had taken up home in her bones, making her feel she might never be warm again. She hurried away from the park and back to her car, regretting that she had to go straight back to work. All she wanted to do was go home, get warm, and forget for a few hours that the world could be a very ugly place indeed.

18:04

Rob opened another can and drank, downing most of it in one go. It was some time since alcohol had gone from being something he needed to block out the pain, to just something he needed. These days, the shakes were so bad he couldn't get out of bed without a drink first. He kept a can of lager or a bottle by the bed just so that he'd be able to function each morning.

Not that it mattered. He took another swig from the can and looked at the photos on the mantelpiece. The biggest one, in the middle, was his favourite. Always had been. It showed Molly the summer after her fourth birthday, two years after Sheryl's death. Two years of sadness mixed with moments of unbearable happiness as he watched his daughter grow, every day becoming more like the mother who'd loved her but never got a chance to know her.

They'd gone on holiday, him and Molly, just the two of them. Hired a little house on the coast near Broadstairs. Sunny days spent building sandcastles, swimming in the sea, and eating over-cooked, overpriced fish and chips from the little chippie down the road from their bungalow.

The day of the photo, the weather wasn't that good and they'd gone for a walk in the countryside instead of their usual trip to the beach. They'd walked across meadows sprinkled with all sorts of wild summer flowers – deep blues, bright yellows and startling whites – the colours bursting from the green grass like a celebration.

Molly loved having her photo taken. Rob had sat her down amongst the flowers and taken ten or twelve shots. In this one, she was staring out at him, her head tilted to one side, holding up a yellow flower and sticking her tongue out. Her wild curls were blowing around her face like they had a life of their own.

As he took the photo, Rob thought he'd never known something could be so perfect. Molly in her purple summer dress, the yellow flower and her beautiful hair, sitting in a meadow surrounded by yellow and blue and white flowers, full of life and love – her whole wonderful life stretched out in front of her. And he knew, even with the sadness that was always with him, that he was lucky because he still had Molly and she made him happier than he'd ever imagined it was possible to be.

After she was gone, he'd thought of nothing except finding the person who'd killed her. He sat in this room, day after day, drinking beer, looking at the photos and letting the hatred consume him. He imagined all the different ways he would track down the killer and make him pay. In the darkest parts of his mind he pictured what he would do to the man, how he would hurt him.

Over time, the hatred burned inside him, growing stronger all the time. Until one day he realised Molly's killer might never be found. Was that when the drinking became something else? A means to an end – his end – and not just a way of getting through each interminable day. Maybe. Maybe not. Either way, it didn't matter. All that mattered was Molly, and she was gone.

In the corner of the room, the TV flickered and spat sounds out at him. The six o'clock news had just started. A little girl's face appeared on screen. A pretty little thing with dark hair and a dimple that reminded him of Molly's. The girl disappeared, replaced by three more faces – a man, a woman and a teenage boy. They all looked as if the blood had been sucked from their bodies. Rob wanted to turn it off, couldn't bear to keep looking at those lost faces. Except he couldn't bear to look away, either. He felt a connection with them. Because he knew. Just like he knew there would be worse to come. The hell those poor people were going to endure was only starting. Those early days, there was still hope. And when there's hope, you can survive anything. It's later, after the unimaginable has happened, that's when life ends and this begins.

He heard her, his Molly, every single minute of every single day. She never left him alone – her screams, her pleading. Not that he wanted her to leave. He owed it to her to endure, just as she had. It's why he kept going. He had to suffer. How else could it be? It wasn't enough, of course. No matter how much he suffered, it was only the tiniest fragment of what she had gone through.

On the TV, the mother was crying and begging for help. Poor cow. Rob felt for her. He really did. But all the begging in the world wasn't going to do her any good. The camera drew back, panned the rest of the people sitting at the table. Rob jerked when he saw the familiar face sitting beside the father. Ed Baxter. Jesus Christ. Wasn't it enough Baxter had fucked up the first time? He hadn't found Molly. Why the hell did anyone think he'd be able to find this child?

When the doorbell rang, Rob considered not answering it. Then it rang again and he changed his mind, thinking maybe it was that detective back again and if it was, he would give her another piece of his mind.

Except when he opened the front door, it wasn't her. Another woman stood in her place. Blonde, this time. With skin the sort of orange you only get from a sunbed. Some sort of spotty scarf tied around a too-thin neck.

'Mr York?' She flashed a set of white-white teeth in his face. 'My name is Martine Reynolds. I'm a journalist on the *Evening*

News. I was wondering if you could spare me a few moments?'

The moment he heard the word journalist, he started to close the door. Muck-raking scumbags the lot of them. The shit they'd said about him after Molly disappeared, even trying to make out it was him who'd taken her.

'Fuck off.'

But she was quick. Moved forward and stuck her foot in the door. Thickly sweet perfume hit him and he looked down at her foot, thinking if she didn't move it, he'd slam the door on it. And he would have, too, if it wasn't for what she said then.

'Please,' she said. 'It's about Molly. I think I know who took her.'

Whatever he'd been expecting, it wasn't that. And even though a part of him knew she was a dirty, lying, scumbag journalist who was probably making it up just to get inside his house, he had to know for sure. So he pulled open the door and stepped back.

'You'd better come in,' he said.

She walked past him, bringing the smell of dead flowers with her into his house. And that's how it started.

21:06

Dai was already there when Ellen arrived at The Dacre. She went to the bar and got the drinks in – another pint for Dai and a half of lager shandy for herself.

'Good health,' he said, raising his fresh pint.

'Cheers.' She nodded and took a sip of her drink.

'You're looking a bit tired,' Dai said. 'I don't remember those dark rings under your eyes when we used to work together. Ed's working you too hard, I'd say.'

'It's not him,' Ellen said. 'It's this case. Well, that and trying to do my job properly while being a decent mother at the same time. I'd sort of forgotten how hard it was to keep all those different plates spinning.'

'You're sure you didn't come back too early?' Dai asked.

Ellen shook her head. 'No way. The day-to-day grind of running a house and looking after two children – there's more to life than that. I'm fine, Dai. It's all fine. Really.'

He nodded. 'Must say, I never saw you as the stay-at-home type. Too much going on in that brain of yours. Too sharp for your own good, Ellen Flanagan. Kelly, rather. She won't be long for uniform, I told Paul. And I was right, wasn't I?'

'Only because you were so good to me,' Ellen said. 'You and Paul, you were both so generous. I learned so much working with you both.'

'Worked both ways,' Dai said. 'We were always on the lookout for any bright sparks to work with us. Trouble is, the bright sparks were few and far between. You were the exception, Ellen. It's why we put so much work your way. Why I supported you when you applied for detective. I knew you could do it. And you proved me right, didn't you?'

Ellen's face grew hot as Dai spoke. He was, she knew only too well, unforthcoming with praise most of the time. She remembered like it was yesterday that first year at Ladywell. She'd been so full of herself back then. So certain she had what it took to make a difference.

'I was such a show-off,' she said, remembering how hard she'd worked in those first few years. How determined she'd been to prove herself. To be the best.

'No more than any of the blokes,' Dai said. 'Difference is you weren't a bloke. Most women in the Met, they like to keep a low profile. Scared of standing out, I suppose, in case it marks them as being different. That never bothered you, Ellen. I always admired you for that. The way you were always willing to stick your head above the parapet and take whatever was thrown at you. You didn't give a shit what anyone thought of you. Pity there's not more like that.'

'You can talk,' Ellen said. She'd never met anyone who cared less about other people's opinions than Dai Davies.

He smiled. 'You're not wrong there. A right stroppy pair we make, hey? And speaking of stroppy, how are the lovely Eilish and Pat these days?'

Ellen took another sip of her drink. Even though the beer was diluted with lemonade it still tasted good. Made her crave a cigarette.

'Fine,' she said. 'Great, really. When they're not doing my head in, that is. What about you? You still seeing that Stella?'

'Nah,' Dai said. 'Things didn't work out between the two of us.

I wasn't that bothered, if I'm honest, Ellen. This whole romance business, it's more trouble than it's worth. I'm giving up on it.'

'I thought she was nice,' Ellen said.

Dai shrugged. 'Nothing wrong with her, no. But she wasn't the woman for me.'

'So who is?' Ellen asked. In all the time she'd known him, he'd never lasted more than a month with any woman. 'Maybe you should have given things a bit more time with Stella.'

'Listen,' Dai said. 'I didn't come here tonight to get advice on my love life, thank you very much. It's enough that I have to put up with it every time I go down home and have to listen to my sister going on at me. I expect better things from you, you hear?'

Ellen rolled her eyes. 'Fine, then. You tell me what I'm allowed talk about and I promise I'll behave myself for the rest of the evening.'

'Well, there was something actually,' Dai said. 'But first of all, why don't I pop to the bar and get us both another drink? This pint went down way too quickly.'

'I'm fine,' Ellen said. 'Don't get me anything.'

While Dai was at the bar, Ellen sipped her shandy and tried to ignore the growing cigarette craving. A memory pushed its way through the nicotine longing. A night out with Dai seven or eight years ago. Both of them more than a little drunk. Conversation veering from maudlin to pathetic. Dai had been going on about some woman. The love of his life. Unrequited love. Ellen couldn't remember much about it. What she did remember was trying to speak to him about it the following day. He'd clammed up, claimed he didn't know what she was on about. She knew he'd do the same if she asked him about it now.

'So,' she said, once he'd settled back with his fresh pint. 'What's the story?'

Dai ran a hand through his hair.

'I hate it that we can't smoke inside, anymore. I could really do with a cigar right now.'

'We could go outside if you want?' Ellen said. She'd already noted where the cigarette machine was. Seeing as she had already caved in this week, she might as well give in and go with it.

Dai shook his head. 'Too cold, isn't it? A man could do his bits some serious damage standing out in that for too long. Especially when those bits aren't seeing as much action as they once did.'

'You should have hung on to Stella,' Ellen said. 'Your bits would be fine.'

Dai tilted his head, an action she recognised as dismissive.

She shrugged. 'So?'

'It's about Helen actually,' Dai said.

Ellen frowned, not understanding.

'Helen Hudson,' he clarified.

Ellen still didn't get it, and told him.

'I know her, you see,' Dai said. 'From my early days in Bristol. You know that's where I worked when I first joined the force?'

Ellen felt a rush of anger. She wasn't sure – yet – what caused it.

'We were in the same writing group, you see,' Dai continued.

'Creative writing, you know. It's what I like to do when I'm not working. But I've told you that, haven't I?'

Only about a thousand times, Ellen thought. Once, a long time ago, she'd made the mistake of offering to read one of Dai's short stories. It was a mistake she wouldn't repeat in a hurry.

'Helen was my writing partner, you see. We would read each other's stuff and comment on it, that sort of thing. God, she can write, that woman. A pity she never took herself seriously enough to give it proper go. With that talent, and the looks to go with it, who wouldn't want to publish her?'

He had a thing for her, Ellen realised. Helen. Her looks hadn't struck Ellen as anything special when they'd met the other day. But stricken with grief, the woman was hardly looking her best. Who knew what she looked like under normal circumstances?

'She was with her first husband then,' Dai said. 'Her name was Helen Lawson in those days. A right bastard he was. Carrying on with another woman behind Helen's back. Helen knew what he was up to, though. Told me all about it. Only every time she confronted him, he denied it. Called her paranoid for doubting him.'

'You offered to help, I take it?'

'I couldn't bear seeing her like that, you see,' Dai said. 'She wanted to leave him, but it's not easy when kids are involved. Part of her thought, what if he was right? What if all those late nights and whispered phone calls were as innocent as he claimed they were? So yes, I offered to help.'

Dai drank deeply from his pint glass before he spoke again.

'I had him nailed down within the week. He was only banging his own secretary. And all the time he was at it, there was poor Helen – going out of her mind. And you know what's so strange about it, Ellen? That secretary. She wasn't a patch on Helen. You'd wonder what it is about some people. Don't know a good thing when it's staring them in the face.'

Ellen lifted her glass, realised it was empty, put it back down again.

'I need a fag.' She stood up. 'I won't be long.'

She couldn't get the cigarettes out of the machine quickly enough. Outside, she ripped open the pack, pulled out a fag, lit it with the lighter she'd brought along 'just in case' and inhaled. She held it in for as long as she could, then exhaled slowly, watching the trickle of smoke float over the empty beer garden.

Damn Dai Davies, anyway. Why did he have to complicate everything? The Hudsons hadn't struck her as a couple in love. And she didn't think the tensions between them were just because their daughter was missing. In fact, the more she thought about it, the more she started to believe the real reason for their marital discord was sitting inside the pub waiting for her.

Damn Dai.

Ellen finished her cigarette, squashed the butt into an overfull ashtray and marched back inside.

'Right,' she said, sitting down opposite him. 'I think I've

worked this out. You and Helen have a little thing going. How long it's been going on for I do not know and I do not want to know. But she's the reason you turned up at the station the other day. She's got in touch and asked you to keep an eye on things. She knows you're not with Lewisham, but she guesses you'll have mates who are. Mates, like me, who are an easy touch. Especially when they've just been through the wringer with the IPCC.

'So, are you going to do a Baxter and convince me Kevin's guilty? I'm guessing that's the handiest option, isn't it? I mean, with Kevin out of the way, you've got a clear path to his missus, right?'

'Wrong,' Dai said. 'And you've got no call speaking to me like that, either. I don't understand why you're so angry. I wanted to tell you the other day, when we met in the corridor, but it wasn't the right time or place. Why the hell do you think I wanted to see you? It was so that I could tell you as soon as I possibly could.'

Then Ellen realised the real reason for her anger. She was hurt. Stupidly, she'd thought Dai wanted to meet for old time's sake. As if.

'I'm already being pushed by Baxter,' she said. 'And now I feel as if you're going to do the same thing. I was so looking forward to being back, Dai. And maybe I sort of built it all up too much in my mind. But I just didn't expect it to be like this.'

'Like how exactly?'

'I'm not sure,' she said. 'Maybe it's Baxter. Or maybe I'm the problem. Maybe it's that I don't like not being my own boss.

With the Hope case, Baxter wasn't around. So I was in charge. Everything we did, it happened because I wanted it to.'

She stopped, not sure if she was making any sense.

'You thought you were on track to becoming a DCI,' Dai said. 'And now you're not and you don't like it.'

She shrugged. 'Maybe. Or maybe I just don't like every man and his dog telling me what to do.'

'I wouldn't do that.'

'Isn't that why you're here?' she said.

'No. I'm here because you're my friend,' Dai said. 'And when Helen called and asked me to help, I wanted to run it by you before I said yes.'

'And what if I say no?' Ellen asked.

'Then I'll tell her that.'

'What does Helen think you can do that we're not doing already?' Ellen wanted to know. 'Besides, what can you do? You're Greenwich. It's a Lewisham case.'

'Listen,' Dai said. 'Her daughter's missing. She'd done what any normal person would do under those circumstances and called the one person in the police she knows and trusts. She's not asking me to take over or go behind your backs. She's just asking if I'll help in any way I can.'

'You can't come into the team,' Ellen said. 'I've already spoken to Ed about getting another body in. He won't even consider it.'

'But if I could help out unofficially?'

Ellen chewed her lip as she thought this over. To have someone else as a sounding board wasn't a bad idea. Except she had to be sure Dai didn't have his own agenda for wanting to help.

'I don't think Kevin did it,' he said. 'If that's what you're thinking.'

She smiled. 'More or less exactly what I was thinking, actually. Tell me why, then. Why didn't he do it?'

'Kevin's a funny chap, right enough. I cannot for the life of me work out what Helen sees in him, but that's neither here nor there. The thing is, he's decent really. And even if he doesn't like the day-to-day grind of – how did you put it? – looking after two kids and running a house, it doesn't make him some sort of child abductor, does it? If that was the case, wouldn't most parents murder their children at some stage?'

'Baxter doesn't see it,' Ellen said. 'Usually, we work pretty well together. It's like when I was with you. You know, we always saw things in the same way. And that's what it was like with Baxter. Until recently.'

'Why's that, then?'

Ellen sighed. The truth was, things had never been the same between them since she caught him with Abby. But she wasn't about to tell Dai about that.

'Molly York,' she said instead. 'Baxter led the investigation when she first disappeared. I was on a secondment to Trident at the time so I wasn't part of the team. Baxter took it hard when Molly's body was found. Blamed himself, I think, for not finding her in time. Now another girl's gone missing. Maybe he's lost his perspective.'

'So what do we do?' Dai asked.

'We need to find her,' Ellen said. 'And we do whatever it takes to do that.'

'Even if it means upsetting Baxter?'

Ellen nodded. 'Yes. There's been too much death in my life, Dai. I don't want any more.'

Dai raised his glass and winked at her. 'No more death. I'll drink to that.'

And just like that, it was done. As Ellen clinked glasses with him, she hoped she was doing the right thing. Because if she wrong, if Dai Davies wasn't being straight with her, she could get into a whole lot of trouble. And with her recent track record, that was the last thing she needed right now.

22:15

Ellen's mother was dozing on the sofa, seemingly oblivious to the noise blaring from the over-loud TV.

'Do you mind?' she said, sitting up as Ellen turned down the volume. 'I was watching that.'

'Sorry, Mum,' Ellen said. 'I thought you were asleep.'

Her mother snorted. 'As if. How was Dai?'

'Fine,' Ellen said. 'Same as always really. He sends his love.'

She sat down on the sofa beside her mother and took her hand, rubbing her thumb along the calluses on her mother's palm. 'Was everything okay here?'

'Grand.' Her mother gave Ellen's hand a squeeze. 'Sure your two are no problem. It's great the way you get them off to bed so early every evening. Some difference to the way yourself and Sean were at that age. A right pair. Used to drive me mad, trying to get the two of you to settle. It's so much easier with Pat and Eilish. For a start, you only have to get one of them off at a time. You two used to wind each other up, get yourselves all excited.'

Ellen smiled. It wasn't like she hadn't heard her mother making this comparison, and hundreds of others, many times before. Inevitably she favoured Pat and Eilish, demonising the young Ellen and Sean. Ellen was sure they were never as bad as her mother made out. She was equally sure she'd probably do the same thing if her own children ever had kids.

It was part of the rituals of families, she supposed, stomach twisting as she thought about Noreen. Her other mother.

'Will you have a cup of tea before you go?' Ellen asked.

'Ah no,' her mother said. 'I'll be getting off. Your father doesn't like it when I'm not there. He won't go to sleep, you see, until he knows I'm home. And then he's a right grump in the morning if he hasn't had enough rest. Speaking of which, you still look tired. I think you're working too hard.'

Dai had said more or less the same thing earlier. She obviously looked a complete wreck.

'I'm fine,' she said. 'Besides, you're the one doing the real work, Mum. If it wasn't for you, I'd have had to tell Ed I couldn't come back. And that reminds me. It's too much for you and Dad, taking the kids every day. How would you feel if I signed them up for the after-school club a few days a week?'

'No.' Her mother's voice brooked no argument. 'You know how your father and I feel about that, Ellen. We love having your kids. Sure, why would we send them off to that God-awful place when they can be with us?'

'It's not awful at all,' Ellen said. 'The kids who go there seem to really enjoy it.'

'Yes, but not Pat and Eilish,' her mother said. 'You know they'd much rather be with us. Or with you.'

Ellen sighed. How could she explain that the idea of not working terrified her? That without work, all she had was the children and no matter how tempting it was, she couldn't let them become the single focus of her life. Because before she knew it, they'd be grown up and the last thing they'd want was some needy mother trying to push her way into their adult lives. Because without Vinny and her job, the children were all she had. And that could be a good thing or a bad thing, depending on how she handled it.

'I'll think about it,' she said. 'Maybe.'

Her mother smiled. 'Good girl. Now then, I'm going to make a move. Check your father's survived without me.'

'Well at least let me call you a taxi,' Ellen said. 'I hate the thought of you walking home on your own.'

Unsurprisingly, her mother wouldn't hear of getting home by any means apart from shank's mare and, reluctantly, Ellen gave in.

'It's only down the road, Ellen. What do you think could possibly happen to me between this side of Trafalgar Road and the other? You need to take a chill pill, so you do.'

Ellen tried not to smile. 'You reckon? Maybe I'll do that. But only if you promise to call me when you get home.'

Muttering something to herself about Greenwich not being anywhere near as dangerous as it was in her day, Bridget Flanagan buttoned up her coat and disappeared into the night.

Five minutes later, she phoned to report her safe arrival home.

Allowing herself to relax then, Ellen poured herself a glass of Merlot and sat in the sitting room, thinking about her meeting with Ger Cox and the brown, bleak landscape of Hoo. There was something about those flat, muddy marshes that got under your skin and stayed there. A sort of ghostly possession.

Vivienne Westwoods and impeccable grooming aside, Ellen liked Geraldine Cox immensely. And her assessment of Baxter had, in Ellen's opinion, been spot on.

If he says Kevin Hudson's your man, then he'll have spent so long working up to that decision that nothing is going to change his mind.

So what was it that made Baxter so certain?

Ellen moved across to the laptop and started reading through news reports on Jodie Hudson's disappearance. All of them ran with the same photo of the pretty ten-year-old with thick dark hair and a smile that broke your heart.

'Where are you, Jodie?' Ellen whispered.

Her mind flashed back to the afternoon last summer when Pat got lost in Greenwich Park. Ellen still couldn't think about it without feeling sick. It was the powerlessness, worse even than the fear, that had nearly killed her. The fact that there was nothing in the world she could do to bring him back.

Pat turned up a few hours later. Jodie Hudson had been missing for three full days. Ellen couldn't begin to imagine what her parents must be going through.

In her bag, Ellen's mobile started ringing. Pulling it out, she saw it was Baxter calling.

'Ed,' she said. 'What is it?'

'I wanted to apologise,' he said. 'For this morning. I was out of order and I'm sorry.'

'It's fine,' Ellen said.

'No it's not,' Ed said. 'I'll try to make sure it doesn't happen again. I've got a lot of shit on my plate right now, Ellen. Unfortunately, you got in between me and that plate this morning.'

'Lovely analogy,' Ellen said. 'Any updates?'

'Nothing,' Ed said. 'I keep going over things, wondering what the hell we've missed. There has to be something, Ellen. What about Kevin? Do you think I'm wrong about him?'

'Maybe,' she said. 'Maybe not. If he's guilty, though, he won't get away with it. You've got someone with him 24/7, right?'

She thought about pushing the Molly York angle again but decided not to. Another angry stand-off was the last thing she felt like right now.

'Two FLOs working rotation,' Baxter said. 'With Abby leading, of course.'

Of course.

'If he's hiding something, we'll find out,' Ellen said, preferring not to dwell on Abby.

Baxter sighed. 'Will we? That's what I said the last time, Ellen. When Molly went missing. I really believed we'd find her, you know. Really believed it, deep in my gut.'

'And what about this time?' Ellen asked.

'This time I don't know what to think,' Baxter said.

Ellen wanted to offer him reassurances, to tell him it would be all right and they'd find her. They'd find her and bring her home and she'd be safe. No one would ever hurt little Jodie Hudson ever again. Except she couldn't find the right words. So she said nothing. Just stayed on the line, looking at the photo of Jodie Hudson on her computer screen, and listening to the endless hum of a dead line in her ear after Baxter hung up without another word.

THURSDAY,
17 FEBRUARY

06.00

There's a window on the wall over the bed. It's got bars across it. Which is stupid because it's way too high for anyone to try to climb through it. The only way out of this stupid place is through the doors and he keeps those locked.

I hate him.

He's mad. Like, really properly mental. And I don't know what you're meant to do with a mad person or how you can get them to not be mad. Can you do that? He's decorated this shed like it's a bedroom. That's because he thinks I'm this Marion, who's his sister. Even though I've told him a million times that I'm not her.

We have a shed. I think it's meant to be for Dad, but we use it for dumping all our stuff. Dad's golf clubs and our bikes and all the things that drive Mum mad if we forget to put them away and they clutter up the hallway. She hates clutter but Dad doesn't care about it.

There's a toilet in here. And a TV. A really crap TV. It's massive and old-fashioned like the one Nanny used to have. All you can watch on it is those videos and they're so stupid and if I have to watch any more of them, I'll end up mad just like him.

Dad let him take me. I think it's because he was so angry at me. He was really angry that morning because we were late and I wouldn't wear my school shoes because they were all dirty and I hate them and I wanted to wear my new trainers. I told him I hated him.

That's why I'm here. It's a punishment.

I've been praying. It doesn't seem to make any difference.
I'm still here.

10:00

Ellen had tried – unsuccessfully – to reschedule her next session with the counsellor.

'If you cancel, you're off the case,' Briony said when Ellen called early on Thursday morning.

'A child is missing,' Ellen said. 'Surely that's more important?'

'If you start skipping your sessions,' Briony replied, 'then I can't guarantee you're in a fit state to lead this investigation. I'll see you at ten.'

The counsellor had hung up before Ellen had a chance to say anything else. And so, on Thursday, when she should have been getting on with the job of finding Jodie, Ellen was sitting on a chair in Briony's bright, airy surgery in Ladywell, talking about things she hated talking about and wishing she could be anywhere else.

Briony Murray was a petite, pretty, perky Antipodean who bore more resemblance to a cheerleader than a shrink. Until she opened her mouth. The two women sat facing each other in comfortable armchairs placed either side of a Victorian fireplace in Briony's office. Like the counsellor, the room was bright and light.

Briony was asking Ellen about Jodie, probing into aspects of the case Ellen would rather not think about.

'It must make you think about your sister,' Briony suggested.

'No,' Ellen said too quickly. 'Why would it?'

Briony smiled. 'You tell me.'

She should have deflected it. Instead, in her efforts to prove her counsellor wrong, Ellen walked right into it.

'Two girls?' she said. 'That's a bit tenuous, surely? My sister was only a baby. Eighteen months old when she … when she died. Jodie's ten. And she's … it's totally different. She's older and she has two parents who love her and an older brother who's devastated by what's happened. And that poor boy. Every time I see him, I imagine what it's like for him. Because it's so difficult for the children. When something like this happens, the adults take over and they're so caught up in their own pain and fear that they forget about the children. It's not on purpose. Of course not. But think about it from a child's perspective. This kid, Finlay, his whole world has just been turned upside down. One minute he's part of a family, then this terrible, unthinkable thing happens and everything's changed and yet no one is there to talk to him about it. No one has the time or the strength to sit him down and explain what the hell is really going on. What has really happened to his sister? Why has the world suddenly shifted? When will things go back to normal? Will they ever go back to normal?'

'Is that what it was like?' Briony asked.

'I don't know.'

In her mind, the memories of it were so mixed up. She was only four when it happened. How can a four-year-old make sense of something like that? How can anyone?

'The noise woke me.' She was barely aware she was speaking. It was as if she had no control over her voice. No idea what words would come out of her. Because when you never, ever spoke about something and then you suddenly did, who knew what you'd say?

'I thought it was … I didn't know what it was. When I think about it now, I can say it sounded like a wild animal. But back then, all I knew was that it was terrible. A terrible howling sound.'

Inhuman. When she thought about it now, that's the word that best described the sound she'd heard that night. And yet, in a way, it was the most human of noises. The sound of pure grief. And yet …

'It was my mother,' she said. 'Such pain.'

And yet …

In the bed beside hers, Sean was still asleep. He never woke, no matter what noises were going on in the other room. Never heard her father shouting at her mother when he was drunk. Or worse. Never heard their baby sister Eilish crying, night after night after night. And he never heard this.

'I remember getting up. Standing in the bedroom shivering. It was so cold in the flat. Always cold. It must have been warm sometimes. In summer, but I don't remember that. All I remember is the cold.'

A banging sound had started up. In her mind, when she remembers that night, the sound is her own heart, thumping loudly inside her. Thinking about it now, she realises it was one of the neighbours knocking on the front door. She imagined that noise her mother was making, seeping its way through the narrow walls and flimsy floors of the flat into every corner of that Peckham high-rise.

'I don't remember leaving the bedroom. All I remember is what happened after that. The light was on in the bathroom. Everything else in darkness. I followed the light because that's where the sound was coming from. I don't know if I called out for anyone. I don't think so. I think I already knew it was her.'

She was back there now. More bits of it coming to her. The chill of the lino against her bare feet as she shuffled along the corridor, past the closed sitting room door towards the slice of yellow light cutting out from the bathroom. Getting closer and closer to that sound.

And then her mother was there. Baby Eilish in her arms. And the look on her mother's face was like nothing she'd ever seen before. And she wanted Mammy to take her in her arms and hold her tight and take her back to bed and cuddle her and tell her it was all right, everything was going to be all right. Except Mammy couldn't do that because she was holding Baby Eilish and something was wrong. Something was so bad and wrong and Mammy was crying and her mouth was open with that bad, bad sound coming out of it and …

Blue lights. A blanket wrapped around her and Sean. Both of them huddled in the back of a car. A man in blue uniform. Police. No sign of Mammy or Baby Eilish. Sean's little face white, his big eyes staring at her, not understanding.

'I want my mammy.' Her voice was so little in the big car with the other noises all around them. Police radio and adults everywhere, whispering and talking, and no one telling them what was going on or where they were going or what had happened to Mammy and Baby Eilish.

And because no one would listen, she opened the door and jumped out and started running back to the block of flats. They lived on the top floor. She could see the sitting-room window. It was easy to see their flat because, unlike most of the others, the lights were on.

She ran as fast as she could, screaming out for her Mammy to come for her. Because she was scared now. So scared that they would take her away and she would never see Mammy or Baby Eilish again. Because something bad had happened. Something so bad to make Mammy make that sound and look like that. And she needed to know. She needed to know what had happened. She needed Mammy.

She was nearly at the building when someone caught her. A large arm wrapped around her middle, lifted her right off the ground. A man's voice, telling her it was okay. But he was a liar and she was kicking him and hitting him and screaming at him to let her go, but it was no good. He was big and strong, much stronger than her and no matter how hard she hit him it did no good. He held her tight, carrying her back to the car, further and further away from her mother and the only home she'd ever known.

'Ellen?'

Briony's hand on hers, squeezing. A box of tissues placed on her lap. Ellen took one and used it to wipe her face.

'Sorry,' she managed.

Another squeeze of her hand. 'No reason to apologise.'

'For the first few days,' Ellen said, 'no one would tell us anything. We were put with this foster family. They were okay, I think. I barely remember them, to be honest. Then one day this woman came and sat us both down and told us that Eilish had died and our mother was helping the police find out what had happened to her.'

'And after that?'

'After that, nothing. Eilish was gone and our mother was taken from us. We were adopted by the Flanagans and I never saw my mother again.'

'How do you feel about that?' Briony asked.

'I'm fine about it,' Ellen said. 'And so is Sean. She killed our sister, Briony. We could never forgive her for that. And the parents we got instead, they're wonderful. We've been so lucky. Why on earth would we want to change that?'

Ellen told herself she was trying to convince Briony. That wasn't true. The person she really needed to convince was herself.

Because now she'd started talking about it, now the memory of that night was fresh in her head again, she'd realised something. She missed her real mother. She'd possibly never stopped missing her. And maybe it was about time she stopped missing her and did something about finding her.

11:00

Rob woke on the armchair in the sitting room. The curtains were still drawn and in the faded yellow light, it was impossible to know what time it was. Morning, he guessed. A brass band thumped and clashed inside his head; his neck was stiff from the way he'd slept. He felt like shit.

On the floor beside him, an unopened can of lager. He bent down, groaning with the effort, picked up the can and opened it. He downed a big mouthful and wiped his mouth with his hand.

He'd been a bit pissed when that journalist showed up, but he'd got his act together sharpish when she told him why she had come. A hard bitch with her fake tan and even faker smile. She said she wanted to help him, but that was bullshit. She wanted a story. And that was fine by him, if she was willing to give him what he wanted.

He leaned back in the chair and closed his eyes, going back over every detail of yesterday's visit.

Her name was Martine Reynolds. She sat opposite him on the sofa, skinny arse hanging off the edge of it like she was scared she'd catch something from it.

'Another girl's gone missing,' the journalist said.

'Tell me something I don't know,' Rob replied.

She surprised him by doing just that. Told him all about Jodie Hudson's step-dad and his conviction for hurting a kid. Told him there was every chance the police would mess up this case, just like Molly's, and wouldn't find Jodie until it was too late.

As she carried on talking, Rob barely listened. His mind focussing on one thing and one thing only. The name. Kevin Hudson.

'I want people to know the truth,' the journalist said. 'About Molly and Jodie and Kevin Hudson. I want them to know that this man is out there and, despite his background, the police are doing nothing about it. His own step-daughter's disappeared and he's still free to walk the streets. How does that make you feel, Mr York? As Molly's father, how do you feel knowing the police have a suspect but they've done nothing about it?'

'How do you think it makes me feel?' he asked.

'Angry?' the journalist said.

When Rob nodded, she scribbled something on the notepad resting on her scrawny thighs.

'What do you think the police should do?' the journalist said then.

'They should arrest him,' Rob said. 'Of course they should. But they won't do it. Mark my words. They'll fuck up again. Just like they did with my Molly. Instead of going after the real bastard, they focussed all their efforts on some poor sap who had nothing to do with it. You telling me they're doing the same thing again? They should be arrested themselves, the whole bloody lot of them. And I'll tell you something else while I'm at it, that bastard Baxter is a useless tosser. He didn't find my Molly in time, so why the hell they have put him in charge of finding this girl, I do not know.'

The journalist left soon after that, promising to be back soon. Not that he gave a shit. He said Hudson's name aloud now, letting the words echo around the silent room, drifting around the photos of his daughter. The name of the man who'd killed her.

It was like a gift. This woman knocking on his door and offering up the name. She hadn't even known what she was doing. Had wanted some soundbites from him for her stupid story. But he was wise to her. Had too much first-hand experience of the way the press operated to be fooled by that cow. Playing the innocent when all along she'd come because she knew, finally, who'd hurt his Molly. And maybe she was a bitch and a piece of shit like all journalists, but if she was serious about this Hudson fella, then who was Rob to argue with her?

Kevin Hudson.

Rob drank more beer and let his mind travel to the dark place. He already knew what Hudson looked like, had seen him on the TV. Now he pictured Hudson's face, screaming and begging for mercy as Rob hurt him. There would be no mercy for Kevin Hudson.

It was time to make a plan. Find out exactly where Hudson

lived, and take it from there. For the first time in a very long time, Rob realised he had something to look forward to. It felt good.

13:15

Ellen was late getting back to work. After her session with Briony, she'd gone for a long walk. A futile attempt to clear her head. Back at the station, Ellen found Alastair Dillon and Malcolm McDonald in the incident room.

'Where's Raj?' she asked.

'Over at the Hudsons',' Malcolm said. 'Abby called earlier. Said she needed some back-up. Place is crawling with journalists and the family are near breaking point.'

'Why didn't she call me?' Ellen demanded.

A blush crept up Malcolm's pale face and he looked to Alastair for assistance.

'Your phone was switched off,' Alastair said. 'At least, that's what Abby told me. To be honest, Ma'am, she's no reason to lie. I'm pretty sure she'd have preferred to speak to you instead of the boss.'

Damn counselling session. She'd have to have a word with Briony. See if she could postpone the sessions until this case was over. She needed to be in contact with her team at all times. Not that it would have mattered in this instance. She was certain Abby never even tried to call. Probably went straight to Raj, who she seemed to have wrapped tightly around her middle finger. Like most of the other blokes in this place.

Turning her back on Dillon and McDonald, Ellen sat at her desk and started trawling through emails. If she concentrated really hard, she might just be able to block out the confusion of emotions this morning's session had stirred up. Damn counselling.

The emails were the usual mix of junk mail and urgent requests. She ignored anything not directly relevant to the case. An email from Ger Cox caught her attention.

Ellen

Good to meet you yesterday. Something I forgot to say and you won't find it in the files I'm sending across. Brian's boss is a guy called Simon Wilson. It may not be anything, but he struck me as a nasty piece of work. Although, in fairness, he's done a good job with Brian. Seems to have taken Brian under his wing when the guy's parents disappeared. Despite that, there's something off about him. Not sure if that helps or hinders your case, but if it was me investigating, I'd take another look at Wilson too.

Files couriered across this morning. Happy reading.

Ger.

Ellen closed the email and swung her chair around.

'Malcolm, I'm expecting a set of files. Coming across from Rochester. When they arrive can you contact me straight away?'

'Sure,' Malcolm said. 'Anything I can do with them when they arrive?'

'Just call me.'

Ellen stood and went out of the incident room, down the corridor to Baxter's office. She nearly went in without knocking, but the image of Baxter with Abby stopped her just in time. None of them wanted a repeat of that.

Baxter didn't answer when she knocked. Tentatively, she pushed the door open. He was sitting behind his desk, talking on the phone to someone.

'He's bound to be like that,' she heard him say. 'What did you expect?' Then, a moment later. 'I don't care how you do it. Just keep me out of it.'

He saw Ellen then and hung up.

'Ellen,' he said. 'What is it?' He sounded tired and looked even tireder.

'Is everything okay?' she asked.

'Fine,' he said. 'Just sorting out a surprise for a mate of mine. His sixtieth coming up and a few of us are organising a few drinks at the golf club for him in a few weeks. Nothing fancy, of course. He wouldn't like that. Just a few pints with some mates.'

The lie was so obvious it startled her. It was none of her business, after all, who he'd been talking to. Unless it was Abby, of course. And even then, it really was something Ellen was better off not knowing about.

'How're things?' Ed asked, obviously as keen as she was to change the subject.

'We're getting nowhere,' she said. 'It's driving me nuts. We need to widen our focus, Ed.'

'Take another look at the Molly York case, you mean?'

She nodded, preparing herself for another argument.

'Maybe you're right,' Baxter said instead. 'Christ, Ellen. I don't want to lose the focus on Hudson because I still think he's our main suspect. There is still no sign that he was where he said he was the morning Jodie disappeared. No CCTV, no witnesses, nothing. On the other hand, as you've rightly pointed out before, there's nothing proving he took Jodie, either. Except the incontrovertible fact that, as far as we know, he's the last person to have seen her. That, coupled with his history and the fact he's her step-father and most children are hurt by people they know, that makes him a suspect. The only one we've got.'

Ellen sighed. What had Ger Cox said? If Baxter believed Kevin was the suspect, the chances were he had good reason.

'I can see that,' she said. 'And I'm not suggesting for a second we lose our focus. Just widen it, that's all.'

'Where to?' Baxter asked. 'Molly York? We've already done that, Ellen, and it's given us nothing.'

'That's because we only looked at Fletcher,' Ellen said. 'What if we widen it a bit? Check out the other suspects? Maybe we'll find something Rochester missed.'

'I doubt it,' Baxter said. 'But it's worth a shot, I suppose. Only if you can do it alongside everything else. Can you do that?'

She thought of the long list of things she had to wade through. The limited time she had to get it done. And then she thought of Jodie.

'Of course,' she said.

Baxter nodded. 'Then get on with it, Ellen. And don't come back here again until you've got something for me. You don't need me to tell you that time's running out.'

15:45

Ellen took the children to the park after school. They had just reached the playground when she felt her mobile phone vibrating in her pocket. Dai. Checking the kids were okay – both of them were on a roundabout being pushed by an older child, their squeals of delight carrying across to where she stood – she took the call.

'Checking I got home alright?' she asked.

'I wouldn't be so patronising,' Dai said. 'Have you got a minute?'

'Sure. What is it?'

'I had a chat with Helen this morning. Told her I'd spoken with you. So it's all above board, you see.'

'Okay,' Ellen said, thinking the news was hardly worth a phone call. It was exactly what she'd expected him to do.

'Only that's not why I'm phoning,' Dai said. 'Not really. It's Kevin, see? Helen wants you to try and talk to him.'

'About what?'

'She thinks he's hiding something from her.'

'Hang on,' Ellen said. 'If that's the case, she needs to come in and make a statement. You know that, Dai. Besides, we interviewed him the other day. Couldn't get anything from him. Tell her to come in.'

'It's not that simple,' Dai said. 'Helen says whatever Kevin is up to, it's got nothing to do with what's happened to Jodie. He loves that little girl like she's his own flesh and blood. That's what Helen told me and I've got no reason not to believe her.'

Ellen took the phone from her ear and looked at in exasperation.

'Just hear me out,' Dai was saying when she put the phone back where it was. 'Kevin had a rough time in prison. Terrible, by all accounts. When he came out, he was a changed man. The experience nearly destroyed him. And because of that, he has a pathological fear of being arrested again. So he won't open up with someone like Baxter who's made it as plain as the nose on his face that he thinks Kevin is guilty. And he won't speak to Helen. She's already tried. You're the only hope we have.'

'Why me?' Ellen asked. 'Why don't you give it a try if you're such a close friend of them both.'

'I never said Kevin and I were friends,' Dai said. 'Fact is, the bloke doesn't like me very much.'

And we all know why that is, Ellen thought.

'Helen likes you,' Dai continued. 'She told me. I think she might trust you more than that Abby person.'

'I got the impression Abby and Helen were getting on fine,' Ellen said.

'Yes,' Dai replied. 'But you're the senior officer. You've got more clout with Baxter, and Helen knows that.'

If only, Ellen thought.

'Helen says Kevin was framed,' Dai said. 'That he should never have been charged for what happened. She thinks he's obsessed with getting justice and she's worried he's about to do something stupid. Or that he already has.'

Ellen sighed. All around her, children were playing. Running and climbing and swinging on swings and sliding down slides. All of them, so happy and carefree. She wondered when that carefree stage passed and life became a big pile of shit that never seemed to be sorted.

'For all we know,' she said. 'Whatever Kevin has been up to may be connected to Jodie's disappearance. Isn't it possible there's a link? What if he pissed someone off and to get him back, they took his child? That makes a sort of sense, doesn't it?'

'Yes,' Dai said. 'And that's why you need to speak to him, Ellen. You're the only one with any chance of getting through to him.'

16:15

The day they left, he sat in the empty kitchen for hours, waiting for them to come home. When he got so tired he couldn't stay awake, he lay down on the kitchen floor and slept there. He couldn't face going upstairs. Without Marion and Daddy the house was too empty.

Early the next morning, he heard a car pulling up outside. He jumped up, his heart racing, spirits lifting. Daddy's van had an odd, creaking noise it made when he braked. As Brian raced outside, he could already hear the old van groaning, and he knew for sure it was them.

He pulled open the back door just in time to see the back of the van disappearing into the garage behind the house. It didn't matter where they'd gone or why they'd left. Didn't even matter that it was so cruel of Daddy just to go off like that without telling him. The only thing he cared about right now was that they were back and he wouldn't be left on his own.

Inside the shed a door slammed and he heard footsteps – the slap-slap-slap of heavy soles against the stone floor. He strained his ears, listening for signs of another person – Marion – but didn't hear anything.

A man walked out of the shed and stopped, looking around him like he wasn't quite sure which way to go. The morning sun was behind him, casting the man's features in shadows, making it difficult to see who he was.

For a moment, Brian let himself believe it was Daddy. Even though the man was too short, too broad to be Daddy. Even though, as the man recognised him and moved towards him and opened his mouth to speak, it was clear he wasn't Daddy at all.

'Hello Brian,' the man said. 'I'm glad you're here. I came over yesterday afternoon but there was no sign of you. I was afraid you'd run off.'

Brian opened his mouth to speak but no words came out. Simon. What was Simon doing driving Daddy's van? And where was Marion? What had he done to Marion?

Without even realising he was doing it, he started backing away. He wanted to turn and run, get back into the house and lock the door and never let anyone inside it ever again, but there was something about the way Simon was looking at him that made it impossible for him to do that. It was like Simon could see inside his mind, reading his every thought.

He managed to get his mouth working.

'What do you want?'

Simon smiled. 'Your Daddy's gone, Brian. But you've probably worked that out already, haven't you? He's taken Marion, of course. Said she deserves better than growing up in this stinking shithole in the middle of nowhere. Asked me if I'd look in on you from time to time, make sure you're okay.'

Brian had backed right up against the house now, there was nowhere left for him to go. He watched as Simon kept walking, getting closer and closer. Daddy wasn't coming back. He knew that now. He'd taken Marion and left him here to rot. Marion! He couldn't live without her. He'd promised Mam he'd look after her, no matter what.

Simon was right up close now, so near that Brian could see the red, broken veins across his cheeks and smell his dirty stinking breath as he leaned even closer, pushing his face right into Brian's.

'Aren't you going to invite me in, Brian?'

He woke up, sweating, the sheets twisted around his body, trapping him. In a panic, he tried to free himself, flailing and thrashing in the bed, not knowing where he was or who he was fighting.

Suddenly he was free. With a roar of triumph he thrust his body forward, out of the bed so he was standing on the cold lino. He looked around, his panic subsiding as he let his mind slowly adjust. He'd done it again. Fallen asleep in the afternoon. Tired all day because he couldn't sleep at night.

Reaching out, he picked up the photo he kept beside the bed. It was old and faded now. In the dim light, it was hard to make out her features, but he could imagine them. He rubbed his thumb back and forth across the outline of her face as if, by doing that, he could somehow reassure himself she was still there.

Through the small curtainless window, the sky was grey tinged with pink and he could see pale sun in the distance, low in the sky, casting its dying glow over the gloomy, endless landscape.

If he tilted his head in just the right way, he could see the roof of the shed through the branches of the trees. He loved that shed. He had started building it years ago. Daddy wanted somewhere he could park the van. Said he needed a proper space, somewhere solid.

Then Daddy and Marion went and the shed remained forgotten for a long time. Until Molly. After that, Brian knew he needed somewhere else. A special place where he could keep Marion safe, if he ever found her.

He'd spent so long decorating it. Saving up the money Simon gave him and buying all that pink wallpaper. Even putting it up by himself. It was difficult, but he'd managed fine after a few false starts. When the room was all ready, he'd been so proud of it. Could hardly wait to show it to her.

Only she hadn't been as excited about it as he'd hoped. Compared to what she'd had before, the room she was in now was like a palace. Okay, maybe Daddy had got her a better room after they'd left, but Brian didn't think so. Daddy didn't care about things like that. Once, he'd called Brian a *fucking fairy* for helping Marion put up a poster of a princess in her bedroom. Daddy had gone mad and ripped it from the wall. Poor Marion had cried for ages, even after Daddy gave her a belt and told her to shut up.

A sudden image flashed in front of him, Marion sitting on the bed with her legs pulled up so he could see her knickers. Almost like …

He shook his head, angry with himself for even thinking it. Something wasn't right, though. It was like she was someone else entirely, not his Marion.

Of course she's not your Marion, you gobshite.

Daddy was off now. Roaring inside his head, confusing him.

Shoot the bitch and be done with it. She's nothing but trouble.

Daddy's gun was under the bed. Daddy left it behind when he went away. It had bullets in it. Brian knew how to load the gun and put in more bullets if he needed to. He'd watched Daddy do it enough times. Daddy used it to shoot rabbits and birds. Brian kept it in case someone broke in and tried to hurt him. If that happened, he'd shoot no problem. He'd probably shoot more than once. And he'd be good at it, too. Wouldn't miss. Just like a real soldier. But to do that to Marion?

Do it!

'La-la-la-la-la-la-la! It's the Rainbow Parade! The Ra-a-a-a-a-a-inbow Para-a-a-a-de!'

Brian sang as loud as he could to block out Daddy's angry roaring.

He was still singing half an hour later when he went outside. He glanced down the yard, towards the shed. Shook his head. Didn't think he could face her today. He hadn't been to see her yesterday, either.

He knew it was wrong to leave her for so long, but she had a real knack for making him feel bad. No matter what he did, no matter how many treats he brought her or nice things he did for her, he was always left with the impression that she wasn't happy.

It's because she doesn't want to be here. Any eejit can see that.

'Somewhere OOOOVER the rainbow, way up high,' Brian

screamed, running for the van and jumping inside. As he fumbled with the ignition, he kept singing, shouting out the words of her favourite song at the top of his voice.

Even after he'd got Daddy's old van going, even after he'd driven away from the house and was nearly at Higham, Daddy was still at it, goading Brian and telling him that the girl in the shed wasn't Marion.

In his heart, Brian knew Daddy was wrong, knew he was only saying that stuff to confuse Brian, trip him up just so he could have a right laugh about it when Brian realised he'd made a mistake.

The problem was, no matter how hard he tried not to think it, there was a tiny part of his brain that was already starting to wonder if maybe, just maybe, Daddy was right. And if he was, and the girl in the shed wasn't Marion, if she turned out to be another mistake, just like Molly, then Brian wouldn't have a choice. He'd have to get rid of her.

18:30

Ellen had a box she kept in the room off the loft that they'd converted into an office. She knew where it was, but never, ever went near it. Until now.

The children had been fed and were playing cards in the sitting room. Grabbing the moment of peace, Ellen crept up there and pulled the box down from the high shelf over the desktop computer she rarely used.

It was a small cardboard box that was once white but was now an indiscriminate shade of grey. Ellen opened the lid. A pale blue teddy bear was inside. Underneath this, a faded colour photo. She pulled the bear out first, held it to her face and inhaled the smell. Was it her imagination or could she still – even now – detect the faintest scent of perfume on it? A smell that seemed, somehow, familiar, even though she didn't know how that could be possible.

She closed her eyes and let the vague, faraway memories of her mother float to the surface. Apart from the night Eilish died, she couldn't recall specific events. All she had was a stash of scattered images and disassociated flashes of memory.

She remembered – vividly – the fear and the hunger, her mother crying as she held Baby Eilish, who seemed to scream all the time, except for that last day, when she did nothing at all. She remembered eating Rice Krispies from a packet, ripping the bag open and scraping the crumbs up with her fingers. Her tummy rumbled when she put her face against the plastic bag to lick it and got the sugary smell of what had once been in there.

There were other, earlier memories, too. Fainter, yes, but definitely there. Her and Sean lying in bed with their mother as she cuddled them and sang a song. What was the song? It was there, she could almost hear it, she tried to focus on it but it was gone.

She opened her eyes and took out the photo. Two young children, a boy and girl, standing either side of a woman with wild dark hair and blue, blue eyes. The woman wore a slash of red lipstick and was smiling. She looked happy.

It couldn't have been easy for Noreen. Abandoned by her husband, stuck in a Peckham high-rise with three young children. Maybe it all just got too much for her. Ellen didn't know how well she would have coped in that situation.

'Mummy!' Pat's voice dragged Ellen back to the present. Except she wasn't ready. There was more to think about. More memories to sift through and try to make sense of.

'Mummy!' Louder and angrier this time.

Ellen put the photo and the teddy back in the box and closed the lid. As she walked downstairs to see what her son wanted, her head filled with the sound of a song. A woman singing as she cuddled her two children close to her, keeping them warm under the duvet on a dark winter's night. And then, as she got to the chorus, two little voices joining in, the three of them shouting the words out, voices rising tunelessly over each other in the warmth of the bed.

Bring back, oh bring back, oh bring back my bonnie to me, to me.
Bring back, bring back, oooooooh bring back my bonnie to meeeeeeee!

According to Pat, Eilish had cheated. According to Eilish, Pat was a sore loser. Ellen didn't care who was right and told them so.

Then, watching Eilish's lip start to wobble, she quickly suggested they make some cocoa in the kitchen together.

'Cup cakes,' Eilish said.

Ellen checked the time. 'It's too late for cup cakes. It's nearly bath time.'

'Cup cakes only take twenty minutes,' Pat said. 'We can make them and then have our bath. Please, Mum?'

Ellen groaned. After making the damn cakes then they'd want to eat some and it was too late for sugary treats and bath time would be pushed back and ... God dammit, couldn't she be more organised?

'Fine,' she said. 'Cup cakes and bath. But if either of you ask to watch TV before bedtime, we'll never, ever make cup cakes this late in the evening again. Got that?'

Eilish jumped at her, wrapping her little arms around Ellen's middle.

'Yaaay! Mummy's the best mummy in the world.'

Of course, the cup cakes took longer to prepare than she'd anticipated and, of course, both children insisted on sampling one before their bath. And after that it was teeth and storytime and, finally, bedtime.

It was exhausting, but worth it. She knew her parents worried that she spoiled the kids, but what choice did she have? They had already lost so much. Any chance to make them happy and she jumped at it. And tonight, at least, they had gone to bed happy. No tears, no temper tantrums. Just kisses and cuddles and smiles. Surely, Ellen thought as she went downstairs, that was worth anything?

In the hallway, the local free newspaper lay on the mat inside the front door. Ellen bent to pick it up and carried it, folded under her arm, into the kitchen. Pouring herself a hefty glass of Shiraz, she moved into the sitting room. Her plan was to have a glass or two of wine, a flick through the local rag and the TV channels, followed by an early night.

This changed when she unfolded the paper and saw the front page. It took a moment to process what she read. She hadn't been expecting it. Her mind raced as she read through it a second time, as she tried to work out how this could have happened. One name jumped out at her, making her stomach drop. Rob York. Another name, further down the same piece that made her want to throw up. DI Ellen Kelly. Shit. Shit, shit, shit.

On the table beside her, the phone started ringing. She picked it up, thinking it was Ed. A woman's voice at the other end, brittle, with a posh Cheshire accent.

'DI Ellen Kelly? Martine Reynolds here. Crime editor for the *Evening News*. I'd like to ask you a few questions about Jodie Hudson.'

Ellen recognised the name. She checked the newspaper just to make sure. Martine Reynolds. The piece of shit who'd written this piece of shit.

'I have nothing to say to you,' Ellen said.

She hung up quickly. Almost immediately, the phone started

ringing again. She lifted it, disconnected the call and left the phone off the hook. Then she finished her wine in one long mouthful, stood up and went for some more. It was going to be a long night.

23:50

It was late and Rob was drunk. Way too drunk. He didn't care. This was a celebration of sorts and he deserved a good drink. His glass was empty. Looking around for the whiskey bottle, he was surprised to see that empty too. He'd thought there was more left.

There was another bottle in the cupboard, but he didn't know if he could be arsed to stand up and find it. He looked at the newspaper, spread out on the table before him. A news story all about Kevin Hudson. The man was a bloody animal.

There was a photo of Hudson with the story and Rob examined it, looking for some external sign of what the bloke was capable of, but he couldn't find anything. There was that case in Austria, the bloke who'd kept his daughter locked in a cellar for all those years, Rob couldn't remember his name but it didn't matter. The thing was, with that bloke you could see just by looking at him that he was a nasty piece of work. A monster they called him, and even if you didn't know what he'd done, you'd look at the photo and think to yourself, there's something not right there.

Not with Hudson, though. Which made him all the more dangerous, if you thought about it. Rob had thought about it. A lot. Done nothing but think since that journalist had called around. Every time a kid went missing it brought it all back. Not that it ever went away, of course, but when you hear of another kid, well, it almost feels as if it's happening to you all over again.

He'd really felt for the Hudsons then. Jesus, you wouldn't wish that on your worst enemy. Worse than dying, it was. At least when you were dead you stopped hurting.

There was only one thing had kept him going over the years, and that was finding the bastard who'd done that to his Molly. In his head, he'd imagined it over and over. Every scenario you could think of, he'd pictured it. Fantasizing about what he'd do if he ever got a chance.

He hadn't expected it to be this easy. Each time he'd gone through it, he'd pictured Sam Spade calling with the news that someone had been arrested. After that, the scene varied according to Rob's mood. The ending was always the same, though. He always made sure of one thing – that the person who'd ruined his life paid for what he'd done.

That woman turning up on his doorstep, it was like a sign. Almost made him believe there was a God. He didn't believe that, of course. You couldn't see something like that happen to your own daughter and believe in anything much after that.

This, though, this was good. The first good thing that had happened in a long time. Kevin Hudson. He looked at the photo again. Didn't look much like a killer. Didn't look like much at all. Ordinary bloke wearing a denim shirt and smiling. As if a monster like that had any right to be smiling.

Just went to show that old saying was right. About not judging a book by its cover. Some bollocks like that. Kevin Hudson. A simple phone call, that was all it had taken. Turn on the tears and Bingo! Amazing what people will tell you if you start crying on them. This called for a celebration. First thing he'd had to celebrate in a long time.

He got up, staggered across the floor and pulled open the cupboard door. At first he couldn't see the bottle. Hidden behind the box of Cornflakes. When he reached in to get it, the cereal box fell onto the floor and Cornflakes scattered everywhere.

Who cares, Rob thought. Only bloody Cornflakes. He didn't even like them. They crunched under his feet as he walked back to the table. He opened the whiskey bottle and looked around for his glass. Couldn't see it anywhere. He drank straight from the bottle. Whiskey ran down his chin and neck but he didn't care. Tidy it all up in the morning.

He felt something under his foot and looked down. Cornflakes all over the floor. How did that happen? Didn't matter. He didn't even like Cornflakes. Just bought them out of habit because that's what they'd always bought. Molly wouldn't eat Weetabix or Ready Brek, but she'd eat Cornflakes until they came out her ears.

He sat back down and looked at the mess of papers in front of him. There was something important in there?

Renata Cash. That's who he'd called. Recognised the road, didn't he? Remembered Renata lived on the same street. What was it called? It was here somewhere. He'd written it down. Hadn't he? He rummaged through the papers, not quite sure what he was looking for but knowing he'd recognise it the moment he found it.

Hudson's face was everywhere. The same photo on all these sheets of paper. Hudson in an open-necked denim shirt, clean-shaven and young-looking, smiling at Rob. Mocking him.

What right did that bastard have to mock him? He'd show Hudson. He'd show him all right. Angry now, he rustled through the pages, trying to find the information he needed. Then he remembered.

Renata was little Rachel Cash's mother. A right dopey cow, Renata, but kind with it. One of the few who'd made some effort to stay in touch with him. She lived on the same road he'd seen on all those news reports about Jodie. Rachel was twelve now. First year in 'big school'. Hired a limo for her party. Renata said they had some great photos and did Rob want her to send him some? Did he fuck. But there was something else she could do for him.

He stood up. The movement was too quick. His body swayed and he grabbed hold of the table to stop himself falling over. The table shook and the pile of papers slid off, landing with a whoosh on the carpet of Cornflakes, Hudson's smiling face in amongst

Molly's favourite cereal.

That wasn't right. Not right at all. Rob got down on his hands and knees and gathered the paper together, brushing the Corn-flakes off as he put them all back onto the table.

Breathing heavily, he grabbed hold of the leg of the table and tried to haul himself up. But he couldn't get his body working and he slipped, fell back down to the ground. His head cracked against the floor and for a moment the whole room spun.

Eventually, things slowed down, stopped. Rob lay where he was, staring up at the bare bulb in the ceiling, noticing the pattern of damp from where the bath leaked. One day, the plaster-work would give and the bath would fall into the kitchen. He supposed he should seal up the cracks around the bath before that happened, but doubted he'd get around to it.

He remembered, then, what he'd been looking for and shifted on the floor so he could get his hand into the back pocket of his jeans. As he moved, his jumper rode up and bits of broken Corn-flakes stuck to his back, scratching him. He pulled out the piece of paper and held it up to his face. He'd told Renata he wanted to write to the Hudsons. Offer his sympathy. It had been that easy.

The words swam and it took a tremendous effort to focus and read what he'd written, carefully transcribing the address as Renata read it out to him over the phone. Finally, his eyes focussed and he read the words aloud, repeating them until they seemed to echo around the kitchen.

Kevin Hudson, 80 Dallinger Road, Lee, SE12 0TJ.

Dallinger Road. Where Rachel Cash lived. Molly used to go there after school. Two days a week while Rob worked. He'd recognised it straight away when he saw it on the TV. Now he had the address, all he had to do was come up with a plan. A way of sorting Kevin Hudson and making sure he never did anything like this again.

To do things right, he'd need help. Earlier that evening, he'd run through a list of people he knew. Kept coming back to one name – Frankie Ferrari. According to Rob's neighbour, Vera, Frankie had got out last week and was back home living with his mum.

Rob glanced at the clock. Nearly midnight. Too late to call Frankie. He'd do it later. Get some sleep first and try to clear his head. He was going to need a clear head for Frankie. A clear head and a good story. There was nothing Frankie liked more than a good story. And nothing he liked less than men like Kevin Hudson. Nonces, that's what Frankie called them. Had his own special way of dealing with them and all.

Rob pushed himself up off the floor, smiling now. He was looking forward to speaking with Frankie and hearing just what Frankie had to say when he told him about Kevin Hudson.

00:01

I keep thinking they'll find me. Because they must be looking for me, right? Mummy and Daddy will be worried. They will be worried, won't they? I miss them. I miss Finlay. He said last week that he hates me, but he doesn't hate me really. I told him I hated him too, but I don't. Of course I don't. I love him and I can't think about him without getting tears in my eyes.

I keep thinking of last summer when we were in Spain. It was really hot. Roasting. And I got sick because I ate some prawns that hadn't been cooked right and I vomited for two days. And after all the vomiting I had to stay in bed and we were in this little house with a swimming pool and the Hutchinsons were in the house beside ours and I hated lying in bed listening to everyone having fun in the swimming pool. And there was this waterfall and they all went one day, except me and Mummy because she had to stay at the house to look after me.

When they came back, Finlay sat beside me on the bed and showed me all the photos of the waterfall and it made me really sad. And because I was so sad he got the small DVD player that we use in the car and he put on The Sound of Music, which me and Mummy love but he hates only he didn't hate it this day and he watched the whole thing with me and he was so lovely and cuddled me and we sang all the songs together. And at the end of it he promised that when we go back to Spain this year, he'll bring me to the waterfall, just me and him and no adults and we'll have the best time ever.

And now I'm here. And I keep thinking about how nice he was to me that day and wondering if we'll go back to Spain and wondering if they'll go without me if I'm still here. And I don't want them to do that. I don't want to be here anymore and I specially don't want them to go to Spain without me. Because the Hutchinsons will be there and Amelie is, like, in love with Finlay, even though she's only the same age as me and he's way too old for her. But if I'm not there, then he'll play with her instead of me and take her to the waterfall and watch DVDs with her, and it's not fair because she's not even his sister and I really, really don't want him to be with her because after a bit he'll forget all about me and if everyone forgets about me, then no one will remember to come and find me and I'll be here forever and ever.

And I can't be here anymore because it's horrible and I feel sick and all I want to do is go home.

FRIDAY, 18 FEBRUARY

09:00

Friday morning, Ellen got to work early, hoping to get in and out of there before Baxter showed up. He'd already left two messages on her voicemail. So far, she hadn't found the courage to call him back.

She went through her emails, made a list of things to do that day and was just getting ready to make an early escape across to the Hudson house when the door to the incident room swung open.

'Ellen!' Baxter's voice boomed through the room. Beside Ellen, Alastair visibly quaked.

'My office. Now.'

Baxter swung around and stomped down the corridor, the sound of his footsteps echoing back to Ellen, who hurried after him. By the time she caught up, he was already inside his office, pulling out the chair behind his desk.

'Close the door.'

He sat down and slapped yesterday's *Evening News* down on his desk.

'Want to tell me what the hell is going on?'

Ellen sat down in the chair opposite and started speaking.

'Sir, I had nothing to do with that piece. The first thing I knew about it was when that dropped through my letterbox last night.'

'You're telling me it's a coincidence?' Baxter asked. 'You turn up – according to Miss Martine bloody Reynolds – asking York about his dead daughter. Something you failed to mention to me, your superior officer, by the way, and the next thing *this* gets published?'

'I should have told you,' Ellen said. 'I'm sorry. Really I am. But surely you can't think my visiting Rob York has anything to do with the story?'

'Are you trying to be dumb or is it just an act?' Baxter snapped. 'Think about it, Ellen. Whatever you said to York, he jumped on it. Put two and two together and made five. Assumed there's some link between Jodie and Molly and this is the result.'

Ellen thought of the broken man she'd met yesterday.

'No,' she said. 'You've got it wrong, Ed. I don't think Rob York would have contacted the press. If you read the story, you'll see this is all inside information. Look, she even knows we haven't got any CCTV footage of him in Lewisham the morning Jodie disappeared. How the hell can she know something like that? And anyway, I never even mentioned Kevin to Rob York. How could he even begin to …'

'Stop it!' Baxter was shouting now, face red with an anger she'd never seen in him before. An anger that, somehow, felt out of proportion for what he was accusing her of doing.

'What is it with you?' Baxter continued. 'Why the bloody hell do you always have to make things so difficult? I made myself very clear on this, DI Kelly. Your job is to investigate Kevin Hudson, find out everything you can about where he was the morning his little girl disappeared. Do you do what you're asked?

Like hell you do! You run off doing your own thing, ignoring what anyone else says if it doesn't agree with your version of reality. Christ almighty! It's like your obsession with Billy Dunston all over again. Once you get something into your mind, you can't let it go. Well this time I'm not giving you a choice. One more fuck-up and you're off the case and off my team. Permanently.'

Ellen pushed her chair back and stood up. She took a moment before she trusted herself to speak.

'You're right,' she said. 'I don't let things go easily. But that's something you've always encouraged. I may have been obsessed – as you put it – with Dunston, but with good reason. That obsession is what led us to Katy Hope. I was the one who found Katy, Ed. And her little boy. I found both of them. And that's more than you can say about Molly York.'

Back in the incident room, Ellen sat at her desk, put her head in her hands and groaned. What the hell had she been thinking? She'd half-expected Baxter to come after her, but so far he'd remained in his office. Probably writing her dismissal letter.

'That bad?'

She lifted her head and saw Alastair's grey eyes staring down at her. He was from a small village in Orkney. Ellen always imagined his eyes were the same colour as the sea he'd grown up beside.

'Worse,' she said. 'Oh God, Alastair. He really let rip and instead of sitting there and taking it, I threw it right back at him.'

'Don't be too hard on yourself,' Alastair said. 'The boss hasn't been himself these past few months. We've all had a taste of it at one time or another. Some of us more than others.'

'I'm sorry to hear that,' Ellen said. 'Who's borne the worst of it? Don't worry, I'm not asking you to tell tales or anything. But if Baxter's upsetting people in my team, then I need to know.'

'He's really had it in for Abby,' Alastair said. 'It's like he's blaming her for something. I mean, I know what happened between them, but that was all over before it even started, if you know what I mean. It was just a fling. And for a while after that they seemed to get along fine. Recently, though, he's really gone for her a few times in briefings and stuff. If you ask me, he's gone too far on more than one occasion.'

Ellen didn't understand. The Baxter she knew had always been a supportive, sympathetic boss. Yes, he could be a pain in the arse at times, but who couldn't?

'I thought it was this case,' she said. 'But you're saying it's been going on for longer than that.'

'A few months at least,' Alastair said. 'I would have said something, but it seemed petty to start moaning about the boss when we've more important things to be getting on with.'

Ellen rubbed her face as she tried to sort her thoughts out.

'Right,' she said after a moment. 'I need to get across to the Hudsons' house and see how they're doing. This business with the *Evening News* has hit them hard. I got a text from Abby last night. She said they're really upset about it.'

'Any idea who tipped off the journalist?' Alastair asked. 'Sorry, none of my business, I know. But Baxter will have their guts for garters when he finds out. I wouldn't like to be in their shoes.'

'He thinks it was Rob York,' Ellen said. 'Molly York's father. Ed's wrong about that, though. He's too angry right now. I'm sure when he calms down he'll realise the leak had to have come from inside. In the meantime, if you have any suspicions, you'll let me know?'

'Of course,' Alastair said. 'Only I can't imagine it was any of the team. One of the uniforms, maybe?'

Ellen sighed. 'Maybe. Anyway, I can't worry about that right now. Whoever the leak is, that's Baxter's problem, thankfully. Not mine.'

She looked at the pile of files on her desk that had come across from Rochester yesterday.

'Alastair, this all relates to the Molly York case. Can you go through them and make a list of suspects they had at the time. Start with Simon Wilson, Brian Fletcher's boss. See what the reports say about him. Once you've done that, give me an update. Ger Cox, the DCI in Rochester, didn't like him. I want to know why. I have a feeling we'll need to have a word with this Wilson bloke. And while you're doing that, I'm going to have a chat with Kevin about Dan Harris.'

'Who's he?' Alastair asked.

'The juvey Hudson attacked. I want to get Kevin's version of what really happened and why he was locked up.

'Baxter's convinced Kevin's behind Jodie's disappearance. Judging by last night's paper and the wider coverage this morning, everyone else thinks the same thing. What about you, Alastair? What do you think? Am I wrong to keep trying to find a connection with Molly York? Or worse, did Kevin take Molly too, like that Reynolds woman is trying to imply?'

'Kevin told us he was in Lewisham the morning Jodie disappeared,' Alastair said. 'He's lying about that. I was the one who went through the CCTV footage, remember? And I was the one who sat with every single uniform and went through their witness statements. No one they spoke to remembers seeing Kevin that morning. And he doesn't appear on a single piece of CCTV footage. He wasn't there. I'd bet my life on it. And if that's the case, there are only two real questions: where was he and why the hell is he lying to us?'

Ellen stood up. 'Thanks, Alastair. I'm going to get over there now. I've spent too long focussing on Molly York when I should have been trying to find out what the hell Kevin is playing at. You'll call me as soon as you're finished here?'

'Of course.' Alastair gave Ellen one of his rare smiles. 'It's a pleasure working for you, Ma'am. Always.'

The compliment, as unexpected as the smile, left Ellen lost for words. She would have hugged Alastair on the spot if it wouldn't have embarrassed the hell out of him. Instead, she gave him a smile of her own and got out of there as fast as she could before Baxter came looking for her and killed the little bit of good feeling the conversation with Alastair had given her.

10:30

Making her way through the media scrum was a challenge. When she finally reached the front door, Ellen had to press the bell several times before Abby finally let her in.

'Any sign of that cow Reynolds?' Abby asked as she slammed the door shut.

Ellen shook her head. 'To be honest, I just kept my head down and pushed my way through. Thought it was the easiest way of getting in here unharmed.'

'It says in the paper that you went to see Rob York,' Abby said.

Ellen gritted her teeth, ready for the attack.

'So?' she asked.

'So, it's strange you didn't think to share that with the team,' Abby said. 'Not that I think it's a bad idea. Far from it. The possible connection between the two cases is obviously something we should consider. And, if I'm honest, I'm not comfortable with the investigation focussing so strongly on one suspect. I'm scared we'll miss something.'

'I thought you'd take Baxter's side,' Ellen said.

'It's not a question of sides,' Abby said. 'Really, Ellen. What sort of simpering idiot do you think I am? My only concern is finding Jodie. Whatever's going on between you and Baxter, that really is none of my business.'

A flare of anger rose in Ellen. Instead of giving in to this, she suppressed it.

'Listen,' she said. 'I think we need to talk. Is there somewhere we could go?'

'Sitting room.' Abby nodded to a door on the left. 'Helen's in the kitchen, watching the news. She won't switch if off and it's horrible. Every news channel is regurgitating all the crap that woman wrote about Kevin. Let me go and check she's okay and I'll be in to you in a second.'

'What about Kevin?' Helen asked. 'Where's he?'

'He's taken Finlay to the park,' Abby said. 'It was my idea. It's horrible in here, Ellen, listening to that crowd outside. I've had to take the phone off the hook. I sent Kevin and Finlay out the back way, through the neighbours' garden. The kid really needed a break from all this. So did poor Kevin.'

'Good idea,' Ellen said. 'Do you think he'll be safe on his own, though?'

'You mean, if someone's read the paper and has him pegged as a paedo?' Abby asked. 'Yes, I did think of that. I offered to send someone with them, but Kevin wouldn't hear of it. Said they needed time alone.'

'Okay,' Ellen said. 'You go check on Helen, then. I'll see you in a minute.'

It was her first time in the sitting room. Unlike the kitchen, this room was tastefully furnished with mismatched, shabby-chic furniture including a leather Chesterfield that wouldn't have looked out of place in Ellen's own sitting room.

Framed drawings and pictures covered the wall above the fireplace. More of Jodie's art work. On the mantelpiece, a range of trophies for football and tennis. Ellen guessed the trophies were mostly Finlay's and liked the way both children's achievements were celebrated in different ways.

Walking over and examining the pictures more closely, she was struck again by Jodie's talent. She thought of the rudimentary pictures Pat produced. There really was no comparison. One picture, more than any, stood out. An ink drawing of a boy's face. The boy had dark hair that flopped down over one eye. A handsome boy. His head was raised slightly and the artist had drawn the shadowy outline of an Adam's apple midway along the neck. The boy was, indisputably, Finlay Hudson. Ellen marvelled that a ten-year-old had the talent to be able to capture a likeness so well.

'Amazing, isn't she?' Abby came into the room and stood alongside Ellen. 'St Anne's has a gifted and talented programme, apparently, and has been supporting Jodie. Helping develop her talent. She starts secondary school in September. Her parents had been looking into getting a scholarship.' She held out a mug to Ellen. 'Here, I brought you a coffee.'

'How's Helen?' Ellen asked.

Abby shrugged. 'Bearing up. Just about. I assume you'll want a word after this?'

'I was hoping to speak to both of them,' Ellen said. 'But if

Kevin's going to be a while, I might come back later.'

'So what was it you wanted from me?' Abby asked.

'It's about Baxter,' Ellen said.

Abby's body stiffened. 'What about him?'

'I need your help,' Ellen said. 'He's not himself. He really lost it this morning and, from what I've heard, it's not the first time. And whatever his problem is, it's distracting him from the case. I'm worried, Abby. Worried Baxter's lack of focus will cause us to mess up.'

'And you think it's me?' Abby asked. 'I'm the reason he's acting the way he is? Well you're wrong. Me and him, it was ... well, it was a stupid mistake. He worked that out straight away. Took me a while longer, I'll admit, but I got there pretty quickly. And once I realised he wasn't interested, I moved on. So did he. At least ... Look, I'm sorry, Ellen. Whatever his problem is, it's not me. I swear to you.'

'How can you be so sure?'

Abby lowered her face to her mug. 'I just am.'

'Why?'

'Just because,' Abby said. 'It's like I told you. Things between us were over ages ago so if he's, if there's something wrong, the problem isn't me. The problem is something else entirely.'

'Something else entirely that you know about,' Ellen said. 'But you're refusing to share with me?'

'No.' Even if Abby hadn't blushed, Ellen would have known she was lying. The rebuttal came too fast. Like she'd been preparing herself.

Ellen put her cup on the ground and stood up. 'I need to find out what's going on with Baxter,' she said. 'I was really hoping to do that with your help. But if you're refusing, I'll still get to the bottom of this. And when I do, if I find out it's got anything at all to do with your stupid fling, I'll have you, Roberts. Got that?'

When Abby looked up, her eyes shone with tears. The second time she'd nearly cried in front of Ellen.

'I'd help you if I could,' she said. 'I swear to you.'

Ellen shrugged. 'For now, I don't have any choice but to believe you. Now, if you don't mind, I'm going to leave you here to have a think about things while I go and have a word with Helen.'

She left the room as quickly as she could. Why did all her dealings with Abby have to be so difficult? Ellen really thought they were getting places this morning. And then, just as the barriers seemed to be coming down, Abby clammed up.

As she walked into the kitchen, a horrible thought struck Ellen. Something that would explain the tears and Baxter's dark mood. How long did Alastair say this had been going on? A couple of months? Ellen thought about turning around, going back to Abby and asking her straight out. But she didn't think she had the strength to deal with that. Not right now.

The door to the kitchen was closed. Ellen could hear Helen inside, crying. She took a deep breath, put her hand on the door, pushed it open and went inside. Right now, Helen Hudson's missing girl was her priority. Everything else would have to wait.

10:45

The park had been Abby's idea. Despite his instinctive distrust of the pretty FLO, Kevin had found himself warming to her over the past few days. Especially since yesterday. Ever since that journalist had turned up asking questions, Abby had been a rock. They'd never have got through last night and this morning without her.

She was doing a good job of looking out for Fin, too. Which was just as well because himself and Helen were too caught up in their own nightmares to spare the boy a second thought. Take today, for instance. As soon as Abby suggested the park, Kevin knew straight away it was the right thing to do. One look at the hunted expression on his son's face should have alerted him to the urgent need to get the boy out of the house for a few hours.

'I'll have my mobile,' Kevin promised, sensing the boy's reluctance to leave the house. 'Mum'll phone straight away if there's any news.'

They'd had to go out the back way. Out front, Dallinger Road was crawling with journalists, professional cameramen and women, and gawpers. People who obviously weren't her for any other reason except to catch a glimpse of the grieving family. Weirdos.

They climbed over the wall into the Picardies' garden, which backed onto theirs. From here, they walked down Holme Lacey Road and along Manor Lane to the park.

Along the way, Finlay was quiet and Kevin, wrapped up in his own thoughts, barely noticed the boy was with him as they plodded along the quiet, suburban streets.

At the entrance to the park, they both hesitated, knowing this wasn't going to be easy. This place, in particular, was full of memories of Jodie.

Kevin put his hand on Finlay's shoulder and squeezed it. 'Come on, son. Let's get this over with.'

The memories came hard and fast – Jodie throwing crumbs to the ducks, teaching her to cycle without stabilisers along that path over there, family picnics in the central grassy area, playing football and rounders with the two children on summer evenings. Passing the playground, he had to avert his eyes because the sight of other children on the swings and the climbing frame and the see-saw felt like it might kill him.

'Shall we grab a hot chocolate first?' he suggested.

Finlay shook his head. 'Don't want to go in there.'

'Why not? A hot chocolate's just the thing on a chilly afternoon.'

'They're a bunch of bastards,' Finlay said.

Kevin frowned. 'Language, Fin. Who are you talking about, anyway? The café is like a second home to me. It's kept me going over the last year and a bit, let me tell you. Come on, I'll race you.'

He started running, but when he reached the entrance to the café, he noticed Finlay still standing where he'd left him, pushing the ball in front of him with his toe. His head was hanging down so Kevin couldn't see his face, but he didn't imagine his son was smiling.

Poor Fin. His parents were so caught up in their own fears they'd barely noticed how any of this was affecting the boy. Kevin wondered if maybe they should arrange some counselling or something, like Abby had suggested. But when did you start doing that? What if they still hadn't found Jodie in three months' time? Or six months, or a year?

Thinking that made him feel light-headed and sick at the same time, like he might faint. This was unbearable. Coming to the park had only made it worse, as well. What had he been thinking? He should be at home with Helen, supporting her and willing the phone to ring with the news that Jodie had been found and she was safe and everything was going to be okay. He had to keep believing that would happen. The alternative, that life would continue like this without them ever finding her, was inconceivable.

Finlay moved forward another few inches. Kevin wanted to go inside and order the hot chocolates but he was seized by the sudden fear that if he did that, he'd come back outside and Finlay would be gone. So he waited.

'Come with me,' he insisted when Finlay finally joined him.

As he stepped inside, Kevin realised people in here had been watching him. The place was unnaturally silent, as if they'd all stopped talking the moment he'd put his foot over the threshold.

Avoiding eye contact with everyone except Judith, the café owner, Kevin ordered two hot chocolates.

'On the house,' Judith said when she handed him the drinks.

'You don't have to do that,' Kevin said, but she shook her head. 'I insist.'

She turned to Finlay. 'I heard about yesterday. Bobby told me. I'm so sorry, Finlay. I've spoken to Steph and I'll make sure nothing like that ever happens again.'

Bobby was Judith's son. He ran the place Monday to Friday. Judith only ever appeared at the weekends.

Kevin looked from Judith to Finlay. 'What happened yesterday?'

'Nothing,' Finlay muttered. 'Come on, Dad, let's go. This place stinks.'

Kevin grabbed him by the shoulder. 'I want to know what happened.'

'Just leave it,' Finlay said. 'I don't want to talk about it.'

Kevin didn't want to leave it. He wanted to know exactly why Judith was looking so guilty and Finlay's face had turned bright red, as if he was on the verge of losing his temper. But there was a tremor in Finlay's voice that he didn't like. The poor kid sounded like he was about to burst into tears.

So Kevin said nothing, just nodded goodbye to Judith and followed Finlay back outside.

At first, Kevin couldn't see him and his throat tightened as he scanned the park. He opened his mouth to call out Finlay's name when he saw him, marching past the ice house on the other side of the park.

There was a jerky rhythm to the way Finlay was walking and it was only as Kevin caught up with him, out of breath from running, that he realised the boy was crying, tears streaming down his cheeks.

'Hey.' Kevin reached out and touched his arm, but Finlay shoved him away.

'I've got your chocolate,' Kevin said.

'They all think you did it!' Finlay screamed, swiping the cardboard cup from Kevin's hand and knocking it to the ground. The lid fell off and the sweet smell of chocolate wafted through the cold air.

'What do you mean?' Kevin wondered how his voice could sound so calm when, inside, an iron claw was scraping through the centre of his body.

'I went there yesterday, in the afternoon,' Finlay said. 'Me and Leo. All I wanted was a bloody can of Coke. The moment I went inside, I knew what they were all talking about. A group of them, girls mainly, and some lads from Thomas Tallis. Leo knew it too and he said we should leave but I thought, fuck them. If they want to talk about me, fuck them. It's a café and I want a Coke. So I went up to the counter and the girl working there ...' he trailed off and looked around, as if he was trying to look for something that wasn't there.

'The blonde?' Kevin asked, referring to the pretty girl who

worked there occasionally. The one Finlay had the mother of all crushes on.

Finlay nodded, wiped his nose with the back of his sleeve and continued. 'She asked me what was it like, and I said what did she mean? I could see the others laughing, like they knew exactly what she was going to say next.'

'What did she say?'

Finlay glanced at him then looked away quickly. 'She asked me what it was like knowing my dad was a paedo. Said everyone knew that's why you come here in the mornings. That you only do it so you can look at the kids in the playground. Then the others started as well, calling you names and saying all sorts of stuff. And the girl, she asked me if I liked little kiddies as well. Said it explained why I hung around the place. She called me a dirty little pervert.'

There was a roaring noise in Kevin's head and he tried to concentrate on the words coming out of Finlay's mouth, but they sounded all mixed up.

His legs crumbled beneath him and he was falling. As he hit the ground, he saw Finlay, moving towards him. He could only see his feet. It reminded him of something and instinctively his body curled into a ball. His arms went up, covering his head, as three words repeated over and over in his head, an incessant drumbeat that he couldn't stop.

Dirty little pervert. Dirty little pervert. Dirty little pervert.

14:00

Dai was waiting for her outside The Pavilion, the old-style tea house at the top of Greenwich park. Ellen was too restless to sit down, so she suggested they got coffees to take away instead.

'You look tired,' Dai said. 'Work getting to you?'

It wasn't just work. She'd been unable to sleep last night, memories of her early childhood whizzing around inside her head, raising all sorts of questions she really didn't want to think about.

'No more than usual,' she said.

They walked along the top of the park towards the statue of General Wolfe. Despite the cold, Ellen was glad to be outside. She loved the park. On clear days like this, she couldn't think of anywhere else she'd rather be.

Being with Dai was relaxing, too. He'd never been one of those people who needed to talk all the time and she preferred it that way.

'I haven't had a chance to talk to Kevin yet,' Ellen said. 'I was planning to do it today but this business with the press, it's thrown everything off track.'

'Helen's very upset,' Dai said. 'Can't say as I blame her, either. Scum of the earth that Reynolds woman. I've had dealings with her in the past. You steer clear of her, Ellen. You hear me? Now then, why don't you tell me why you called and needed to see me so urgently.'

'There's something I need you to find out,' she said. 'If you can. But it's awkward.'

She drank some coffee as she tried to work out what to tell him.

'It's to do with Baxter,' she said. 'I've been thinking. What if he was involved in the Dan Harris case somehow?'

'Remind me who Dan Harris is?' Dai said.

'He's the guy Kevin assaulted. A fifteen-year-old kid. If Ed knew the kid, wouldn't that explain his fixation on Kevin?'

'But wouldn't you know if he'd been part of that?' Dai asked.

'In theory,' Ellen said. 'But maybe there's some other connection. Something I don't know about.'

'And you want me to do what exactly?'

'Have a word with Helen,' Ellen said. 'Off the record. See if she can think of anything connecting Baxter with Dan Harris.'

Dai took a sip of coffee. 'You're not being straight with me, Ellen.'

They reached a pond and paused to watch a group of ducks sliding around each other on the iced-over surface. Like they were putting on a display.

'I mean,' Dai continued. 'I can see why you think there might be a connection with the Harris case. And it's worth asking the question. But there's something else. Something between you and Ed that you're not telling me. I sensed it the night we met at The Dacre.'

'You're right,' Ellen said. 'Only I'm not sure I can tell you. You see, I found out something about him last year. Something he doesn't like me knowing. I need to know if that's why he's acting strange. Or if there's another reason. Does that make any sense?'

'Not really,' Dai said. 'Maybe you should tell me what it is you found out?'

'I can't do that.'

Dai shrugged. 'I can't help you then, Ellen.'

She looked across the park. Like every other day of the week, it was bustling with people everywhere. Did it ever stop, she wondered. Did life ever slow down enough for you to take time to catch your breath and work out what the hell you were doing here?

'Ellen?'

She looked back at Dai and saw nothing but compassion in his brown eyes. Embarrassed, she looked down, found herself staring at his hand, hanging loosely by his side. It was an old man's hand. Gnarled knuckles, deep wrinkles and dark patches of skin, which hadn't been there when she first met him.

'Are you okay?' he asked.

Resisting the urge to reach out and squeeze his hand, she nodded.

'If I tell you,' she said, 'do you promise it won't go any further?'

This time, it was Dai who reached out. His big hand wrapping around her smaller one. The calluses on his fingers rubbed over her own knuckles, comforting her.

'Just tell me,' Dai said.

And because she couldn't see any other way, she told him.

20:35

I hate him.

Except the weird thing is, it's nearly worse when he's not here. When I'm on my own …

He's here now. Putting on another video. I want to hit him and pull him away from the video player and tell him I never, ever in my whole entire life want to watch another episode of the stupid Rainbow f-word Parade.

Except I don't say anything. I'm too scared.

Today he brought bon bons. I don't really like bon bons but they're okay, I suppose, and I'm hungry. Really hungry.

He's beside me on the bed now and his hand is on my leg. I want to pull away so bad it's like if I don't, I'll explode or something. I don't look at him. I watch the TV instead, thinking even the f-word Rainbow is better than having to look at his face.

In a bit, he'll start going on about Marion. F-word Marion who disappeared years ago and how could he even think I'm her when she'd be an adult now, anyway? But I know it's because he's mad and that's why. Mad people don't think the same way as normal people.

And when he starts on about Marion then he'll cry. You'd swear he was some sort of baby, instead of a big old man. I'm not surprised Marion and Daddy left him. Who'd want to live out here with a lunatic like him?

'Are you okay, Marion?'

'Fine.'

I'm trying to ignore his hand on my knee. Except it feels so disgusting and I can't stop thinking about how dirty his fingernails are. I keep chewing on the toffee bon bon, making myself keep going until it's soft enough to swallow.

'You're very quiet,' Brian says. 'You were never this quiet before. Chatter, chatter, chatter, from morning till night. It was one of the things I missed most.'

Oh God. Here we go.

'The silence nearly killed me to start with. That first night, I slept in the kitchen. On the floor. I couldn't bear to go upstairs on my own. It was Simon who found me the next day, curled up asleep on the kitchen floor. Can you believe it? If it wasn't for Simon, I don't know how I'd have coped. I mean, I know we never really liked him before. Well, we had our reasons, I suppose. But he was good to me after you left, Marion. Say what you like about him, but he's looked out for me over the years. You wouldn't believe what he's done to keep me safe.'

I know there's more. There's always more. In a moment, he'll ask me where 'I' went and why 'we' didn't take him with us. As if that's not obvious. Then the tears will start. Wah-wah-wah.

His hand moves, slipping off my knee and resting a bit higher.

I hate him.

'I wish you'd tell me where Daddy took you. It was such a shock, you see. Coming home and finding you both gone like that.'

I can feel his nail, scraping against my skin. I'm thinking if I'm really careful, and if I don't speak or move at all, maybe he'll forget about me in a bit and move his hand away.

He's still talking and I'm trying not to listen. I'm watching the TV but thinking about 'iCarly', my favourite programme. I'm imagining that Carly and Sam and Freddie are in the room with me and any moment now Freddie's going to smile and tell me everything is okay and before I know it, I'll be back home with Mum and Dad and Finlay and mad Brian will never, ever be able to find me.

SATURDAY,
19 FEBRUARY

11:30

Saturday morning. Ellen was greeted with a cloudless blue sky and a wind so cold it almost cut her in half as she threw the previous day's newspaper into the green recycling bin, along with an empty wine bottle. It wasn't the first bottle inside the bin and seeing them piled up like that, Ellen knew she'd have to cut back. The wine was in danger of becoming something she relied on. If it wasn't already.

She looked up at the sky and considered her options for the morning. She had a few clear hours before work started. On a day like this, there was only one place to be. She went back inside to the children.

'Right,' she announced. 'Let's all get dressed and go to the park. It's a beautiful day out there.'

'It's cold,' Eilish moaned. 'Don't want to go out in the cold.'

'The fresh air will do you good,' Ellen said. She sounded so much like her mother sometimes it was a worry. 'We'll go and see the deer, have a hot chocolate in The Pavilion and later, if you're both really good, we'll have an early lunch in Pizza Express.'

Wrapped up well, the three of them left the house and walked the short distance from Annandale Road to Greenwich Park. Despite the cold, every other family seemed to have had the same idea. Ellen's progress through the park was slow as the children encountered several friends along the way. By the time they reached The Pavilion for their hot chocolate stop, their group had increased to include three other parents – two mothers, one father – and five more kids.

Ellen was relieved when she spotted Kirstie Jakes among the group. Kirstie was the mother of Rufus, Pat's best friend ever in the whole wide world. She was also, like Ellen, a single parent. In the traditional community of St Joseph's Primary School, single parents were the exception rather than the norm. Kirstie, a divorcée, was even more of a source of gossip than Ellen, a mere widow.

Once they'd purchased their drinks, the group walked to the deer enclosure at the top of the park. Ellen mentally planned how the rest of the morning would go. The deer, followed by a trip back down the hill to the playground where the kids would run around for a good hour, if she was lucky. Then Pizza Express, drop Pat and Eilish off at her parents' for the afternoon and rush off to work. She tried not to look at her watch every few minutes, willing the time to pass quickly so she could be at her desk sooner rather than later. Her mind was full of Jodie Hudson and finding the space to concentrate on her own children was proving difficult.

Kirstie walked with Ellen, sipping her chocolate and bitching about Peter, her ex.

'This was his weekend with the kids. Bastard phoned me last night to say he had to work.' She snorted. 'Work my arse. He sounded half-pissed and I bet he's picked up some tart and was planning to shag her stupid all weekend instead of spending time with his own kids.'

'Rufus and Izzy must be gutted,' Ellen said. 'Life's so crap for kids sometimes, isn't it?'

'Yeah, but they're resilient as well,' Kirstie said. 'I mean, look at them now. You'd never guess there was anything wrong with them, would you?'

She was right. Rufus and Pat were playing some sort of *Star Wars* game, whacking each other with imaginary light sabres. Izzy was huddled in a group with Molly Prendergast and Eilish, giggling and whispering girlie secrets to each other.

Kirstie's kids looked for all the world as if there were no clouds on the horizon of their little lives. Likewise, to look at Pat and Eilish, you'd never know that they still cried regularly for their own father – dead for over three years.

'We're going to Pizza Express later,' Ellen said. 'Why don't you join us? The kids are having a great time together, it seems a shame to break them up.'

Further down the hill, conversation with the other parents turned to secondary schools – specifically the lack of decent ones in Greenwich – and Ellen found her mind drifting. Pat had two years of primary school left, so worrying about what secondary school he would attend wasn't high on her list of priorities right now. Plenty of time to worry about that once Year Four was behind him.

On mornings like this, the park was the best place in the world to be. It swept out in front of her, all the way down to the colonnaded splendour of the Maritime Museum. Behind the museum, the Naval College stretched along the Cronin of the Thames, itself a sheet of silver in the early spring sun. On the other side of the river, the glass and concrete buildings of Canary Wharf stood out against the clear blue sky, out-of-place and futuristic, contrasting sharply with the rest of the city, tumbling away behind it.

Ellen took a moment to soak up the view, reminding herself how good her life was. She might have stood there a while longer, savouring her moment of stillness, if she hadn't been distracted by someone calling her name. She looked around, and her stomach somersaulted when she saw Jim O'Dwyer walking towards her.

The kids had spotted him as well and threw themselves at him, giving Ellen time to straighten her mouth out so she wasn't smiling like a loon.

'We're going to the playground!' Eilish screeched.

'Yeah, come with us,' Pat roared. 'Please, Jim! You can chase us.'

'And you can have pizza with us afterwards,' Eilish added helpfully, her voice rising even higher than before. Not something Ellen would have thought possible.

Smiling, Jim untangled himself from the children and nodded at Ellen. 'Shouldn't we check with your mother first?'

Eilish giggled. 'She won't mind.'

'I'm sure Jim's got better things to do on his weekend than

chase you two around a playground,' Ellen said, cringing at how prim she sounded.

Jim rolled his eyes. 'What could be better than chasing these two about the place?'

And before she could stop him he had raised his arms like claws and started making growling sounds. On cue, Pat and Eilish fled, screaming and squealing. He gave them three seconds, winked at Ellen and ran after them.

'Who the hell is *that*?' Kirstie hissed.

Ellen shrugged. 'Just a guy I went to school with. Primary school, actually. Sort of a family friend, I guess.'

Kirstie sniffed. 'Family friend, my arse. And speaking of arses, he's got a fine one. Ellen Kelly! Is that a blush I see rising up those porcelain cheeks of yours? Come on, spill the beans. You and him?'

Ellen shook her head and almost succeeded in frowning. 'God, no. Nothing like that. Seriously, Kirstie.'

Now here he was, standing in front of her again, smiling in that bloody irritating way of his. When he smiled, a dimple appeared under his left eye and she found herself staring at this now, mesmerised.

'Ellen?'

She blinked. 'Sorry, what did you say?'

'I was just asking how you're doing. It's been a while since I've seen you.'

'Fine,' she said. 'How about you? You're looking good.'

For Christ's sake. What possessed me to say that? Control yourself, woman.

The dimple deepened. 'Not looking so bad yourself. Kids seem good, too. Listen, I'd love to come along to the park for a bit. But only if you're sure I won't be getting in the way or anything?'

Wildly, Ellen glanced around for Kirstie, but her friend had mysteriously melted away, leaving Ellen alone with him.

'Um,' she said.

Green eyes. Seemed greener against his dark skin. How'd he get to be so tanned at this time of year?

'Great,' he said. 'That's decided then. Come on, kids. I'll race you down the hill.'

Ellen opened her mouth to say something else, possibly to protest at the way everyone assumed she was happy with what had just been decided. Except before she could get any words out, the others were already halfway down the hill and she had no choice but to follow them.

'Not so fast, Eilish!' she called out. It was a futile exercise. Since Jim had appeared, Ellen might as well be invisible for all the attention they paid her. As she hurried after them, snippets of yesterday's conversation with Dai came back to her. She'd felt guilty, at first, for telling Dai about Ed and Abby. Then angry when Dai seemed neither surprised or particularly shocked.

'It happens,' Dai said. 'Especially in a job like ours, where you spend more time with the people you work with than you do with your own family.'

'But not Baxter,' Ellen argued. 'He's been happily married for as long as I've known him. What's he doing, throwing that away for a fling with some stupid blonde half his age?'

'Sounds like she's your problem,' Dai said. 'Not Ed.'

Maybe Dai was right. She didn't like Abby Roberts. And it wasn't just because of the affair. What Ellen hated was women who used their looks instead of their brains to get what they wanted. In doing so, they undermined all women, everywhere.

She'd reached the playground now and needed to gather up the kids and go for the pizza she'd promised them. A rash promise, now she thought about it. She would have been better off bringing them straight around to her mother's and getting into work as soon as possible. But one look at their little faces and she knew she was incapable of letting them down. Pizza Express was a highlight for them – they'd be devastated if she called it off. And nothing was worth that. Life, after all, was too short not to do everything you could to make it as perfect as possible for those you loved most in the world.

13:00

Simon was saying something, but Brian wasn't listening. His head too full of Marion to concentrate on anything else.

'You okay, mate?'

He felt Simon's hand on his shoulder and jumped.

'Fine,' he said. 'Just a bit tired. Not sleeping so well, you know?'

'Never a problem for me,' Simon said. 'Not in this job. I'm knackered by the time I get home in the evenings.' He paused and looked closely at Brian. 'You do look a bit shagged, now you mention it. Anything you need to talk about?'

Fear clutched his stomach and he shook his head.

Simon looked at him a moment longer then shrugged. 'Well if you're sure. Hey, look over there. It's her, isn't it?'

For a terrible moment, Brian thought he meant Marion. It was the girl's hair. Long and dark. As he watched, she turned and started running down the hill, black hair streaming out behind her like a river.

She was laughing as she ran – a lovely sound that carried across the park and lifted his spirits. Was that strawberries in the air or was he only imagining it? Strawberry shampoo. In a red bottle in the bathroom. Mam used it to wash her hair.

He had a sudden, clear memory of a summer's day, a long time ago, when he'd made her a daisy chain. It had taken him ages to thread the delicate stems. Like Daddy, he had big hands that weren't suited to such a delicate job. But he'd managed it in the end and it had been worth it for the smile she gave him as he placed the crown of flowers on her head. And how beautiful had it looked sitting on top of that blue-black hair of hers?

'See?' Simon said. 'It's definitely her. Bitch from Manor Park. I've a good mind to go over to her now.'

Then Brian realised.

Simon wasn't talking about the girl. It was the woman. Tall

and slender, she was hurrying down the park after the girl, calling out to her.

'Not so fast, Eilish!'

Eilish. Relief rushed through every part of his body. It wasn't Marion. She was still at home. Safe. Besides, what was he thinking? The girl running down the hill was too young – couldn't be more than six or seven, he guessed.

He examined the woman again, and shook his head. He couldn't place her. Faces were a problem for him. Always had been. When he was little, men would drift in and out of the house – friends of Daddy's. Bad men who hurt him. Afterwards, Brian was always able to remember the things they'd done to him, the different ways they'd hurt him, but never their faces. It was why it had taken him so long to find Marion. So many girls out there who looked like her, it hadn't been easy.

'Jesus, Brian.' Simon shook his arm. 'You're away with the fairies today. Listen, mate, why don't you take a breather? Go grab a coffee or something. I'll be fine on my own. We've nearly finished this section, anyway.'

'Thanks, Simon,' Brian said, relief rushing through him. 'Appreciate it. Really, I do.'

He pulled off his gloves and walked away from Simon. His head felt like it might explode and he tried to think of something else. Except it was impossible. Every bit of his brain was stuffed with thoughts of Marion.

Part of him wanted to tell Simon, share his good news with

someone. And who else did he have except Simon? Maybe he could. Maybe this time Simon would understand, know that even if Brian had made mistakes in the past, things were different now. Maybe ...

He turned around, ready to go back. Stopped himself just in time.

What was he thinking?

Simon would only twist things. Try to persuade him it wasn't Marion. That he'd messed up. Again. And before he knew it Simon would start on about Molly. He felt himself starting to sweat. Impatiently, he unzipped his jacket and held it open, letting the cool air rush in, wrapping around his body as he hurried down the hill, as far from Simon as he could get.

Simon was only looking out for him. He knew that. It's what Simon did. What he'd always done. Brian felt bad lying to him. Simon was his best friend. His only friend. The one person in the world who'd always been there for him. No matter what. He owed Simon, big time.

Breathing deeply, he forced himself to calm down, think sensibly. There was no need for Simon to know anything about this. All he was doing was keeping his promise. Mam had made him swear to look after Marion and that's what he was going to do. If that meant lying to Simon or the police or anyone else, well, so be it.

Except ...

No. He had to stop those thoughts. It wasn't easy, though. It was Marion's fault. She was making things so difficult. Making him doubt himself, start to wonder if he might have made a mistake after all.

Unbidden, other images came to him then. Molly. A pretty little girl. Even after he'd worked it all out, realised she wasn't Marion, even then, he'd never meant for her to get hurt. If only she'd listened, kept quiet like he'd told her to. Instead of carrying on the way she did – screaming and crying and making all that noise. It wasn't like he hadn't warned her.

That's women for you, Brian. Never listen to a word you say. Bitches, every last one of them.

He shook his head, trying not to listen.

'Shut up!' he hissed. 'Just shut up!'

But once Daddy got started there was no stopping him.

You've done it this time, boy. A right royal mess you've got yourself into. She's tricking you. Are you so stupid you can't see that?

'No!' The roar out of him was louder than he'd meant and a group of children coming along the path towards him stopped suddenly and looked at him. He brushed past, ignoring them, all his efforts focussed on blocking out that relentless sound of Daddy's voice, beating away at him.

He couldn't shut Daddy up completely but if he tried, really hard, he was able to ignore the voice. It was a bit like turning the volume down on the radio – the noise was still there, but not so loud that it interfered with anything else you were doing.

The best way to turn the volume down was to think about nice things. Like Marion and all the things they'd get up to together over the next few months. There was so much to look forward to now that she was back.

He smiled, feeling better now. It was all going to be okay. There was a bakery he passed on the way home every evening. He'd pop in there later and buy her something special. A few cakes would persuade her to tell him where she'd been all these years. It was worth a try.

He zipped his jacket back up and turned around. Time to get back to work. The sooner he finished, the sooner he could get off home. To Marion. She'd be all happy when she saw the cakes. They could make an evening of it, sitting on the bed, eating cakes and chatting away as they watched *Rainbow Parade*. Just like they used to. It was going to be a great evening. He could hardly wait.

14:15

Ellen phoned Abby and arranged to meet Kevin Hudson in his house after lunch. As she drove across, Jim O'Dwyer's face flickered in and out of her mind with increasing frequency.

It was that dimple. No it wasn't. Well, not entirely. There was his body, too. Looked like he worked out. Not a look she'd ever gone for in the past, but every time she saw Jim O'Dwyer she had an almost irresistible urge to sink her teeth into him.

After the pizza, Pat and Eilish had gone to the toilet and she was left alone with him.

'Would you like to go for that drink sometime?' he'd asked.

Was it her imagination or had he seemed nervous?

'Um.'

Later, she'd pat herself on the back for her quick wit and charm. No wonder he was so keen to go out with her. What man could resist?

He smiled. 'Um yes or um maybe?'

'I might have been working up to a no,' she said.

'Ah, but that would be too cruel,' he said. 'Besides, what have you got to lose? Come out for a drink with me, Ellen. Just two old friends having a drink. Nothing heavy, no pressure. If we both enjoy ourselves and don't find each other's company too offensive, we may even decide to do it again.'

She smiled then. Might even have come up with something witty if the kids hadn't come rushing back right at that minute.

'Let's make it a maybe,' she said as Eilish clambered onto her lap. 'Call me next week.'

And now, even though she knew she'd hate herself for it, she was already hoping he wouldn't let her down and not bother to call. She thought she might be gutted if that happened.

On Dallinger Road, the crowd of journalists seemed to have dissipated slightly, although there were still far too many of them. As she ran towards the house, Ellen heard a woman calling out her name. Recognising the voice, she turned to face a skinny woman with a too-orange tan and too-blonde hair.

'Have you come to arrest him?' the woman asked. 'Or is he still *helping you with your enquiries*?' As she said the last bit, the woman made quotation marks with her fingers, indicating the phrase was nothing more than a euphemism. If there hadn't been a gaggle of her counterparts around, Ellen might have slapped her.

'Kevin Hudson's done nothing wrong,' Ellen said. 'And you lot should be ashamed of yourselves, hounding a grieving family like this. Piss off, the lot of you.'

As if they'd do what she asked. The sooner Ed nailed the senseless git who'd leaked the story, the better. Ellen turned from them in disgust and ran on to the house. This time, there was no need to ring the bell. Abby must have been watching out for her. The door swung open as Ellen approached the house and she let herself inside, grateful to escape the press pack.

'Kevin's in the garden,' Abby said. 'It's cold out there, but he said he'd rather be outside. He's a smoker and they don't smoke inside the house because of the kids.'

In the garden, Kevin was sitting on a wooden bench, smoking as Abby had predicted. Ellen's relief at seeing a gas garden heater beside him was short-lived when she realised the heater was switched off.

'Thanks for agreeing to see me,' she said, sitting beside him on the bench. Immediately, damp started seeping through her jeans and she knew, within minutes, she'd be freezing.

'Cigarette?' Kevin held out a pack of Marlboros and Ellen took one, grateful for any warmth she could get.

'So,' Kevin said, once Ellen had lit up, 'more questions, I take it?'

'I'm not here to set you up,' Ellen said. 'Or to trick you into saying something you don't want to. I'm here because I need your help, Kevin. You see, I don't think you took Jodie.'

'What do you need?' he asked.

She needed him to tell her where the hell he'd been last Monday morning. If she asked him outright, though, she wouldn't get anywhere. Direct questioning hadn't worked before, so there was no reason to think it would be any different this time around.

'I want to know about Dan Harris,' she said instead. 'I mean, I've read the old files but I want to hear your side of things. Can you do that for me?'

Kevin blew a trail of smoke into the air. Ellen watched it drift upwards and disappear into the grey, late winter afternoon. There was a long pause and Ellen was just thinking of asking a second time when Kevin suddenly started speaking.

'I think our lives are defined by moments,' he said. 'A single moment in time that determines everything after it. You don't know it when it's happening, it's only later when you look back, you realise that's the way it is.'

Ellen thought of Vinny, lying in the middle of their road, his body crushed from the car that had driven into him deliberately.

She knew exactly what Kevin meant.

Misunderstanding her silence, Kevin gave a half-laugh. 'Probably talking nonsense,' he said. 'I'm just trying to explain, that's all. After Helen split from Mark she moved to London with the kids. Wanted a fresh start, I suppose.

'She was a friend from way back. I'd known her for years. Always had a thing for her, if I'm honest. I was gutted when she moved to Bristol and married Mark. When I heard she was back in London, I got in touch.

'Just friends at first, but we grew closer over time. I still think if things had turned out differently.' He paused. 'Well, no point thinking about that now.

'When she first came to London, Helen had no money. Her parents' house is tiny so she decided to rent. The only place she could afford was a flat in Downham. The estate was a dump. Ruled by a gang of hooligan kids – all of them on ASBOs but should have been locked up by rights.

'The first time I stayed over, I couldn't believe it. These guys were animals. They did all sorts – dogshit through her letterbox, stones through the front window, name-calling every time she went anywhere. Those bastards made her life hell.'

'Why?' Ellen asked. 'I've been involved in cases like that and I know how stressful it is for the victims, but there's usually something that triggers it.'

'There was another family on the estate,' Kevin said. 'Immigrant family with a disabled child. A teenage girl. She had learning difficulties – not sure what exactly – and a funny way of walking. She couldn't speak properly, either. Local kids picked on them something terrible. Helen made the mistake of intervening, tried to get them to stop.'

'So they turned on her instead?' Ellen guessed.

Kevin nodded. 'I begged her to leave, move in with me, but she wouldn't have it. Said she'd already made enough mistakes and we'd move in together when the time was right – if the time was right – and not before then.'

He stopped.

'I felt I had to protect her,' he continued quietly. 'So I started staying over more and more. If I'm honest, I'm not sure either of us were ready for that but, the thing is, I couldn't bear to think of her facing those bastards on her own.'

'What about the police?' Ellen asked. 'Lewisham has a good record of dealing with anti-social behaviour. Surely Helen complained?'

'Oh she complained all right. That was the problem. A policeman came around to the house, took a statement. Did no good, though. Quite the opposite. They really had it in for her after that.

'Harris was the ring-leader. You know, when I think about that time, I'm convinced if it wasn't for Harris, they'd have left us alone. It was like he was obsessed.'

Kevin turned to face Ellen. 'I went out for coffee one evening. Just a jar of coffee, that's all. She'd run out. Told me it didn't matter, but I wouldn't have it. Didn't see why I should let a group of lowlifes stop me from going across to the local shop. Besides, it was just across the road. Neither of us imagined …' his voice trailed off.

Ellen wasn't sure she wanted to hear the next bit. It was a familiar story, one she'd witnessed time and again in the deprived areas of Lewisham. Families virtual prisoners in their own homes. Their lives ruined by the thugs who ran wild on the council estates across the borough.

'I heard the girl first,' Kevin said. 'Crying, pleading with someone. I didn't know who she was but I went to see what was going on.

'They were down the alleyway that ran behind the row of shops. Harris and two of his mates. They had the girl – the one I told you about. Cassie, her name was. I remember that. Harris was holding her. They'd ripped her top open and were taking photos of her with their phones. Laughing at her. I heard Harris asking if she'd like to take things a bit further. Go somewhere private.'

Ellen swallowed and tried to think of something to say. Something that wouldn't sound trite. She couldn't think of anything.

'I didn't know what I was doing,' Kevin said. 'I just went straight for Harris. At one point, I heard someone screaming, it must have been the girl. The next thing, it was only me and Harris. His mates must have run off. Harris, he was lying on the ground. Not moving. I remember lifting my hands and they were covered in blood.'

Ellen's stomach burned as if she'd swallowed acid. There was a lot more she wanted to ask but she couldn't bring herself to speak. Beside her, Kevin continued talking.

'Harris was fifteen years old. Legally, he was a minor. That's what did it for me. I was sent down for hurting a kid. Police made out like I was some kind of child abuser.'

'Even after you told the police what he'd done?' Ellen asked.

'We tried our best,' Kevin said. 'Helen begged Cassie's family to come forward, but they were too scared. Said they couldn't face the consequences of what might happen. They were seeking asylum, you see. Waiting to see if they could stay. Her father said he was sorry, but they didn't want to do anything that would jeopardise their asylum claim. Helen's got a pal at Greenwich Station. Dai Davies. She asked him to intervene, but there was nothing he could do.'

'So Harris got away with it?' Ellen asked.

Then Kevin did something that surprised her. He smiled.

'For a while. Can't get away with it forever, though, can he?'

'What do you mean?'

'Just that, Ellen. In the end, everyone gets what they deserve. It's simply a matter of time.'

A sudden thought struck her. 'Is it Harris?' she asked.

'What do you mean?'

'Is he the reason you won't tell us where you were on Monday?' One look at Kevin's face told her she was right. And also that she'd gone about it totally the wrong way.

'You don't know anything,' he said. 'Thought you said you weren't trying to set me up. You're a liar. That's what you are. Just like every other cop I ever met. You don't really care about me or what happened with Harris. You only came out here to get me to say something you could use against me. Well I'm done talking to you, DI Kelly. I'm going inside now and if you try to stop me, I'll be on the phone to my solicitor before you've even had time to leave.'

He stood up and walked inside the house. Ellen called after him but it was no good. She could have kicked herself. She'd got so close, only to blow it at the last moment. And now she was left with nothing except a bum so cold she couldn't even feel it any longer.

She took her phone out and scrolled through her address book, wondering which of her team to call. Decided on Raj Patel.

'It's me,' she said when Raj answered. 'I need a favour. Can you get some info on Dan Harris? I want to know where he lives, what he does and who his friends are. And as soon as you've got all of that information, I want you to call me. Got that?'

'Sure thing,' Raj said. 'I'll get onto it straightaway.'

Satisfied, Ellen hung up. In the distance, a police siren screamed out. Ellen pictured the police car, rushing through the grey streets on its way to some other tragedy. Another broken life in a city full of broken lives. Tragedy heaped upon tragedy. Nothing ever changed, and probably never would.

15:30

Rob checked his watch again. He'd been waiting almost forty minutes. The adrenalin that had driven him until now was gone. He felt tired and dispirited. He'd give it another five minutes. No more than that. If Frankie hadn't showed by then, he wasn't coming.

He'd known all along Frankie mightn't turn up. Frankie had promised, right enough, but you could never really trust him to do what he said. To call Frankie Ferrari unpredictable would be like Rob describing himself as a bit upset by the events in his life.

Frankie Ferrari. Rob's best mate all through primary school. Two little kids bound together by an obsessive love of football and *The Beano*. It didn't last, of course. They went to different secondary schools, their lives diverging even further in the years beyond that. Rob met Sheryl, married, had Molly. He worked a regular job and played football on Friday nights with a group of lads from The White Hart. Meanwhile, Frankie went from wild to wilder. Drink first, then drugs. Uppers, downers, inbetween-ers. You name it, Frankie was doing it. Encouraged by Sheryl, who said Frankie freaked her out, Rob started seeing Frankie less and less. Got to the point where whole years would go by without the two men meeting up.

Ten years ago Frankie was arrested and charged with murdering his step-father, Ian. Rob remembered Ian from when they were kids. He hadn't liked him much, but could never have suspected the abuse Ian had dished out to Frankie over the years. For the first time, Rob thought he understood why his old friend had gone so badly off the rails during his teens and early twenties.

After Frankie was put inside, Rob started visiting him. Not often. Three times in total. Not nearly enough when you considered Brixton nick was only a few miles down the South Circular. Still, as Frankie himself said, it was three times more than any other bastard they'd been to school with.

When Molly died, Rob felt he understood what Frankie had done to Ian. Knew he'd do the same if he ever got his hands on the man who'd killed his baby. On his last visit to Frankie, two years ago, Frankie offered to help track down Molly's killer 'and show him what happens to nonces who hurt little girls'.

At the time, Rob thought it was all talk. And maybe it was. After all, if Frankie had been serious about helping him, surely he'd have turned up today.

When Rob called Frankie and told him what he needed, Frankie couldn't have sounded keener. Rob found himself having to talk Frankie down, persuade him they couldn't go straight over there. Said they needed to make a plan first.

Except Frankie hadn't showed.

Rob was glad he hadn't given Frankie any details over the phone. It wasn't like Frankie hadn't asked, either.

'Just a name, Rob. That's all. You can fill me in on the rest when we meet.'

But Rob resisted, knowing if he gave Frankie a name, that

would be it. Frankie would go after Hudson himself, a one-man revenge machine, and Rob wouldn't get a look in. He had half-expected Frankie to think of the news reports about Jodie Hudson and put two and two together, but then, Frankie wasn't the type to be up on current affairs. Rob didn't even know if he could read. Wouldn't be surprised at all if he couldn't.

He checked his watch again. Gone half-three now and still no sign. He felt deflated, pulling his jacket tight around him, getting ready to leave.

He was nearly at the exit when he heard someone calling his name. He turned and saw Frankie, waving frantically, jogging up the hill from the Catford end of the park.

'Rob! Over here, mate!'

His stomach tightened with anticipation as he ran to greet his old pal. This was it, then. No going back now.

'I didn't think you were coming,' he panted, drawing up alongside Frankie.

'Only been waiting here the best part of a fucking hour,' Frankie said, putting a huge hand on Rob's shoulder and squeezing.

'I said by the café,' Rob replied, trying not to wince as his shoulder was crushed. 'Why would I want to meet you down there? That's where all the druggies and muggers hang out, Frankie. Jesus, mate.'

'Freezing me bleedin' nuts off,' Frankie continued, as if Rob hadn't spoken. 'Colder than a fridge out here today. Some bloke over there with his kid giving me funny looks an' all. Like I'm some nonce or something. Nearly went over to him and asked him what the fuck he thought he was looking at. Would have done an' all except I didn't want to frighten the kid. Right little cutie she is, in her red dress and hat.'

Rob nodded but kept his mouth shut, thinking the sight of Frankie Ferrari coming for you would terrify anyone, not to mind a little kid. His size itself – six foot seven, weighing at least twenty stone – was enough to give a child nightmares. Then there was his face, which looked as if wars had been fought and lost in it.

They were standing near the empty playground, cold weather driving families indoors, out of the biting wind. Apart from a group of park-keepers throwing dead branches into a trailer, there was no one else around.

On days like this, the park was a depressing place to be. Rob regretted the impulse that had made him suggest they meet here. The park, of all places, where he used to come with Molly and where he mostly avoided now because it was unbearable to be here without her.

Jesus Christ, he thought. His throat was dry as sand and he had a stinking headache. It wasn't fresh air he needed, it was a pint.

'Come on,' he said. 'I'll buy you a pint and tell you why I wanted to meet.'

Four pints later and Rob was starting to feel better. Frankie had mellowed as well, to the point where Rob thought it was safe to bring up the reason for the meeting. So far, Frankie hadn't offered to buy a drink but Rob wasn't bothered. What he needed from Frankie was worth more than a few pints. Much more.

'See, the thing is Frankie,' he began, after he'd got another round in. 'The reason I wanted to see you. It's to do with my Molly.'

'They found the fucker that done that yet?'

Frankie lifted his glass and swallowed half the pint in one go. 'I tell you, Rob, they ever get that bastard, we'll pay him a visit. Just you and me, fella. What do you think?'

'I know who he is,' Rob said.

Frankie slammed his glass down on the table, so loud the noise made Rob jump.

'Well what we doing here then?' Frankie roared. 'Why aren't we out there teaching him a lesson?'

'Take it easy, Frankie,' Rob muttered. The big man was already standing up and Rob put his hand on one of Frankie's huge arms.

Frankie glared at him. For a second Rob thought he was about to be whacked. But Frankie sat down instead.

'Just hear me out,' Rob said quickly.

Frankie nodded but didn't say anything. Just sat looking at Rob, breathing deeply through his flattened nose.

As briefly as he could, Rob told Frankie about his visit from the policewoman and then from the journalist and what he'd learned about Kevin Hudson.

'So what you're telling me,' Frankie said when he'd finished, 'is that this psycho's already hurt one kid and they let him back out so he could do the same thing again to someone else?'

Rob shrugged. 'Looks that way to me.'

Frankie was doing that funny breathing thing again and holding onto his glass so hard, Rob thought it might shatter. He remembered what Vera, his neighbour, had said about him.

'He's still not right in the head,' Vera said. 'Poor Maggie is at her wits' end. Blames herself, see? Says she should have known what Ian was like. You can see her point. I mean, didn't take a genius to work out that he was no good, that bloke. No good at all. She says prison's made Frankie worse. Says he was bad when he went in but he's worse now.'

Vera had leaned forward and lowered her voice. 'The other day, Maggie came home from the shops and found Frankie out in the garden, banging his head against the wall. Like he was a proper loony. You ask me, that boy should be locked up.' She paused and sniffed. 'It's not right letting people like that out when they're in that state.'

Thinking of that now, Rob could see the fresh scars on Frankie's forehead, presumably from where he'd smashed it against the wall. A memory flickered through his head. Him and Frankie as young kids.

'We used to play football.' He surprised himself by saying this out loud. Hadn't meant to. The beer was kicking in.

Frankie looked surprised. 'That's right, fella. In the park across the road there. You, me and Aidan Potter. He was good, Aidan. I remember that.'

'Not as good as you, though,' Rob said. 'My dad always said you were good enough to turn professional. Here, didn't you try for Palace once?'

It was like Frankie just shut down. His face sort of closed up and he picked his pint up and drained it, eyes looking at something far away. Rob knew whatever Frankie was looking at, it wasn't anywhere here in The White Hart. Made him regret he'd ever said anything and he cast around his drink-muddled mind for a different topic of conversation.

Except it was like everything else had faded away and no matter how hard he tried, the only thing he could think of was Frankie Ferrari, aged about ten years old, chasing a ball that had been kicked high in the air by Aidan Potter. The ball flew across the green playing field with little Frankie chasing after it, his legs moving so fast it looked like they were engine-powered. And then, as the ball started to drop, Frankie was right there beneath it. At the time, Rob remembered this clearly, it was like Frankie's head and the ball were connected with some sort of invisible thread. The ball drifted down as Frankie's head rose. Then, and this was the beautiful thing, Frankie's head tilted sideways and jerked forward, hitting the ball and sending it flying forward again, this time in the opposite direction.

And then Rob and Aidan were running forward, already screaming and roaring with joy as the ball seemed to hang in the air for an impossibly long moment before dropping right into the back of the goal, behind Rory Abbs, the goalie who just stood there looking as if he didn't know what the hell had just happened.

In the distance, he could hear Frankie's voice, asking if he was all right. Then Frankie's damaged face was in front of him, and his big, meaty hands were on his shoulders shaking him.

'Rob, mate? You all right?'

He tried to say something but he couldn't because he was crying, tears streaming down his face, his nose running, salty slimy snot in his mouth and smeared across his face.

Frankie there in front of him, and in his head, a little boy running like the wind after a football as his friends cheered him on.

21:30

Helen was sitting at the kitchen table. In front of her, a photo of Jodie in a silver frame. Beside that, a glass of white wine. Judging by Helen's face, it wasn't her first drink of the day.

'Where've you been?' she asked, putting emphasis on the 'you' like it was a dirty word. Like the very thought of him filled her with disgust.

She picked up the photo, examining it. As if, if she looked hard enough, it would offer up some clue to Jodie's whereabouts.

Kevin went and stood behind her. He wanted to reach out and stroke the back of her neck. She'd got her hair cut short last year.

He hadn't liked it at first but he'd got used to it and that bare spot at the back of her neck, just below the hairline, never failed to move him. It reminded him, in a way nothing else did, of her vulnerability. Her skin there was so soft, like a child's.

He didn't reach out, of course. She would have brushed his hand away if he'd touched her. Instead, he turned and went to get himself a glass of water.

They'd married after he was released from prison. Helen's idea. He knew she blamed herself, believed somehow that if she'd moved as he'd suggested, all that business with Harris would never have happened.

She'd done her best, though. Tried everything she could to get Cassie's parents to come forward. And afterwards, when he was inside, she visited at every opportunity. Even though it couldn't have been easy for her, not with him the way he was.

Naïvely, they'd both believed they could put it all behind them. That they would marry, move on with their lives and things would return to normal. How stupid could a person be?

'I asked where you've been this past two hours,' Helen said.

'Out walking,' Kevin said. 'Nowhere in particular.'

Behind him, Helen said something he didn't catch. He was distracted by what he could see through the window over the sink. Finlay in the back garden, kicking a football against the wall, again and again.

Helen stood up. She staggered sideways and fell against the table, knocking over her glass. Ignoring it, or possibly not even noticing, she grabbed the phone.

'Gonna call Abby,' she said. 'Ask her what she's playing at. She went out to get me something to eat. Doesn't take this long to go to the chippie and back. Stupid cow's probably gone off doing something else.'

'That's not a good idea.'

Kevin grabbed the phone from her hand and held her to prevent her from falling.

'Gimme that!' She lashed out at him and tried to wrestle the phone from him. Her fist hit him in the chest and he fell back, shocked by the power behind the blow. For someone who could barely stand up, she was well able to pack a punch.

'Helen,' he lowered his voice and tried to wrap his arms around her. She was crying now, her face all crumpled up and tears rolling down it. When she cried she reminded him of Jodie and he couldn't bear it. He just wanted to hold her and stroke her hair and tell her that everything would be all right.

'Give me the phone!' she screamed. Her fists were pummelling into him now, two hard little hammers beating against his shoulders and chest. A punch landed in his stomach and he grunted as the air rushed from his body, leaving him light-headed and desperate.

He was starting to panic. Couldn't breathe, could barely see. Blood pumped in his ears, merging with the other sounds in his head – men chanting as fists and feet punched and kicked him.

Get him, get him.

Helen's angry face kept going in and out of focus, like he was looking at her through a camera. The noises in his head grew louder and he felt his legs giving way as the blackness descended and her face disappeared entirely and all that was left was her punches raining down on him and the men's voices, growing louder and louder in his head.

Get him, get him.

'Kevin?'

Hands on his shoulder, someone shaking him. He opened his eyes and saw Helen.

'Oh Kevin,' she whispered. 'I'm sorry, love. So sorry.'

He struggled to sit up, get away from her.

'I'm sorry,' she repeated. But she didn't try to stop him when he scrabbled backwards out of her reach, and he was grateful for that. He sat up, pulling his legs up so his chin was resting on his knees, and wrapped his arms tight around himself.

'It's okay,' he said. His tongue felt thick in his throat, making it difficult for him to get the words out. 'Not your fault. You hate me. I don't blame you. I hate me too. It's my fault. All of it. I know that.'

He tried to say more but he couldn't get his mouth to work at all now and before he could stop himself, he was crying, sobs ripping through his body. His face was wet from tears and snot and he tried to wipe it dry with his sleeve but it was no good. He couldn't stop. He kept thinking of Jodie, how angry he'd been with her that morning. And all for what? Because he'd thought there was something more important he should be doing. His mind so focussed on revenge he wasn't thinking straight. Wasn't concentrating on what was important – Jodie. Rushing her like that, as if he couldn't wait to get her out of his sight.

'I thought I was doing the right thing,' he gasped. 'I never knew this would happen. I'd never have done it, Helen, I swear, if I'd ever thought ...'

She sat down beside him on the floor and wrapped her arms around his shoulders.

'Don't.' He tried to pull away. 'Please, Helen, just leave me.'

She didn't move, though. Instead, she pulled him tighter and held him as he sobbed into her warm, soft body. Somewhere in the distance, he could hear a ball banging as it was kicked against a wall, again and again. The sound was soothing, something reassuring about the steady repetition of the rhythm, like it might keep going forever, long after everything else around it had ceased to exist.

22:00

I hate him.

But I'm going to try to be nice to him. I'm thinking if I try really hard, he might let me out of this stupid pink shed. He might even let me go home.

He gets really cross sometimes. Like when he asked if I liked the videos and I said they were a bit babyish. And I didn't say it in a mean way or anything, but he got this look on his face and I got really scared so I said they weren't really and I was sorry and it was okay after that.

Even though it's not really okay because the videos are so stupid. A load of stupid people and their stupid animals all living on a street that's on top of a stupid rainbow somewhere stupid. How old does he think I am?

Oh God. He's coming. The pain in my tummy gets worse when he's here and it's starting now. All tight and hard and sore. Quickly, I switch on the TV and press the Play button on the video machine. The music starts up and makes my tummy worse. My friends would slaughter me if they ever saw me watching something this stupid.

I've started sucking my thumb again. Mum will go mad but I don't care.

The door opens and he's in the room now, looking down at me. 'I brought you some supper.'

Stupid f-word Brian. I hate him.

I pull my thumb out and try to smile. 'Thanks.'

I can't look at him, so I keep watching the TV. He sits down beside me. The fat man and the dog are playing a game of Snakes and Ladders. There's a cat as well. She's saying something mean to the dog, but I can't hear her because stupid, f-word Brian is speaking.

'Coco Pops.'

He's pushing a bowl onto my lap. I love Coco Pops. There's too much milk and some of it spills onto my hand and my school skirt, but it doesn't matter. The skirt is filthy already. And me. I probably smell as bad as he does. I thought about asking him if I can have a bath, but then I got this picture in my head of him in the bathroom with me and it made me feel a bit sick so I haven't said anything. And now I'm thinking of it again and my tummy's so bad, I don't know if I can eat the Coco Pops.

Except he's staring at me. With that funny look he gets, like he's in love with me, or something.

I lift the spoon and chew a few Coco Pops. They don't taste of anything and they're all soggy and disgusting.

'They're nice.' I'm such a liar but I don't care. I know it's what he wants me to say.

The little girl who owns the animals is on the TV now, but I don't know what she's doing because I'm not really paying attention. All I can think of is Brian, sitting beside me, watching me.

Oh God.

He shifts closer and the bed shakes and I can feel his breath on my face and it's hot and wet and disgusting and I want to scream at him to go away. Except I wouldn't even say go away I'd say something worse. A swear word.

'I thought you liked Coco Pops.' When he speaks, little bits of his spit land on my cheek.

'They're lovely. I'm just trying to watch this.'

'It was always your favourite,' he says. 'Old man Ted and his family of pets. And cheeky little Annie. She's a right monkey, hey? Imagine if we ever spoke to Daddy the way she speaks to Ted!'

Oh thank you God. He sounds all happy now. I take another

spoonful, really piling the spoon up this time. It's nearly at my mouth when he touches me. It sends this shock right through me. I jump away from him and the bowl falls out of my lap and there's Coco Pops and milk all over the pink rug and he's shouting – Marion, Marion – and then he's down on the floor trying to clean it all up and I can't stop crying and telling him I'm sorry.

I'm trying to hide in the smallest corner of the room. There's nowhere to hide. And he's here now, standing over me like one of those giants in Jack and the Giant Slayer and that's all I can think of. Those giants and what they did and Brian is saying something but it's all mushed-up sounding and I can't understand any of it.

And then it's later and we're sitting on the bed again and there's another video playing and Brian is speaking to me.

'Where did you go?' he asks.

He doesn't look like a monster now. More like a sad gorilla, with his big head drooping and his hands hanging down.

'What do you mean – where did I go?'

Oh God. His eyes are all wet. Again. And I know the crying will start in a bit. I really hate that.

'When you left here, Marion. Where did Daddy take you? It was awful, you know. I promised Mam I'd take care of you. No matter what happened. And I was doing that. I was going to get us out of here. I was going to get a job and everything. Save up money and get us both out of here. Except you were gone before I could do any of that.'

And now he's off. Wah-wah-waaaaah. His big body shaking so bad the bed rocks like a boat. I should probably do something to make him stop but I don't know what, so I sit there, watching him cry and listening to that horrible sound and wishing my mum was here.

When I get out of here, I'm going to be with her forever and ever. And I'll probably never even have to go to school again, or anything. Just live at home with my mum and spend all my time with her and never think about this place ever again.

SUNDAY,
20 FEBRUARY

11:55

Sunday morning meant Mass, which Ellen hated as much as the kids but endured for the sake of her parents and a Catholic education for her children. Before that, she made two phone calls. The first to Raj Patel, for an update on Dan Harris.

'Not a nice character,' Raj informed Ellen. 'Harris is a low-life crim who's been done for everything from drugs through to burglary and D&D. The last time our lot had a run in with him was when his girlfriend accused him of assault. He beat her up pretty bad, by all accounts. Except when the case came to the Magistrate's, the girlfriend withdrew her statement. Said someone else had carried out the attack.'

There was a subtext there that Ellen and Raj both understood without needing to discuss it. Something they saw again and again. Women being abused by their partners but, when it came to the crunch, too scared to do anything about it. The partners threatened them and, nine times out of ten, the broken women succumbed to the threats.

'Pretty much backs up how Kevin described him,' Ellen said. 'I don't suppose Harris could have had anything to do with Jodie, could he? I know it's a long shot, but is there a revenge angle here, maybe? Kevin was done for GBH. What if Harris was on some sort of revenge mission?'

'Doesn't sound like he's got the brains for something like that,' Raj said. 'But I'll look into it. He lives in Bromley. Want me to head over there later, have a quiet word?'

'Good idea,' Ellen said. 'Let me know how you get on. Thanks, Raj.'

Her second phone call was to Alastair. She wanted to find out what he'd uncovered about Simon Wilson, Brian Fletcher's boss. When her call went to voicemail, she left a message asking Alastair to call her back. Then she packed work away for the rest of the morning and went to collect her children and parents for the weekly visit to St Joseph's church.

After Mass, Ellen drove through the Blackwall Tunnel to Limehouse. She had a tonne of work to do, but the prospect of a few hours in the company of her brother and his partner was a welcome break. Sunday lunches in Limehouse were something of a family tradition and one Ellen cherished.

Usually her parents were an obligatory presence at these lunches with Sean and his partner, Terry. Today, though, they were going to a seventieth birthday party at the Irish Centre in Lewisham.

'Mick Taylor,' her father had explained as they'd stood freezing outside the church earlier that morning. 'My old pal from Spiddal. We went to school together, imagine that. And here we are now, nearly sixty years later, living it up in the Big Smoke. You couldn't make it up, could you?'

Beside him, Ellen's mother tutted and rolled her eyes. 'I'll be calling you later, Ellen, when he falls asleep on the sofa and I'll need to carry him up to bed. All himself and Mick do when they get together is drink themselves into oblivion.'

It was a vast exaggeration, of course. If he was lucky, her father would get away with two, maybe three mild lagers, before his wife put a stop to any further drinking.

Sean and Terry lived in a modern, riverside apartment in Limehouse. From the outside, the building was all glass and clean lines. Inside it was neutral colours, open-plan and the definition of taste.

'Something smells good,' Ellen said, as Sean opened the door of the apartment.

'Stuffed roast pork,' he said, putting his arms around her. 'Free range and organic. Full of goodness.'

She luxuriated in his embrace, feeling his absence sharply when he pulled away and turned his attention to Pat and Eilish.

'Hey guys! Long time no see. High-five, Pat. Eilish? Oh wow. What's that? A Peppa Pig princess. Fantastic. Come on, let's go and show it to Terry. He loves princesses almost as much as you do.'

'Men don't like princesses,' Eilish said, putting her little hand in Sean's and letting him lead her into the apartment, Ellen and Pat trailing close behind.

'That's not true,' Sean said. 'Terry loves princesses. And pink. It's his favourite colour.'

'Is that because he's gay?' Eilish asked.

Sean pretended to consider this seriously for a moment, then nodded. 'I guess so, Eilish. What about you, Pat? Is pink your favourite colour as well?'

'Euurgh!' Pat pulled a face and pretended to strangle himself.

'Hey, don't do that!' Terry called, from somewhere far away in the other corner of the living room. 'At least not before we've had a chance to go through this.'

He held up *Match*, Pat's favourite football magazine.

'Cool!' Pat yelled, jumping forward. 'Is it this week's one?'

'Sure is,' Terry said, coming forward to greet them. 'And this is for you, Eilish. Her name's Roxy.' In his other hand he held some sort of doll that looked like a funked-up, saucier version of Barbie. It had a nest of dark hair, breasts at least five times the size of any other part of her, and was wearing a short, figure-hugging red dress that would have looked better on a hooker than a child's toy.

Terry smiled at Ellen. 'A friend of mine makes a whole line of them. This one is the most, er, subdued version. Most of the others are bespoke models used in various bondage clubs in the City. Roxy was the only one I could find that didn't have her nipples pierced.'

'Nipples?' Pat started sniggering. 'Why would someone pierce a doll's nipples? That's disgusting!'

'Indeed it is,' Ellen said, relieved her father wasn't here. She could just imagine the questions he'd ask about bondage clubs and body piercings. Only last week, the mother of one of Eilish's friends had to have a quiet word with Ellen about Eilish teaching her child the word eejit.

'As in *fecking eejit*, apparently,' the concerned mother informed Ellen. 'Eilish told Freya her grandfather had been very specific about that.'

Ellen bit back her first instinct, which was to laugh, and promised the woman she would have a word with her father. Something she had no intention of doing, of course. He would treat any such intervention with the disdain it deserved and, she was sure of this, would go out of his way to teach Eilish other, even less suitable phrases to shock her friends with.

Lunch was the full works. Alongside the pork, they had Heston Blumenthal roast potatoes, Delia's apple sauce, and a selection of sublime roast vegetables. Dessert was Baked Alaska and whipped Cornish cream. Ellen thought she might never be able to eat again.

Afterwards, they went for a walk, heading west along the river towards Wapping and Tower Bridge. Sean walked ahead with Pat and Eilish, while Ellen lingered behind with Terry.

'You've got something on your mind,' Terry said, linking his arm in hers.

She looked at him, surprised. 'How do you know that?'

He grinned. 'I'm a lawyer, Ellen. Part of my job is paying attention, working out whether people are trying to hide something or not.'

'I'm not trying to hide anything.'

'I know. But you're distracted. Work getting to you? Must be hard being back. Although you were suited to being a stay-at-home mother. All that time spent worrying about the state of the neighbourhood and fretting over your next gym class.'

Ellen smiled.

'Why does everyone think being a housewife is so unrewarding?' she asked. 'It's bloody hard work looking after two kids, let me tell you. Hey, maybe we should swap places for a week. Let me take on the Home Office and you can deal with the yummy mummies at St Joseph's and use your lawyer skills to negotiate a deal between Pat and Eilish on which TV programmes they can watch before bedtime.'

Terry laughed. 'Point taken. So come on then. What's worrying you? And don't say *nothing*. I can see something's the matter. Sean's noticed too. He kept glancing over at you during lunch, like he was checking you were okay. Only you were so distracted you didn't even notice, did you?'

Ellen looked into Terry's kind eyes and thought, not for the first time, how lucky Sean was to have met him. On paper, you'd never have put the two men together. Sean, the working-class boy from South-East London, and Terry, public school education, Oxford graduate, partner in one of the UK's top human rights law firm and a regular human rights commentator on radio and TV. Sean was into clubbing and house music and recreational drugs. Terry preferred opera, fine wine and country walks.

Except somehow, their relationship worked. Perfectly.

Before Terry, Sean had never had a serious partner, just a series of one-night stands in seedy clubs with names like Fist and Shaft.

A carpenter, Sean met Terry when he was asked to build a set of shelves for the library of Terry's old house on Fournier Street, near Spitalfields. One week into the job, Sean had moved in and the two men had been together ever since.

'Ten years,' Ellen said now. 'That's how long I've known you, Terry. Don't you ever get sick of this?'

'Sick of what?'

'Me,' she said. 'Me and all my shit. You and Sean, everything in your life just seems so simple. Straightforward. The only crap you ever have to deal with is mine.'

Terry smiled and wrapped his arms around her. 'That's not true, Ellen. Believe me, my life is every bit as complicated. I'm just not as good at dealing with stuff as you are. I prefer to lock my demons away in a box at the back of my mind and pretend it's not there. And that, my dear, is not a very healthy way of managing it, I can tell you. Now then, why don't we take the children to the park for a bit? I'll entertain them while you and Sean can chat about whatever it is you need to get off your chest.'

'Thanks, Terry,' Ellen said. Her face was pressed up against his cashmere coat and her voice came out all muffled. Which was just as well because it hid the tremor in it. It also meant he wouldn't be able to see the tears that had, inexplicably, filled her eyes as he'd been talking.

At King Edward Park, true to his word, Terry took Pat and

Eilish into the playground while Ellen and Sean wandered across to the railings overlooking the river.

'Spit it out then,' Sean said. 'You've got that look on your face. What's wrong?'

She tried to smile, didn't quite manage it.

'I've been having these counselling sessions,' she said. 'You know, to help me deal with all that Dunston stuff. Or something.'

Sean nodded. 'I know that, El. I thought the sessions were going well. Are you saying there's a problem with them? You could always ask for a different counsellor, you know.'

'It's not that,' Ellen said. 'The counsellor's great. But something came up in the last session. I started talking about what happened with Eilish. And since then, I can't stop thinking about our first mum. Noreen. I want to find her, Sean. I need to know what happened.'

A pulse twitched at the corner of his eye. Apart from that, he stayed still.

'What do you think?' she asked. Stupid question, but she asked it nonetheless.

He turned to face her. He looked so bloody vulnerable. She forgot, sometimes, how soft he was. Mostly with Sean, all you ever saw was the sunny, carefree front he put on for the world. It was easy to forget that underneath there was a sensitive man who didn't cope well with change or unexpected news. It was easy to forget that the haunted, lost look on his face now was one she'd seen too much of in the first four years of their life.

'It's a terrible idea,' he said. 'But I would say that, wouldn't I? Because I'm not like you. All I've ever really wanted was this, what I have with Terry. A home, someone to love me, a job I enjoy and the rest of my family living close by. You're different. You've got this drive and this need to get to the heart of things. It's not something I understand. Eilish, our mother, everything that happened, how can you cope with digging up all of that? It was horrible. A horrible, ugly time and I never want to think about it or have to deal with it or talk about it or whatever it is you're meant to do with all that stuff. I just want to forget about it.'

Ellen took his hand in hers. She felt him tense but he didn't move away and she took that as a good sign.

'It's because of Vinny,' she said.

Sean frowned. 'What do you mean?'

'It's difficult to explain,' she said. 'But when he died, it left me feeling dirty somehow. Like this bad thing that had happened had tainted me. I know it's ridiculous, but that's just how I felt. And then there was all that business with Dunston. I'm not sure, but I thought if I confronted him it would make everything better. Only it didn't. It made it worse.'

'Oh Ellen.' Sean pulled his hand away and wrapped his arm around her shoulders, pulling her close. 'You should have said something.'

'I don't think I could have explained it properly,' she said. 'At the time, I wasn't even aware that's how I was feeling.'

'I still don't see what any of this has got to do with her.' Sean spat out the last word like it hurt his mouth.

'It's Eilish,' Ellen said. 'I can't stop thinking of her. Surely you think of her too from time to time?'

The edges of his lips tightened. 'Of course I think of her. Jesus, Ellen. She was my sister too.'

'I need to know what happened,' Ellen said. 'It's like I can't move on with the rest of my life till I find out. I feel I owe it to her.'

'You know what happened,' Sean said. 'Our mother got pissed, Ellen, and drowned our baby sister in the bath. That's all there is to it. There's no deep, dark secret. She was an alcoholic who had three kids and she couldn't cope. So she drowned one of us. It's that simple. And if you really care about your own kids, then I suggest you do everything you can to keep them as far away from that evil, murdering cow as you can.'

14:00

'It's about Dan Harris.'

Kevin's grip on the phone tightened as he struggled to breathe. 'You still there?'

The man's voice sounded far away, like he was speaking to him through a long tunnel.

'Who is this?' Kevin managed.

Images assailed him. Harris and Cassie. Phones being used as cameras. Cassie's face, all scrunched up from crying. Harris falling to the ground, fists and feet pounding into him. Hands on Kevin, pulling him off.

'I know something about Harris,' the man on the phone was saying. 'Something that might interest you.'

Blood rushed to his head, pounding in his ears, pressing against his skull. His heart thudded wildly, so rapidly it felt like any second it would explode, bursting through the insubstantial wall of his chest.

He closed his eyes, saw Harris and opened them again. Harris lying face up on the floor of his sitting room. The hole in his chest, the dark stain across his white shirt. Eyes wide open, staring at nothing, devoid of life.

'What about him?' Kevin whispered.

'Not over the phone,' the man said. 'We need to meet. Tonight. The Northbrook. Seven o'clock. Don't be late.'

14:04

Rob hung up and looked at Frankie, sitting across from him on the only other chair in the sitting room.

'Tonight, then.'

Frankie raised his can of beer in the air. In his hands, it looked too small, like a can made for a child, not a grown man.

'Who's this Harris bloke, then?'

'The kid he hurt,' Rob said. 'The one he got sent down for.

Thought if I mentioned his name, it'd work. Bet he thinks I'm some mate of his or something.'

Frankie belched loudly. 'Good thinking, Rob. So, fella, seven o'clock it is. Christ, I can hardly wait.'

Rob said nothing. He wanted to feel good about it. Everything was working out just the way he'd planned. Except, he couldn't shake off the feeling he'd got when he heard Hudson's voice for the first time. The guy sounded scared. More than scared. Terrified. He hadn't been expecting that.

He picked a fresh can from the ground, opened it and drank, trying to block the uneasy feeling in the pit of his stomach. He drank long and deep, trying to focus on Molly, reminding himself he was doing all of this for her.

'You all right, Rob?' Frankie asked.

He took another slug of beer and nodded.

'Fine,' he said. 'Just fine.'

It was the truth. Almost the truth. And even if he wasn't quite right about it yet, he knew he would be. He'd come this far. No way he was turning back now. No matter what happened. He owed it to Molly.

This was payback time.

18.30

'Police are investigating the murder of a man found dead in a flat in Bromley but have refused to give any details of the victim's identity.

Early speculation is that this is another example of the escalating problems between rival drug gangs in the Bromley area ...'

Ellen's mobile rang and she pulled it from the pocket of her jeans. At the same time, she pointed the remote control at the TV, turning it off.

It was Dai.

'I need to see you,' he said.

'Sure,' she said. 'When were you thinking?'

'Are you free now?'

Ellen glanced across at Abby Roberts, sitting at the other side of the oversized kitchen table.

'Not really. Have you got something for me?'

'Yes,' Dai said. 'But I don't want to do it over the phone.'

'I'm busy this evening,' Ellen said. 'And most of Monday. How about we grab a quick coffee late afternoon? Unless it can't wait till then?'

'It can wait. I'll see you tomorrow. The Dacre at five. They serve coffee, if that's your thing.'

He hung up before Ellen could say anything else and she looked at the phone, as if it might give up some clue as to what Dai had discovered.

'Everything okay?' Abby asked.

Ellen nodded. 'Fine. Are you ready to go? Only I told my mother I'd pick the kids up by nine.'

Abby pushed her chair back and stood up. 'I'm ready,' she said.

'I thought we could walk across, if it's all the same with you. I'm doing this excruciating diet at the moment and I'm trying to fit in as much exercise as I possibly can. You know how hard it is trying to stay healthy in this job, right?'

'Right.' Ellen looked at Abby's exquisite little body and wondered what part of it Abby could possibly be unhappy with. Unless …

She'd invited Abby over to her place for a coffee so they could talk about the Hudsons. Which they'd managed to do without killing each other. And after all the talking, they'd reached the same conclusion they always did. That there was something Kevin Hudson wasn't telling them. Ellen was convinced it related to Dan Harris. To her surprise, Abby agreed with her. So they decided to pay Kevin one more visit. Together. Almost made Ellen feel like she and Abby were a team.

'What do you think of that murder in Bromley?' Abby asked, nodding at the TV as she zipped up her jacket.

'That?' Ellen asked. 'Who cares? Some drug-dealer killed in a turf war. You know what pisses me off, though? It's not even a week since Jodie's gone and already she's not headline news any more. Instead, the press are more concerned about some guy who probably got what was due to him.'

'He's still dead,' Abby said. 'Even if he was dealing, he didn't deserve to die. No one does. No matter what they've done. That's why people like us don't believe in the death penalty.'

'Who says we don't?'

Abby looked genuinely shocked and, for a precious moment, she seemed lost for words. Making the most of the moment, Ellen put on her own jacket and suggested that, if they were walking, they'd better get a bloody move on.

Outside, they marched up Vanbrugh Park to the point where Greenwich ended and Blackheath began. After a while, Abby gave up trying to make conversation and they progressed in merciful silence.

When they reached the heath, Ellen paused to look over the dark expanse of open space to the twinkling lights of Blackheath village on the far side.

'I love it up here,' Ellen said. 'You know, if I ever come into money, that's where I'll live.' She pointed to the row of Georgian houses lining the edges of the heath towards Blackheath. 'I used to come here as a little girl and imagine I'd own one of those houses one day.'

'You'd need to find yourself a different job,' Abby said. 'Or a rich husband. Oh God. I didn't mean that. Shit …'

Ellen bit her lip to stop herself smiling. It was the first time she'd heard Abby swear.

'Don't worry,' she said. 'I get it all the time. People say things without thinking. And why shouldn't they? I don't expect the whole world to tippy-toe around me, watching every word that comes out of my mouth. And I certainly don't expect you to do that, either.'

'You said you came up here when you were little?' Abby said.

'All the time,' Ellen said. 'I grew up the other side of Trafalgar Road. My parents still live there, in fact.'

'So you're a Greenwich girl born and bred,' Abby said.

'More or less. Well, Peckham for the first few years, then we moved to Greenwich when I was four.'

'Your parents must have been relieved when they moved from Peckham to here,' Abby said with a laugh. 'That's what I call moving up in the world.'

'I don't remember that much about it,' Ellen said. 'And we weren't with our parents then. Sean and I are adopted.'

'Oh,' Abby said. 'I didn't realise. But I wouldn't, I suppose. And Sean's your brother?'

'Twin,' Ellen said. And then, for no reason she could think of, she continued speaking. 'Our mother went to prison. For killing our baby sister.'

There was silence for a moment and even in the dark, when she glanced over, she imagined she could see Abby trying to work out how to respond. Ellen wondered what on earth had made her come out with it in the first place.

'Well,' Abby said eventually. 'I can't even pretend to know what that would be like. But it must have been pretty awful for you both.'

This time, Ellen did smile. 'You could say that.'

They walked in silence across the heath. There was something Ellen needed to ask Abby. She was trying to think of a tactful way to approach the subject when her phone rang. Raj Patel.

'Have you seen the news?' Raj panted.

Behind Raj, Ellen could hear another man speaking. Her insides contracted as she recognised the voice. Mark Pritchard, the forensic pathologist.

'Is that Mark?' she asked. 'Jesus, Raj. What the hell has happened? Please tell me it's not Jodie.'

'It's Harris,' Raj said. 'Dan Harris. The bloke you asked me to speak to. Only by the time I got across to Bromley, I was too late. Local boys already here. Neighbour discovered the body earlier today.'

'Any idea how he died?' Ellen asked.

Kevin's words were swimming around her head: *In the end, everyone gets what they deserve.* Surely he didn't mean …?

'Too early to tell,' Raj said. 'But two things I can tell you. Harris has been dead for a good few days. And he didn't die a pretty death. This is definitely a murder investigation.'

'Listen to me,' Ellen said. 'Abby and I are on our way to Hudson's place right now. We need to get to Kevin. Now. Raj, we'll be there in under ten minutes. I need you to radio ahead for backup. But tell them to wait outside. No, better still, wait for us on the corner of Holme Lacey and Dallinger. We'll meet them there. Can you call Baxter as well? Tell him what's happened.'

'No need,' Raj said. 'He's just arrived.'

Great, Ellen thought. Just what she needed. Baxter storming into this mess with his ready-made assumptions. She needed to get to Kevin first.

'What's wrong?' Abby asked as Ellen hung up.

'Dan Harris is dead,' Ellen said. 'No details yet, but we need to get across to Hudson's place right now. Who's with them at the moment?'

'Malcolm,' Abby said. 'He's covering so I could come see you.'

'Call him,' Ellen said. 'Tell him not to let Kevin Hudson out of his sight. And bugger this walking business. Let's find a cab.'

Ellen started running, hoping Abby could keep up, not caring if she couldn't. The only thing she cared about now was getting to Kevin Hudson and finding out exactly what, if anything, he had to do with the murder of Dan Harris.

18.48

Frankie was saying something. Rob leaned closer, but he still couldn't make out the words.

'Wha'sat?' He grabbed Frankie's arm to get him to slow down.

They were running. On a road in Lee somewhere. Or rather, Frankie was running while Rob staggered along beside him, trying to keep up. They'd kicked off the evening with a feed of pints in a pub near Eltham station before jumping on a bus and coming here. For his size, Frankie couldn't half move quickly.

'Would you keep it down,' he hissed, pulling his arm free. 'We don't want to be drawing attention to ourselves, do we?'

'I can't remember the house,' Rob slurred. He looked around, confused. The houses swayed and blurred in front of him as he tried to recall which one was Hudson's.

''S'alright,' Frankie said. 'Number eighty. 'S right up there. See?' He grabbed Rob's head and twisted it so he was looking up the hill at the white house near the top.

'You all right, Rob?' Frankie asked. 'Looking a bit sick, mate, if you don't mind me saying so. Sure you're up for this?'

Rob nodded. The dizziness passed. As he got his breath back, the wave of nausea that hit him a moment ago started to fade. He belched, releasing some of the trapped air in his stomach. Jesus, how much had they had? Five pints? Something like that. Too much on an empty stomach.

It was all right for Frankie. He'd eaten a huge roast dinner with his beer. No food had gone near Rob's stomach since yesterday. He was nervous. Excited of course, yeah. But nervous too.

''Slike.' He started to explain it to Frankie but had to belch again. His mouth filled with the taste of beer. 'Like when you're a kid and you've been waiting so long for Christmas and by the time the day itself comes you're so sick with the excitement of it all, you can't enjoy it properly. Sort of like that but without any of the fun, if you know what I mean.'

Frankie grabbed him by the shoulders and shook him hard. 'Listen, Rob. You know what we've got to do here tonight, right? It ain't going to be something you'll forget and it sure as hell ain't going to bring your little girl back, so you better think about that before we go any further. You got that?'

Rob closed his eyes and saw Molly, smiling at him and holding her arms out, the way she did when she wanted him to pick her up. Almost at once, before he had any time to savour it, the image disappeared, replaced by her ruined little body the day he'd gone to identify her. He opened his eyes.

'Yeah,' he said. 'I know all that, Frankie. But at least I'll sleep easier knowing that bastard paid for what he done to her. That's why I'm doing this. No other reason.'

Frankie let go of his shoulders and nodded. 'Glad we got that sorted. So, you ready?'

Rob looked along the road towards number eighty. He could see lights on in the downstairs windows, and imagined Hudson in there, safe and warm. Maybe even pretending to comfort his wife, who probably had no idea what sort of an evil bastard she was married to.

Up ahead, there was a noise. Frankie nudged him, his huge elbow slamming into Rob's side, winding him.

'Here he comes,' Frankie hissed.

The two men moved back into the shadows of the garden behind them and watched, with growing excitement, as Kevin Hudson appeared and started walking along Dallinger Road, towards Rob and Frankie.

18.50

Helen was still in the kitchen. She hadn't spoken to him. Hadn't said a word, not one word since she'd watched the news. The hallway was dark but he didn't turn any lights on, not wanting to draw attention to himself. Quietly, he slipped into his coat and buttoned it up. He should really tell her he was going out but it would only upset her, and he'd caused more than enough upset already.

He had the front door open and was nearly outside when she appeared.

'Running away?' she asked.

'Just going out for a walk,' he said. 'Need to get some fresh air, that's all, Helen.'

'Where, Kevin?' Her voice rose and she was starting to sound hysterical. 'Who are you meeting? I heard you. On the phone yesterday. You're meeting someone in The Northbrook. It's to do with *him*, isn't it? It always comes back to this.'

She grabbed his sleeve, pulling at him, trying to drag him back into the house. Upstairs, he could hear Finlay moving about, the floorboards creaking and the sound of the TV in his bedroom being switched on.

'Stop it,' Kevin pleaded, trying to lift her hand off him. 'Please, Helen.'

'You said you'd let it go,' she shouted.

Above his head, the TV grew louder and Kevin imagined Finlay lying on his bed trying to block out the sound of his mother crying.

'Helen.' He tried to wrap his arms around her but she lashed out, fists pummelling into his chest until he pulled back, letting her go.

'You said it didn't matter anymore. That's what you said, Kevin. You said the only thing that matters now is Jodie. But you're a liar, aren't you? A bloody goddamn good for nothing liar!'

'I won't be gone long,' he said.

Another lie. He had no idea what he was going to face or how long he'd be gone. All he knew was he had to go. Now that the body had been found, he didn't have a choice.

'Besides,' he continued. 'I'll have my phone with me.' He held it up as evidence that, this time at least, he was telling the truth. 'If there's anything, anything at all, you only have to call. I'll come straight back.'

She had stopped crying now and was wiping her face with her sleeve. He went to move towards her again but she put her hand up, stopping him.

'Just go,' she hissed. 'Just bloody go if you have to. And if something happens to you, Kevin Hudson, then to hell with you. I won't come looking for you. The only thing I care about right now is Jodie. I don't have time for anything else. Do you understand that?'

He wanted to tell her he understood perfectly. That if he was in her shoes, he'd feel exactly the same way. It was his fault. All of it. And that the only reason he was going out now was because he had to try and fix things. He didn't know if he could, or if it was too late for that, but he had to try at least.

Except he couldn't tell her that. She had already gone. Into the kitchen, shutting the door behind her, leaving him alone in the hallway.

He sighed, and turned to open the front door. A blast of icy air engulfed him. It wasn't too late to change his mind. If he wanted, he could go back inside and give up on this whole thing. He shook his head. He'd started this whole business and now he had to finish it. Once and for all.

As he pulled shut the front door, he heard the detective's mobile phone ringing. Malcolm. The guy they'd sent across to replace Abby. Some instinct told Kevin to get away from the house as quickly as he could in case, for some reason, Malcolm came looking for him.

The road was quiet. The last journalist had moved on yesterday. Jodie would only become interesting again when she was found. If she was found.

Out here, Kevin could still hear the TV. Blasting from Finlay's bedroom, following him down the street as he hurried to The Northbrook for his seven o'clock meeting with a man who, if Kevin's suspicions were right, wanted to speak to him about the recent murder of Dan Harris.

18.55

The Northbrook was a swift ten-minute walk from Kevin's house. He walked quickly, footsteps pounding out against the pavement, echoing into the still night. He tried not to think about Helen, or the way he'd left things. He didn't blame her for being angry. He'd lied to her. Made a promise, then broken it. She'd begged him to keep away from Harris, saying he'd damaged their family enough. She was right, of course. If it wasn't for Harris, none of the rest of it would have happened.

Jodie.

Each time he thought of her, it was like being stabbed in the heart. He'd let her down. Let them all down. Of all the cock-ups in his life, this was the worst. Images of her flooded his mind and he speeded up, trying not to let them overwhelm him. As if he could run away from them. In fact, the faster he walked the more images there were and the faster they flashed before him, until it felt like he was drowning in them.

He was so caught up with what was going on in his head, he didn't notice the man in front of him until it was too late. He ran straight into him, his body thrown back with the impact as he bounced off the bigger man.

He started to apologise. A hand reached out from nowhere and wrapped itself around his throat and he was dragged backwards. Instinctively, he lashed out, kicking wildly, arms swinging as they tried to make contact with whoever was holding him.

The figure in front of him moved closer. Kevin saw a fist coming down and tried to duck, but with the arm around his neck he couldn't move. There was an explosion of pain as the fist smashed into the side of his face.

Then another blow, this time in the stomach, punching the air from his body and leaving him gasping for breath. The arm around his neck tightened and he struggled against it, body screaming for air.

The person holding him was still dragging him back, lifting him so his feet swung in the air. He tried to kick out, but his legs had no strength left in them. Suddenly, the pressure around his neck lifted, and he was shoved forward. He fell to the ground and tried to pull himself up but a foot pressed into his back, pushing him down.

A face appeared in front of him. Up close. It was too dark to make out the features but he could smell the man – beer and cigarettes. He tried to pull back but the man grabbed him by the hair, dragging him closer.

'Kevin Hudson,' the man whispered. 'Thought you could get away with it, didn't you?'

Kevin tried to speak. The man pulled his hair, yanking his head up, and he screamed instead.

'Hurts, doesn't it? Nothing compared to how my Molly felt, I bet. Do you remember her, Hudson? Molly York?' Another tug on his head, pulling it back even further.

'Think! Molly York, it was only three years ago, you bastard. Surely you haven't forgotten her already?'

Molly York. He recognised the name.

'I don't know what you're talking about,' he shouted. Half mad with panic, he struggled to break away. His fists lashed out uselessly, flailing around without hitting anything.

'Molly York!' the man roared.

A weight on his back like someone had dropped a block of concrete down on him. Inside, something cracked. Stabbing pain shot through his side.

Then another voice, so close it felt like it was coming from inside his head.

'Fucking nonce. Want to find out what it feels like?'

Hands pulling at his clothes. Cold air slapped his back as his coat was ripped open. Then more hands, tugging at his trousers.

'No!' He tried to fight it, using everything he had to shove the man off him. The other man was still holding his head. He was saying something now, but Kevin couldn't hear him. All he knew was the man on top of him and the hands on his body, tearing his clothes.

Something moved, loosened, inside him. Warmth and wetness down the insides of his thighs.

'Fucker's pissed himself.'

The weight on his back disappeared. He scrabbled forward but they were on him again, kicking and punching.

Get him, get him.

He tried to curl into a ball, pull his arms over his head, protect himself. Someone grabbed him, half-lifting, half-dragging him off the ground.

The smaller man held him, lifting his head and forcing him to look at the other man.

'You're going to pay for what you did, Hudson.'

'Hold him tight,' the big man said, moving towards them.

He smiled, a flash of teeth against a dark face, and for a moment Kevin thought it was going to be all right. Thought they'd done whatever it was they'd come to do and they would leave him now. Then he saw the knife in the other man's hand and knew they hadn't finished at all. He knew they'd only started.

The man lifted the knife and with blinding, horrible clarity, Kevin knew what they were planning and why they'd pulled his trousers down.

He opened his mouth to scream but a hand clamped over his mouth, blocking any sound.

18.59

'What's that noise?'

Ellen stopped, holding up her hand as Abby started to speak.

'Shhh,' she said. 'I heard someone screaming. Listen.'

'Nothing,' Abby said after a moment. 'Seriously, Ellen. You're imagining it.'

'I didn't imagine anything,' Ellen said. 'Strange. Probably a fox or something. Loads of them around this part of London.'

'Foxes?' Abby asked. 'Why would a fox choose to live here in the city, surrounded by people?'

Ellen shrugged. 'People mean food, I guess. As far as I know they live off all the stuff we throw away – leftover food, that kind of thing.'

'Poor little things,' Abby said. 'Driven out of the countryside by all that fox hunting, I wouldn't wonder.'

'I don't think that's the reason,' Ellen said. 'Besides, fox hunting's illegal. Or didn't you know that?'

Before Abby could answer, a loud noise ripped through the air. This time there was no mistaking the sound. A man roaring a girl's name.

'Molly York!'

'What the ...?' Abby began, but Ellen had already grabbed her arm and was dragging her forward. They were almost at Dallinger Road. The journey from Blackheath had taken longer than expected. There were no taxis about and the minicab office near Blackheath train station had no cars for another hour so Abby and Ellen had been forced to walk, after all.

Ellen pointed to a narrow lane, leading off the main road, a few yards in front of them.

'It came from down there,' she said. 'I'm sure it did. Come on. Quick.'

They raced forward. Ellen could make out the outline of two or three figures. One of them was crouched on the ground but as she watched, the person – a man? – seemed to pull himself off the ground until he was standing.

As her eyes adjusted, she saw there were three people. One of them was being held between the other two and appeared to be struggling.

The voice she'd heard earlier kept running through her head as she inched her way down the lane towards the silhouetted figures. Molly York. Is that what he'd really said or had she only imagined it?

The closer she got, the clearer the outlines became and when she finally worked out what was in front of her, she reacted automatically.

'Police!' she shouted at the top of her voice. 'Freeze! Nobody move. Do not *move*!' she added as the hulking figure in front lifted his arm. Her legs turned to jelly when she saw what was in his hand.

'Drop your weapon.' She inched forward. Without needing to check, she could sense Abby beside her, moving when she did, stopping when she did, following her every move.

Behind the giant, another voice spoke. 'Put it down, Frankie.'

Ellen peered through the darkness. 'Mr York? Rob? Is that you?'

She took another step forward and the stench of fresh urine hit her. She was now close enough to see the three men more clearly and she didn't like what she saw.

She felt Abby's hand on her arm, warning her, but she shrugged it off and rushed forward, her only thought to help the poor creature being held. She had nearly reached him when, out of the corner of her eye, she saw the giant man moving towards her. She tried to duck, but he was too quick for her.

His arm swung down, hitting the side of her head. As she

crashed to the ground, she reached out, still trying to save Kevin Hudson. But he seemed, suddenly, too far away. A great shadow appeared over her. She tried to pull herself up but he kicked her in the stomach, knocking her back again.

She lay there, unable to move, struggling to get her breath back. He moved towards her again. She screamed as he grabbed her around the neck, squeezing tight, making it impossible for her to breathe. She tried to fight him off, but he was too strong. Her fingers grappled uselessly with his huge hand. She felt her body slipping away from her and no matter how hard she tried, there was nothing she could do to stop it.

19:08

Through the window, I can see there's a big moon. The window's my only way of knowing when it's night time. Outside, I can hear the rumble of a train. I hear trains going by a lot.

I'm really cold. Shivering. And my teeth are chattering. I want Mum. I think of how warm she'd make me, cuddling up to me on the bed, telling me how much she loves me. And thinking all that makes me cry, even though I thought I'd cried so much there was nothing left. You could cry enough to fill a river or a sea and there'd still be more tears left over.

There's this programme Finlay used to watch. Some sort of cartoon with a dog. I hated it, but sometimes I'd pretend to watch it just so I could sit beside him. He was always nice to me then and we'd snuggle on the sofa, watching the dog do stupid things. In one episode, the dog was in a desert and he was walking for miles and kept on saying: 'water, water. I need water.'

Finlay kept laughing and I laughed too, even though I couldn't see why it was meant to be funny but I knew if I asked Fin, he'd be mean to me. And I'm only thinking of that now because I know just how that dog must have felt. Even though there's no desert and no sun here. Even though it's the opposite of warm.

I keep thinking where can I get water and I can't think of anywhere. But then I get an idea. It's a bit disgusting, but I'm so desperate I don't care. I get out of the bed, keeping the quilt wrapped around me because it's so cold.

There's a tank thing on top of the loo where the water's kept. I can't remember what it's called, but I'm thinking the water in that should be clean enough. I flush the toilet four times first. Each time I wait till the tank is full before pressing the handle again. I'm a bit worried Brian will hear so I'm ready to run back to the bed if I have to, but nothing happens. No footsteps or anything.

The lid of the cistern – cistern! – is really heavy but I can drag it enough so that there's room to dip my fingers into the water. Oh God. The first drops land on my tongue and it's such a good feeling. It tastes fine so I go again, only this time I cup my hands and fill them with water. It goes everywhere but I'm drinking and it's amazing.

When I've had enough I get the lid back into place and race back to bed. I curl into the tightest ball, trying to keep warm. I squeeze my eyes closed and pretend I'm at home, in my own bedroom at the back of the house.

It's not that hard to imagine that's where I am. After a while, I even start to think I can hear Dad, breathing in that heavy, nearly-snoring way he has. And Fin, moving around in his room next door.

Outside, an owl hoots. I imagine it flying around out there, big wings flapping as it swoops over the fields looking for mice and things to eat. And I imagine then that I'm flying too, floating in the clouds. It's a nice feeling. I try to hold onto it.

19:18

'I've given him a sleeping pill and put him to bed,' Helen said, coming into the sitting room. She sat down heavily on an arm-chair and looked at Ellen and Abby.

'What the hell happened out there?' she asked.

Her voice was slightly slurred, as if she'd been drinking. And she looked so lost, Ellen thought, like a child.

'There were two of them,' Abby said. 'Difficult to ID, that's the problem. Even with the moon it's still dark out there. One of them was big, though. The one who … well, he was big. Scary big.'

Ellen thought of the knife the big man had been holding, and what he'd been planning to do with it. The memory of Kevin with his trousers bundled around his ankles, the air full of the smell from his emptied bladder – it wasn't something she would forget.

She touched the side of her face where she'd been hit. It hurt like hell. Her head felt unbalanced, as if the injured side was somehow heavier than the other.

'Do you need ice for that?' Helen asked, seeming to notice Ellen's face for the first time.

Ellen shook her head. The movement caused another wave of pain, and she wished she hadn't.

'It's fine,' she lied.

She glanced over at Abby. 'I still don't understand how you managed to take on the two of them.'

Abby blushed. 'I didn't have to do anything. They just ran off. The big guy, he, one minute he was attacking you, the next, the other guy was pulling him off and they pushed past me and ran off. I should have stopped them. I tried but …'

Ellen frowned, trying to recall pieces of what had happened. She could remember being hit, and kicked. Abby's voice, shouting something about assaulting an officer of the law. Had she really said that?

Then she remembered something else. Rob York. York and Hudson – was there something she'd missed? Unless she'd been mistaken …

'Did you hear him?' she asked Abby. 'One of them. He shouted something about Molly York.'

'I really couldn't say,' Abby said. 'I'm sorry. It all happened so quickly.'

A moment later, when she lifted her mug of tea to take a sip,

Ellen noticed Abby's hands were shaking. Poor kid. Dealing with an alley fight probably wasn't a standard part of a FLO's working day. Mind you, she'd handled herself well out there. Ellen was impressed.

Outside, in the hallway, Ellen could hear the hum of voices as Malcolm briefed the uniforms. Another door-to-door was underway to try to find out if anyone had seen the two men who'd assaulted Kevin. So far, there was no sign of Baxter. Small mercy but better than none, Ellen supposed.

She went into the hallway and caught Malcolm's eye.

'Got a moment?' she asked.

When he came over, he looked scared. She didn't blame him.

'I'm sorry,' she said. 'I shouldn't have lost my temper. I know it wasn't your fault.'

Malcolm shook his head. 'No. You were right, Ma'am. I should have stopped him from going out. It's just, I heard him at the door and was coming out to stop him, but then Abby called and I thought that might be more important so I took the call instead. By the time I'd finished with Abby, Kevin was already gone. I did look for him on the street, but there was no sign.'

'It doesn't matter,' Ellen said. 'Anything back from uniform yet?'

'Nothing,' Malcolm said. 'But we'll keep trying.'

Back in the sitting room, Abby was asking Helen about Kevin.

'Where was he going, Helen?' Abby asked.

Helen's eyes dipped away, refusing to make contact with Abby or Ellen. Hiding something. Ellen caught Abby's eye and the FLO nodded. She'd spotted it as well.

'Helen?'

'He had to go out,' Helen said. 'Told me he was meeting someone, but wouldn't tell me who.'

Ellen sat on the sofa beside Abby and looked directly at Helen. 'I don't believe you.'

Helen's eyes widened. 'I'm sorry?'

Ellen shrugged. 'You heard me. You're hiding something. And here's the thing, Helen. If you're holding out on us, then whatever it is you're not telling us, it might help us find Jodie. How do you think you're going to feel if we can't find her because of something you haven't told us?'

'You don't know what you're talking about,' Helen whispered.

'Helen,' Abby's voice was soft, persuasive. 'If Kevin's done something, you have to tell us. Better out than in — there's a reason people say that, you know.'

Helen's eyes filled with tears and when she looked up, Ellen knew she'd made her mind up. Whatever secret her husband was hiding, Helen would tell them. Well done, Abby.

'He should never have gone to prison,' Helen said. She stood up. 'I'm sorry. If I'm going to do this, I need a drink. Can I get something for either of you?'

At the same time as she said this, the doorbell rang. Helen rushed to answer it.

Ellen followed her into the hallway, just in time to see Helen pulling open the door. Behind Helen, Ellen saw Baxter, framed in the doorway.

Helen gasped. 'You've found her?'

Baxter shook his head and pushed past Helen, into the hall-way, Raj Patel close behind him.

'This isn't to do with Jodie,' Baxter said. 'Where is he?'

'Ed.' Ellen stepped forward. 'Kevin's not well. The attack, it was pretty brutal. He needs rest.'

Baxter turned to Raj. 'Upstairs, Detective' he said. 'You heard her.'

'Please,' Ellen said. 'Can't this wait?'

She caught Raj's eye and he looked away, obviously embar-rassed to be caught in the middle.

Baxter pushed past Ellen, headed for the stairs.

'Come on, Patel. No time to lose.'

19:22

Upstairs, Kevin wasn't sleeping. Helen had made him take a sleep-ing pill, but he'd slipped it under his tongue without swallowing it. He needed to be alert, work out what had happened tonight, and why. Finlay was still in his bedroom, TV blasting out as he tried to block out the real world. Kevin was glad the boy hadn't seen the state of him when the two investigators had brought him back. Despite his best efforts, his mind kept revisiting that moment, when he'd realised what the men were planning to do to him. In the bed, he shivered and drew his arms tight around his body, trying to shut the memory from his mind.

The thing was, he'd recognised the voice. Not the big fella but the other one. The one who'd held him. It was the same man he'd spoken to on the phone. The man had a raspy voice that sounded as if too many cigarettes had done permanent damage to his vocal chords. It was the same voice that had roared out that name – Molly York.

After Helen went back downstairs, Kevin had sat here in the bed, repeating the name to himself. Molly York. The little girl who'd disappeared three years ago. When the men had grabbed him, he thought he knew what they were about. They were mates of Harris. The people who'd made the phone call. They didn't want to talk to him. They wanted to punish him.

Except then they'd started going on about something else entirely and Kevin thought they were the ones who'd made the mistake. He shook his head. It wasn't that simple, though. If they thought he was someone else, why had they made the call?

He remembered something else. Something Kelly had shouted when she found him. Kevin threw back the duvet and got out of the bed. He needed to go downstairs, talk to her right now.

He grabbed some clothes off the chair and got dressed, the pain in his side slowing everything down. Every move was torture. He was at the bedroom door, ready to go downstairs when the doorbell rang. Automatically, he shot forward, his mind instantly focussed on Jodie.

Then he heard Baxter's voice, telling Helen that wasn't why he was here and for a moment Kevin's body stopped working. The sudden rush of adrenalin subsided and he felt as if every last bit of energy had been squeezed from his body and he didn't even have enough left to keep his heart beating or his lungs breathing.

Bits of the conversation in the hallway drifted up to where he stood. It was difficult to hear what they were saying with Finlay's TV in the background, but he could make out the gist of it. Enough for him to know that Baxter wasn't here to see how Kevin was doing after the attack.

Baxter sounded serious and Kevin knew, with dull certainty, how it would play out. They would take him in for questioning. Then, once it was clear Baxter knew what Kevin had been doing the morning Jodie disappeared, that would be the end of it. They'd lock him up again.

Down below, Helen was asking Baxter to let her explain. But he was ignoring her. Telling someone to move upstairs.

Kevin moved across to the sash window overlooking the garden. He heard footsteps on the stairs and pushed open the window. Moving as fast as he could. Ignoring the screaming pain in his side. Down below, he could make out the shapes of the garden furniture that Helen had been nagging him for months to dismantle and put away, insisting the wood would be ruined from the damp and the cold.

Glad he hadn't already done that, Kevin slid his body out the window. Not letting himself think about what he was doing, he pushed himself away from the window frame and jumped towards the solid wooden table beneath him.

22:15

'Marion?'

He stood outside, branches brushing the top of his head and the sides of his face, waiting for her to answer. When there was no sound, he pulled back the bolts, opened one of the doors and peered inside.

She was curled up on the bed, her back to him, completely still.

'Marion!' He leapt towards her.

She jumped up and started scrabbling away from him, until her little body was pressed against the wall. He felt a momentary wave of relief when he saw her tear-streaked face and realised she'd only been crying. Not dying, like he'd first thought.

Then he tensed again, watching the way she cowered away from him. He moved forward, making sure to keep his voice calm and quiet.

'It's okay, Marion, I'm not going to hurt you. I just want to check you're okay. That's all. You gave me a right fright lying there like that, making those funny noises.'

He sat down on the bed and put his hand on her knee. She whimpered and tried to pull her leg away, but he increased the pressure until she stopped wriggling. Her skin against his palm felt warm and soft. It was nice and she shouldn't be so difficult. All he was doing was looking after her. Why did she have to give him such a hard time?

She was scared. It wasn't fair. There was no need to be scared. He'd never hurt her. Not like Daddy, who'd done terrible things to all of them. He wanted to give her a hug, tell her not to worry about a thing and that she was safe now. Except the way she was acting, if he tried to hug her she'd probably start screaming or something. It was a bad business altogether and he wished Mum was here. She'd know what to do.

Mam was nothing like Daddy. She was kind and gentle and gave Brian kisses and told him he was her little man.

Marion's leg felt nice as he rubbed it. A melting sensation started in his tummy. It was nice, but he knew the feeling was part of the Bad Thing. Marion didn't try to stop him, though, so maybe it was okay, what he was doing.

'She was a great mam, wasn't she, Marion?' he said, hand stroking – up and down, up and down – liking the way it felt, but being careful not to let it take over. That was the important bit. If you weren't careful with the Bad Thing it took over and suddenly you'd find yourself doing all sorts. Keep in control, Brian, that's the key.

Marion made a noise and he looked at her, feeling something like anger when he saw she was still crying.

'Stop that now,' he said, using his firm voice. 'All those tears. There's no need for that at all. You're safe here. Daddy doesn't know where you are. He'll never find you down here. I promised Mam I'd take care of you and that's just what I'm doing. You'd think you'd be glad of it instead of crying like a baby all the time.'

'Have you got anything to drink?' she whispered.

Brian sighed. 'I brought you Coco Pops last night and all you did was knock it on the ground. I'm sorry, love, but you need to learn. If you're a good girl today, I'll bring you something again tomorrow. How about that?'

She started crying harder and the noise was really annoying. Could she not stop it? Just leave it out for once?

'Please,' she begged. 'Just a drop of water. Please?'

She looked up at him then, big blue eyes looking at him like he was a king or something. When she did that, his stomach went all funny. It was nearly like she knew what she was doing, knew when she looked at him like that, it made him want to do the Bad Thing.

He felt sorry for her then. It wasn't her fault she was scared. God only knew what Daddy had put her through over the last few years. His hand was still on her leg, stroking her soft skin. She was so tense. He could feel her body trembling and it made him sad that she was like this, even with him. Without thinking, he moved his hand higher up her leg.

Her whole body jerked, like he'd hit her.

'Jesus!' He jumped up and stood over her. His breath was coming so hard he was almost snorting. Made him sound like a pig. Or a monster.

She'd pulled her legs up tight against her body. It made her skirt hitch up and from where he was standing he could see her knickers.

Pull your skirt down, little bitch.

Daddy!

Brian swung his head from side to side, eyes darting around the small room. He couldn't see Daddy, but that didn't mean anything. Daddy was clever. Brian should have thought of that. What if Daddy had come back here looking for Marion?

If Daddy knew what Brian had been up to, he'd hurt him. Like the time Daddy caught Brian in his bedroom, doing the Bad Thing. He'd beaten the living daylights out of him that night. Brian understood, though. Daddy said it was for his own good, and Brian believed him. Just like he believed him later, when Daddy came back into the bedroom and showed him just what happened if you listened to the monster inside your head and let it do whatever it wanted.

'See what happens?' Daddy said afterwards, standing over Brian and buttoning up his trousers with his face all red, and breathing through his nose, making a snorting sound, like a pig. Or a monster.

Now he'd started thinking of Daddy he couldn't stop. Couldn't get Daddy out of his head, remembering the way he'd hurt Brian, over and over, all the time telling him it was for his own good. He crouched down in front of Marion.

'Where is he?' he asked. 'Where's Daddy, Marion? Where did

he take you?'

She didn't answer him, just kept crying. Silvery slivers of snot were running from her nose down into her mouth. She wasn't even bothering to wipe them away. It made him feel sick just to watch her. He couldn't stand it anymore.

'Shut up!'

He shouldn't have said that. He tried to tell her he was sorry but she put her hand over her ears, blocking him out.

His tummy felt funny, like he might get sick. He turned away from her. He was tired. Exhausted. It wasn't fair. Here he was, making all this effort to keep her safe and all she did was sit on the bed crying and not being any fun at all.

Without another word, he walked out of there, taking care to lock up properly after him. Behind him, as he walked down the garden to the house, he imagined he could still hear her crying.

MONDAY,
21 FEBRUARY

11:30

After the morning briefing, Ellen drove across to St Anne's school in Lee. Celia Roth, the headmistress, was home from Australia and back at work and Ellen was keen to see her.

The school was a modern, sprawling, red-brick building at the end of a nondescript, suburban street. The gates were locked and Ellen had to ring a bell and explain who she was before being buzzed in.

As she crossed the large expanse of concrete playground a tall, slender woman strode out to meet her.

'Celia Roth,' the woman said, holding out her hand. 'Pleased to meet you.'

Ellen liked her instantly and readily returned the woman's smile and handshake.

'Ellen Kelly. Thank you for agreeing to meet me, Mrs Roth.'

The other woman smiled. 'It's Miss, not Mrs. But I'd much rather you called me Celia. Let's go inside to my office. This way.'

Inside, Ellen was ushered into an immaculately tidy office where she was offered a seat while Celia made fresh coffee from a machine on the window-sill behind her desk.

'Sorry if I sounded wary on the phone,' Celia said, as she handed Ellen her coffee. 'My first instinct, when you called, was that you might be a journalist. You wouldn't believe how many of them have been trying to get in to see me. And I've only been back at work a few hours.'

'Of course,' Ellen said. 'I was sorry to hear about your mother.'

'Thank you,' Celia said. 'That's kind of you. It hasn't been easy. And then to come back to this. It's inconceivable. Naturally we're all praying that Jodie will be found but ...'

Abruptly, she put her cup down on the low table between them and stood up, turning away from Ellen to look out the window.

'Are you okay?' Ellen asked.

Celia nodded. 'I'm sorry, Mrs Kelly. Something like this, it has such a devastating effect on our little community here at St Anne's. It's knocked us all for six, I can tell you. Do you have children?'

'Two,' Ellen said. 'A boy and a girl. Pat, my son, is nine. Eilish is seven. And please, call me Ellen.'

Celia smiled. 'Pat and Eilish Kelly. Where do they go to school?'

'St Joseph's in Greenwich,' Ellen said.

'Ah, Simon Cahill's school. He was deputy head here before he went to St Joseph's. Did you know that?'

Ellen shook her head. 'I didn't, but it hardly surprises me. Everyone seems to know everyone else in this part of London. It's scary.'

Celia smiled and sat back down. 'It is strange, isn't it? But lovely as well, I think. In a city the size of London, we're lucky to feel part of any sort of community, don't you think?

'Take us two, for example. You probably don't remember me, but I certainly remember you, Ellen Flanagan.'

Ellen looked closely at the woman sitting opposite her, trying to find something familiar in her face. Grey eyes, strong cheek-bones, great skin, she figured Celia Roth was in her mid- to late-fifties. Anything up to fifteen years older than Ellen.

'St Ursula's,' the other woman said. 'Oh, I'd left by the time you started, but my best friend's cousin used to have a thing for you, you know. We used to tease him terribly about you. Poor chap.'

'The poor bloke,' Ellen said. 'Did I ever find out about this crush?'

Celia shook her head. 'You started going out with someone else and I think that was the end of it. Poor Jim decided you were a lost cause, I think.'

Ellen's heart did a somersault. 'Jim?'

'O'Dwyer,' Celia said. 'His cousin, Kathy, was – still is – my closest friend. Of course, I don't get to see her so much these days. Not since the family moved to Broadstairs.'

Ellen could have happily sat there all afternoon, hearing about the crush Jim O'Dwyer had once had on her and speculating – wildly and wrongly, no doubt – about whether he still held a torch for her. But that wasn't why she was here.

'I'm conscious of time,' she said, making a show of glancing at her watch. 'Is it okay if I ask you some questions about Jodie?'

'Of course,' Celia said. 'I do apologise. A trip down memory lane is all well and good, but it's not going to help us find Jodie. What do you need to know?'

'Let's start with her father, Kevin.'

'What about him?'

Ellen leaned forward in her seat. 'I'd like your honest opinion about him. What's he like as a parent? Do the kids seem happy with him? Have you picked up any sense that his marriage is happy? Unhappy? Why do you think he stays at home while Helen goes out to work? What do the other parents say about him?'

'If you've only come here to ask questions about Kevin, I'm not sure I'll be able to help you,' Celia said.

'I don't think he's guilty,' Ellen said, 'if that's what you're thinking. I know my colleagues have already asked your staff about him. I'm sure lots of the parents are talking – believe me, I know only too well how parents like to bitch and gossip about other parents at the school gates. I think you might be better placed than some others to give me a balanced view.'

Celia sighed. 'Kevin Hudson is a good man. I like him. And Helen. They're devoted parents and have two lovely kids to show for it. Kevin's had a hard time of it over the years and that shows. He's not the easiest man in the world to get along with, but once you get past that awkward exterior there's a really lovely person underneath.

'Now, you haven't asked me directly if I think he could have harmed Jodie but, for what it's worth, I'll tell you what I think. St Anne's is quite a conservative community. Kevin and Helen are an exception – in more ways than one. Now, I know there's a good reason why Kevin and Helen have chosen a different route. The problem is, that's not something they want to share with the other parents.

'Of course, there are other fathers who don't work, and many families where both parents work part-time and share the child-care equally. But these families, they're always ready to explain their reasons for doing things a certain way. Kevin and Helen, they've got a reputation for being secretive.'

'Which is understandable, given the circumstances,' Ellen said.

Celia nodded. 'Exactly. You know Kevin's background. It's something we've kept from the other parents. Kevin and Helen didn't want anyone knowing and I respect their decision. Just as I respect the fact they trusted me enough to tell me about it in the first place.'

'Do you know what he went to prison for?' Ellen asked.

Celia nodded. 'Yes. I also know the alleged victim was a minor in the eyes of the court.'

'What do you mean – alleged?'

'I mean,' Celia said, 'that things aren't always what they seem to be. You're a detective, Ellen, you know that. I despise gossip of any sort. If you want the details of Kevin's incarceration, I'm afraid you've come to the wrong person. It's not my place to discuss that with you. I suggest it's something you raise with Kevin himself.'

Sensing the subject was closed, Ellen moved the conversation on, asking everything she could about Jodie. She learned nothing she didn't know already – Jodie was a bright, hard-working girl with a cheeky streak who loved a laugh. Popular with almost everyone, her two best friends were Grace Hooper and Holly Jones. If Ellen was lucky, she'd find both girls' mothers waiting outside at pick-up time. As far as Celia knew, the only thing connecting Molly York and Jodie Hudson was that the two girls lived in the same part of London. Celia doubted Kevin had even heard of Molly York before she disappeared.

After she left Celia, Ellen got back into her car and called Alastair. Kevin Hudson's disappearance had changed everything, but Ellen still wanted Alastair's update on Simon Wilson.

'Any sign of Hudson?' she asked, once the greetings were out of the way.

'Nothing yet,' Alastair said. 'But we've gone national on it. He won't get far.'

The worst thing about it, Ellen thought, was that by running away, Kevin had made his situation far worse. Baxter's fixation had moved from believing Kevin abducted Jodie to a conviction the man had killed Dan Harris.

'What about Molly York?' Ellen asked.

'I've got that list you asked for,' Alastair said. 'Although to be honest, Fletcher was always their only real suspect. I did a bit of digging into Wilson, like you asked for, but he's clean. Respectable businessman with his own landscaping firm. Owns a string of properties across North Kent. And several verbatims saying what a decent bloke he is and how well he's looked after Fletcher.'

Another dead-end.

Ellen thanked Alastair and hung up. Her face throbbed from last night's injury. And the inside of her skull. It was an effort to concentrate on anything apart from the constant pain. She pulled down the sun shield and looked at her reflection in the mirror. The side of her face was swollen, but make-up had covered the worst of the bruising. A pity it wasn't so effective at covering the dark rings under her eyes. She looked like shit. And felt it too.

She closed her eyes, tried to remember every detail of the attack. It wasn't easy. Her brain kept focussing in on one thing: poor Kevin with his trousers around his ankles and the look of terror on his face. That wasn't what she wanted. There was something else.

Yes. There it was. She opened her eyes and got her phone back out. Pressed the re-dial button.

'Alastair, it's me. Can you get across to Hither Green in the next fifteen minutes? We've got a job to do.'

12:05

Kevin limped to the end of the platform, as far as possible from the huddle of passengers, all waiting for the Eastbourne train. It was a bright, cold day with a bracing wind and he had no coat. Right now, that was the least of his worries.

He'd spent the night in a cheap hotel near Victoria Station. Now, he was getting out of the city. Earlier, he'd walked across to

Westminster and withdrawn as much as he could from an ATM. He knew the police would be able to trace him from the transaction and hoped the Westminster location might wrong-foot them for a while longer.

He wanted to call Helen, but was afraid if he heard her voice he'd crack and end up going home. And that would mean handing himself over to DCI Ed Baxter. He couldn't do that.

Everything was such a mess. The six months he was locked up, all he could think of was getting out. Stupidly, he'd imagined everything would go back to the way it was before. Him, Helen and the kids making a life together. He'd thought that all the trauma, all the horror would, somehow, magically disappear.

He had been a fool. There was no going back in this life. You only got one chance. If you messed it up, you were done for. It was that simple. The whole idea of redemption, living through a trauma and emerging the other side, butterfly-like, was a load of bullshit.

Working that out was a revelation. He'd tried so hard, at first, to find the positives. Helen was still with him, things were strained, sure, but at least she hadn't run off and left him. There were the kids, as well. Not his by birth but, in every way that mattered, they were his and he loved them more than he'd known it was possible to love anyone.

Even that, pure and uncomplicated love, had been destroyed. Jodie was gone. His life was in tatters. A jigsaw puzzle he'd spent his whole life endlessly, painfully piecing together. Then, just as he was putting in the last few pieces, along came Dan Harris and smashed it into a thousand tiny pieces.

The jigsaw could never be mended. Redemption wasn't an option, but revenge was. A dish best served cold and all that. Although frankly, Kevin didn't give a shit how it was served.

It had all seemed so simple, so blindingly obvious. Until now.

Now, Harris was gone, but that didn't help because so was Jodie. The train pulled onto the platform. As he waited for the doors to slide open, Kevin made a promise to himself. He would get her back. One way or another. And after that, he would hand himself over to Baxter and let him do his worst. Because once Jodie was home again, safe, then Kevin didn't care what happened. Jodie was all that mattered. She was all that had ever mattered, if he'd only realised it.

12:40

Ellen banged on the door again and waited. Still no answer. She stepped back and looked up at the house. With the curtains drawn tightly in each room, it was impossible to see if anyone was in there or not.

She bent down and tried to peer through the letterbox into the house.

'Mr York!' she yelled through the narrow slit. 'Please answer the door. It's DI Kelly. We need to talk.'

She thought she saw the glow of light underneath the closed

door leading into the kitchen, but she couldn't be sure if it was an electric light or just daylight that seemed brighter against the darkness of the rest of the house.

Her back started to ache and she stood up and looked at Alastair.

'We could break it down,' Alastair said. 'Take ten minutes max to get some back-up.'

Ellen pictured Rob York sitting inside the house. Huddled in that dark, dank sitting room surrounded by images of his dead daughter. She shook her head.

'I'd rather not. Let's give it another try.'

She started banging on the door again and calling out his name.

'He won't answer, you know.'

Ellen turned round and saw an elderly lady with bright orange, dyed hair and a perm so tight it could have been painted onto her head.

'Even when he's at home, he rarely comes to the door,' the woman continued. 'Besides, I don't think he's there. He went off somewhere yesterday evening and I haven't seen him since. Of course, he keeps odd hours, Rob. Up all night and sleeps during the day. Poor boy. It's a wonder he keeps going at all, when you think of it. I suppose he doesn't have a choice, really. All he has to hope for is that they'll find him one day. The man who killed poor little Molly.'

The woman stopped talking and looked from Ellen to Alastair, then back at Ellen again.

'Who are you, anyway?' she asked. 'Police? You look like police. Oh dear, he's not in any trouble, I hope? He's a good lad, Rob. I mean, he's not right in the head anymore, not really. Him and Frankie make a right pair, the two of them. Sad when you remember them as little lads. I still think of them like that sometimes. Even though I know that's silly. You can't help it, though, can you? It's like with my friends. They all look the same to me as they did when we were in our twenties and thirties. Even though we're all the wrong side of seventy these days. We're old now. All of us. And that's sad too, I suppose.'

There had been two men last night. Rob and another, larger man.

'Who's Frankie?' Ellen asked.

The woman squinted as she focussed on Ellen. 'You never told me who you are, dear. If you're police, I expect you'll know Frankie already, won't you? Frankie Ferrari? No?' More squinting. 'You're not police then?'

Ellen smiled. 'We are, actually.'

'But you're not here to cause trouble.' This was said as a fact not a question. 'Tell me your name, dear. If I see Rob, I'll tell him you came looking for him. Can't say fairer than that now, can I?'

'I guess not,' Ellen said.

She gave the woman a card with her details on it, telling her it was urgent Rob called her as soon as possible.

'What next?' Alastair asked, as the woman walked away from

them. 'I've had a few dealings with that Ferrari guy. He's a right nutter. Want me to get him in?'

Ellen sighed. This latest business with Kevin was, as her father might say, one unholy mess. First, the discovery that Dan Harris was dead. Murdered in his flat in Bromley. Then the assault on Kevin. Finally, Baxter showing up to arrest Kevin. For murder.

'Maybe I was wrong,' Ellen said. 'Maybe it wasn't him I heard last night.'

'You don't really think that,' Alastair said.

'No,' Ellen agreed. 'The thing is, I'm not certain enough to go breaking his door down. I do want to speak to him about last night, but not like that. I suspect if we put pressure on him, he'll clam up.'

'So we just let them get away with it?' Alastair asked. 'Apart from anything else, Ma'am, it was an assault on an officer.'

Ellen reached up and touched the side of her face.

'I'll come back for York,' she said. 'And Ferrari. Our priority for now is still Jodie. With everything else that's happened in the last twenty-four hours, we're in danger of forgetting that. Whatever Rob York did or didn't do, one thing we can be pretty sure of is that he isn't the person who has Jodie. Yes, we need to have a word. But my guess is that Martine Reynolds told Rob that Kevin was our main suspect and there was every chance he was the person who killed Molly, too. In his fragile state, there's every chance that tipped poor Rob over the edge. I'll tell you one thing, Alastair, don't let that Reynolds woman come anywhere near me.

If she does, I won't be held accountable.

'Come on. I need caffeine. Let's grab a coffee in the park and decide on our next steps.'

Like the last time, Ellen sat outside the café in Mountsfield Park, enjoying the view. She watched a pair of workmen clearing a section of the park beside the playground. A van was parked nearby, she could just make out the name Medway Maintenance printed along the side of it.

'Remind me,' Ellen said. 'What was the name of the firm Fletcher worked for?'

'Medway Maintenance,' Alastair replied. 'They're here today, too. Look.'

Both workmen were dressed in green overalls and, even from where she was sitting, it was obvious from their body language that the shorter, older man was the one in charge. Every so often, he'd point to a new area of the park, issue some instructions and the bigger man would lumber over obediently and start doing whatever it was he'd been told to.

'Back in a sec.' Ellen drained her coffee and wandered across. It was only when she got closer that she realised she'd seen them before. The shorter man was the one who'd nearly run her over in Manor Park.

He obviously recognised her as well and didn't seem too eager to speak when she approached him.

'We've got a lot on this morning,' he said. 'This better be quick. Who did you say you were again?'

'I didn't,' Ellen said. 'Just said I wanted to ask you a few questions, that's all. Starting with your name, sir?'

The man leaned on the spade he was carrying and looked at her. 'And what makes you think I'd talk to you?' he asked.

'Because you don't have a choice.' Ellen flashed her warrant card. 'You can either answer my questions here or we can pop across to Lewisham station. Might take a few hours and bugger up your day but, believe me, your well-being is way down my list of priorities right now.'

The man shrugged. 'What is you want to know?'

'Molly York,' Ellen said. 'Remember her? Little girl taken from this very park three years ago. One of your staff was in the frame for it, if I'm not mistaken.'

'They let him go, though, didn't they?' the man said. 'Not fair on him if you lot start digging all that up again. Not fair at all.'

'We'll decide what's fair and what's not, Mr ...?'

'Wilson,' he said. 'Simon Wilson.'

'And you were Brian Fletcher's boss at the time?'

Wilson's eyes slid across to the big man, who had stopped working and was standing beside a pile of branches, staring at Ellen. Fletcher, she realised with a jolt. A tall, overweight man in his mid-twenties. Right now, he looked terrified.

'What about it?' Wilson said. Then, shouting across to Fletcher. 'Get back to work, Brian! Nothing for you to worry about here. I want those branches cleared now, you hear?'

'Not a bother, Simon,' the other man said. 'I'll get to it now.'

'Good of you to keep him on after all that business with Molly,' Ellen said. 'Not many people would do a thing like that.'

'His old man and I were mates,' Wilson said. 'Sort of mates, at any rate. See, Brian's mother died when he was only young and then a few years ago his father fucked off. Couldn't cope. Just upped and left poor Brian to fend for himself. I came out to the house one morning and found him there all alone. Don't know what he would have done if it wasn't for me. Look, officer—'

'Detective Inspector,' Ellen corrected.

Wilson shrugged. 'Whatever. Brian's had a hard time, see? He's not a bad bloke. A few sandwiches short of a picnic, but that's all. That business with Molly, he'd never do something like that. He's too soft. Besides, he was innocent. Your lot had to admit that in the end. It wasn't right, you know, the way they focussed on Brian. Just because he's a bit backward. Wasn't right at all. The last thing he needs is to have to relive it all again. That wouldn't be right. Do you understand?'

Ellen understood all right. For whatever reason, Wilson saw himself as Fletcher's protector. And his determination not to let her speak to Fletcher left her wanting to speak to him more than ever. Something she planned to do sooner rather than later.

Thanking Wilson for his time, she said goodbye and went back to Alastair.

'Drink up,' she said. 'Let's get back to the station. I want to read everything you've pulled together on Wilson and Fletcher. There's something funny going on there and, whatever it is, I want to get to the bottom of it.'

She walked back to the car with Alastair. At the park gate, she turned and looked back at the two Medway Maintenance men. Simon Wilson was standing where she'd left him. Hands on his hips, staring across the park right at her. Ellen remembered her first encounter with Wilson and, with great restraint, resisted the urge to flick her middle finger at him a second time.

12:45

The banging on the door felt like it would never stop. Every time she hit it, the noise was a train running through his head. There she went again, bang-bang-bang, and shouting out his name.

Rob groaned and curled his body tighter into himself, pulling his legs up and wrapping his arms around them. He was sitting on the kitchen floor, pressed up against the washing machine. It wasn't comfortable, but he didn't have the energy to get up. He had no idea how long he'd been sitting here.

He was having problems concentrating. His memory of last night was fragmented, like he was trying to see his reflection in a broken mirror. He couldn't get the bits to fit together properly.

Every time he closed his eyes he could feel Hudson struggling against him and the stench of the man's piss was stuck to the insides of his nostrils. He'd thought it would feel good. Finally get the bastard who'd hurt his little girl. Except at the time, well, it hadn't felt the way he'd expected.

Frankie had bloody loved it. Shit, he was off his head. Worse than Rob had thought. At least Frankie wasn't a coward, though. When it came to the crunch, Rob had chickened out, hadn't he? Seen the fuzz and freaked. Threw Frankie off the copper and legged it.

On Burnt Ash Hill they walked back to the bus stop together. Frankie never said, but Rob could sense his disappointment. He'd expected more and Rob had let him down. Let everyone down. Especially Molly.

Outside, the policewoman banged on the door again. *Go away*, Rob pleaded silently. *Just go away and leave me alone.* There was a bottle lying on the floor beside him. He picked it up and emptied what was left into his mouth. Hot whiskey burned his throat, his gut twisting as it landed in his empty stomach.

'What now?' Frankie had asked after they got off the bus.

Rob shook his head. 'Catch up with you soon,' he'd said, turning and leaving his mate standing alone in the street. He knew Frankie didn't want to stop. Mad fucker probably wanted to carry on drinking, but Rob had had enough. He felt sick. He just wanted to come home and get some sleep.

But he hadn't been able to sleep. He'd sat in here all night, drinking and crying and trying not to think about the way he'd felt when he'd seen the knife and knew what Frankie was planning to do with it.

Later, he'd gone upstairs to get some sleep, but he couldn't face the empty bed and the silence of the bedrooms. So he came back down and sat here instead.

As the first cracks of daylight pushed their way underneath the red blind in the kitchen, Rob's mind started to clear. He had to finish off what he'd started. Kevin Hudson still had to pay. Only this time, Rob would do things the right way. On his own, without involving Frankie.

Frankie meant well, but he had been a mistake. Rob shouldn't have listened to him. Should have made his own plan. He tried to stand up, but his legs gave way and he fell down again. He lay on the floor, sorting things out in his head.

He was still there many hours later, long after Ellen Kelly had been and gone, and long after the light behind the blind had started to fade, marking the end of another day, in a string of endless days, that he had to get through on his own, without Molly.

17:00

It had been a pig of a day and the prospect of a half-hour break and a cool beer was all that got Ellen through the afternoon. She was late getting to The Dacre and Dai was already inside, waiting for her. The pint glass in front of him was nearly empty. Ellen bought him a refill, along with a half of lager for herself. A pint would have better served her needs but she was driving.

'You were right,' Dai said, once Ellen was settled in the chair opposite him.

Ellen, glass midway to her lips, paused. 'What about?'

'Ed. He's been keeping something from you.'

Ellen drank some lager, thinking the liquid might help the sudden dryness in her throat. It made no difference. She thought of the time spent over the past few weeks with Abby Roberts. The way her feelings towards the FLO were gradually changing. She hoped Dai wasn't about to tell her something that would change them back again.

'He's sick,' Dai said. 'Very sick. Cancer. Hodgkin's Lymphoma. In the advanced stages, I'm afraid.'

Ellen opened her mouth to say something. No words came out.

'I had a hell of a job finding out what was going on,' Dai continued. 'It's clear Ed doesn't want anyone to know.'

'Advanced stages,' Ellen said. 'What does that mean?'

She knew the answer, but needed to hear Dai say it.

'The cancer's spread,' Dai said. 'He doesn't have long left. Six months at most.'

'No.' She wouldn't believe it. Ed had looked tired recently and he hadn't been himself. But cancer? It wasn't possible. He didn't look ill enough for one thing.

'You've made a mistake,' she said. 'I'm not sure who your source is, but whoever it is, they're not reliable.'

'Andrea told me,' Dai said. 'She's going out of her mind. Can't get Ed to stop working. There's no mistake, Ellen, love. None at all, I'm afraid.'

There was a photo on Baxter's desk. It appeared in Ellen's head, lodged there, refusing to move. Baxter and Andrea on holiday in Cyprus. Both of them tanned and smiling. Ed was looking directly at whoever took the photo, so that when you looked at it, it seemed he was smiling straight at you. Andrea, on the other hand, was looking up at her husband. Smiling. Her feelings for him as evident as if she was speaking the words. *I love you.*

The photo had only been taken a couple of years ago. Before Baxter messed things up. Ellen wondered if Andrea knew about the affair.

'What's he playing at?' she asked. 'Why isn't he with his family making the most of every moment he's got left? What the bloody hell is he thinking?'

'He can't face it,' Dai said. 'That's what Andrea thinks. He's thrown himself into work as a way of blocking out what's happening. And, of course, he sees this as his last chance. He couldn't save Molly but, with a bit of luck, he might just be able to save Jodie before it's too late.'

'That's bullshit,' Ellen said. 'If he's serious about saving Jodie, can't he see he's a liability, not an asset? He's too messed up to focus properly on what we need to do.'

'I know that, and you know that,' Dai agreed. 'But the question for both of us is, how do we convince Ed?'

20:00

There's pink wallpaper with a pattern of tiny trains on it. Rows of little trains, all different colours. Green and red and yellow and blue. There are children inside the trains. I can see their faces. They're smiling and wearing hats that match the colour of the train they're sitting in.

I think the trains are going to the seaside and the children are on a school trip. Except when I think of a school trip, it makes me think of my own friends, especially Grace and Holly. And when I think about them, it makes me sad. I wonder if they think about me a lot. Do they wonder where I am? Do they miss me? I hope so.

There's this one thing I keep remembering. A sleepover at Grace's during the Christmas holidays. We stayed up really late, watching films on the little TV in her bedroom. And afterwards the three of us went to bed in the big airbed that Grace's mum put up for us.

And we talked about all the things we want to do when we get older. Grace made us promise we'd be best friends forever. We linked hands and said it over and over: 'Best friends forever.'

I'm saying it now. Whispering it the way we did that night because we didn't want Grace's mum to hear us.

'Best friends forever. Best friends forever.'

And if I try really, really hard, I can imagine they're here with me. Grace and Holly. I imagine I can feel their fingers in mine and they're whispering it too. And when we say it, it's to the rhythm of the trains and it's all beating like a piece of music in my head.

Best friends forever, best friends forever, best friends forever ...

21:30

Ellen sat in the sitting room, a glass of Merlot by her side and Count Basie on the sound system. Music to make you want to get up and dance. Made her think of Vinny, how he'd never let his total lack of rhythm get in the way of a good bop.

She closed her eyes and let herself remember him. She pictured him at their wedding reception. The two of them dancing to Dean Martin. *Amore.* Naffest song in the world. Her and Vinny, surrounded by all their friends. All of them singing along. Moon hitting their eyes like a big pizza pie. World shining like they'd had too much wine. *Amore.*

Dean Martin followed by Nick Cave's *Into Your Arms.* Vinny's choice. She still had all his CDs. Never listened to them. She couldn't. Even now, if she heard Johnny Cash or Nick Cave, she had to block out the sound. Their voices evoked too many memories.

And now, more sadness. Ed Baxter's face joined Vinny's. Ellen opened her eyes. She needed to speak to Ed. Should have done it today, right after she left Dai. Only she couldn't face it. How did you even begin to have that conversation?

Her glass was empty. She could do with more wine, but knew that was a bad idea. Instead, she rinsed her glass in the sink, drank some water and switched the lights off. She would have a long, hot bath and get an early night for once.

She was at the top of the stairs when the doorbell rang, the sudden sound making her jump. She waited, holding her breath to see what would happen next. She rarely had unannounced visitors and never this late. An image of Billy Dunston flashed before her. The day she'd seen him outside her house, staring in at her through the dining-room window. Trying to intimidate her. Frighten her from pursuing the truth about her husband's death. As if.

At least it couldn't be Dunston this time.

When the bell went again, she sneaked downstairs and into the dining room, where she was able to peek out the window. A figure stood in the doorway. It was too dark to make out anything except the silhouette.

The bell rang again and Ellen opened the door quickly, before the noise woke one of the children up. Her irritation turned to fear when she saw Abby Roberts standing on her doorstep.

'Jodie?' Ellen asked.

'Oh gosh,' Abby said. 'No. I'm sorry. I just, well, I wanted to make sure you're okay.'

'Okay?' Ellen asked. 'Course I'm okay. Why wouldn't I be? Listen, Abby, I don't mean to be rude but I'm shattered. I was just on my way to bed, actually.'

'Sorry,' Abby said again. 'I should go. It's just, I can't stop thinking about what happened. Yesterday, I mean.'

'And that's it?'

Abby nodded. 'Some guy punched you in the face and kicked you in the stomach. It was nasty. I know because I was there. And I feel awful that I didn't stop that horrible man before he hurt you. I can't stop thinking about it. Can't stop seeing it, over and over in my head. The big man coming for you. I tried to stop him, Ellen. I really did. But he just shoved me off him like I was, like I was a little fly or something. I'm so sorry.'

Ellen didn't know what to say. It hadn't occurred to her for a second that Abby would hold herself responsible for what had happened. Why should she?

'Abby.'

The FLO looked on the verge of tears. Crying was the last thing Ellen could cope with right now.

'Oh bugger it,' Ellen said. 'Come in. You look as if you could do with a drink.'

Ellen refilled her wine glass and held the bottle towards Abby, who shook her head.

'I won't be able to get out of bed in the morning if I have any more,' she said. 'I've no head for wine. I don't know how you do it.'

'Do what?' Ellen asked.

'Knock back the wine like that,' Abby said. 'I'd be on the floor if I drank that much.'

There was nothing accusatory in Abby's voice, but Ellen felt defensive nonetheless. What business was it of Abby's how much she drank, anyway?

'I'm not much of a drinker,' she said. 'Actually, rephrase that. I wasn't much of a drinker. Since Vinny died though, I do seem to drink more. Loneliness, I suppose.'

And depression, she thought, but didn't say. The wine just made things more bearable. Things like finding out someone you'd worked with for the last fifteen years had a terminal illness and wasn't going to be around for much longer.

She drank more wine without tasting it, keen for it to do its job and take the edge off the dark mood she couldn't seem to shake.

'Are you okay?' Abby asked.

Ellen nodded. Then shook her head. 'Sorry. I'm crap company, I know.'

'Do you want to talk about it?' Abby asked.

Ellen wondered if Abby knew. She'd assumed the tension between the FLO and Baxter was to do with their affair, but what if Abby had somehow found out about Baxter's illness and had confronted him about it?

'I know so little about you,' Ellen said. 'Do you have family? A boyfriend? Brothers and sisters? Tell me something about yourself.'

Her eyes flickered to Abby's ring finger. No ring.

'I had a brother,' Abby said. 'But he died a few years ago. Now it's just me. Both my parents have been dead for years. Andy, that's my brother, he looked after me when Mum died. I was only sixteen. If it wasn't for Andy, I doubt I'd have coped, to be honest. I adored him.'

She looked so vulnerable when she said that. Hunched up on the sofa, hands wrapped around her empty wine glass, Abby seemed closer to Ellen's children's age than her own.

'How terrible,' Ellen said.

Abby shrugged. 'It wasn't easy. Still isn't. He'll be dead four years this summer. God, even saying that. It seems so impossible that he's gone. I went through a period of trying to understand why it happened. Trying to find some meaning in it. You see, I couldn't accept that it was possible for him to be there one minute – so full of life and love, so vital – and then he's just gone. I thought, I think I thought there had to be some reason for it. But there's not, is there?'

'Shit happens,' Ellen said. 'All the time, bad things happen to good people. It's the hardest lesson to learn, I think. And I hate the fact my own kids have had to learn it at such a young age. It doesn't seem fair.'

She stopped speaking, aware that she was babbling. The wine's fault. If she wasn't careful, she'd be sharing all sorts of intimacies with Abby Roberts that she would inevitably regret.

'Andy was in a car accident,' Abby said. 'Like your husband.'

Vinny's death was no accident, Ellen wanted to tell her. Billy Dunston killed him on purpose.

'What happened?' she said instead.

'He was driving home after a night out. Car coming in the other direction. Driver was drunk and lost control. Crashed head-on into Andy's car. He was dead by the time the ambulance arrived. Oh listen to me, would you? I'm sorry. I didn't come here to talk about myself. I just wanted to make sure you were all right. That's all. I really should be going.'

She stood up, her face flushed, although whether from embarrassment or wine, Ellen couldn't tell.

'Don't go yet,' Ellen said. 'There's something I need to ask you. Sit down.' Then, when Abby hesitated. 'Please?'

'It's about Ed,' Abby said. 'Isn't it?'

'I've heard he's had it in for you these past few months,' Ellen said. 'I wanted to check if you're okay or if you need to talk about it.'

'Really?' Abby asked. 'Or is this your opportunity to gloat? You made it clear at the time how you felt about what happened. Why would you care now whether I'm okay or not?'

Fair point.

'CID is tough for everyone,' Ellen said. 'Possibly even more so for women. There aren't many of us. Not enough, in fact. The least we can do is stick together and try to help each other out. I don't approve of what you did. You're right about that. But that doesn't mean I'm going to stand by and watch you be treated badly, either. We're in the same team, Abby. And, as a more senior officer, I'm responsible for looking out for you.'

'It's not easy,' Abby said. 'But not for the reasons you think.'

'You don't know what I think,' Ellen said.

'No, but I can guess. Okay. Look. Me and the boss. It was a one-off. Well, maybe more than once, but it was never serious. A fling. I knew it. He knew it. And when it ended, we were both fine with it.'

'So what changed?' Ellen asked.

'He did,' Abby said. 'He came up to me at work one day. A few months ago. Asked if I was free to meet for a drink. I could see something was wrong so I agreed, even though I wasn't sure it was what I wanted. I assumed his wife had found out about us and that's why he needed to speak to me. Except it wasn't that.'

'He told you about the cancer,' Ellen guessed.

Abby's eyes widened. 'You know about it?'

'Yes, but don't ask me how I found out,' Ellen said. 'Christ, Abby. If you've known all this time, why the hell haven't you done anything about it?'

'Don't you think I've tried?' Abby replied. 'We've had a massive argument over it. I've told him he has to tell someone, but he's refusing point-blank. I thought he'd come around and maybe he would have. If it wasn't for this case. I can't get through to him, Ellen. He's so bloody determined to find Jodie first and he swears that once he's done that, he'll step down.'

'You're sure there's nothing else?' Ellen asked.

'Like what?'

'Like, you're definitely okay,' Ellen said. Then, with the help of the wine, she decided just to come out and say it. 'I've been worried maybe you were pregnant and that's what the fall-out with Baxter was all about.'

Abby burst out laughing. 'Oh my Lord. Did you really? Oh no. I don't look pregnant, do I? You're not trying to tell me I've got fat. I've been so good recently. I thought I was losing weight, not putting it on.'

'You look fine,' Ellen said. 'It was just a mad idea. Would have explained, I suppose, why Baxter was being so horrible to you. Mind you, he's being horrible to me too and I'm certainly not up the duff, either.'

Later, Ellen called a cab for Abby and walked her to the front door when it arrived. As they said goodbye, Ellen asked about the driver who had killed Abby's brother.

'He served six months,' Abby said. 'And when he got out, the first thing he did was get in touch with me. Said he couldn't live with what he'd done. Begged my forgiveness.'

'What did you do?' Ellen asked.

'I forgave him,' Abby said. 'When it came down to it, I didn't see that I had a choice. I could see he was devastated by what had happened. In his own way, he was hurting as much as I was. Meeting him, hearing how sorry he was. It helped. Really.'

Briefly, Ellen's nostrils filled with the smell of charred flesh. She remembered the way Dunston's blood had felt on her skin, warm and sickening.

'I'm not sure I could do that,' she said. 'Forgive, I mean.'

'I found it easier,' Abby said. 'The alternative, to let it eat away at me until it destroyed me, I couldn't do that. Life's too precious to waste it obsessing over things that have already happened. At some point, we all need to close the door on the past and focus on appreciating what we've got now. That's my take on it, anyway.'

'You think I was wrong,' Ellen said. 'Don't you?'

'Dunston?' Abby asked. 'It's none of my business. You think I slept with Teddy just to get my promotion. That's none of your business, either. Maybe we'd both get on better with each other if we remembered that.'

Ellen giggled. She couldn't help it. Blamed the wine, even though she knew it wasn't just that.

'Teddy?' she asked.

Abby's mouth twitched, like she might smile too any second now. 'I think he prefers to be called Baxter at work,' she said. 'Teddy's what he calls himself in, um, private.'

The picture was there again now. Abby and Baxter in his office. Abby on her knees, his trousers down around his ankles. Ellen shook her head.

'I hope to Christ it was for a promotion,' she said. 'I'd hate to think you did it because you actually liked the old bastard.'

'Maybe I found him attractive,' Abby said. 'Or maybe he reminded me of someone. My brother, say. Either way, it doesn't matter. Just as it doesn't matter what really happened with you and Billy Dunston. Goodnight, Ellen. Thanks for the wine and the chat. I'll see you tomorrow.'

And before Ellen could respond, Abby turned and ran out to

the taxi waiting for her outside. She jumped inside and the car pulled away, leaving Ellen standing alone on the doorstep.

The rumble of traffic from Trafalgar Road drifted through the quiet night air. Here on Annandale Road, all was quiet. So quiet that, for a moment, it was possible to believe time had stopped and she would stand here forever. A lone figure in a darkened doorway, looking blankly into the night, unable to move or speak, her mind full of images she didn't want to see and the silent screams of every child who'd ever disappeared or ever would. And she wished the children would disappear from her mind, but they wouldn't. They never did, and she knew they never would.

22:10

Brian tried to lift the cup, but his hand was shaking so badly he only succeeded in spilling the tea. Not that it mattered. It was cold by now anyway. It had slopped onto the sleeve of his jumper and that felt cold as well. Cold and damp, like his trousers. He could smell the stuff on his trousers too, and when he moved it felt all sticky between his legs. Sticky and smelly. With stuff that had come from him.

Disgusted, he pushed himself off the chair, and started ripping his trousers off, right there in the kitchen. He'd have to throw these slacks away. Even if he washed them properly, he didn't think he'd ever get rid of the smell.

He didn't want to look but couldn't help himself. It was all smeared along the inner legs of his trousers, little bits of it glistening on his thighs and the hairs around his you-know-what. Sticky and slimy. Like glue.

The images still flickered in his head, snap shots of what had started it. Marion on the bed with her skirt up, showing him her knickers. The feel of her soft skin when he touched her. The way she let him touch her. Smiling up at him. Whispering in his ear, her breath all hot and tickly.

'It's all right, Brian. You know I don't mind.'

Abruptly, Marion disappeared, erased by other images, other memories. His hands smeared with Daddy's stuff. The sick, salty taste of it. Daddy's voice in his ear now, his hand on his head, telling Brian if he was a good boy, he'd do what his Daddy told him to. Except afterwards, Daddy called him a dirty little bastard and hit him.

Marion should have stopped him.

Little bitch probably did it on purpose.

No point arguing with Daddy when he was in a mood. Besides, maybe Daddy was right and Marion had done it deliberately, just to make him feel bad or something.

But it wasn't Marion! She hadn't even been here. It was all in his head. He looked fearfully around the kitchen, checking he was alone, that it really had just been his imagination. His dirty, monstrous mind.

Marion would never do something like that. She was good

and kind and everything that was right about the world.

Except …

He couldn't help noticing it. She was getting awful dirty, so she was, and there was a funny smell off her that seemed to be getting worse.

She's a dirty little cow, that's why.

'Twinkle, twinkle, little STAAAAR.' Another Marion favourite. Mum used to sing it when she put them to bed.

Why do you think she's so keen for you to touch her?

'How I wonder what you ARE.'

Marion was crying when he went to see her yesterday. Threw herself at him the minute he walked through the door, screaming and begging him to let her go. Snot running down her face. Sticky and slimy.

He shivered. It was freezing here in the kitchen. He needed another cup of tea. One he would drink this time, not let go cold while he lost himself. The Bad Thing wouldn't happen again. He didn't know what had got into him. It was like he'd gone mad for a minute.

On the shelf by the kettle there was a box. It had donuts inside. He'd bought them on his way home. Donuts with pink icing on the top. He was looking forward to seeing her little face light up when he showed them to her.

Outside was dark. How had it got dark without him even noticing? At this time of year, the days were so short you'd wonder how to fit anything into them at all. Night again and it felt like the last one had only been gone a few hours.

Using the dirty trousers, he wiped himself down as best he could before going upstairs to put on his other pair. After that, he'd have a nice cup of tea and take the donuts out to Marion. Donuts and a bit of the *Rainbow* crowd. What more did they need?

In the background, Daddy was still talking, but Brian ignored him. Just upped the singing a bit and concentrated really hard on blocking out the voice and pretending Daddy wasn't here at all. It was a good trick that. Already Daddy's voice was fading and the words had stopped making any sort of sense. Just random sounds, floating around the inside of Brian's head like someone had accidentally dropped them in there.

Little tart. Dirty bastard. Like her mother. Like that, Brian. Good boy.

'Stop!'

He opened his eyes, the sound of his own voice frightening him. When he realised what he'd done, he started laughing. Roaring like a bloody mad man in his own kitchen. Pull yourself together, mate. Shouting like that and half-scaring yourself to death.

It was only later, after he'd drunk his tea and was carrying the donuts down to the shed that he realised Daddy's voice had gone from his head. He smiled then. It was going to be a fine old evening, all right. He unlocked the door, pulling back the bolts one by one. A fine old evening indeed.

TUESDAY,
22 FEBRUARY

09:20

The phone call came as Ellen was pulling into the car park at work. She didn't recognise the number and nearly didn't answer. Changing her mind at the last moment, she flipped it open and held it to her ear.

'Ellen Kelly.'

Silence at first, then a man's voice. 'I need to see you.'

It took a moment before she recognised him.

'Kevin? Where the hell are you?'

'I'm in Eastbourne,' he said. 'Can you come?'

Before leaving for Eastbourne, Ellen attended the morning briefing. The PM on Harris was back. Time of death anything between a week and ten days. Which put Hudson nicely in the frame. The report also confirmed what they already knew. Harris had been shot. Single bullet between the eyes. In Ellen's opinion, it bore all the hallmarks of a professional hit and she didn't see how Kevin Hudson could have done something like that. Baxter disagreed. Which was why, after the briefing, Ellen decided not to tell him where she was going. Mumbling something about following a lead, she got out of there as quickly as she could and hot-legged it to Eastbourne.

She drove south, the suburbs of South London disappearing as green countryside replaced Victorian terraces. London – there one minute, gone the next. Just like Jodie.

Ellen had arranged to meet Kevin in a café on the seafront.

When she arrived, he was waiting for her, sitting on the decking area right on the beach. He was smoking and the smell of nicotine sent a surge of longing through her.

'Thanks for coming,' he said, throwing the cigarette to the ground and stubbing it out with his foot.

She nodded at the café. 'It's too cold to sit here. Let's go inside.'

'Too many people,' Kevin said. 'Can we walk instead?'

'Let's go then,' Ellen said, lifting the collar of her coat as a bracing sea wind wrapped itself around her neck.

They walked along the seafront. A scatter of childhood memories distracted Ellen – day trips to seaside towns when she was a child. Running along Brighton pier to the arcade at the end, the air full of the smell of chips and salty sea. Melted ice-cream dripping down her wrists, trying to walk on the pebbled beach and falling over, hurting her knees. Her parents. Michael and Bridget Flanagan, who'd given Sean and Ellen the best childhood possible.

'I wasn't sure you were going to show,' Kevin said.

He looked wrecked, she thought. Like he hadn't slept or washed or eaten in days.

'I told you I would,' she said. 'Where are you staying, anyway?'

'A cheap and nasty guesthouse. It's a dump, but I can't afford anything better.'

Ellen stopped walking. 'What's going on, Kevin?' she asked.

'It's to do with Dan Harris,' he said.

'I worked that one out,' Ellen said. 'He's dead, but then, you know that already.'

'I didn't do it.'

'Right,' Ellen said. 'Let's find somewhere warm and you can tell me all about it.'

They chose a trendy bar in Little Chelsea that was almost empty at this time of day. Ellen ordered two cappuccinos and they sat down at the back of the cavernous space.

'No one will hear us back here,' she said. 'Besides, even if someone was trying to listen in, they wouldn't be able to over that damn music.'

'Not a fan of house, then?'

'I don't even know what that is,' Ellen said. 'Right. Here's your coffee. Tell me about you and Dan Harris.'

'Prison messed me up,' Kevin began. 'Big time. Because Harris was underage, the other prisoners had me down as a nonce. I had the shit kicked out of me more times than I can remember. By the time I got out I was a total fuck-up. I still am. Look. See the way my hands shake? Never stop. Haven't been able to work, I'm on anti-depressants and my relationship with Helen is non-existent. Even before this business with Jodie, we'd more or less stopped talking to each other.

'I became obsessed. It started nearly a year ago. Around the same time I realised nothing was ever going to be the same again. And I realised it was all Harris' fault.'

'So you decided to track him down,' Ellen guessed.

Kevin nodded. 'I wanted to confront him, let him know what

he'd done. No, that's not strictly true. I wanted to hurt him. Revenge. That's what I wanted.'

'And how were you going to get it?'

'I don't know,' he said. 'Hadn't thought it through properly. At first, I just concentrated on finding him. It was easier than I thought. His mother still lives in the same house in Downham. I started watching the place. Harris came to visit one day, and I followed him. All the way back to his flat in Bromley. It was that easy.'

He paused and drank some coffee. When he started speaking again, he wouldn't look directly at Ellen, preferring to focus on a spot somewhere over her head.

'I just wanted him to pay. It was little things at first. Rubbish through his letterbox; another time I super-glued his doorbell. After that, I got a bit spooked, thought he'd start looking for whoever was doing that stuff. I tried to stay away, but it was no good. Like I said, I was obsessed. I knew I had to confront him. Face to face.'

Kevin's eyes slid to Ellen's and he gave a small laugh, utterly devoid of humour.

'Man to man, I suppose. So I left him another note. Slipped it through his letterbox and told him I wanted to meet. I didn't give my name. Just a time and a place.'

'Monday, 14 February?' Ellen guessed.

A brief look of surprise crossed Kevin's face before he nodded.

'It's why I was in such a hurry,' he said. 'I'd arranged to meet

Harris in Bromley that morning. I didn't want to be late.'

'What were you planning to do when you got there?'

Kevin shrugged. 'I just wanted him to know, if that makes sense.'

Ellen thought of Billy Dunston and nodded. It made perfect sense.

'We'd arranged to meet at the entrance to the Glades,' Kevin continued. 'You know, the big shopping centre in Bromley? But he didn't turn up. I knew he wouldn't. So I went to his house. He lived on this shitty estate in North Bromley. Ground-floor flat. One of those places with the front doors all facing out onto a communal square of concrete. Full of druggies and alkies. No families as far as I could tell. Perfect place for a scumbag like Harris.

'I knew he was dealing. I'd worked that out for myself, watching the steady trail of visitors to the flat. When I say dealing, Ellen, I'm not talking big-time. Shots of skunk to the local crackheads. Pretty sure he was on something himself. Seemed fairly out of it the few times he ever came out of the place.

'First thing I noticed, his door was open. Not wide open, just a bit. I half-thought he'd done it on purpose, pictured him waiting inside for me. I nearly turned then and went home. I remember the way my heart was that morning, thumping so hard it hurt. I was shit scared.

'I don't know how long I stood outside before I got enough courage to step inside. There was this terrible smell. Shit and piss and something else as well. Burnt flesh. As I walked down the hallway towards the room at the back, the smell got worse.

'I think I knew, even before I reached the room. It was like being in a dream, though. I wanted to turn back, but I couldn't stop myself. My body just kept moving forward, getting closer and closer to that smell.

'Everything was so still and quiet. A dead silence all around me that added to the feeling of being in a dream. When I reached the door, it took a moment for me to work out where the smell was coming from. He was behind the sofa. I saw his legs at first. Two feet, toes pointed up towards the ceiling. No shoes or socks.

'I don't know why I went in there. I keep going over that. Wondering if there was some sick part of me that wanted to know.' He shook his head. 'I haven't told anyone until now. He was dead, of course. Lying face up, eyes wide open, staring straight at me. Dead eyes. And he had this big hole in his forehead. I can't stop thinking about it.'

Ellen reached across the table, took his shaking hand in hers. As she held it, she wondered how on earth she was going to persuade him to hand himself over to Baxter and tell him the truth about the morning Jodie disappeared.

11:00

'I'm not Marion.'

There. I've said it. He's at the door, but when he hears me he turns *around, and there's something in his face I don't like and I'm wishing I could swallow the words. Grab them back from the air and pretend I'd never said them. It's too late for that.*

He walks back to where I'm sitting and stands over me. 'What do you mean?'

And that's such a stupid question that I get angry so I say it again. 'I'm not Marion.'

Then he gives one of those big, stupid sighs and he sits down beside me and puts his hand on my leg. Stupid, stupid Brian. I pull my leg away even though I know he hates when I do that, but I don't care.

'Why are you saying this now?' he asks. His voice is all quiet, but I can see he's angry. I hate him.

'I asked you a question.'

He's staring at the TV, even though it's turned off. I wonder if he's so stupid, he thinks there's something there. Probably.

'I'm not just saying it now,' I tell him. 'I told you loads of times to start with, but you wouldn't listen. I'm not your sister. My name's Jodie. Jodie Frances Hudson. Frances after my Nanny.'

There's this girl in Year 3. Kayla Jackson. She has Down's Syndrome and it makes her face look a bit funny and she's a bit simple. Kayla's brother, Ben, is in my class. No one treats Kayla like a normal person. The teachers and other parents are always super-nice to her and the other kids are never allowed to be mean to her. Not ever.

I wonder if that's what Brian's got or if it's something else. Whatever it is, I don't care.

'Stop it.' He stands up so quickly I fall back when the bed lifts.

I hit my head against the wall and it hurts. Really hurts. Above me, Brian is shouting.

'Stop playing games with me, Marion. If you carry on like this, Daddy will be in to sort you out and you don't want that, do you?'

I try to get up, but he shoves a big hand into my chest, pushing me back and then he's leaning down, pushing his face into mine.

'Do you?'

Do I what? I don't know what I'm meant to say. He's too close and my head hurts and I can feel that I'm starting to cry. I don't want to cry. Don't want him to see me, but it's too late. His hand reaches out and I think he's going to hit me even though he doesn't. He's trying to wipe my tears away. When his finger touches my cheek I think I'll be sick.

'Give over,' he says 'There's no need for tears. You were only playing with me, weren't you? It's just if Daddy hears you, he'll lose it. You know that.'

And then it's like a volcano erupting inside me and I'm screaming at him and hitting him and telling him what a stupid, fat idiot he is and how much I really, really hate him and his stinky body and dirty clothes. And he's just staring at me, his face all sad like I've done something wrong. Like this is my fault. And that's what does it.

I pull my head right back and fill my mouth, then spit as hard as I can right into his big, stupid face.

13:00

'You can't stay hiding forever,' Ellen said. 'And the longer you stay on the run, the worse it'll be. Not just for you. Think of Helen and Finlay. Jodie, too. She's going to need you when she comes home, Kevin. Imagine what it will be like if you're banged up inside when she comes back?'

'I'm terrified,' Kevin said. 'Surely you can understand that?'

'Of course I can,' Ellen said. 'But that doesn't change anything. The best thing you can do is face up to this now. Running away, it won't help. Let me take you back to London. I'll do everything I can to make sure you're treated properly. You tell me you didn't kill Dan Harris and I believe you. But you need to believe me, too. Otherwise, how can you expect me to help you?'

'It's not you I'm worried about,' Kevin said.

'Ed Baxter's a good copper,' Ellen said. 'It might seem like he has it in for you, but that's not really the case. I swear to you, Kevin. Baxter's no fool. If there's no evidence to prove you killed Harris, then Baxter will be as keen as anyone to see justice done.'

'You really think so?'

'Yes,' Ellen said, trying to sound like she meant it. 'I really do.'

In the end, it wasn't as difficult as she'd thought it might be. Being on the run for two nights had been enough to show Kevin that hiding from his problems wasn't the answer to anything.

'Bromley will be handling this,' Ellen explained on the drive back to London. 'I know the DCI there. Ray Cunningham. He's a good guy. I've already called, told him we're on our way. You've already earned some brownie points by handing yourself in.'

'I'll be kept in overnight?' Kevin asked.

'Yes,' Ellen said. 'But you'll be held at the station. And they can only keep you for twenty-four hours. There's every chance you'll be back home by tomorrow evening. Even if it's on bail for now. You'll need to call Tom Abbot. Get him to meet us at the station. He'll make sure you're taken care of.'

She glanced across at Kevin. He looked apprehensive, she thought, rather than terrified.

'You're doing the right thing,' she told him.

He nodded. 'I know. I just wish it wasn't so damn difficult. You know, if it wasn't for Jodie and Finlay, I don't know if I'd even have called you. Me and Helen, our marriage was on the rocks long before any of this happened. I could probably have walked away from it. But those kids. I love them, Ellen. Love them so bad. And Jodie, I still wonder if it's really happening. I don't think, even now, it's hit me properly. I keep expecting someone to tell me it's all been a mistake. I keep remembering my life, the way we were just over a week ago. And it wasn't perfect but it wasn't so bad, either. Only I never realised, you see. I spent too much time focussing on the bad stuff and not enough time, nowhere near enough time, thinking about just how lucky I was.'

She could have churned out the usual clichés. How none of us really knows our luck until it runs out. Or some guff about life moving too fast and never having enough time to just sit back and be grateful. In the context of losing a child, all those senti-ments sounded too trite. So she stayed quiet and the rest of the journey passed in silence.

14:35

The door to Baxter's office was closed. Ellen knocked, then opened it without waiting for a reply. Ed was sitting at his desk, a half-eaten sandwich on a plate in front of him. He looked grey and tired and like he'd rather be anywhere else.

'I was wondering when you'd show up,' he said. 'Well done on catching Hudson. I'm not too happy about the way you did it, but you got him in the end. That's what matters.'

'It doesn't get us any closer to finding Jodie,' Ellen said.

'Maybe,' Baxter said. 'Maybe not. Hudson's not off my list of suspects, that's for sure. I should be angry with you, Ellen. I really should. But I'm just so glad we've got the bastard in custody. Well done.'

'Thanks,' she said.

'Was there something else?' he asked. 'Only I've got a bloody tonne of stuff to get through this afternoon.'

'Actually,' she said. 'There was something. The thing is, Ed, I'm worried about you.'

Silence. A red glow rose up Baxter's neck and across his cheeks. Oh Christ, she'd really done it now.

'And what might you be worried about?' he asked.

'You shouldn't be here,' Ellen said. 'I know you're not well. I'm sorry, Ed, but I can't sit back and pretend I don't know. It's not fair on you and it's not fair on the team. Or Jodie.'

He put his elbows on his desk and leaned forward. 'I might have known you'd work out something was wrong. And it doesn't take a genius to guess who told you, either.'

'It was no one on the team,' Ellen said.

Baxter held up his hand. 'I don't care who it was. The point is, my health is none of your damn business, Ellen. I am in charge of this investigation and I will continue to be in charge of this investigation until we find Jodie. And nothing you do or say will change that. Now, if there's nothing else, you can leave now. I've a pile of work to get through.'

'It's not working,' Ellen said. 'You're trying to solve the case quickly for the wrong reasons. I can understand that. To a point. I want to find Jodie, too. As soon as we can. But not at the expense of a proper investigation. We need to do this properly or we won't find her.'

Baxter's face now matched the stain of ketchup on the plate in front of him.

'Leave,' he said. 'Now. Before you say anything else and I'll be forced to kick you off the case for insubordination.'

'Ed, please.' She tried again. 'You need to tell someone.'

'Your last chance,' he said. 'Go. Now.'

It was useless. Like trying to punch her way through a concrete wall. She left without saying goodbye. Outside his office, she stood in the corridor, leaning against the wall and wondering what the hell to do next. The logical step was to go above his head. Speak to Nichols, Chief Superintendent. Except the man was a gobshite and the last thing Ellen wanted was any contact with Nichols that wasn't absolutely necessary.

She looked back at the door to Ed's office. Imagined him sitting in there, in pain but trying not to show it, wading his way through the pile of files on his desk, determined to find Jodie and atone for past mistakes. What then? At the end of this case he would go. She was sure of that. And that would be the end of something. Another ending in a life that seemed to have too many endings.

She couldn't think about that now. Instead, she pushed herself away from the wall and started walking down the corridor to the incident room. The afternoon was still young and she had work to do.

15:15

Brian hacked angrily at the thick stems of dead foliage near the front of the wild area. This was a section of the park they tended only twice a year, keeping it as nature intended for the rest of the time so that wildflowers could grow and the caterpillars that fed off those flowers had a chance to flourish.

Simon said they needed to start clearing out the dead remains of those plants that hadn't survived the killer frost earlier in the year. Brian had offered to do the job. It meant he could work alone and not have to chat with Simon, who was starting to drive him mad with his questions.

He knew Simon suspected something, but he didn't care. Ever since yesterday, it had been hard to care about anything. He didn't even want to think about it, but the whole incident kept replaying over and over in his head like some bloody film on a never-ending loop.

He could still feel the wet splat of her spit. Kept seeing her face, unrecognisable with rage.

My name's Jodie!

Blimey. The way she'd screamed at him. And then the big mouthful of spit, right in his face. No wonder he'd lost it. No one could blame him for that. Even Daddy would understand. If anything, Daddy would be proud of him. Tell him he handled it like a man and not some bloody pansy.

Afterwards, he'd sat outside for the longest time, looking out across the dark expanse of empty landscape towards the marshes. At nights, it was so dark where he lived you'd be mistaken for thinking that all around the house and land was just an empty void. If it wasn't for the occasional train passing in the distance, you'd think there was nothing in the world left apart from himself and his little house.

Empty. That's how he'd been feeling ever since. Once the anger died away, he was left with nothing. It was like Marion had come back with the sole purpose of destroying him all over again.

Only she wasn't Marion. He knew that now. His Marion was still out there somewhere, waiting for him to find her. And he would do that. Soon. First, he had to sort out this mess with the other girl, the one who'd pretended to be Marion but really wasn't. And once that was done, he'd be free again to focus on the only thing that mattered – finding Marion and bringing her back home.

16:30

Ellen left her car at the station and took the DLR home, thinking the walk through the park would do her some good. In fact, it just made her late. Her parents had collected the kids from school and taken them to Ellen's house. She'd arranged to meet them there and cook supper for her parents.

She walked through the park, moving fast. It was bitterly cold. The air was damp and misty and clung to her hair, skin and clothes. She wouldn't be doing this again in a hurry.

As she walked, she went back over her day, mentally ticking items off her long list of things to do. Baxter was an outstanding. She still hadn't decided what to do about that situation. Then there was Kevin. Still being held at Bromley. Ellen needed to find out how Helen was coping. She'd left a message for Abby but, so far, the FLO hadn't returned the call.

As Ellen took out her phone to try again, a group of men caught her eye. Park workers, all dressed in green overalls, cutting dead branches from the trees along the side of One Tree Hill. Some were up on ladders, while others were carrying the cut branches into a trailer parked nearby.

She swerved off the path and walked across to the men. The name on the van said Medway Maintenance, but there was no sign of Simon or Brian.

'I'm looking for Brian,' she asked the man closest to her.

He looked at her, taking his time to answer as he sized her up. 'Fletcher?' he said at last. 'Not here today. Boss has got him over at Manor Park finishing off some job.'

'By boss you mean Mr Wilson, right?'

The man nodded before bending down to gather up a fresh pile of chopped branches.

'Hang on,' Ellen said, following him as he walked over towards the trailer. 'I'd like to ask you some questions.' She showed her warrant card.

The man dumped the branches into the trailer and nodded. 'Go on then.'

'Brian Fletcher,' Ellen said. 'What can you tell me about him?'

The man sniffed and shook his head. 'Hardly know the bloke. I've only been working with Wilson's lot for a couple of weeks. Alex is the guy you need to see. I'll get him for you. Alex!' He called to the man up the ladder, cutting branches from the tree. 'Lady here wants a word.'

'Detective Inspector,' Ellen said. For all the good it did. The man had already walked away and was busy gathering up the next pile of branches.

Alex turned out to be Alexandru, a Romanian who'd been living in London for the past eight years, as he informed Ellen within the first two minutes of talking to her. He was a short, stocky man with long, dirty blond hair, piercing blue eyes and a cheeky smile.

'You speak good English,' she said. 'If I didn't know, I'd say you were from Lincolnshire or Yorkshire.'

'I worked up north first when I came to this country,' Alex replied. 'Had a girlfriend from Scunthorpe. You know Scunthorpe? It's a shithole. But this girl – Sandra Allen – she was worth it.'

'So what happened?' Ellen asked.

Alex shrugged. 'She dumped me for my best friend, Stanislav. It was a bad time. I got into a lot of trouble after that. If it wasn't for Simon, I'd have been sent back to Romania. He gave me a job, and a reference. I owe him. Big time.'

'And what about Brian?' she asked.

'What about him? Brian is a good guy, too.' Alex paused. 'He's not in any trouble, is he?'

'Not yet,' Ellen said. 'I'm investigating a missing persons case. A little girl.'

The smile dropped from Alex's face and he stiffened. Until then, he'd seemed relaxed, laidback even, using his arms expansively when he talked, and giving every indication that here was a man totally at ease with himself.

Now, he crossed his arms tightly in front of himself like a barrier.

'Brian is a good guy,' he repeated. There was a robotic tone to his voice that was new as well. 'If you think he has anything to do with this girl, then you're wrong. He's a simple guy, sure. You police, though, you get an idea into your head and that's it. Once you've decided someone is guilty, that's it. In your minds you've already got them locked up. Now, if you'll excuse me, I need to get back to work. Still a lot of branches to clear before we can finish for the day.'

As he turned to go, Ellen reached out and touched his arm. 'I'm sorry. I didn't mean to upset you.'

'You haven't,' he said. 'But I have nothing more to say to you.'

'Wait. Just one second.' She pulled a card from her wallet. 'My details. If you think of anything else, call me. A child is missing, Alex. A little girl called Jodie. I'm just trying to find her before it's too late.'

'Jodie Hudson?' Alex asked.

'You know her?'

He shook his head. 'Heard about it on the news, that's all. Like I said, I don't know anything about it. Goodbye.'

And then he was gone, picking up his electric saw and climbing back up the ladder to continue cutting dead branches.

Ellen stayed for a moment, half-hoping he might change his mind, climb back down the ladder and tell her something else. But he never even looked back at her. Eventually she turned and headed across the rest of the park, towards home.

18:00

'He's not himself this afternoon,' Ellen's mother said, following her into the kitchen. 'Has he said anything to you?'

'I haven't had a chance,' Ellen said. She'd barely been home an hour. Just enough time to get supper ready for her parents and children. She knew Pat was out of sorts, but had already decided there was nothing she could do about it until after supper.

She handed her mother a bowl of salad. 'Can you take this through, Mum?'

Mrs Flanagan eyed the salad suspiciously. 'Your father won't eat this, you know. What is it, anyway?'

'Rocket with balsamic dressing and Parmesan shavings,' Ellen said.

Her mother snorted. 'What's wrong with a bit of lettuce?'

Squeals of laughter erupted from the sitting room, making Ellen smile. Her father was playing the monster game. This basically involved him prowling around the room trying to catch Pat and Eilish. Whenever one of them got caught by the monster, the punishment was death by tickling.

'He's like a child himself,' Ellen's mother said, but she was smiling as well, and Ellen felt a sudden surge of love for her.

'I'll have a chat with Pat,' Ellen said. 'I promise, Mum. I know there was a memorial service in school today for that boy who was killed. Jamie Rider? He used to be a student at St Joseph's.'

'And you think it's reminded him of Vinny?' her mother asked.

'Sometimes everything reminds him of Vinny,' Ellen said. 'Don't worry, Mum. Whatever it is, I'll deal with it. Now, come on. Let's eat. I'm starving.'

'That rocket stuff is grand, isn't it?' Ellen's father said once the meal was over. 'Bridget, why don't we get some of that? Beats the shite out of lettuce any day of the week, I'd say.'

'Mum,' Eilish piped up. 'Why is Granddad allowed to swear but we're not?'

'Because he's a stupid old man,' Ellen's mother said. 'Who doesn't know any better. I keep telling him he's got a mouth like a sewer, Eilish, but do you think he listens to me? Of course not.'

'What's a sewer?' Eilish asked.

Ellen made eye contact with her father and smiled. 'Fancy giving me a hand clearing this away?' she asked.

In the kitchen, she turned the TV on so they could catch the news as they tidied up. Clearing the dishes and washing up had always been her father's job. The one little piece of housework her mother trusted him with.

On the news, two stories still dominated – the murder in Bromley and Jodie's disappearance. So far, the press hadn't made a connection between the two cases, mainly because Harris' ID hadn't been made public yet. Soon, that would change and Ellen knew the first journalist to come sniffing around would be Martine bloody Reynolds, joining the dots and making a gruesome picture she could use to shift copies of her rag.

'Is that the girl you're looking for?' Ellen's father asked as Jodie's face appeared on the TV screen. 'Terrible business. Did I read somewhere that the father's the main suspect?'

'Don't believe what you read in the papers,' Ellen said. 'You know that, Dad.'

Before her father could answer, disruption from the sitting room distracted them both. Pat was shouting. This was followed by the sitting-room door slamming shut and the clunk-clunk of his footsteps running up the stairs.

Ellen rolled her eyes at her father. 'This has been coming all evening,' she said. 'Leave him to me.'

Upstairs, the door to Pat's bedroom was closed. Ellen pressed her ear against it and listened. Heard Pat crying. Big, shuddering sobs that cut through her. She knocked on the door and went in without waiting for him to answer.

He was lying face down on his cabin bed, arms wrapped around his head, his little body shaking as he cried.

'Pat?'

Ellen climbed the ladder and lay down beside him. Tentatively, she reached out and put her hand on his head. He didn't brush it away, which she took as a good sign.

'Pat, love. What is it?'

'We were playing Blink with Nanny, and Eilish cheated and

Nanny let her and it's not fair because I was winning. Nanny always lets Eilish cheat just because she's younger than me. But I don't get why we have to let her. I hate them both. I hate Nanny and I hate Eilish and I'm not playing any more stupid games with either of them.'

'I'll have a word with Eilish,' Ellen said. 'Cheating isn't nice, you're right. And it's not fair on you. I do understand that. But it's not worth getting so upset about either, Pat.'

'How do *you* know? Just 'cause you don't get upset about anything.'

Where the hell had that come from?

'Of course I get upset,' she said. 'But sometimes when I get upset I try not to show it because I think it might upset other people.'

'You don't get upset about Daddy anymore.'

Now they were getting somewhere. At last.

'Pat.' She stroked his head, fingers lingering on the silky softness of his dark hair. She longed to press her face against his neck, like she used to do when he was little, and breathe in the lovely, unique Pat smell.

'I do still get upset about Daddy,' she said. It was an effort to keep her voice from wobbling. 'I miss him. All the time. Every single day. And I always will. Just as I know you and Eilish will, too.'

'It's not fair,' Pat said. 'I'm the only boy in my class who's dad is dead. None of my friends have a clue what that's like. And if you miss him so much, why don't we do something special to remember him?'

'Like you did in school today for Jamie Rider?'

'We had this, like, really stupid mass we had to go to and everyone was talking about him and saying what a great person he was. And I didn't even know him, Mum, but I had to go to this mass. It's not fair. Why do they do something for someone I don't even *know*. They didn't do anything when ... after Dad's accident. Nothing. And all my friends were nice enough for a bit, but now it's like they've forgotten all about it.'

'They haven't forgotten,' Ellen said. 'It's just difficult for them to understand because it hasn't happened to them. And you're right, Pat, it's not fair. I absolutely hate that you and Eilish have lost your dad. I hate it so much I can't tell you. But the thing is, darling, sometimes people die. It's horrible and sad and I wish it didn't have to happen, but it does.'

'What if the same thing happens to you?' Pat asked. 'And don't say it won't or it can't because that's not true.'

Ellen hated these conversations. He was right, of course. She couldn't promise something that wasn't true. And yet, she couldn't bear to think of him living with such uncertainty.

'I will never, ever lie to you about this,' she said. 'But think about it logically. You said it yourself, you're the only boy in your class who's lost a parent. The chances of the same thing happening to anyone else in your class are extremely low. The chances of something happening to me are even lower than that.'

'They're not in the police.'

'What's that got to do with anything?' Ellen asked.

'Rufus' dad works in a bank,' Pat said. 'Leo's dad is a plumber and Aidan's dad is a teacher. They're all normal jobs.'

'A policewoman is a normal job.'

'It's dangerous,' Pat said. 'I looked it up on the internet. Being in the police is the fourth most dangerous job you can do. The only things worse are deep-sea worker, bomb squad and construction worker.'

How long, Ellen wondered, had this concern been knocking about inside that head of his? And why the hell hadn't she picked up on it before now?

'I want you to give it up,' Pat said. 'Please, Mum. I want you to do something else. Something that's not so dangerous.'

'I can't do that,' Ellen said. 'It's not as easy as you think, moving jobs, Pat. Being a policewoman is the only thing I know how to do.'

'But you don't need to do it,' Pat said. 'I heard Nanny telling Granddad. You don't need to work because we have, like, loads of money from Dad. So why can't you just give it up?'

Ellen tried to think of an answer that made sense, but nothing came to her. In the end, she wrapped her arms around him, held him tight and told him she'd think about it. She owed him that, at least.

21:00

Dallinger Road was quiet when Ellen pulled up outside the Hudsons' house. While it was a relief not to have to run the press gauntlet anymore, the lack of media presence was depressing. Before long, the press would move on to the next big story, forgetting all about Jodie.

Ellen ran from the car to the house, shivering on the doorstep as she waited for someone to let her in. The door was eventually opened by Finlay. The hope in his face, when he saw Ellen, was painful to see.

'Is your mum around?' Ellen asked.

'Have you found her?' Finlay asked. 'Is that why you're here?'

'I'm sorry,' Ellen said. 'No news. I just wanted to see how you were all doing. Listen, Finlay, would you mind if I come inside? It's freezing out here.'

'So you've got no news at all?' Incredulity made his voice sound high-pitched and childish.

'I'm sorry,' Ellen said. She nodded to the inside of the house. 'May I?'

He stood back and let her pass.

'Is Abby around?' Ellen asked.

'She's in the sitting room,' Finlay said. 'We've been watching TV together. Her brother died. Did you know that? But she said she doesn't think that will happen to Jodie because you're a really good detective and Abby said you'll find her. You will find her, won't you?'

'I hope so,' Ellen said. She went to go into the sitting room, but the boy started speaking again.

'Mum wants me to go back to school tomorrow,' he said. 'She says I've missed too much already and school's important.'

'She's right,' Ellen said. 'I know it's difficult, Finlay, but sometimes, even when really bad stuff is happening, we have to carry on with our normal lives.'

He frowned. 'That's what Abby said. But you don't know what it's like. None of you have a fucking clue what this is like for us. And how does going back to school make anything better? I hate school and I'm going to hate it even more if I go in and everyone's talking about me and pointing at me. And they all know what's happened. Do they know about my dad, too?'

'What about him?'

'He's been arrested,' Finlay said. 'Mum told me earlier. That's why she's in bed. She had to take a sleeping tablet. I heard her telling Abby she can't sleep and she's stressed. She kept getting sick. The first day Jodie went. She kept throwing up. I never saw my mum being sick before. I didn't know adults got sick. I know that's stupid, but it's the truth.'

He looked so vulnerable. Reminded her so much of Pat. Poor kid. A flash of rage hit her at the cruelty of it all. Some perverted bastard had caused all this. Her hands curled into fists as she remembered her promise to Ger Cox. A promise Ellen had every intention of keeping.

'Did your mum say why the police have arrested your dad?' Ellen asked.

'It's nothing to do with Jodie,' Kevin said. 'It's, like, just a formality or something, right?'

'Right,' Ellen said. 'And your friends in school won't know anything about it. We've been really, really careful not to let the press find out about this.'

'Like you were the last time?'

'That won't happen again,' Ellen said. 'I promise. Listen, Finlay. You have my number if you ever need to talk, right? Call me if you have any questions at any time. I'm always here for you. And so is Abby. Right now, my parents are babysitting and I promised I wouldn't be long. I'm just going to pop into the sitting room for a quick word with Abby. Then I'm out of here. But you call me if you need anything. Got that?'

'Okay.'

There was nothing new from Abby. Helen was sick with worry about how Kevin would cope overnight. The sleeping pill had been Abby's idea. A good one, in Ellen's opinion.

'I'll be here all night,' Abby said. 'I'll make sure Finlay's okay and I'll check Helen regularly as well. There's nothing for you to worry about here, Ellen. Get home to your own family.'

Finlay was still in the hall when she came out. Ellen said goodnight, reiterated her request that he call if he ever needed her, and left. Outside, she closed the front door and leaned against it, exhausted. She admired Abby's stamina. Being inside that house for any length of time wasn't easy.

While she'd been with Abby her phone had rung. It was Dai Davies. She'd let the call go to voicemail and now she took the phone from her bag and listened to his message.

'*Been having a bit of a think about this Fletcher bloke, Ellen. We only have his boss' word for it that Fletcher's innocent. For all we know, the boss could have reasons of his own for covering for Fletcher. I think we should take a trip out to Hoo and see what else we can dig up. Maybe even have a snoop around his house. How are you fixed for tomorrow?*'

A trip to Hoo. Why not? It was worth a shot at the very least. She closed her phone and put it back in her bag.

A fat, silver moon hung low in the sky. Ellen thought of Kevin Hudson, locked up in Bromley nick. Words from a poem drifted through her head. Something she'd learned in school. Most of it was long-forgotten, just a few bits of it remained, floating through her head like dandelion clocks on a still, summer's day. Something about a little tent of blue and drifting clouds with sails of silver.

She was tired. Weighed down with exhaustion. She didn't want to be doing this anymore. It was no life.

Pushing thoughts of Kevin from her mind, Ellen ran to the car, climbed in and drove home. It was only much later, after her parents had left and she was sitting with a glass of wine in her hand, *Sinatra at the Sands* on low – comfort music – that she remembered the name of the poem, and why she'd thought of it right at that moment on the doorstep of Kevin Hudson's house.

22:00

The children are smiling and waving goodbye. I want to wave back, but I can't lift my arm. It's too heavy. One of the girls leans out the window.

'Come with us, Jodie! It'll be fun.'

My eyes are closing so it's hard to see. I'm too cold. The seaside's no good when it's cold. Mum always wants us to go in wintertime, but why would we do that? It's only fun in the summer.

Everything's broken in here now. Even the TV. He broke it all.

There are more trains. I can hear them. I use my last bit of energy to keep my eyes open. All the children are smiling.

Some of the wallpaper's starting to peel away and little bits are missing. I've done that. I tear off some more. The paper dissolves on my tongue like Holy Communion but if I imagine really, really hard, I can pretend it's toast. Little slivers of toast with jam on. And runny butter.

I think I'm getting better at this. I can smell it. The warm, buttery smell mixed with the toast and the sugary jam.

'Jodie, come with us!'

A boy this time. He's waving, too. I try to tell him I can't come. I'm stuck in this room. But when I speak, there's no sound.

I'm thirsty. But the toilet is so far and I'm so tired and my ankle's still sore from the other night. It's all swollen up and so stiff I can hardly move it. Maybe it's broken.

My throat's so dry, even breathing hurts. I want to get up but I really don't think I can. Maybe if I sleep for a bit ...

He's coming back. The branches rustling. They do that when he pushes through them to get here.

No.

I try to get up. I can stand but can't walk because my leg's too sore. I'm begging God to make him go away.

But God does nothing.

Bolts — crack, crack, bang. Then the door's open.

I try to get back on the bed, but I get it wrong. Hit my tummy against the bed frame and it hurts. I slip and don't make the bed. Land on the floor instead. Leg hurts bad now.

Footsteps. On the floor. Coming towards me. I try to get onto the bed but before I can make it, he's there, hands around me, lifting me.

I try to kick him but he's too big and too strong and no one can hear me, anyway.

WEDNESDAY, 23 FEBRUARY

01:04

Ellen dreamed of Vinny. In the dream, he was still alive. He hadn't been killed by Vinny Dunston. In the dream, they were on a family holiday in Greece. On a white, sandy beach with turquoise blue sea. It was a happy dream and when she woke, Ellen was happy too. Until she remembered.

She had fallen asleep on the sofa. As a result, she was cold and stiff. And angry. Dunston was dead, but that didn't change anything because so was Vinny. Killing Dunston hadn't given her children back the father they loved and needed. And it hadn't done anything to dilute the hot rage that still burned inside her whenever she thought about what Dunston had done to her beautiful husband.

She was thirsty. In the kitchen, she poured water into a glass and drank greedily. There was a big window over the sink and Ellen's reflection in this was as clear as if she was looking in a mirror. She didn't like what she saw.

Briony had asked if Ellen felt guilty about what she'd done.

'Not one little bit,' Ellen replied, seeing the shock on Briony's face before the counsellor could hide it. Ellen didn't care. There were a lot of things she didn't care about these days. And only one thing that really mattered, anymore. Protecting the rest of her family from any further harm. Would she do it again if she had to? Damn right she would.

She'd tried to explain this to Briony.

'Billy Boy Dunston was a pig,' Ellen explained. 'That's the name he went by. A local Greenwich thug who scared the shit out of everyone he came into contact with. He attacked a young guy in a pub one night. Sliced his face open with a broken bottle. There were lots of people who witnessed the attack, but Vinny was the only one prepared to step forward and make a statement.

'He was run over the day before he was due to appear in court to testify against Dunston. And we could never get Dunston for it because he had an alibi for the time of the hit and run.'

When Briony asked Ellen how she could be so sure Dunston was to blame, Ellen didn't even bother answering. Didn't tell Briony what Dunston had whispered in her ear moments before she shot him.

Your precious husband got what was coming to him. Now it's your turn.

Half his face disappeared with the first shot. Didn't kill him though. In her head, Vinny was there and she was speaking to him. Telling him it was all right, everything was going to be all right. Then she'd lifted the gun, put it against Dunston's ruined face and pulled the trigger a second time. He gave one final twitch and, after that, nothing. William – Billy Boy – Dunston was dead.

In the window, Ellen's reflection smiled out at her. She smiled back. Guilty? Like hell. She'd do it again in a heartbeat.

Upstairs, she checked the children before going to her own room. Pat first, then Eilish. Both of them were fast asleep. Pat, as

371

always, was buried beneath his duvet. Gently, she lifted it off him, folding it back so that his head, at least, was outside the covers. She stroked damp hair from his face and kissed his flushed cheek, breathing in his warm, familiar smell.

In Eilish's room, Ellen knelt by her daughter's bed and wrapped her arms around Eilish's little body. She lay her head on the pillow beside Eilish and thought of Vinny as she watched her daughter sleeping. There were moments like this, when it still felt so inconceivable that he was gone. That the three of them would lead a life in which he wasn't a part.

You were meant to accept it, somehow. Get over it, move on, beat incessantly against the pain and anger and be grateful for what you had. But there was something no one ever told you. That to do that, to move on and get through the rest of your life, you had to kill everything inside you that felt real. The urge to lift your head and howl until your throat was raw from howling. To open your heart and mind to the rage that burned inside you, an anger so hot and dangerous you knew it would kill you but you didn't care, because anything was better than this half-life. This pretence at living.

On the pillow beside her, Eilish stirred. She mumbled something – Ellen didn't catch what – then was silent again. A rush of love then, so powerful Ellen's breath caught in her throat. She leaned forward, kissed Eilish twice on the top of her head, then stood up.

She walked back into her own room and got ready for bed.

Later, as she lay there, waiting for sleep to take her, her mind filled with memories and images of her children. She started to relax, consoled by the all-consuming love. Knowing how privileged she was to be able to enjoy Pat and Eilish, to be with them on their amazing journey through life. It was a rare and wonderful thing indeed. Her eyes closed and she drifted into a deep, dreamless sleep

08:30

Ellen knew, as soon as she woke up, what she needed to do about Ed. She called him straight after breakfast.

'You need to tell Nichols what's going on,' she said. 'And if you don't, then I will.'

'Are you threatening me?' Ed asked. 'Because if you are …'

'Stop it,' Ellen said. 'It's not about threats. It's about doing the right thing, Ed. Think about it. You're not well. It's not fair on the rest of the team if you continue to lead this investigation. More important than that, it's not fair on Jodie. You tell Nichols. Today. And if you don't, then I'm going to see him first thing tomorrow morning and speak to him myself.'

She hung up then, before the conversation turned into another argument, and gathered the children to take them to school.

At the school gates, she kept to herself, standing slightly apart from the other parents, mothers mainly, although a sprinkling of fathers were in evidence as well. She caught snippets of conversations as she waited, enough to make glad she wasn't part of any of them.

'Three times last week he came home without his jumper. I told him, that's it. If he doesn't have it with him this afternoon, then no TV this evening.'

'It's the parents' fault. Children need rules. You see her with her tie-dyed jeans and tattoos and you can tell, can't you, that she'll let the kids run wild.'

'No way I'd let my son go around with his hair that long. Halfway down his back! My Nat says the other kids tease him no end. Call him a girl. It's not right.'

Even if she'd wanted to, Ellen didn't think she'd have been able to pretend to care about jumpers, tattoos or inappropriate hairstyles. Her head was full of Jodie and Kevin. He'd been kept in last night and she was worried about him. She'd told the duty sergeant in Bromley to keep a close eye on Kevin. Knowing his fear of being locked up, she didn't want to take any risks.

'Hello, Ellen.'

She jumped at the sound of the familiar voice, and felt the blush rising up her neck and cheeks as she realised who it was.

'Jim! What are you doing here?' She nodded across at the other parents. 'You need a child to qualify hanging around here in the mornings.'

He laughed. The dimple appeared under his left eye. It was all she could do to stop herself reaching out to touch it. She looked away, angry with herself. She seriously needed to get a grip. He was, after all, just some bloke she went to school with a hundred years ago.

Who just happens to be so damn handsome.

She gritted her teeth, blocking out the evil voice inside her head that was tempting her to think all sorts of things she shouldn't be thinking, like what it would feel like to place her palm flat against his bare chest and slide it slowly downwards ...

'What are you doing here?' she repeated.

The question came out harsher than she'd intended. Briefly, he looked surprised, then his face cleared again.

'Dropping off Anna.'

'Anna?'

'Anna Amato, Susan's daughter. You remember my cousin, Susan, right? She married an Italian bloke. Lived in Italy until last summer when they moved back here. Susan's got workmen in so we've been helping out with Anna. I met your mum here the other day, in fact.'

'Yeah, she's been great,' Ellen said. 'I've got a lot on at the moment and she's been a total star. Oh,' she noticed the man standing slightly behind Jim. 'Raymond, isn't it?'

The man blushed and nodded.

'Sorry,' Jim said. 'Ray, this is Ellen Kelly. We were in school together. Do you remember her?'

Ray nodded again but didn't say anything.

'Haven't seen you in years,' Ellen said, smiling. She cast through her mind for things she remembered about Jim's older brother. Seemed to recall he'd had some sort of breakdown a few years back, but she didn't know any more than that. Looking at him now, shuffling from foot to foot behind his brother, she thought he looked like a less vibrant version of Jim. The same dark hair, similar features, although in Ray's case they had melted into the folds of flesh caused by excessive obesity.

Something about him reminded Ellen, momentarily, of Brian Fletcher. Raymond had the same air of vulnerability about him, like the everyday business of getting on with life was a challenge he wasn't able to cope with.

'You used to play the piano,' Ellen said, remembering. 'You played at the end of year concert when I was about nine. You were amazing.'

Ray glanced at her and she thought she saw the shadow of a smile.

'Still play,' he said. 'Do a bit of teaching as well. You don't play yourself?'

'No,' Ellen said. 'But it's something I've always wanted to do. You wouldn't consider it, would you?'

For a fleeting second, he looked as if the prospect terrified him. Then he shrugged. 'I'd need to check. See if I've got any free spaces. I don't, em, if I teach too much, you know, I find it difficult. But, em, if you phone me, maybe in a few days, and I could see, you know, what might be a good time.'

'Okay,' Ellen said. 'I'm in the middle of a case right now. How about I call you in a few weeks, when things quieten down a bit?'

Ray smiled – properly this time – and it transformed his face. Again, Ellen remembered him as a young boy, head bent over the school piano, fingers flying along the keyboard, creating a sound she could only ever dream of making. For some reason, the image made her sad.

'Is that why you haven't called?' Jim asked. 'You've been too busy?'

He'd left a message a few days earlier. She'd forgotten all about the call. Until now.

'Something like that,' she said.

She was about to say more. Tell him that she really would like to go for a drink with him sometime, that she was still a right mess but she thought she was getting better and, even if she wasn't ready for anything heavy, she might – just about – be ready to start having some fun again.

But before she could say any of that, the school bell rang and Eilish was running towards her for a final hug before she went into class. Ellen looked around for Pat. He was with a group of friends and seemed to have forgotten all about her. Which she took as a good sign. He hadn't mentioned her job this morning and, so far, seemed to be in a good mood.

By the time Ellen had said goodbye to Eilish, Jim and Raymond had wandered off. As she left, she looked around, hoping Jim might still be there, waiting for her. But there was no sign of him anywhere and she continued to her car, trying to ignore the heavy feeling in the pit of her stomach as she scanned the street again and realised that Jim O'Dwyer was long gone.

10:05

It was a cold, damp day – low, grey clouds heavy with the threat of rain. Bursts of white mist puffed from Rob's mouth every time he breathed out. The thick gloves weren't enough to keep his hands warm, and the longer he stood there, the colder they became. He wriggled his fingers, trying to get some circulation going. Pain shot up his hands as the movement made the cold blood move more quickly.

Apart from Rob, the street was quiet. The crews of cameramen and journalists had all moved on to the next story. To them, Jodie was yesterday's news. Already forgotten. Judged irrelevant by a press that cared only for the story with no thought to the people behind it. The ones with the ruined hopes and shattered dreams that fed their mindless machine.

In a house across the road, the front door opened. Rob bent down, pretending to tie his shoelace, and watched the woman throw something into the green recycling bin. When she'd finished, she stood and looked up and down the street, like she was trying to find someone. Like she knew he was there, right across from her, watching.

She had short, cropped hair and a tight little body. He recognised her from the news. Helen Hudson. Jodie's mother. He was too far away to see her face but from the way she held her body, he thought she looked tired. Like she barely had enough energy to keep herself upright.

Of course, that could have been just his imagination but all the same, it was what he thought when he saw her. As he watched, her body seemed to slump even further. For a moment, he felt a surge of pity for this poor woman whose daughter had disappeared.

Then he remembered why he was there, and the feeling disappeared again. By the time she'd turned and gone back inside, slamming the front door behind her, his moment of weakness had passed.

He'd been here the best part of two hours now. Half-frozen and still no sign of Hudson. And he needed to piss. Again. He walked along to the tree further up the road and unzipped his trousers. Cold air hit the lower part of his body as a burst of warm liquid gushed out, splashing against the tree. The remains of earlier visits to the same spot glittered in the hazy light like pieces of broken amber. Strange the way something like piss, which wasn't nice at all, could look so lovely.

He should go over there. No point standing out here freezing his nuts off if Hudson was in there. And, let's face it, where else would he be? There was only the two of them left. Hudson and his missus. The boy had gone off to school soon after eight. And the other woman, the pretty one with the dark hair and the perky walk, had left soon after. Rob thought she might be the police liaison. If she was, then he'd better get over there before she came back.

He was going through it in his mind, how it would play out, when he saw someone walking up the street on the opposite side of the road. Rob's heart beat faster as the figure drew closer and he recognised who it was. A new – better – idea started forming.

Even from here, you could see he was a good-looking fella. Thin but not skinny, with shaggy dark hair that kept falling across his face. Every time the boy brushed it back, it flopped forward again a moment later. It was probably annoying for him, but there was something attractive about the way he flicked it back that made you think the girls would fall for someone like that.

Except Rob didn't like to think about boys and girls stuff because it only reminded him of Molly and how she'd never know the thrill of first love. That feeling you got when you fell for someone – like it was the most important thing ever and no one could possibly understand what it was like to be so in love. The way Rob felt when he first set eyes on Sheryl. The way he'd always felt about her, right up until the day she died. His first and only love. Her and Molly. They were all he'd ever wanted.

He pulled off a glove and reached into his coat pocket, fingering the knife, thinking through his revised plan. They'd got it wrong last time, him and Frankie. Going for Hudson the way they had, like a pair of animals. Not this time. He didn't like it. Course not. But it was a means to an end. In war, any means were justified, and this was a war, no question. A war against people who hurt little kiddies and destroyed lives.

The boy was closer now. The Hudson kid. No doubt about that. The image of his little sister, Jodie. Both pale-skinned with dark hair. Like the mother. Although how the boy got to be so tall was anyone's guess.

Rob walked slowly down the road, making like he was looking for something. The kid paid him no attention. He was kicking a stone and that was about the only thing he seemed to notice.

When he thought it was safe, Rob crossed over and started walking behind the boy. Take it easy, he warned himself. That's all you need to do. Take it easy. He wasn't into scaring kids, but he had no choice. This was his last chance. No way he was going to mess things up. He felt again for the knife, wrapping his hand around the handle, getting ready.

He moved forward, his grip tightening on the knife, knowing exactly what he had to do.

10:07

Ellen had arranged to meet Abby at Danilo's. The FLO was already there when Ellen arrived. Ellen ordered a double espresso and went to join Abby.

'Thanks for meeting me,' Ellen said. 'I wanted to update you on the Ed situation. And we need to talk about Kevin and what happens next.'

'I can't stay long,' Abby said. 'I've left Helen on her own.

Couldn't get hold of Malcolm or anyone else at such short notice. Don't worry, though. She'll be fine for an hour or so. It's a bit easier there now that the press have moved on.'

'Any update on Kevin?' Ellen asked.

'He's doing fine,' Abby said. 'Helen spoke to him this morning. He's still at Bromley, but she said, all things considered, he didn't sound too bad. I think she was really worried about how he'd cope, being kept in overnight.'

'Of course,' Ellen said. 'Any sign that they're going to charge him?'

'I've been trying to get through to the duty sergeant for the past hour,' Abby said. 'I'll get onto it again as soon as we're finished here.'

'Do you think he did it?' Ellen asked. 'Do you think Kevin killed Dan Harris?'

'Harris was shot,' Abby said. 'I don't think Kevin would know the first thing about how to get his hands on a gun. Plus, I know he hated Harris, but even still. I just can't see it. Can you?'

'No,' Ellen said. 'But he was inside, don't forget. It's quite possible he's better connected than you think.'

'Yeah, maybe,' Abby agreed 'I guess we'll know soon enough. What about Ed? You said you had an update.'

'Have you been over there yet?' Ellen asked, nodding in the direction of the station.

'Just for a few minutes,' Abby said. 'No sign of Ed.'

'I've given him until the end of the day to tell Nichols,' Ellen said.

'Or what?'

'Or I tell Nichols myself.'

Abby's eyes widened. 'You'd do that? Wow. You're braver than me. But you're right, of course. Yes, absolutely. It's the right thing to do. I'm sorry. I should have told you ages ago.'

'It doesn't matter,' Ellen said. 'I know now. And I'm not going to sit back and do nothing about it. We'll get this sorted, Abby. I promise. And once we've got Ed facing up to what he needs to do, we can focus on finding Jodie.'

'And Molly York?' Abby asked. 'We still looking into a possible connection?'

'Yes,' Ellen said. 'I've got Alastair working on it. Dai Davies has been doing a bit of digging as well. Off the record. In fact, right after this I'm going to take a drive out to Higham, see what I can find out about Brian Fletcher.'

'Is Alastair going with you?' Abby asked.

Ellen shook her head. 'Baxter doesn't know about it. I can get away with making some excuse, but it's tricky if two of us are out for the whole afternoon. Don't worry, though. I won't be alone. Dai's coming with me.'

Abby's face turned pink. 'Is that wise?'

'What do you mean?'

'I mean he's not part of the investigation,' Abby said. 'Plus, he's a friend of the family. Helen told me. Isn't there a conflict of interest?'

'If there was,' Ellen said. 'I wouldn't have let him be involved. He's offered to help and I've said yes. God knows, we need all the help we can get.'

'So what will I tell Ed if he asks where you are?' Abby said.

'Whatever you want,' Ellen said. 'Just don't tell him where I am.'

'You want me to lie?' Abby asked.

'Yes, please,' Ellen said. 'After all, you're pretty good at it. Shouldn't be a problem, I wouldn't have thought.'

10:10

The boy was strong, but he was no match for Rob, who grabbed him from behind and pressed the knife against his throat. Before the kid had a chance to react, Rob dragged him off the road and into the garden of the Hudsons' house, where they wouldn't be seen by any passersby.

The boy's instinct kicked in and he started to struggle, trying to break free. Rob pulled the boy's arm up behind his back and pressed tighter on the knife. The frantic bobbing of an Adam's apple vibrated along the blade and up through Rob's arm.

'Don't move,' he hissed. 'If you fight me, I'll hurt you. Got that?'

The boy nodded.

'Right then,' Rob said. 'Give me your keys. We're going inside.'

He waited while the kid fumbled in his pocket, pulled out a

single key and held it up for Rob to see.

'Front door?' Rob asked.

More nodding.

Rob shoved him forward. Still holding the kid's arm, he put the knife in his mouth and used his free hand to put the key in the lock and open the door. As soon as he'd done this, he held the knife to the boy's throat again.

'One sound from you and you're dead.'

He manoeuvred them both through the front door and into the house.

'Fin?' A woman's voice. The mother. As Rob tried to work out where she might be, eyes darting around, taking in the stairs and the three rooms leading off the hallway, the door straight in front of him opened and there she was. The same woman he'd seen standing in the garden earlier.

For a split second, she looked confused, her mouth forming into a silent 'O' of shock. This quickly changed as horror and fear blurred her features and she shot forward, arms held out, ready to grab the boy. As if Rob was going to let that happen.

He took a step back, tightening his grip on the boy's arm, causing him to yelp in pain. Helen stopped dead.

'Stay where you are and he won't get hurt,' Rob said. 'All I need is information. That's all. You tell me what I need to know and I'll be gone and neither of you will be hurt in any way.'

'Let him go,' she said quietly. 'Please. Just let him go. Whatever it is you want, don't you think we've been through enough?'

'Where is he?' Rob said. His arms were getting tired, especially the right one, still vibrating from the movement in the boy's throat. And the sound of the kid's breathing, *in-out-in-out-in-out-in-out*, so loud and fast, as if he'd just run a race. A rapid, raggedy sound like a storm inside his head, making it difficult to concentrate on the woman and what she was saying.

'Your husband!' he shouted. 'Tell him to get himself out here, show his face. I'm not letting the boy go until I see that bastard.'

She shook her head, hands pressed against her face like it would fall apart if she didn't hold onto it.

'Harris,' she whispered, and it seemed at first like she was talking to herself. 'I knew it would come back to this.'

Her voice changed as she looked at Rob.

'He didn't do it, you know. Whatever it is you want, whatever you think Kevin's done. It wasn't him. He had nothing to do with what happened.'

The boy's breathing was getting worse. *In-out-in-out-in-out-in-out*. Faster and louder and messing up Rob's head. And why was Hudson's wife going on about Dan Harris? Rob didn't give a rat's arse about Harris. He started to tell her that, but she was off again before he could get his head straight enough to speak.

'What is it with you people?' she asked. 'Why can't you just leave us alone?'

Deluded bitch, Rob thought. Husband beats the shit out of that poor Harris kid and she's still willing to defend him.

'And what about my Molly?' he hissed. 'You think I should let that go, and all? You know raping her wasn't enough for that sick bastard? When they found my little girl, she had cigarette burns all over her body. Do you know that? What sort of sick fuck does that to a child?'

Her face shifted, features rearranging themselves. Anger switching to sorrow. And something else. Pity. Followed by horror.

'You're not saying ...' her voice trailed off. Rob guessed she was imagining those same, terrible things happening to her child.

'My name is Rob York,' he said. 'My child, Molly, was taken from me three years ago. She never came home again.'

'Rob York,' the woman whispered. 'Of course. I remember your name.'

Her voice was all soft, as if she really cared. As if she didn't already know all about Molly and what her bastard husband had done.

'I'm so sorry,' she continued. 'What happened?'

In his arms, the boy was shaking and Rob realised he was crying, big, shuddering sobs that sent tremors through Rob's stomach. He felt tears landing on his wrist and it was hard to concentrate on the woman, knowing the only reason the boy was crying was because of him and what he was doing.

In-out-in-out-in-out-in-out. Getting worse as he tried to breathe through the crying.

What was he doing, anyway? Threatening a kid like this. And he called Hudson a monster.

'Where's your husband?' he shouted, louder than he meant to, but how else could he get them to listen? He needed to get out of here. Find Hudson, force him to admit what he'd done and turn himself in. That was all he wanted.

'He's not here,' the wife said. 'He's in police custody. They think he killed someone. He didn't, of course. But they don't know that. Not yet. I'm not lying to you. You can search the house if you want. You won't find him.'

In-out-in-out-in-out-in-out. An out-of-control train charging around his head, it was. Made it impossible to think. Search the house, she'd said. But how could he do that if he was holding the kid like this?

'Hudson!' he roared at the top of his voice.

'He's not here,' the woman repeated, speaking slowly now, as if he was some sort of half-wit.

The boy moved suddenly and Rob grabbed him tighter, pressing the knife against his throat.

'Why won't you listen to her?' the boy yelled. 'He's not here. What's wrong with you? Why won't you believe her?'

'Shut up!' Rob screamed.

The hand holding the knife felt slippery and when he looked down he was surprised to see blood. Took him a moment to realise it had come from the boy.

Two things happened at the same time then. The boy cried out and the woman leapt forward, screaming. Rob felt her body crashing into them and, a moment later, he was falling backwards.

All three of them crashed to the ground, the back of Rob's head smashing against the doorframe. A flash of white exploded in front of his eyes. He felt the boy and the woman on top of him and he couldn't breathe or move from the weight of them.

Suddenly, the pressure on his stomach lifted and he tried to sit up, but something walloped against his forehead, knocking him back again. Then feet were kicking him, in the stomach and in the side.

Grunting, he tried to pull himself up and around, away from the blows. He couldn't see, something wet was running into his eyes. Blood, he thought. His head felt like a bomb had exploded inside it. He still had the knife and he lunged forward, aiming for the legs attacking him. It connected and, above him, someone screamed. The kicking stopped.

He pulled himself up. Wiping his face with the back of his sleeve, his vision cleared and he saw the woman. She was lying on her side. There was blood on the floor around her.

He looked around for the boy. No sign of him. The woman groaned but didn't move. Sweet Jesus, what had he done?

'Are you okay?' He knelt beside her, trying to locate the source of the blood. He reached out and touched her shoulder. Her body twitched as she turned to look at him.

He wanted to tell her he was sorry. That he hadn't meant to hurt her or the kid. That he was just so frustrated with trying to get justice for Molly. Driven insane. Images of what she'd endured. That he'd reached a point where he knew he'd be better off dead than having to endure one more second of it. That the only reason he hadn't topped himself long ago was the hope that one day, he'd see justice done. Once that happened, it would all be over. He would go to the seaside and walk into the sea and just keep on walking until the water engulfed him, until, finally, the images inside his head disappeared forever.

He opened his mouth to tell her this. At the same moment, something smashed into the back of his head. Briefly, he saw Helen Hudson's face. It was full of sadness and sorrow and something else that he didn't understand. Before he could work it out, he fell forward, into the darkness.

11:00

Ellen drove across to Dai's house in Lee. The most punctual person Ellen had ever met, it was no surprise to see Dai standing on the street waiting for her when she arrived. He was on the phone but when he saw her, he waved and slipped the phone into his pocket.

'I've been trying to get through to Helen,' he said. 'Only she's not answering her phone, which is most unusual. Nothing's happened, has it?'

'Not as far as I'm aware,' Ellen said. 'Were you calling for a particular reason?'

'Just checking in,' Dai said. 'Like I've done most days since this business with Jodie. She's a good friend and I'm worried about her. Nothing wrong with that, is there?'

Isn't there a conflict of interest?

Goddamn Abby.

'No,' Ellen said. 'Nothing wrong at all.'

'So then,' Dai said. 'This Higham place. Where is it and will I like it?'

Before Ellen could answer, her radio buzzed with a message from base. Claire Allsop's sweet, girlish voice, calling for emergency back-up to 80 Dallinger Road.

Ellen glanced at Dai. Dallinger Road was less than a five-minute drive away. She spoke into her radio, confirming she was on the way. Then she swung the car around and started driving.

11:05

You useless lump! You can't get anything right, can you? You're nothing but a waste of bleedin' space, you know that?

Daddy was angry. His voice loud inside Brian's head, cross words banging around like a drumbeat clattering against his skull.

'Stop it!'

Brian pressed his hands against his ears, trying to block out the sound, but making it worse instead. The voice intensified, rising into a scream of such rage that Brian knew what would happen next. Daddy would pull the belt off his trousers and start laying into him.

It was his own fault. He knew that. The one thing Daddy couldn't stand was someone who didn't do what he'd say he was going to do. Brian had made a mistake and he'd promised Daddy he'd sort it out.

He'd tried. Really tried. Had gone in there so sure of himself, knowing exactly what he needed to do. Even took Daddy's gun. Checked it had bullets in it and told himself he'd use it if he had to. She wasn't Marion, after all.

He could hear her crying before he ever opened the door, but he didn't let that stop him. Pulled the bolts back and pushed his way over the bits of broken furniture towards the bed, where she was all curled up like some puppy.

It was only when he lifted her up and felt her little body in his big hands that he knew he couldn't go through with it. She was all warm and he could feel her tummy going in and out with her breathing. It messed with his head and before he could stop it, he was seeing all sorts of things he didn't want to be seeing right then.

Marion with the crown of flowers on her head, smiling at him like he was a king or a god or the best thing she'd ever seen. Then she was gone, replaced by Molly. Molly with the lovely soft hair that smelled of strawberries for the first few days. Molly whose bottom lip always trembled right before she started crying.

The minute the lip started, he'd tell jokes and prance about the place, anything to keep her from crying. It never worked, though. No matter what he did, the tears would start and then the wailing – that horrible sound that cut through him like a knife.

Marion, Molly-not-Marion, Jodie-not-Marion. Girls with dark hair and big blue eyes, crying and smiling, in his head and in his arms until he couldn't stick it a second longer and before he knew what he was doing he was dropping her back onto the bed and stumbling from the room, only just remembering to lock up as he left.

It wasn't easy having two parents to keep happy. There was Mam, begging him to look after Marion and keep her safe. And he tried his best. God knows, he tried. Except every bloody time, he got it wrong.

Being with Mam was the best. She was kind and warm and told him he was a great boy and she loved him and wasn't he the best big brother in the world to his little sister?

'You'll always look after her, won't you?' Mam would ask him.

And Brian would nod his head really hard and say, 'I promise I will, Mam.'

It wasn't easy, though. Not with Daddy around. But a promise is a promise is a promise, and there was no way Brian was going to break that one. No way.

Except words are easy and actions are hard. Especially when you come home one evening and he's taken her and you think you'll never see her again and you wonder how you'll manage to spend your whole life living without her, knowing you didn't keep the promise you made.

If it wasn't for Simon, he'd never have got through those first months. Simon offered Brian a job. Said working was better than staying at home all day, feeling sorry for himself. Brian was nearly a man, Simon said. Time to start earning his own money. Simon couldn't subsidise him forever.

He liked working with Simon. Some of the other blokes, they were a bit hard to take, but mostly Brian kept to himself and didn't let them get to him. Took his orders from Simon and got on with it.

That afternoon, he'd been in Mountsfield Park, weeding one of the few beds that was worth looking after, when he looked up and there she was. Skipping along the path towards the playground. She skipped right past him, didn't seem to notice he was there at all. Not that he minded. The way he felt then, nothing could have upset him. It was as if he'd spent his whole life waiting for that moment.

Even then, he wasn't one hundred per cent sure it was her. But then he heard Mam whispering in his ear, and he knew.

You promised, Brian. Bring Marion home and keep her safe. For me.

So that's what he'd done.

Only you fucked up, didn't you?

Brian shook his head, as if somehow he could shake out the sound of Daddy's voice.

Didn't you?

It was so confusing. How could you tell if someone was lying to you or not? He'd spent a long time worrying about that. Wondering if she was only pretending to be Molly, but really she was Marion. But why would she lie?

He shivered. Looking around, he realised he was standing outside, midway between the house and the shed. Daddy's gun was on the ground beside his feet. He didn't remember dropping it.

In the distance, he could hear a train coming. As a boy, he'd loved going to see the trains. He'd stand at the top of the bank and watch them whizz by. There were never any people on them. Freight trains only. He used to imagine the trains were full of presents, being delivered to all the boys and girls in the world.

Once, after a bad afternoon with Daddy, he'd gone down there, clambered down the grassy bank and waited for the train to come. If he put his ear to the track, he could feel it – the metal vibrating against his ear.

He'd thought about crawling across the track and lying there, feeling the vibrations growing stronger as the train got nearer, picturing the shadow appearing above him and the pressure of the train running over his chest and stomach and legs and the emptiness that would follow. But then he thought about Marion and Mam and how sad they'd be if he left them.

So he sat up and climbed back up the wet, grassy slope, and ran back to the house, where he knew they'd be waiting for him.

11:06

The scene that greeted Ellen and Dai was bizarre bordering on tragic. Rob York was sitting at the kitchen table. Finlay had pulled up a chair behind him and was pressing a bag of ice against the back of York's head. Dried blood stained one side of York's face. Helen was sitting beside him, holding his hands, bound together at the wrist with police-issue handcuffs. She had what looked like an old T-shirt wrapped around her head. Ellen could see blood on this.

Abby stood behind York, looking like she would whack him if he dared to move.

'Mr York was looking for Kevin,' Abby explained. 'He threatened the family with a knife. Luckily, Helen and Finlay managed to overpower him before he did anything stupid.'

'My God.' Dai pushed past Ellen and knelt in front of Helen, grabbing her free hand. 'Are you both okay, Helen?'

Abby glanced from Dai to Ellen but refrained from commenting.

'I'm fine,' Helen said. 'Stop fussing, Dai. Please.'

'I've cuffed him,' Abby said. 'As you can see. And read him his rights. Just waiting for someone to get him out of here now.'

Ellen was already on the radio, sending through an update and requesting more back-up.

'Malcolm and Raj are on their way,' she said. 'They'll take him down to the station. Mr York, you will be charged. You know that, don't you? You can't just break in here with a knife and start threatening people.'

'He thinks Kevin hurt his girl,' Helen said.

Ellen nodded. She knew for sure now it was Rob York she'd heard that night Kevin was attacked. She thought about how close they'd got to doing what they'd set out to do and shivered.

She wanted to ask him what he'd been thinking but she couldn't. That would have to wait until they got to the station. He looked defeated, sitting there like that. Poor man.

'I thought he did it.' He looked at Ellen, his eyes wet with tears. 'I haven't been able to think about anything else since that journalist showed up on my doorstep. You can't know what it's like for me. Sheryl and Molly, they were my whole world. Now, all I do is spend my days drinking and thinking. Not good thoughts. Especially not when I think about Molly, and what happened to her. Mostly, that's all I ever think about. That, and what I'd do to the bloke that hurt her if I ever got my hands on him.

'You spend too long doing all that thinking and your mind goes funny. You start seeing the world different. You become a different person. See, with me, there's nothing left I care about. Not a single thing. So when you ask me what I was thinking, well, I can't answer that. I can't separate my thoughts from what's real and what's not anymore. It's not that easy.'

'I don't blame him for wanting revenge,' Helen said. 'Under the circumstances, I can't say I'd have done any different.'

'How did you get Kevin to meet you that night?' Ellen asked.

Abby had already cautioned him, so whatever he said now was up to him.

'Told him I was a mate of Dan Harris. That journalist told me all about it.' York said. 'Said I had something Hudson might want. It was a long shot. Didn't expect him to jump so quickly, but he couldn't wait to meet me.'

'Except you got the wrong man,' Abby said. 'Kevin hadn't done a thing wrong but that didn't stop you and your thug of a mate, did it?'

'What about this Harris bloke?' Rob asked. 'He was a kid, wasn't he?'

'Dan Harris was a thug,' Helen said. 'Fifteen years old he might have been but Kevin had good reason to do what he did, believe me. And he certainly wouldn't harm Jodie. In the meantime, she's still missing and none of this is helping, is it? No one is any closer to finding my little girl.'

Helen tried to say something else but she started crying instead. Ellen was about to stand up, go over and comfort her. But Dai got there first, holding Helen while she sobbed against him. Holding her, Ellen thought, like he might never let her go.

13:30

He wished Daddy would shut up, but he wouldn't. He kept roaring and shouting and calling him a stupid cunt. Cunt was a bad word. You weren't allowed to use it. If Mam heard you saying it, she'd be cross. But Daddy didn't care about that. Daddy didn't care about anything at all except slapping Brian about the head and roaring at him and getting him to sort out the mess he'd created.

Daddy was right. Brian's mess, his responsibility.

He'd spent the last hour clearing out the back of the van, getting it ready. Had even put some blankets in there so she'd be comfortable. He didn't like to think of her in there getting banged around on the hard metal surfaces.

It would be easier if he didn't have to do this but he had no choice. She was getting worse every day. He felt sad thinking about it. Pictured coming home this evening and there'd be no one there.

He started thinking about all the nice times they'd had together watching *The Rainbow Parade* and eating cakes, but then he had to stop that because it made him feel a bit sick, thinking there'd be no more evenings like that.

He'd gone down there earlier and sat with her for a while. Told her what he was planning to do. She didn't say a word. Just lay on the bed with her back to him the whole time he sat there. In the end, he'd said good night to her and gone back to the house. Truth was, it had been a relief. It was no fun being with someone who didn't speak or even look at you.

After he left her, he'd caught himself humming the tune from *The Rainbow Parade*. 'It's Parade. The Rainbow Parade. Come and join us for colourful fun! The Parade. The Rainbow Parade.

Come and join us for colourful fun!'

He thought about going back, waking her up and singing it to her, thinking that would make her smile. Maybe then she'd turn around and the next thing she'd be chatting away to him, telling him about her favourite episodes and asking him why Fergus Fox was always so sly and mean.

He might have done it, too, but Daddy started up then, driving him on up the stairs and into bed, pushing him around and telling him what to do and not listening when Brian started crying and begging Daddy not to hurt him.

Later, Daddy's voice whispering in his ear, telling him it was for his own good and the least Brian could do was be a good boy and do what Daddy wanted after all the trouble he'd caused.

He'd tried shutting Daddy out but he couldn't do it. His voice was there now, louder than ever. Tormenting him.

You need to get rid of her. Little tramp like that, needs teaching a lesson. Show her who's boss. You can't let them get the upper hand, sunshine. They'll walk all over you if you're not careful.

He'd started singing – blocking out Daddy's voice as best he could, and clearing the van, getting it ready. He got Daddy's gun and put it in the van. Just in case.

He was so caught up with it all he didn't hear the car pulling up. It was only when he heard the footsteps, right up close, that he realised there was someone else there.

'Brian.'

His heart jumped as he recognised the voice.

Quick as a flash, he slammed closed the doors of the van and swung around but he was too late. Simon was already beside him, looking over his shoulders and peering inside the windows of the van.

'Jesus, Brian, what the fuck have you been up to now?'

13:35

Ellen had arranged for Rob to be taken in for questioning. With a bit of luck, he'd be back home by the end of the day. Helen had refused to press charges. Under the circumstances, Ellen couldn't blame her. As for Frankie Ferrari, Ellen was going to leave that for Kevin to decide what to do. If he wanted to press charges, fine. If not, Frankie would be off the hook, too. For now.

Higham turned out to be a string of connected hamlets trickling down from the Gravesend–Rochester road towards the river. Ellen drove. Out along the A2, turning off just before Rochester.

'Twenty miles,' Dai said, as Ellen parked outside a boarded-up pub beside the train station. 'That's all that's separating us from the end of civilisation.'

'It's not that bad,' Ellen said. 'According to the file, Brian lives in a house owned by his boss, Simon Wilson.' She frowned. 'You know, there's something odd about the relationship between those two.'

'In what way?' Dai asked.

'Wilson acts like Brian's guardian,' Ellen said. 'Giving him a job, a house, looking out for him. It's odd.'

'I think it's rather sweet,' Dai said. 'Not many people would be so kind to a young man with learning difficulties.'

'That's just it,' Ellen said. 'Wilson doesn't strike me as the kindly type.'

She stepped out of the car and looked around. The place reminded her of the black-and-white photos in her parents' house of old Irish towns. It gave her that same feeling that she was observing somewhere from a time long past. Apart from a scattering of houses – a mixture of semi-derelict Victorian cottages and cheap, flat-roofed eyesores – there was nothing else.

They had parked at the edge of the village and, from where she stood, the landscape sloped down to the Thames marshes, bleak and desolate under the heavy sky.

'Listen,' Dai whispered.

Ellen frowned. 'What? I can't hear anything.'

'Duelling banjos,' he said. 'I knew it. *Deliverance* country. We're not safe in a place like this.'

'Not sure what gives you the right to slag off a place like this,' she said. 'I mean, Wales is hardly the cosmopolitan capital of the world, is it?'

He started explaining to her that Cardiff wasn't Wales and, as a Cardiff man, he had every right to feel superior, but she didn't bother listening. Instead, she pulled up the collar of her coat to keep her neck warm and headed towards what appeared to be the main street.

A bit further along, they found a shop that looked as old as the village itself. Inside, it was empty apart from an overweight teenage girl with electric pink hair working behind the counter.

A moment's interest flickered across her face when Dai and Ellen walked into the shop, but it didn't last. She had already gone back to reading her magazine by the time the door creaked closed behind them.

'Vicky Pollard eat your heart out,' Dai muttered.

'Excuse me,' Ellen said, shoving her elbow into Dai's stomach.

No answer from the girl.

'She's wearing headphones,' Dai said. 'Listening to her iPod, man, innit?'

Ellen knocked hard on the counter, making the girl jump. Slowly, she took the headphones from her ears and looked at Ellen.

'Yeah?'

Ellen's mind fast-forwarded ten years to a terrible image of Eilish with pink hair, a weight problem and a bad attitude. Dismissing the picture as quickly as she could, she concentrated on the girl.

'I'm looking for Simon Wilson's house,' she said.

'Who?'

'Simon Wilson,' Ellen repeated. 'He owns a local business, Medway Maintenance. You know him?'

The girl moved her head slightly. It might have been a nod of recognition, but Ellen couldn't be sure.

'My brother done some work for him last summer.'

'He has a house in the village somewhere?' Ellen pressed.

The girl frowned. Ellen hoped this meant she was concentrating.

'Don't know about that. Thought he lived in Rochester. Or Upnor. Yeah, that's right. He's got a place in Upnor. Right posh it is, too. Gary went there once. Said it was well nice.'

'He owns a house here in Higham as well,' Ellen said. 'Rents it out to a bloke called Brian Fletcher. Maybe you know him?'

Something like a smile appeared on the girl's face.

'Smelly Brian. Yeah. He don't live there no more, though. Ain't no one lived in that place for a while. We was well pleased when he moved out. Dirty git. Wouldn't want a bloke like that living near you. Not with kids around. Know what I mean?'

'Not a clue,' Dai said. 'Perhaps you'd be good enough to enlighten us?'

The girl shrugged. 'Speak to anyone around here. They'll tell you the same thing about Brian. He's a kiddie fiddler. You know he was arrested a few years back? He took this kid. Only problem was you lot couldn't get your act together to prove he did it.'

'Maybe because he didn't,' Ellen suggested.

'Yeah, whatever,' the girl muttered. 'Like I said, you won't find no one at that house. Been empty for ages. It's at the end of the village, on the right as you're heading towards Rochester. Small bungalow. You can't miss it.'

'Jesus, spare me from small-town bigots,' Dai muttered as they left the shop and made their way across the town in the direction of Rochester.

'No bigots in Cardiff, then?' Ellen asked. 'Come on. Rochester's this way. Let's see if we can find the house.'

The house was as easy to find as the girl had said. An ugly, 1950s bungalow, it stood at the edge of the village in a small patch of concrete, about 500 yards from the nearest house.

It was obvious, as they approached, that no one was inside. They walked around the property, peering through grimy windows into the dark, empty interior. There was no sign that anyone had been there for a long time.

'Layers of dust everywhere,' Dai said. 'Mouse droppings all over the kitchen floor. Cobwebs thick as my arm. It's a ghost house, Ellen, that's what it is. So, what do we do now? According to Babe back there, Fletcher hasn't lived here for ages. So, if he's not living here, then where the hell is he?'

Ellen kicked at some weeds sprouting up through cracks in the concrete.

'I don't know,' she said. 'I really don't know, Dai.'

13:40

'You haven't been straight with me, have you, Brian?'

Simon was angry. Brian could tell from his voice and the way he was looking at him. Like he wanted to kill him for lying. There was something else in his face too, something Brian remembered from before but didn't want to think about. Not now when he was so close to getting rid of the girl.

'I asked you a question,' Simon said. 'See, I know you, Brian. And I know when you're hiding something from me. I'm your friend, remember? You can trust me. I should never have let you move back out here. At least in the village it was easier to keep an eye on you. It's the girl, isn't it? What have you done to her?'

'Nothing!' Brian roared. 'I haven't done anything to her. I'd never hurt a little girl, you know that Simon. I'm not like that.'

Simon's face hardened. 'What's that supposed to mean?'

'Sorry,' Brian stuttered. 'I'm sorry, Simon. I didn't mean anything by it, I swear. Listen, can't you just go? I'm trying to sort out my things here and I can't concentrate with you going on at me like I've done something bad when I haven't.'

'What about the girl?' Simon asked. 'Jodie Hudson. Pretty little thing she is. You know the first thing I thought of when I saw her picture on the news? I thought, now there's a girl who looks like Molly. Do you remember Molly, Brian? Yeah, course you do.'

Brian shook his head.

'Where is she?'

Simon took a step closer, pressing Brian up against the back of the van, so close Brian could feel Simon's hot breath on his face. He had a sudden rush of memories – Simon's hands holding him down, the sound of his breathing, hard and fast in Brian's ear. He tried to move, to push Simon away from him, but suddenly it was like being a little boy again and he was too terrified to do anything in case Simon hurt him.

'So then,' Simon whispered. 'You going to help me, Brian? Or do I have to go looking for her?'

'There's no one here, Simon,' Brian gabbled. 'On my life. I know I made a mistake before with Molly but I'd never do anything like that again. No way.'

'Glad to hear it,' Simon said. 'So, if she's not here, you won't mind me having a look around anyway, will you? How about I start with that lovely bedroom upstairs? The one with the pink wallpaper and the posters? The room where you kept poor little Molly.'

'Look all you want,' Brian said, relaxing as he realised Simon didn't know about the shed. He'd been so clever, letting the trees and bushes grow over it like that. If he played his cards right, he could make sure Simon didn't even notice it.

But Simon must have seen something in Brian's face.

'Ah,' he said. 'Cleverer than I thought. You've hidden her somewhere else. I wonder where.'

'Stop it!'

Brian couldn't stand it a moment longer. The feel of Simon's body against his, the smell of his breath and the heat of it against his face, the knowledge of what Simon was capable of . . .

Using every bit of strength he had, he shoved Simon away from him.

As Simon fell to the ground, Brian tried to step back, away from him. But Simon grabbed him by the ankle and Brian lost his balance and went tumbling down.

He landed on his elbow. Pain shot up his arm. He cried out, but his voice was lost in the other sounds racing through his head. Daddy, shouting and roaring like he always did. And Simon, hitting him and screaming at him. Fists punching into his face and the top half of his body.

Brian rolled away, trying to get away from the punches, trying to not listen to Simon, who had really lost it now and was screaming all sorts of things that Brian didn't want to hear.

'Never coming back. I've told you that a million times but you won't believe me.'

Brian dragged himself up. His only concern was to get away from the fists laying into him and the voice banging on relentlessly. He wouldn't listen. All he had to do was concentrate. Block out the sound of Simon's voice.

'I made sure of that.'

'Somewhere OVER the rainbow.'

If he could only get inside the van. The key was already in the ignition. Just switch it on and drive off.

Simon grabbed his hair, trying to pull him back down. With his other hand, he punched Brian in his lower back. For a moment, the pain blocked out everything else. Then, as it cleared, Simon's voice was still there.

'Little bitch had it coming.'

'Way up HIGH.'

'Your father shouldn't have been so greedy. Didn't want to share her.'

He shook Simon off and yanked open the door of the van.

'There's a land that I dream of once in a lullaBY.'

The key!

Turn the key and get the door closed.

Simon's hands were all over him, trying to drag him from the van. And all the time, he continued talking, his voice drilling through Brian's head, forcing him to listen to things he didn't want to hear.

Brian lifted his foot and shoved it into Simon's stomach. With a grunt, the other man fell back, leaving Brian free to grab the door and slam it shut.

'He left me no choice!' Simon roared.

He tried to turn the key, hand shaking so bad it took several attempts. By the time he'd got the engine started, Simon was up again, battering the side of the van, roaring in at him.

'They're gone. Don't you get that? I'm all you've got left.'

Brian swerved the van to one side, knocked into Simon and sent him flying. As the van roared off down the lane, Simon's voice gradually faded away. So did Daddy's. Until the only thing that was left was the sound of his own voice, screaming out the words of Marion's favourite song, over and over again.

13:45

'Can I help you?'

Ellen looked around to see a young uniformed officer with a

bright face and inquisitive eyes smiling at her.

'We're looking for Brian Fletcher, the guy who used to live here,' she said, walking over to the man.

'And you are?' the PC asked.

'DI Kelly,' she said holding her hand out. 'Lewisham CID. This is my colleague, DI Davies.'

The man looked from one to the other as he shook Ellen's hand. 'What do you want with Brian?'

'Just a few questions,' Ellen said. 'Routine stuff. Nothing for you to worry about.'

'PC Rhodri Jenkins,' the man said. He smiled at Dai. 'A fellow Taff. And I'm not worried, DI Kelly. Curious, though, I must admit. And keen to help if I can. I know Brian. He's a harmless enough chap, I've always thought. I know there was that business a few years ago, but from what I understand he was cleared of any suspicion, right? It was before my time. I only took up this post last year. You're looking at Higham's only law enforcement officer.'

'What the hell brought you out here?' Dai asked.

'A girl,' Jenkins replied with another smile. He smiled a hell of a lot, Ellen realised. 'What else drags a man to a place like this? To be honest with you, it's not so bad. Beautiful countryside in this part of the world, you know. Wonderful wildlife too.'

'Can you help us find Fletcher?' Ellen asked. The last thing they needed was a pitch from the Hoo tourist board.

'You won't find him here,' Jenkins said.

'Be good if you could tell us something we don't know,' Ellen said.

'Ah, right. Well, he used to live here a few years ago, see? But I don't think village life suits him, to be honest. He seems to spend most of his time back in the shack he grew up in. It's not much of a place but he seems to prefer it.'

'And where's that?' Dai asked.

'Better if I show you,' Jenkins said. 'You got a car? We could go out there now if you're not doing anything else.'

'Great,' Ellen said. 'Thanks. Let's go'

Dai sat in the back while Jenkins settled into the passenger seat beside Ellen. He directed them down a series of country lanes until they were well outside the village, surrounded by flat marshland leading to the Thames in the distance.

'Brian's place is down there somewhere.'

Jenkins pointed to a lane even narrower and windier than the one they were currently on.

'What do you mean *down there somewhere?*' Ellen asked sharply. 'I thought you knew where he lived.'

Jenkins shook his head. 'Never been out here in my life. I only know Brian from the odd time he comes into the village. He comes and goes from that house but never lasts long. I don't know why Wilson keeps offering it to him. He'd be better off renting it out, making some money from it.'

'So how do you know about the place out here?' Dai asked.

'Brian told me,' Jenkins said. 'I chat to him occasionally. Feel sorry for him, I suppose. Doesn't take a copper to work out the poor man is special needs. I spoke to Wilson about it. Suggested he got some help for Brian. Gave him a few numbers to call. But I don't know if anything ever came of it.

'He told me – Brian, that is – that he misses this place when he's not here. Said his sister and his mother were here and he needed to get home to be with them.'

'I thought his parents abandoned him years ago,' Ellen said.

Jenkins shrugged. 'I'm only telling you what he told me.'

As she turned into the narrow lane, Ellen's phone rang. She pressed the hands-free button to answer it.

'DI Kelly.'

'This is Alex.' A man's voice. Northern accent. Ellen couldn't place him.

'We met yesterday in Greenwich Park,' the man explained.

Alex. The Romanian gardener who sounded like he'd been born and reared on the Yorkshire Dales.

'Of course,' Ellen said. 'What can I do for you?'

'Brian is harmless, Mrs Kelly. Please, you must believe that. And maybe I'm not doing the right thing by calling you. But I don't know what else to do. Because there is a little girl missing, like you said.'

The car was still moving forward, bumping its way along the narrow track. Peering out the window, Ellen could see no sign of any house. She hoped Jenkins wasn't bullshitting them.

'Alex,' Ellen said. 'What are you trying to tell me?'

'It was a long time ago now,' Alex said. 'I'd only just arrived in London. Was lucky to get a job with my record. Simon, though, he's not too worried about stuff like that. Says if a bloke does a good job, that's good enough for him. And I'm a good worker, Mrs Kelly. But I knew as well, you see, that I owed him. He made that very clear. And when he asked me to do it, I didn't see the harm. See, I knew Brian by then. Knew what sort of man he was. And I knew, as well, what prison would do to him. He wouldn't cope, Mrs Kelly.'

Ellen stopped the car. 'Alex, what are you saying?'

'Simon lied,' Alex said. 'Brian was there, in the park, the day Molly disappeared.'

'Why the hell didn't you tell someone?' Ellen asked. 'Jesus Christ, Alex. This means Brian might be guilty.'

'But that's just it,' Alex said. 'He's not. If I thought for a second he was capable of something like that, you don't think I'd have come forward? I'd never have let Simon talk me into it. It was his idea. Said all I had to do was tell the police Brian was with us that day. We were in Greenwich Park. Just the two of us. Simon told the cops Brian was with us and I went along with it. It got Brian off the hook and kept Simon sweet. I didn't see the problem.'

He didn't see the problem!

It took supreme effort not to scream at him when she asked her next question.

'So why are you telling me this now?'

'Because of this other girl,' Alex said. 'I'm not feeling too good about things. I can't stop thinking, what if I was wrong? Will I get into trouble for this?'

Not bothering to answer, Ellen ended the call and grabbed Jenkin's arm.

'The house,' she hissed. 'Where the hell is it?'

'It's there.' Jenkins pointed to something in front of them. 'Down that hill. Look.'

Ellen clicked her safety belt open and turned to Jenkins. 'Call for back-up. Rochester's closest, right? Get a team out here asap. Turns out one of Brian's alibis lied about where he was when Molly York was snatched. He could be our man, after all.'

Ellen jumped out of the car and started running. It looked, at first, like nothing but a pile of rocks. It was only as she got closer that she saw it was some sort of dwelling.

Behind her, she heard Dai and Jenkins slamming the car doors and running after her.

The front door was closed and Ellen threw herself against it. She tried again. When it still didn't move, she turned to Dai.

'You try,' she said.

'Around the back,' he said. 'Let's see if we can get in that way.'

The back of the house faced onto flat, open countryside with views right down to the Thames. Apart from an overgrowth of bushes and trees near the house, the landscape was unrelentingly barren. In the distance, Ellen heard a train passing.

'Hoo Junction over there,' Jenkins said helpfully, pointing to a random spot in the distance. 'That line behind the house gets surprisingly busy. Freight trains mainly. The only sound you ever hear in a place like this.'

Like the front, the door at the back of the house was a plain wooden door with a Yale lock and a metal handle. Unlike the front door, this one opened easily when Ellen tried the handle. Immediately, the door swung inwards, away from her. She stepped inside.

13:46

The trip to the seaside hasn't worked out. The children all look so sad. In a green train, a little girl in a green hat is crying.

Even though the trains are right beside her, they seem so far away, like the ones I can hear late at night. I want to help the girl who's crying but I don't know what to do.

When I lift my hand to touch her, it takes ages to reach her, even though it's hardly any distance at all. She's so tiny, my finger covers her completely. And when I move my finger away, she's stopped crying.

I'm happy at first, but then I see why she's stopped. Her eyes are wide open and staring at me. Dead eyes. I'm sad but not surprised. You live and then you die and God doesn't care.

The bushes started up outside. Brian. I don't care. Maybe he'll kill me this time and I'll be in Heaven then with the girl from the train. That would be okay. I try to find the girl but it's difficult. So many children. And my eyes. Like someone's rubbed Vaseline over them. Everything blurry.

I squeeze my eyes shut and open them. My heart has gone all funny and it's difficult to breathe.

No! They're dying. In some trains it's already too late. I'm trying to shout at them to wake up, don't die, stay with me, please, please stay with me. Except my voice is gone and this time I know it's not coming back. It's a little whisper and soon there'll be nothing at all.

I put my hands out, nails digging into the flaky paper, pulling at the dead faces as if I might be able to bring them back to life. And it's such a stupid thing but I can't stop and in that red train there are two boys, smiling at me.

'What happened?' I whisper.

They don't answer. Just carry on smiling. Except now one of them's not smiling. I press my thumb against his face. Can't bear to watch it. When I take it away he's not smiling anymore.

And then I'm ripping wallpaper, my nails pulling it off in strips and I've got all this energy, suddenly. The faces are all disappearing, turning into flakes of paper, floating in the air and landing on the bed and the floor.

I'm ripping harder and faster, until there's a snowstorm and I'm in the middle of it.

Little white flakes of dead faces.

13:50

Ellen stood in the kitchen, Dai beside her. Jenkins hovered in the doorway. None of them spoke as they took in the details of the room. It was like a kitchen but, with the exception of a small fridge, without any of the electrical appliances you'd expect to see in a modern kitchen.

The room was dark and it took a while for Ellen's eyes to adjust. As they did, she noticed several things. The creeping growth of mould around the door of the fridge. On the table a packet of cup cakes in a garish, pink box. Beside these, a pile of old-fashioned videos tapes, and a key ring with several keys on it. She stepped forward to examine the videos and felt a stab of recognition. *The Rainbow Parade* – an old TV programme for children. She and Sean were subjected to endless episodes when they were growing up. Her father loved it.

'Pink cup cakes,' Ellen said. 'And these videos. What use does a grown man have for pink cup cakes and a collection of children's videos, Dai?'

'Jodie,' Dai said. 'They're for her. Has to be.'

Ellen turned to Jenkins.

'Where the hell's the back-up? Call again. Tell them what we've found. Tell them to get their arses here as quickly as they can.'

Directly over her head, Ellen heard a noise. Floorboards creaking, as if someone was walking on them.

'Someone up there,' Dai whispered.

Another sound from above. No mistaking it this time. A footstep. Then another. Ellen tensed. Someone was walking through the house, along the floor upstairs, now coming down the stairs, towards the kitchen.

Dai nudged her and pointed to the side of the kitchen. She nodded. If they moved that way, they'd be behind the door when it opened, catching Fletcher unaware when he came in.

Together, they edged their way sideways until they were pressed against the corner. At the same moment, the kitchen door swung inwards and a man appeared, stopping dead when he saw Jenkins, still standing in the doorway.

Dai stepped forward.

'Brian Fletcher?'

The man spun around.

'Mr Wilson,' Ellen said quickly. 'What are you doing here?'

'I could ask you the same question,' Simon Wilson said. 'This is private property. You people are trespassing.'

He looked at Jenkins. 'I assume you brought them here? You should keep your nose out of other people's business, PC Plod. Brian doesn't need the likes of you interfering.'

Jenkins' face hardened. 'And I suppose you only ever had the boy's best interest at heart, is that right?'

'We just want a word with Brian,' Ellen said. 'We're not here to upset him.'

'Well you can't,' Wilson said. 'He's not here. You can see that for yourself. I don't know where he is. I came over this morning to check he was okay, he's been acting a bit funny this last week or so, but when I got here there was no sign of him.'

'So you decided to have a snoop around while he was out, is that it?' Dai asked.

'And you are?' Wilson asked.

'Detective Inspector Dai Davies. I'm working on the case of a little girl who's gone missing. Jodie Hudson – heard of her?'

Wilson frowned. 'What's that got to do with Brian?'

'Where is he?' Ellen asked.

'How the hell do I know?' Wilson said. 'Jodie Hudson. Course I've heard of her. Been following the story on the news. Terrible business. But it's got nothing to do with Brian, if that's why you're here.'

'How can you be so sure?' Ellen asked.

Simon smirked. 'Well she's not upstairs, I can tell you that. Besides, I don't have to explain myself to you or anyone else. I think you should all leave.'

'Maybe if Brian spoke to the two detectives,' Jenkins suggested. 'Then it would clear things up quick and easy.'

'Maybe if you shut up and stopped interfering in other people's business, then they wouldn't be here in the first place,' Wilson said.

'Hang on,' Dai said. 'Listen. What's that sound?'

It was faint at first. Growing louder. An engine. Someone was driving towards the house.

Ellen got outside just in time to see a dilapidated white van stopping at the side of the house. The driver, a giant of a man, she recognised instantly. The same man she'd seen hiding behind Wilson the day she'd spoken to him in Greenwich Park. Brian Fletcher.

13:51

Things were unravelling. His head was too busy with images and sounds. Mam. Marion. *The Rainbow Parade.* Trying to sort out the different girls he'd watched it with – Marion, Molly, and now the one who called herself Jodie.

Except he couldn't even picture the other girls. When he tried, it was only Marion's face he could see. Her smile, her voice, her little hand slipping into his big one, asking him to make her a crown of daisies for her princess hair.

'Little bitch had it coming.'

Simon was still at the house. He knew she was there. That's why he'd come. And if he found her …

Brian braked. The van swerved sideways. Pulling hard on the steering wheel, he managed to turn it around, accelerating back in the direction he'd just come from.

Things were going wrong, slipping out of control, like they always did. It wasn't his fault. He'd been so careful, done everything the way he'd planned it, and now look at the mess he found himself in.

Your father shouldn't have been so greedy. Didn't want to share her.

With Daddy out of the way, Simon didn't have to worry about sharing any more. He had Brian all to himself and, later, Marion. No, not Marion. Molly.

The police thought he'd done it, putting him through it again and again. Words he'd never heard before but knew, just by the sound of them, that they were bad words.

Sexual assault, rape, strangulation.

Simon did that. It was Molly's fault. She'd started crying. Brian could still remember the look on Simon's face when he heard her. All delighted with himself, like he'd just found a sack of gold or something. He'd gone up there straight away.

After that, he'd made Brian go back to the house in Higham and told him not to worry about her. Said he'd sort it out.

Sexual assault, rape, strangulation.

Stop! He couldn't think about all that. Not now. He needed to concentrate. He was nearly home. All he had to do was get there before Simon found her.

The keys. What had he done with them? He'd need them to get into the shed. In the kitchen. He'd left them on the table. Even if Simon found them, he wouldn't know what they were for.

Brian swung the van into the laneway. He could see the house now. Nearly there.

He skidded through the gate, switched off the engine, grabbed Daddy's gun from the passenger seat, jumped out of the van and raced towards the shed. Then he remembered the keys on the table inside. He turned around, and that's when he saw them.

Simon and a man he thought he recognised. The policeman. The nice one. What was his name? Two other people as well – a man and a woman. The man was tall with sandy hair the same colour as Daddy's.

He opened his mouth to ask them who they were, what they were doing here. Simon stepped forward and said something, but Brian couldn't hear him. In his head, Daddy was screaming at him, telling him he'd done it now. The police were here, they'd find the girl and then they'd kill him for what he'd done.

'I didn't do anything!' Brian shouted.

But no one was listening to him. In his head, Daddy was still shouting, telling him to run. Simon was coming closer. Behind him, Brian could see the other man, the one who looked like Daddy, coming towards him as well. Not stopping to hear what either of them had to stay, Brian turned and ran.

13:52

'Wait here for the back-up,' Dai shouted. 'I'll catch Brian.'

For a big man, Fletcher moved quickly but Dai was fast too. The two men raced across the flat, open countryside towards a barbed-wire fence.

Ellen turned to Jenkins. 'You stay here,' she said. 'Keep an eye on Wilson.'

She waited until Jenkins nodded, then chased after Dai and Fletcher. She didn't like leaving Wilson. Didn't trust the man an inch. But Fletcher had a gun. She couldn't let Dai handle him alone.

Fletcher slipped through a gap in the fence and disappeared

out of sight down a hill the other side. Seconds later, Dai did the same. By the time Ellen reached the fence, Dai was sliding down the steep, grassy incline towards the railway track at the bottom. Fletcher was there already, running along the track itself.

Ellen squeezed through the gap. Her jumper caught in something. Barbed wire. It scraped painfully along her back. She yanked the jumper free. A cold blast of air sliced her skin as she slid down the slope after the two men.

* * *

Daddy was chasing him. He was going to kill him. Brian ran as fast as he could but no matter how fast he ran, Daddy was there behind him. He thought Brian had killed Marion.

He ran for the train tracks, the only place he could think of where he might be able to get away. As he ran, a memory flickered through his mind. Sitting here one afternoon, wondering what it would feel like if he lay down on the tracks and let the train drive right over him.

Daddy crashed into him, and they both fell onto the tracks. Then they were rolling over and Brian could see Daddy's face close to his. In his head, Marion was there and Daddy too. He was hurting her. Making her cry.

No more. Daddy wouldn't make anyone cry again. He had him now, slamming his head against the metal tracks, over and over, making him stop. Keeping his promise so Daddy would never hurt anyone again.

* * *

She had almost reached the track when Dai surprised her by launching forward and tackling Fletcher, rugby-style, sending both men crashing onto the tracks.

Dai had the advantage, but not for long. Fletcher managed to roll them sideways so he was on top. He grabbed Dai by the collar of his jacket and slammed his head against the metal track beneath him. Then lifted him and repeated the action.

Ellen raced forward, screaming at Fletcher to stop. She saw the gun in Fletcher's hand and stopped. Dai saw it too, tried to grab it. He missed and Fletcher dropped the gun. Fletcher's fist flew up, swung through the air and smashed into Dai's face.

There was a cracking sound. Dai cried out as blood exploded from his broken nose. Ellen was clinging onto Fletcher's back, her hands on his huge shoulders, trying to pull him off Dai.

Fletcher threw his shoulders back, putting the weight of his body behind the action, sending Ellen flying backwards. She landed heavily on the rocky ground.

When she sat up, Fletcher had the gun again and was pointing it at Dai.

'No!' Ellen dived for him, her body crashing into his. But it was like hitting a tree. He swayed but didn't fall. A gunshot exploded, echoed across the empty fields.

For a split second, the world stopped.

Then Fletcher took aim again.

With the smell of burning in her nostrils and the sound of gunshot in her ears, Ellen lashed out, hitting wildly, trying anything that would stop him. She grabbed the arm with the gun, put all her weight into dragging that down, away from Dai. She bit into the hard muscles in his upper arm, her teeth sinking through the rough material of his shirt, biting into the flesh itself.

Fletcher cried out and the gun clattered to the ground. At the same time, his other arm swung around, punching Ellen in the side of the head, knocking her off his arm. Dazed, half-mad with fear, adrenalin and rage, she managed to grab the gun again.

Her head was pounding where he'd hit her, felt like it was going to explode. Her fingers tightened around the gun and she aimed.

'Freeze! Stop right there, Brian, or I'll shoot you.'

* * *

Someone else was there now. On top of him. Brian hit out, trying to shake off the person who had grabbed him. As he fought his way free, he saw the gun, got hold of it, aimed it at Daddy and pulled the trigger.

It was harder than he'd expected, the impact of the gunshot throwing him back so he nearly fell again. Hands grabbed him, fists pummelling his upper arm. Teeth sank into his flesh, making him shout out with the pain of it.

The gun fell from his hand and he shoved the other person off him and ran on, his only thought now to get away.

'Freeze! Stop right there, Brian, or I'll shoot you.'

Mam?

No, when he turned he saw it wasn't her. A different woman. A flash of rage burned through him. What was she doing? He hadn't hurt anyone. Why was she pointing the gun at him?

'It wasn't me,' he shouted. 'Why won't you believe that? I wasn't the one who hurt her. I'd never do that. It was Simon. He did all those things to her. I thought she was Marion.'

But she wouldn't listen, just pointed the gun at him like he was the bad person, not Daddy. Not Simon.

* * *

'I thought she was Marion.'

To her surprise, he stopped and turned around. When she saw his face, she winced. He was crying. Coming towards her now. Still talking. Still crying. Instinctively, she took a step back.

'Don't come any closer,' she warned.

Suddenly, it wasn't Fletcher in front of her. It was Billy Dunston. His head already half gone and she was holding the gun up, ready to pull the trigger again.

'Please, Brian. Stand back.'

But it was like he couldn't hear her. He just kept coming for her. She raised the gun higher, her hand shaking badly now, her head full of Billy Dunston.

Behind Ellen, there was a new noise. A roaring that started at the same time as the tracks under her feet started vibrating.

Instinctively, she jumped sideways, off the track.

'Brian!' she screamed. 'Get off the track. Now!'

He didn't seem to hear her. Didn't seem to notice the rumbling along the track as the train got closer. Dai dragged himself towards Brian, grabbed the big man's ankle. Realising what he was trying to do, Ellen ran forward to help.

Brian stumbled but didn't fall. His swung his fist at Ellen's face. The impact knocked her off her feet. She staggered back, then crashed down to the ground, the back of her head smashing against a stone. An explosion of colour and pain and noise blocked out everything else.

And still the train was coming closer.

She dragged herself up to sitting. Saw Brian and Dai on the track. Brian on top of Dai, fist smashing into his face. Over and over.

Ellen's fingers tightened around the gun. She aimed at Fletcher. Dunston was there again. Not just his face. The smell as well. The smell of burning, where the bullet hits the flesh, scorching it as it enters the body. She pressed her finger against the trigger, tried to pull it, but couldn't do it. Head full of the stench of burning flesh. Vinny's voice, a reminder of who she'd once been.

What you doing, Blue?

* * *

He was crying so bad it was hard to see, but he could feel Daddy, hitting him, pulling at him. Blindly, Brian lashed out, fists landing on Daddy, punching him as hard as he could.

Somewhere, he could hear screaming. That was blocked out by another noise, distant at first, then getting louder. Briefly, a shadow appeared in front of him, replaced immediately by Marion's face. The crown of daisies was on her head and she was running towards him, laughing – a lovely sound full of life and love.

* * *

Ellen's scream was no match for the roar of the train or the deafening screech of the warning signal or the screaming of the brakes as the driver tried to stop the train.

In a dreamlike moment, Dai Davies and Brian Fletcher disappeared as the blue and yellow engine of the huge freight train smashed into them, crushing their bodies into the railway track. Killing them instantly.

14.10

The train driver was speaking. She could see his mouth moving, but couldn't make out the words. Her ears were still full of the sound of the train, brakes screaming as it ploughed into the two men. Behind the driver, lying on the grass like he'd casually kicked it off, was one of Dai's brown brogues.

Her mind had fractured. All the different parts were working, but separately from each other. Images and sounds floating around that she couldn't make any sense of. There was a woman as well, wearing the same blue uniform as the driver. Had she been in the train, too? Someone had wrapped a blanket around her shoulders and she hugged this around her body, but it didn't seem to be doing any good. Wasn't helping warm up the deep cold that had set in.

Cup cakes on the kitchen table. Pink packaging. A selection of old-fashioned children's videos but no television. Tears streaming down Fletcher's face as he came for her.

'Jodie.'

She looked around, trying to force the different sections of her brain to click into place. This was important. Fletcher had said something. She had to remember what it was. She looked up. Somewhere, the other side of the railway bank, was Fletcher's house.

She turned and started climbing the hill, forcing herself to concentrate on putting one foot in front of the other. The train had cast a shadow over them, right before it drove over them. Meant that right at the very end, the only thing she saw was the shadow, not Dai.

At the top of the hill, she could see the house at the far end of the field. Something felt heavy in her hand and she looked down, surprised to see the gun still in it. She should have fired it. If she had, Dai wouldn't have died.

From the house, a girl's scream broke through the noises in Ellen's head and suddenly she remembered. The blanket slipped from her shoulders as she ran towards the sound as fast as she could.

* * *

No children. Nothing now. My tummy's sore but so is everything else so it doesn't really matter. Cramps are getting worse. I suck my thumb harder because that helps sometimes.

Mum's here now. Beside me on the bed, snuggled up close, stroking my head and whispering that I'm her little princess and she loves me and everything's going to be okay.

'I love you too, Mum.'

The words are only in my head, but I know she's heard me because she smiles.

We're on a picnic blanket. The sun is bright and even though my eyes are closed I can feel it, warm on my face. I have to be really careful and stay so still because if I move, even a teeny bit, then everything disappears: Mum, the picnic blanket, the sun, everything.

Then there's this big crash and it's all gone anyway. I open my eyes and see him. Standing in the doorway, his face all red as he stares at me. It's not Brian.

Now he's coming towards me. His body's blocked everything else out so it's like there is nothing except me and him. I try to sit up, but he gets to me first.

'Mum!'

I scream. Just once. Then there's nothing.

His eyes are black.

The children's faces are all white.

He's too strong and I'm screaming again for Mum to come back, *but it's all inside my head and no sounds are coming out and he probably thinks I don't even care that he's lifting me. But I do. And his hands are crushing me. And I want him to stop because I can't breathe. I think he's killing me ...*

14:15

A man was lying on the kitchen floor. Ellen saw his feet first, and moved forward slowly, dreading what else she'd find. His body was face down, unmoving apart from the slight rise and fall in his middle when he breathed. He was wearing a navy blue, standard issue police uniform.

She knelt beside him, wishing she could remember his name. She shook him gently.

He groaned and his eyes flickered momentarily.

'Where is he?' she asked. 'Where's Wilson.'

But she got no answer. Whatever reaction her initial contact had triggered disappeared. She could see blood matted into the hair at the back of the head and guessed that Wilson had hit him with something. She looked around, trying to work out where he could have gone. Her eyes swept across the videos and pink box on the table. She frowned. Something was missing. Keys. There had been a set of keys there, right beside the videos.

Quietly, she pushed herself off the ground and moved through the house. Beyond the kitchen, there was a tiny hallway and a wooden staircase, leading to the upper floor. The kitchen was the only room downstairs.

She still had Brian's gun. Holding it in front of her with both hands, Ellen moved silently up the wooden staircase, testing each step for creaks before putting any weight on it. At the top, two doors led off the tiny landing. One was already open, revealing a room with a single, unmade bed, a pile of clothes on the floor and not much else.

The other door was shut. Ellen pressed her ear against it, listening. When she didn't hear anything, she put her hand on the handle and slowly turned it. The door creaked open and she jumped forward, gun out, swinging it from side to side as her eyes swept the room.

Empty. Whatever child Fletcher had been hiding in here was long gone. And there was no doubt this was a child's room. A girl's room, at that. Walls painted pink, decorated with some old, tattered posters. Another image from Ellen's childhood – the fox from *The Rainbow Parade*, winking out at her from a poster with only one corner still adhered to the wall.

In theory, Fletcher could have been keeping Jodie here, but something about the room made her doubt this. There was no furniture, for starters, and no sign that anyone had been in here for a long time. If he'd kept her here, wouldn't there at least be a blanket or something for her to sit on? Unless he was a complete animal and didn't care at all about the comfort of his victim.

Which was entirely possible.

The room smelled musty, as well. If a girl had been locked up here for days on end, you'd expect to get some human smell as well, but there was nothing. Ellen examined the door. It looked like there'd been locks on it at one time, you could see the marks in the wood, but they weren't there now.

On the way out, she took a look in the other room. More smells. This time, an overpowering pong of body odour and feet. Apart from the bed, there was no other furniture in this room, either. Ellen turned to go, keen to get away from the smell, when something by the bed caught her eye.

It was an old photo, unframed and frayed at the edges. Time had faded the image to a point where it was difficult to make out the details of the girl's face. Ellen stared at it. At a glance, you'd easily think you were looking at a photo of Molly York or Jodie Hudson. Like them, this girl had dark hair and, even though the image was poor, you could just make out the gap between her front teeth. Like the one she'd seen in the photos of Molly and Jodie.

There was something in the girl's hair. Ellen held the photo closer. It looked like a daisy chain, the sort she made for Eilish from time to time. This girl looked older than Eilish, though. Somewhere between eight and ten, Ellen guessed.

Outside the house, someone was moving around. Foot-steps crunching on the uneven concrete. Jumping up, she ran to the window and peered outside. She could see Wilson creeping towards the dirty white van. He was carrying something over his shoulder – it looked like a bundle of clothes at first. But then it moved.

Ellen threw herself from the room, clattering down the stairs and out the back door.

'Freeze!' she screamed.

He had the back doors of the van open and was shoving the girl inside.

When he saw Ellen, he dragged the girl back out, holding her in front of him like a shield.

'Drop the gun,' he said. 'If you don't, I'll break her neck.'

She was so little. So small in Wilson's arms, eyes wide and terrified in her white face as Wilson's arm wrapped around her neck.

'Let her go,' Ellen said.

Wilson smiled.

Ellen raised the gun.

She imagined she could smell it – bullet-scorched flesh, bitter and burning and impossible to forget.

She aimed for his head. Later, that's what she'd remember. She wanted to kill him.

His arm tightened around Jodie's neck.

Ellen lowered the gun.

Wilson nodded. 'That's it. Drop the gun and no one gets hurt.'

She pulled the trigger.

Blood erupted from Wilson's foot. He screamed, dropping

Jodie as he fell to the ground. Ellen aimed the gun at the same spot and fired again.

Wilson's screams filled her head as she dropped the gun, ran forward and gathered Jodie Hudson into her arms.

ONE WEEK
LATER

Ed was waiting for her by the statue of James Wolfe, at the top of Greenwich Park. Ellen stood beside him, looking across the park to London, stretching out in front of her.

'Shall we grab a coffee?' Ed asked.

'I'm not in the mood for coffee,' Ellen said. 'Mind if we just walk instead?'

She was vaguely hungover. Probably a good thing. It went some way to numbing her feelings about what she needed to talk to him about.

'I've spoken to Nichols,' Baxter said. 'Told him what's going on. And that's it. I'm gone. As of today my career in CID is over. Thirty-eight years. All done now. Not that it matters a damn. It's only a job. Life's far more important. I just wish I'd worked that out earlier. Don't make the same mistake, Ellen, you hear me? The funny thing is, if it was just me affected by this, I'm not sure I'd care that much. It's Andrea and Melissa I can't stop thinking about. They're my world. I can't bear to think of them being hurt by this.'

And what about Abby, Ellen wondered.

'I know I messed up,' Baxter said, as if he knew what she was thinking. 'And that's something I'll have to deal with. Somehow. The only thing I'm grateful for is Andrea doesn't know. About Abby, I mean.'

'How's Melissa holding up?' Ellen asked, keen to change the subject.

Baxter shrugged. 'Putting on a good face, you know.

Underneath, though, she's suffering. Of course she is. And that's not easy to watch, either. I mean, she may be thirty-two but she's still my little girl.'

His daughter was the same age as Abby. Men could be such idiots.

'How do you do it, Ellen?' Baxter asked. 'How do you make sense of something like this?'

'You don't,' she said. 'Because there is no sense to it. So you keep going. You keep going for Andrea and Melissa and all the people in the world who care about you. And that's not easy, either. But you've got to do it.'

His forehead creased in that way she knew so well.

'Why?' he asked. 'Why bother?'

'Because you've got no choice,' Ellen said. 'What else can you do?'

They walked around the edge of the park, down past the tennis courts, along the edge of the Maritime Museum and back up the hill on the east side towards One Tree Hill and the bench dedicated to the first Queen Elizabeth. All the time, Ellen kept wondering when she'd find the courage to ask the question she'd come here to ask.

'How are you holding up?' Baxter asked. 'You're not looking that great, if you don't mind me saying so.'

'I'm fine,' Ellen said.

She wasn't fine. Not at all. It was like her life had rewound, back to those first, early days after Vinny's death. Getting through each day was a struggle. Some days, she didn't think she'd make it. The kids were the only thing that kept her going. That, and the promise of a few hefty glasses of wine each night to help her sleep.

She'd tried some dry evenings, but it was pointless. Without the anaesthetising effects of the wine, she'd lie in bed endlessly reliving the moment on the train tracks. Three nights of this were enough to convince her now was not the time to become teetotal.

First, she needed to concentrate on getting her head sorted. Then she'd think about cutting back on the wine. But how was she meant to get past something like that? She could look at it whatever way she wanted, but it always came back to the same thing. If she'd reacted differently, Dai wouldn't have died.

The wine helped with sleep but did nothing to stop the dreams from coming. She was plagued with variations on the same one – night after night. Standing by the railway, aiming the gun at Fletcher. But when she tried to pull the trigger, her finger froze. She could hear the train coming, see the shadow blocking out the light until all three of them were in total darkness. And still she couldn't pull the trigger.

At the moment the train hit, she would wake up, sweating and panting, unable to get back asleep after that, no matter how much wine she'd drunk.

Over the last few days, she thought maybe things were getting easier. Jodie coming out of hospital, that felt like a big step forward. And knowing the girl would be okay, in the long-term, was a huge relief. Helen and Kevin were still together and told Ellen they would stay that way, united in their determination to heal their daughter. Bromley Police had charged a local dealer for Harris' murder and Kevin was no longer a suspect.

Wilson was in custody. With a bit of luck, he'd never be released to hurt anyone ever again. He was still denying any involvement in the abductions of Jodie and Molly, but the evidence was rapidly stacking up against him.

A search of his home had revealed a number of things, among them a dress that Rob York identified as belonging to his daughter. A claim substantiated by subsequent DNA analysis. Taking apart Wilson's computer, Forensics also found over two thousand images of child pornography. A contact in the Child Protection Unit told Ellen they were among the worst he'd ever seen.

Three bodies had been found buried in the flat fields behind Fletcher's place. A woman on her own near the slope leading down to the railway and, closer to the house, a man and a girl. When she heard about the child, Ellen thought immediately of the photo she'd seen on the floor beside Fletcher's bed. As yet, the police hadn't identified the bodies. All they were able to tell at this stage was that the woman had died much earlier than the other two unfortunates.

'Ellen?'

Ed's voice made her jump.

'Hey.' He put his hand on Ellen's arms. 'Are you all right? You were miles away, so you were.'

Ellen tried to smile, nearly managed it.

'I was wrong,' he said.

'About what?'

'Kevin. I couldn't concentrate. At work, there was so much to do but all the time, when I should have been thinking about Jodie and nothing else, I couldn't get focus. I'd find myself in briefings, Ellen, and halfway through I'd realise I didn't have the slightest clue what someone was telling me. I thought if we could just arrest him, get him behind bars, then we'd find Jodie and that would be the end of it.'

Here was her chance.

'Is that why you went to the press?' she asked.

Silence.

'Ed?'

They were at the top of the park again, standing in the spot where they'd met. Down below them, a woman was playing with a young boy, swinging him by his hands, swirling around and around. The sound of the boy's laughter drifted up the hill to Ellen.

'I was desperate,' Ed said. 'We weren't moving quickly enough. I know what Martine's like when she gets the bit between her teeth. I thought a bit of press interest might make Hudson trip up, do something stupid. How did you work it out?'

'It couldn't have been anyone else,' Ellen said. 'And that day in your office, you were on the phone to her then, weren't you? That story about your friend's sixtieth birthday. I knew you were lying, Ed.'

'Does it really matter now?' he asked.

Damn right it does, Ellen thought.

'You blamed me,' she said. 'You shouted at me and said it was my fault.'

'I know,' Ed said. 'And I'm sorry. I was wrong. I've already said I was wrong. What more do you want?'

'What would have happened?' she asked. 'If I'd suspected someone else, would you have let me go ahead and accuse them of doing it?'

'Of course not. What sort of person do you think I am, Ellen?'

She wasn't sure how to answer that. Not anymore.

'It doesn't matter,' she said. 'It's done now.'

An awkward silence fell between them.

'I should go,' Baxter said eventually. 'Andrea will be expecting me.'

Ellen walked him to the exit.

'Take care,' she said. 'And keep in touch, won't you?'

Unexpectedly, he grabbed her and hugged her. She hugged him back, shocked at how frail his body felt under the bulk of his clothes.

And then he was gone. Out the gate, walking down Croom's Hill, getting further and further away from her. She noticed the slump in his shoulders, the heavy way he walked, as if every step was an effort. At the bottom of the hill, he turned and waved. She waved back, tried to smile. Realised she was crying instead so she moved away quickly, hoping he hadn't noticed.

When he was gone, she walked back through the park, carrying the image of his face as he'd waved to her. He'd looked so lost. Like a little boy separated from his parents. It made her think of her own children and she hurried forward, keen to get home to them as soon as she could, hoping the sight of them would push away the image of Baxter's lost face. At least for now.

* * *

Later that night, with just a bottle of wine for company, Ed's words came back to her.

It's only a job.

The Merlot was finished. It wasn't even ten thirty yet. If she went to bed now she'd be awake by three am and would spend the rest of the night thinking, unable to get back asleep.

She went into the kitchen and pulled another bottle from the wine rack. It was a different wine, but that hardly mattered. Blocking out reality was the only thing that concerned her right now.

Don't make the same mistake.

No chance. She took a mouthful of fresh wine and went back into the sitting room, where she put on *Sinatra at the Sands*, her favourite CD.

She settled in one of the Art Deco armchairs, listening to Sinatra, Count Basie and the boys having a right old time of it. Out of the corner of her eye, she could see the red light of the answer-machine flashing. Two messages. She'd already listened to them. One from Jim O'Dwyer. The other from Abby Roberts. Abby's message had been there for over a week. Jim's a bit longer. One day soon, she'd get around to deleting them.

She should call them back. She should do lots of things. She'd get around to all of them. One day soon.

The opening chords to *You Make Me Feel So Young* started up. Ellen's eyes closed and she fell asleep holding her empty glass, dreaming of herself and Sean as young children, running through the meadows like the character in Frank's song. Eilish was there, too. In the dream, she was still alive, racing beside her older brother and sister, laughing as the lush meadow grass tickled her bare legs, young and carefree and happy, her whole life stretched out in front of her, like some wonderful adventure.

MORE FROM BRANDON CRIME

Young homeless women and drug addicts are being abducted before being brutally mutilated and murdered, and a city is held in the grip of unspeakable terror. By abducting Katie, the young daughter of private investigator Karl Kane, the killer has just made his first mistake, which could well turn out to be his last.

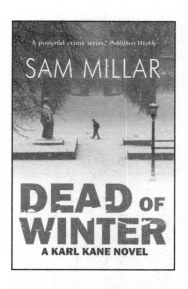

'A powerful crime series.' *Publishers Weekly*

SAM MILLAR

DEAD OF WINTER

A KARL KANE NOVEL

Private Investigator Karl Kane returns to the streets of Belfast investigating the discovery of a severed hand. Karl believes it's the work of an elusive serial killer, but the police are claiming a simple vendetta between local criminals. Karl embarks on a nightmarish journey as he attempts to solve the mystery and soon he's suspecting Mark Wilson, his detested ex brother-in-law. But as the winter days become darker, Karl discovers that Wilson is more than a match for him when it comes to dirty dealing and even dirtier fighting, as he battles to keep from becoming the next victim.

BRANDON